THOUGHT LITTLE OF HER
CAN'T FORGIVE HER
STRONG REVULSION
LONG
RESISTANT AT FIRST,

ARISA MORISHIGE
WAS A SUBDUED PRESENCE IN THE CLASS AND WAS BULLIED. AFTER THE ACCIDENT, SHE REVERSES HER STATUS AND REIGNS OVER THE OTHERS, BUT HER HEART IS SHAKING AFTER SHE LOSES HER "SCYTHE."

A SUDDEN BUS ACCIDENT THAT OCCURRED ON THE WAY TO AN EXCHANGE CAMP CHANGES EVERYTHING. THERE ARE ONLY A MERE FIVE SURVIVORS, ALL GIRLS. KONNO'S PERFECT, ORDINARY LIFE THAT WASN'T EVER SUPPOSED TO CHANGE COMPLETELY CRUMBLES AWAY.

MORISHIGE SEIZES POWER, AND CONTROLS THE FIELD THROUGH FEAR. USUI BECOMES CONSUMED BY HER OWN ANXIETY AND RUNS OFF. HOWEVER, WITH THE APPEARANCE OF THE ONE AND ONLY BOY, HINATA, THE SITUATION REVERSES ABRUPTLY. AFTER HEARING HINATA SAY "LET'S ALL GO HOME TOGETHER," KONNO'S FLAGGING TRUST TOWARDS HER COMPANIONS IS RESTORED. MEANWHILE, A DESPAIRING MORISHIGE'S SUICIDE ATTEMPT FAILS. IN THE DARK OF THE NIGHT, SHE SWINGS HER BLADE AT SOMEONE IN HER VICINITY.

MORNING ARRIVES. USUI IS DISCOVERED, DEAD.

HARUAKI HINATA
INITIALLY ON HIS OWN AFTER THE ACCIDENT, HE HAS NOW JOINED THE OTHERS. HIS POSITIVE ATTITUDE GIVES THE OTHERS COURAGE.

CHIEKO KAMIYA
HAS AN ABUNDANCE OF KNOWLEDGE REGARDING NATURE AND RESCUE. HAS HAD A COLDHEARTED SIDE, BUT IS SLOWLY CHANGING.

contents

Scene. 12 – Facts and Truths

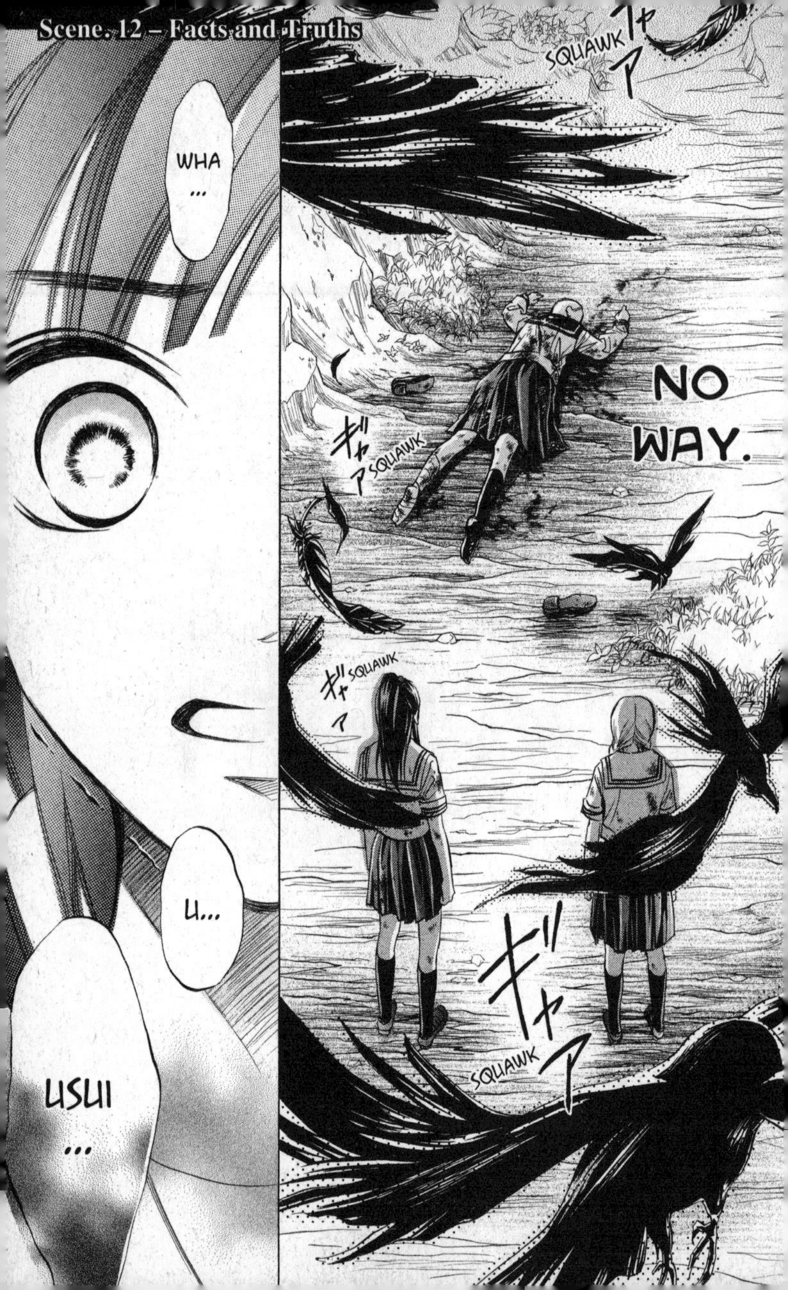
ギャア
SQUAWK
NO WAY.
ギャア
SQUAWK
ギャア
SQUAWK
ギャア
SQUAWK
WHA ...
U...
USUI ...

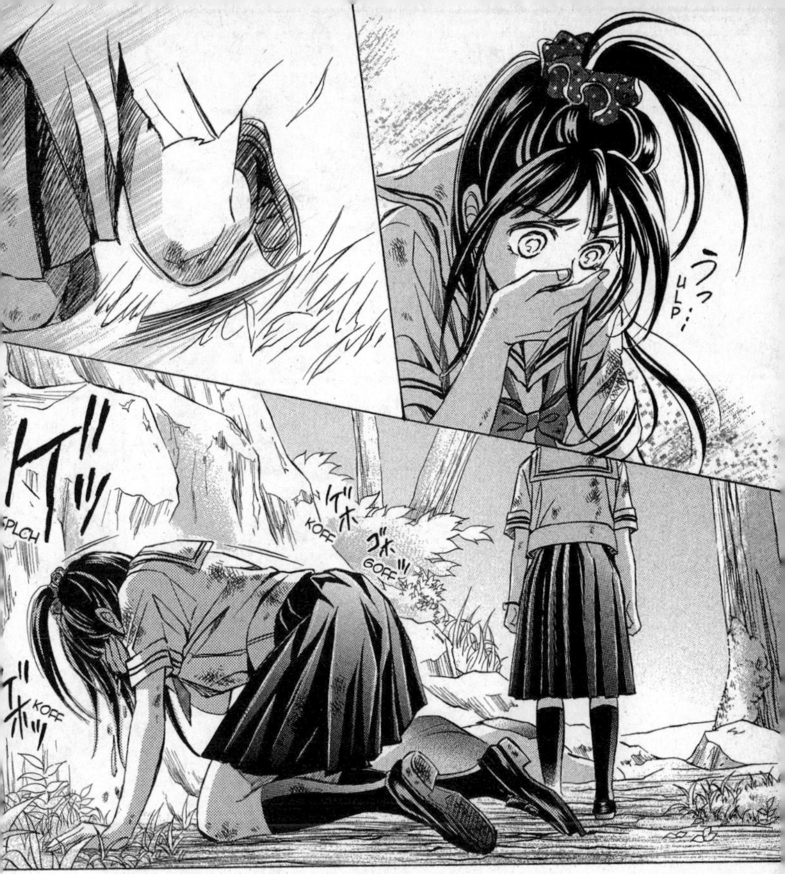
うっ…
ULP
ゲホ
KOFF
ゴホッ
GOFF
ドッ
SPLCH
ゴボッ
KOFF

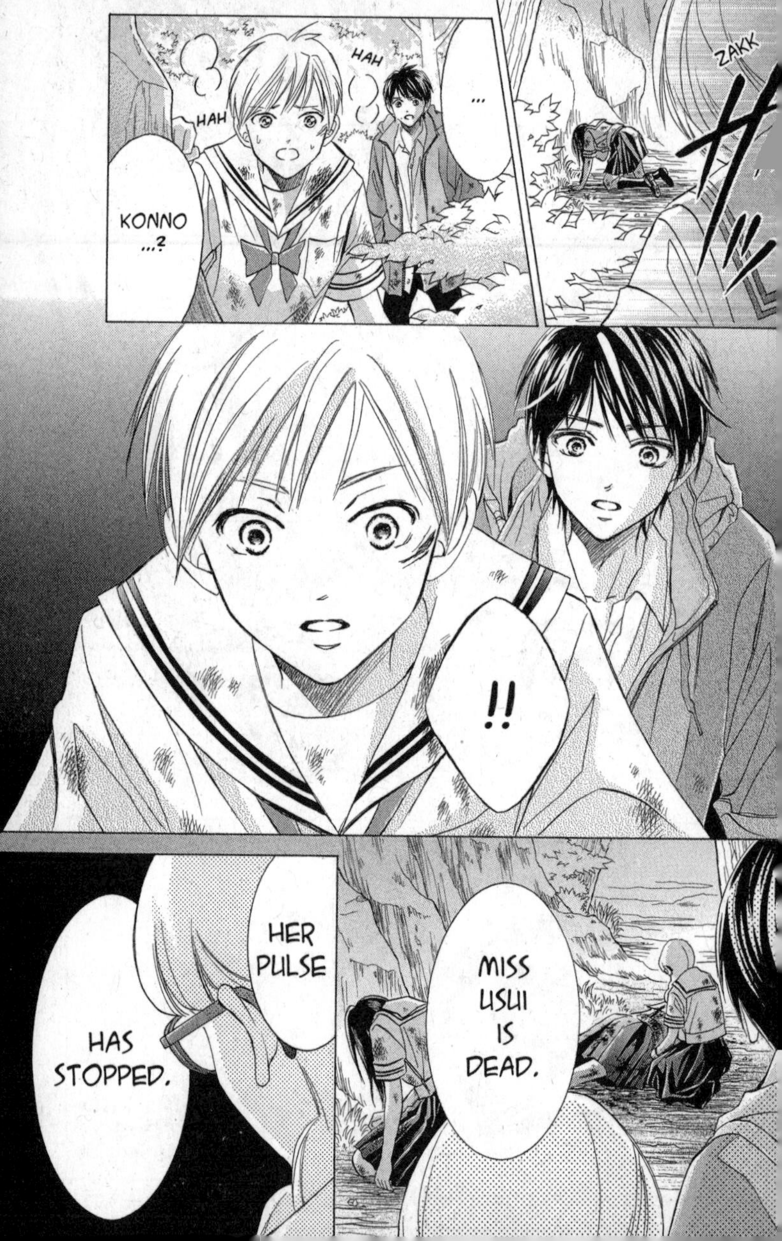
ZAKK
...
HAH
HAH
KONNO ...?
!!
MISS USUI IS DEAD.
HER PULSE
HAS STOPPED.

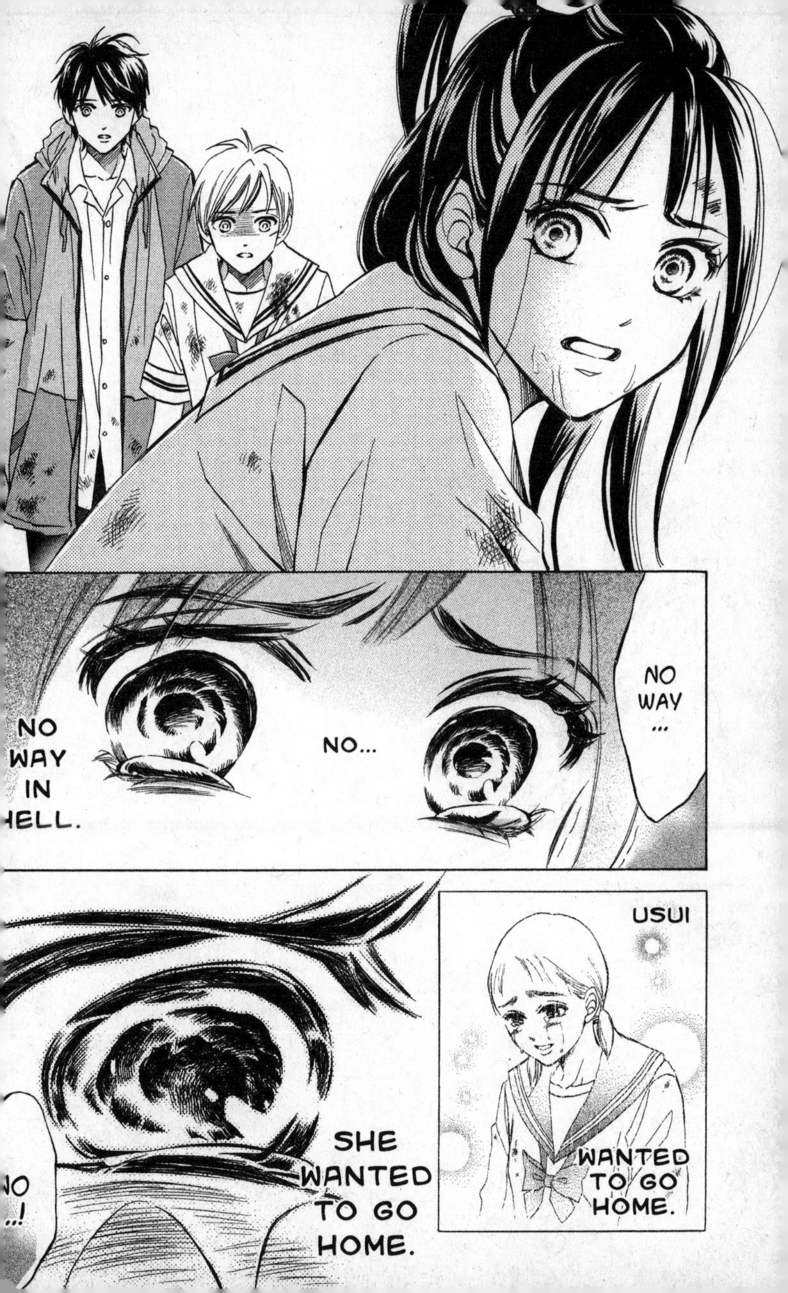

NO WAY ...
NO...
NO WAY IN HELL.
USUI
WANTED TO GO HOME.
SHE WANTED TO GO HOME.

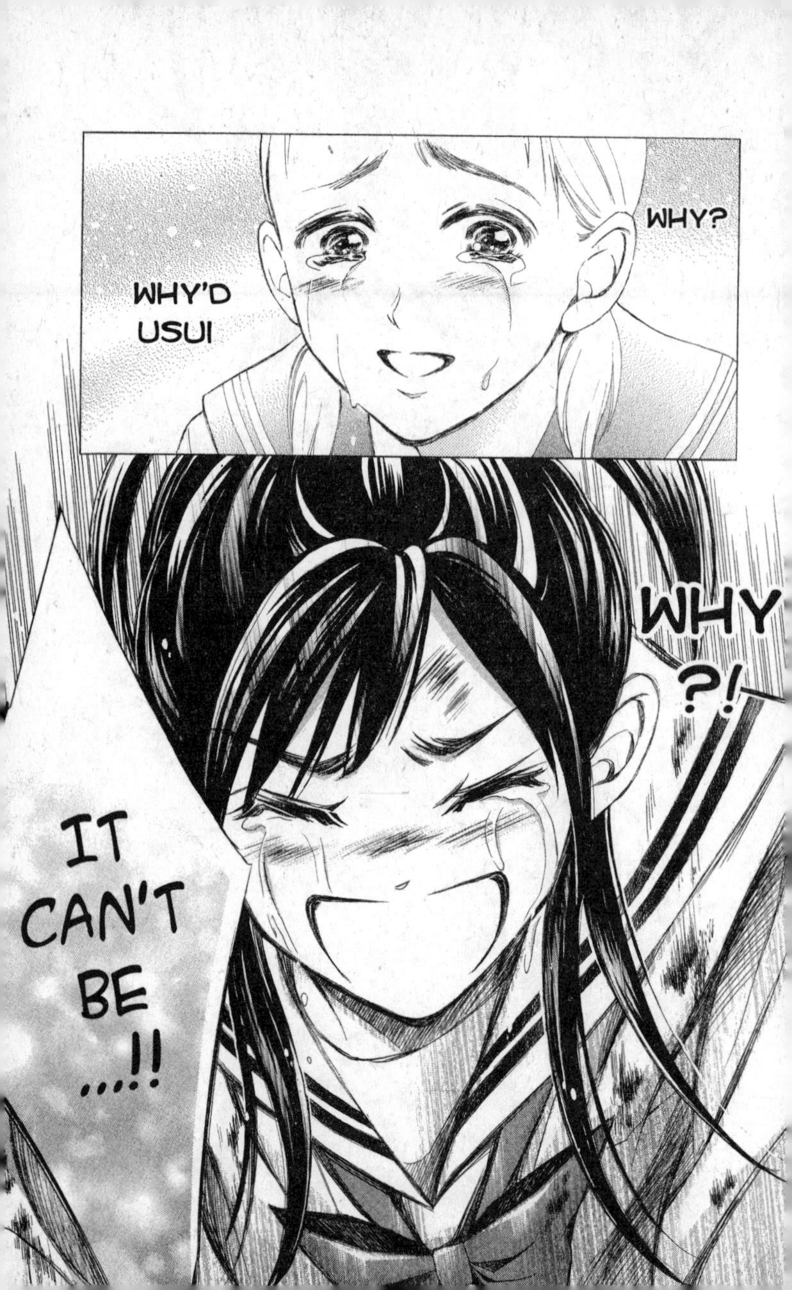
WHY?
WHY'D USUI
WHY ?!
IT CAN'T BE ...!!

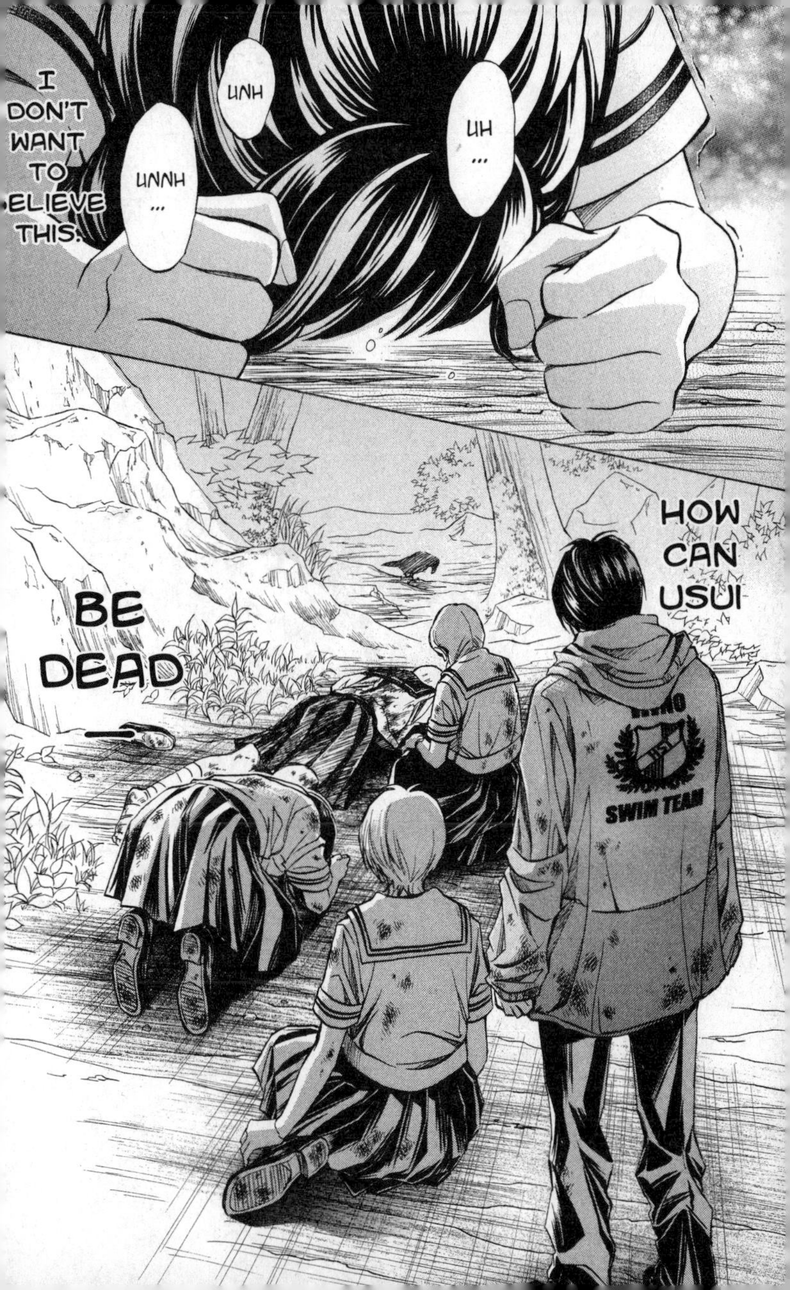
UH ...
UNH
UNNH ...
I DON'T WANT TO ELIEVE THIS.
HOW CAN USUI
BE DEAD —
SWIM TEAM

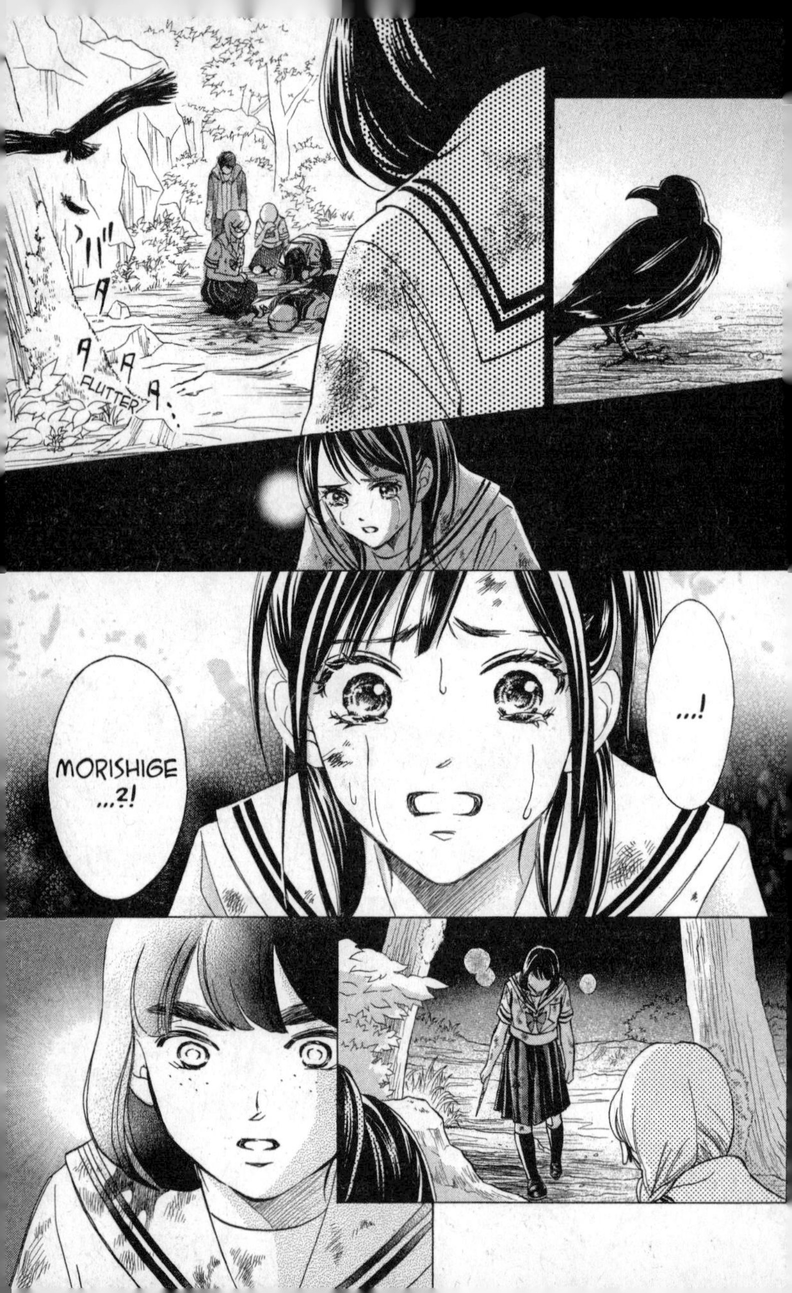
FLUTTER
...!
MORISHIGE ...?!

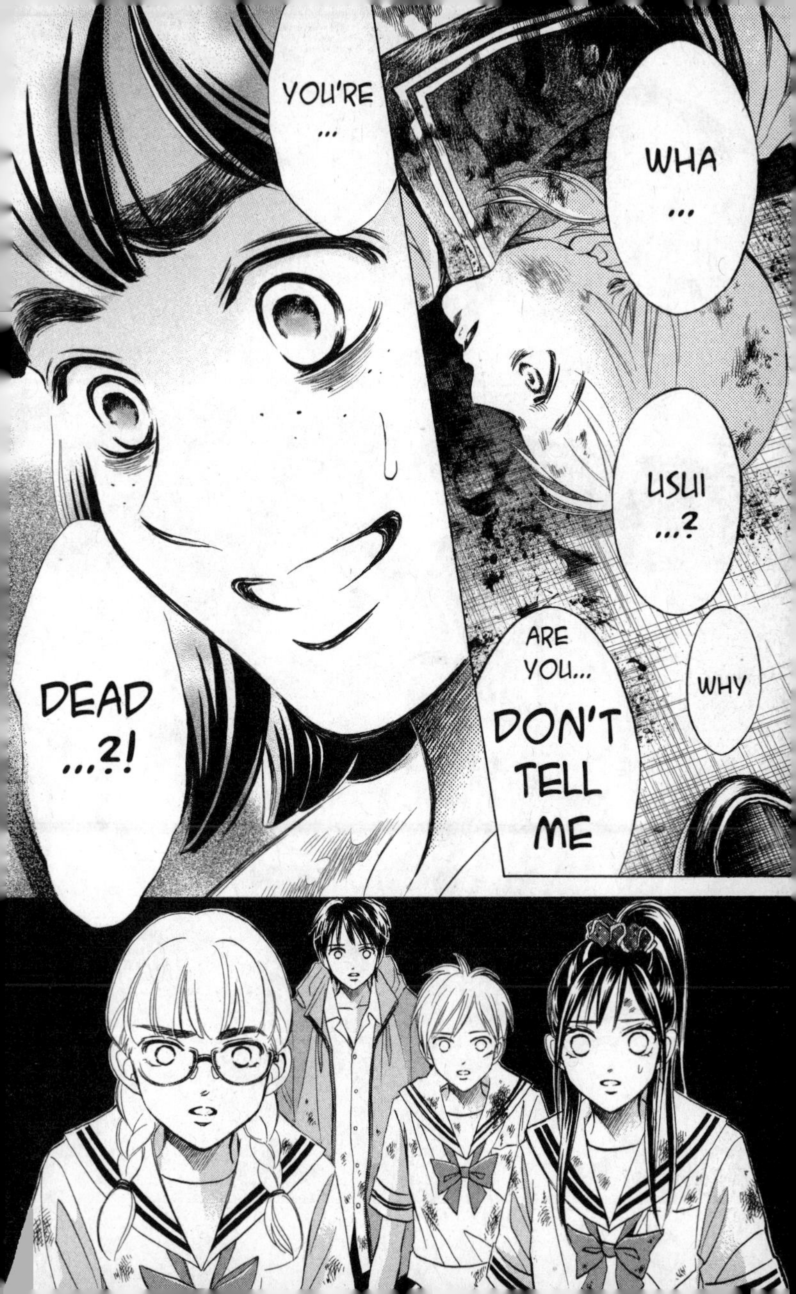
WHA ...
USUI ...?
WHY
ARE YOU... DON'T TELL ME
YOU'RE ...
DEAD ...?!

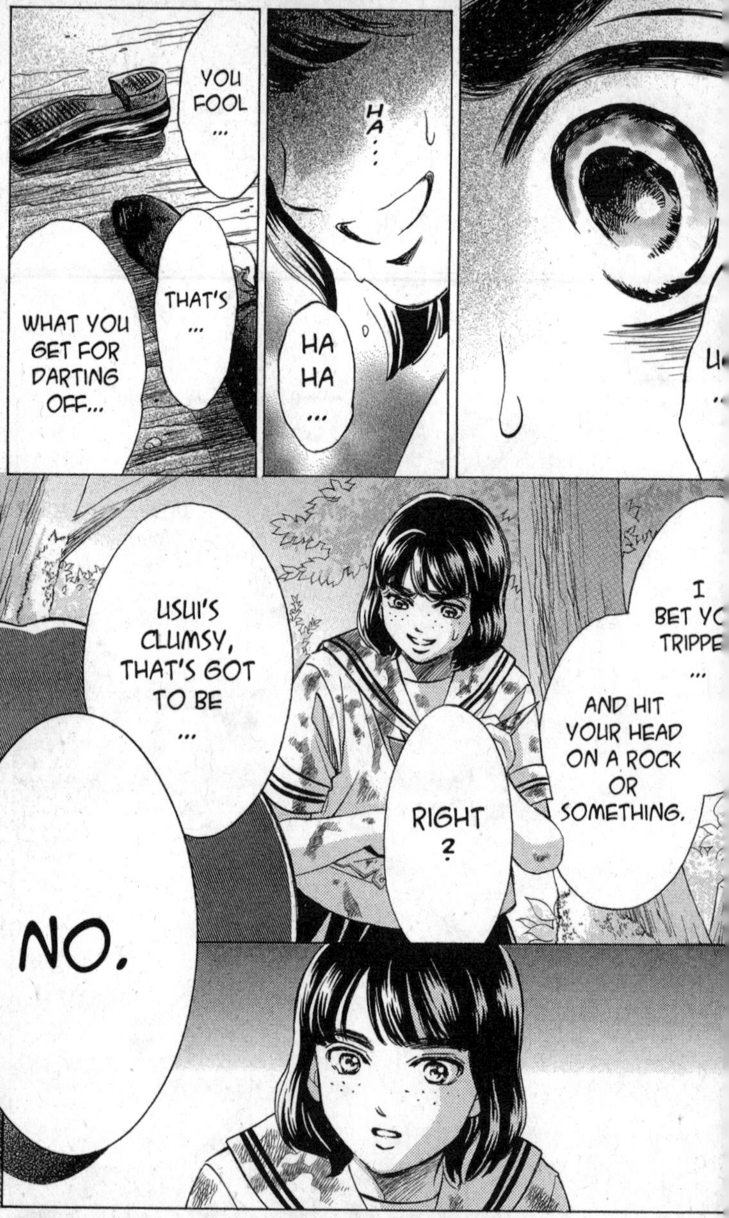
HA...
HA HA ...
YOU FOOL ...
THAT'S ...
WHAT YOU GET FOR DARTING OFF...
I BET YO TRIPPE ...
AND HIT YOUR HEAD ON A ROCK OR SOMETHING.
RIGHT ?
USUI'S CLUMSY, THAT'S GOT TO BE ...
NO.

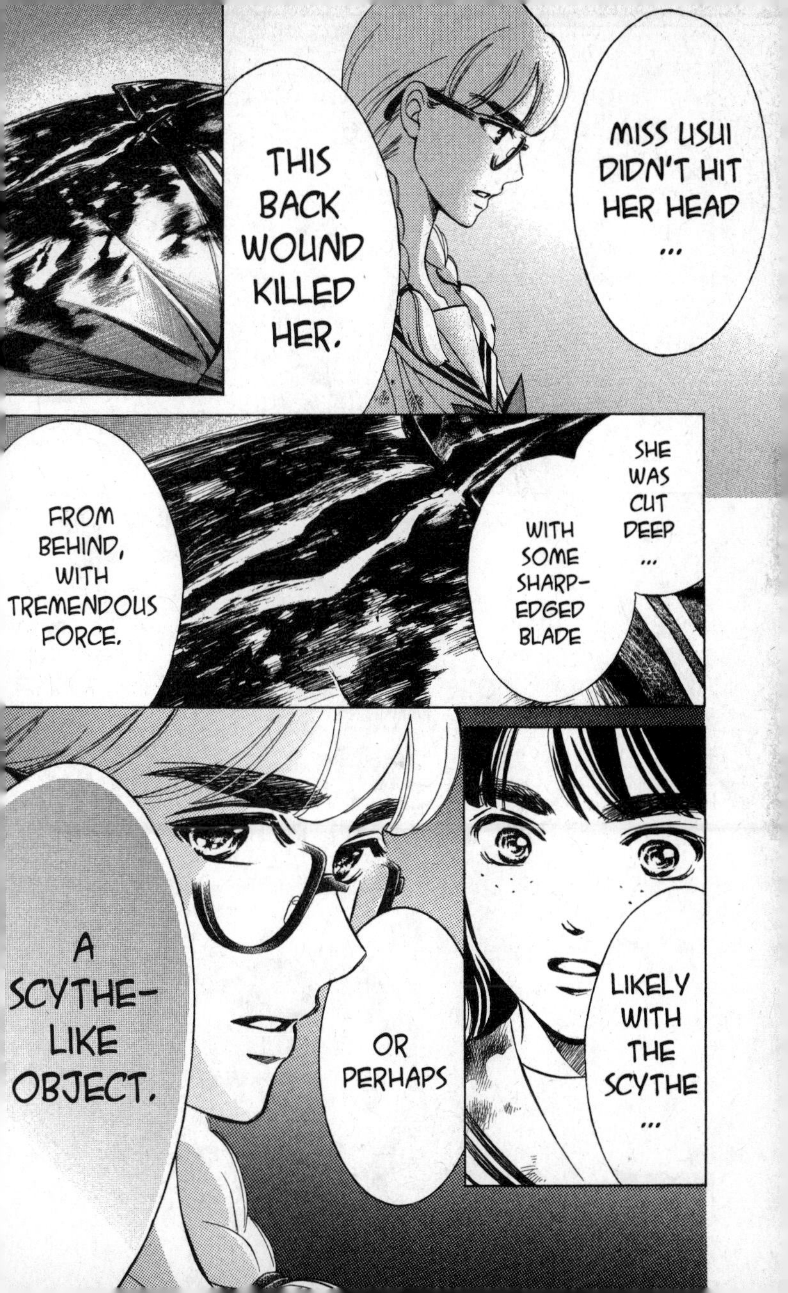
MISS USUI DIDN'T HIT HER HEAD ...
THIS BACK WOUND KILLED HER.
SHE WAS CUT DEEP ...
WITH SOME SHARP-EDGED BLADE
FROM BEHIND, WITH TREMENDOUS FORCE.
LIKELY WITH THE SCYTHE ...
OR PERHAPS
A SCYTHE-LIKE OBJECT.

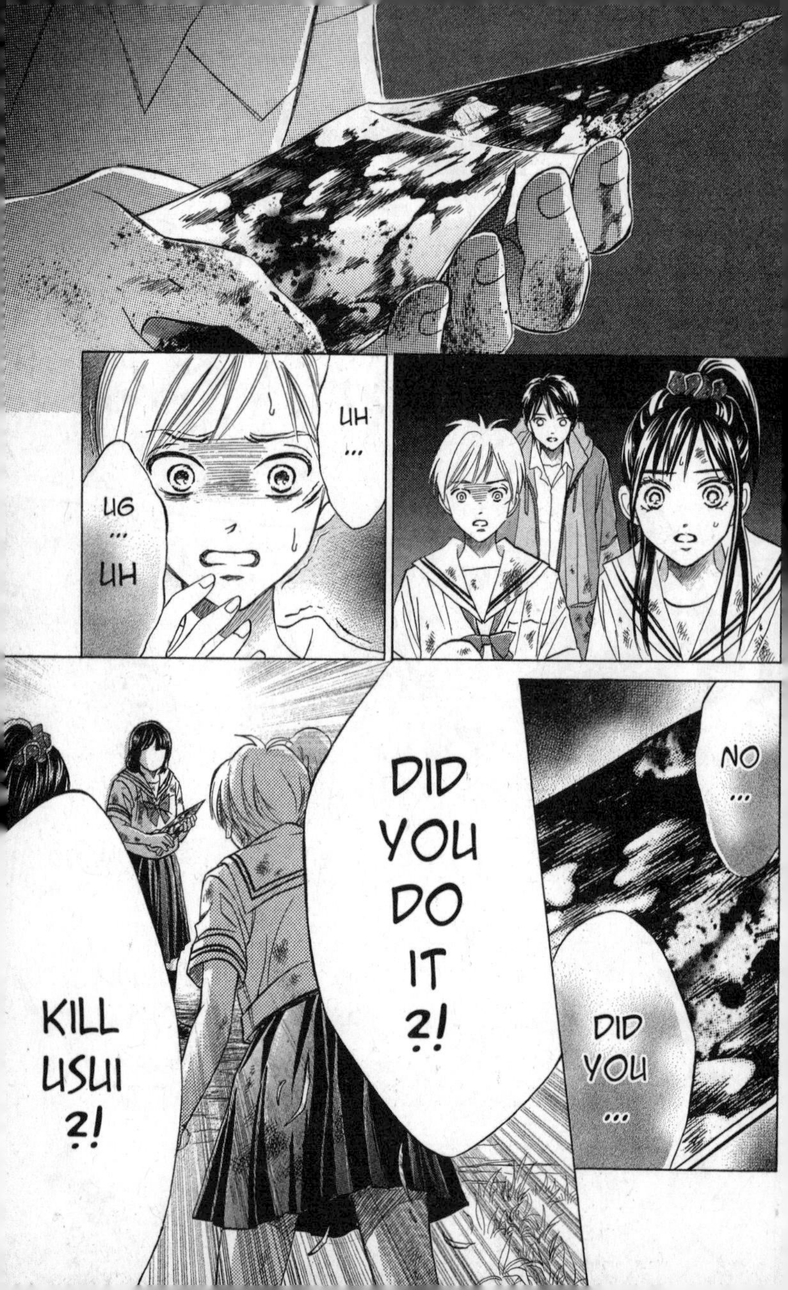
UH ...
UG ... UH
NO ...
DID YOU ...
DID YOU DO IT ?!
KILL USUI ?!

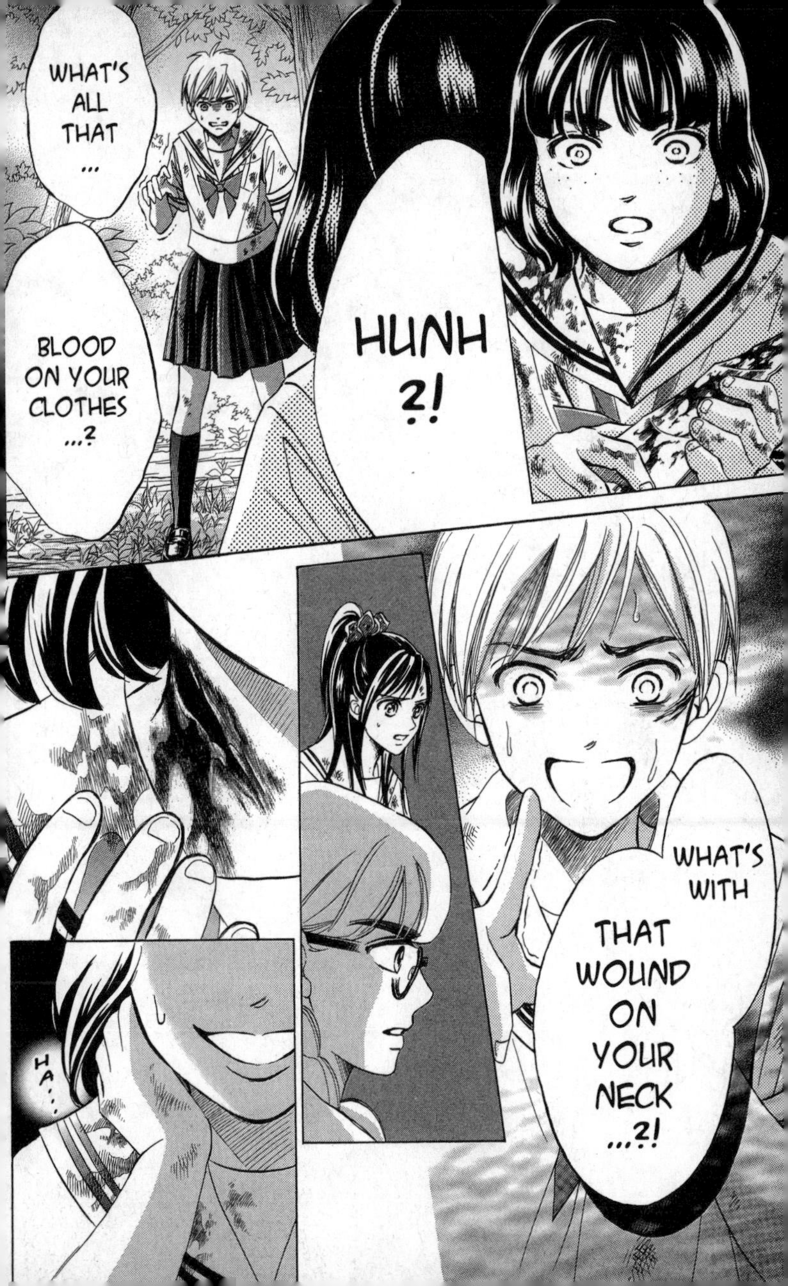
WHAT'S ALL THAT ...
BLOOD ON YOUR CLOTHES ...?
HUNH ?!
WHAT'S WITH THAT WOUND ON YOUR NECK ...?!
HA...

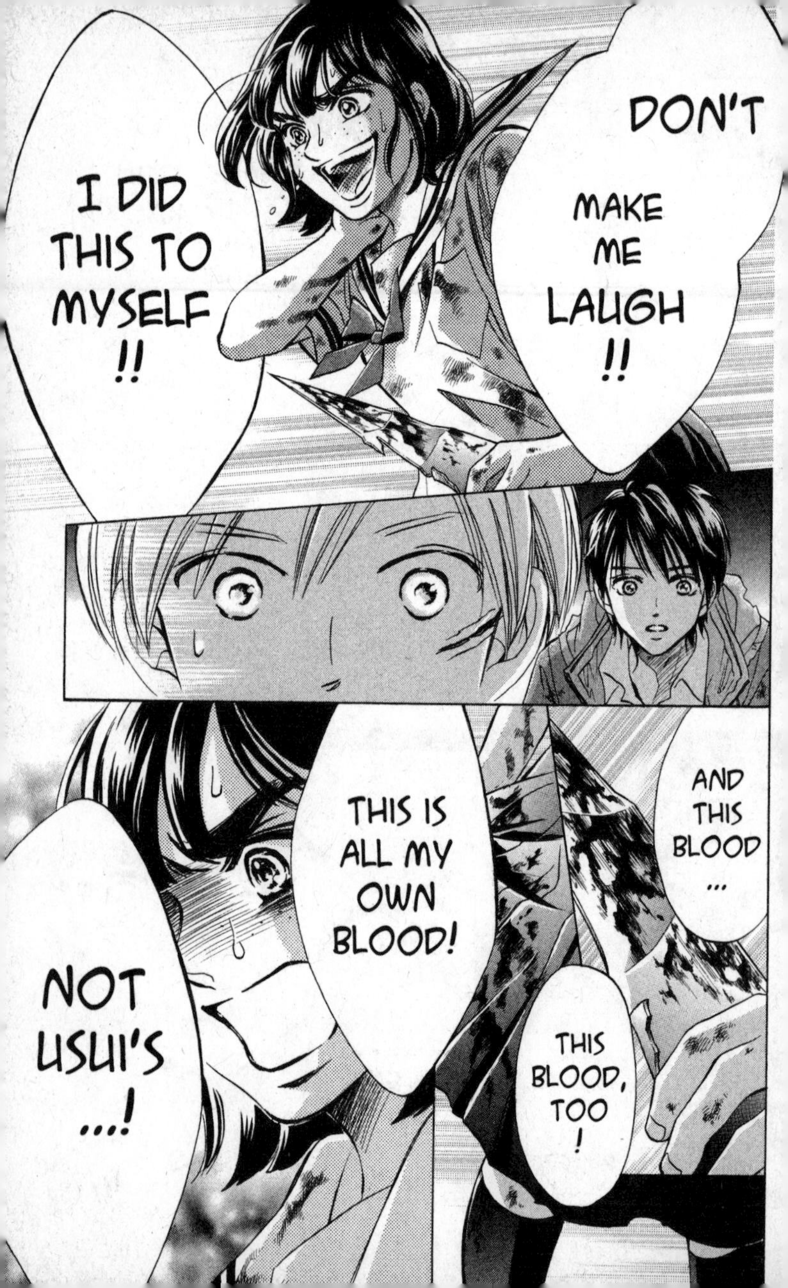
DON'T MAKE ME LAUGH !!
I DID THIS TO MYSELF !!
AND THIS BLOOD ...
THIS BLOOD, TOO !
THIS IS ALL MY OWN BLOOD!
NOT USUI'S ...!

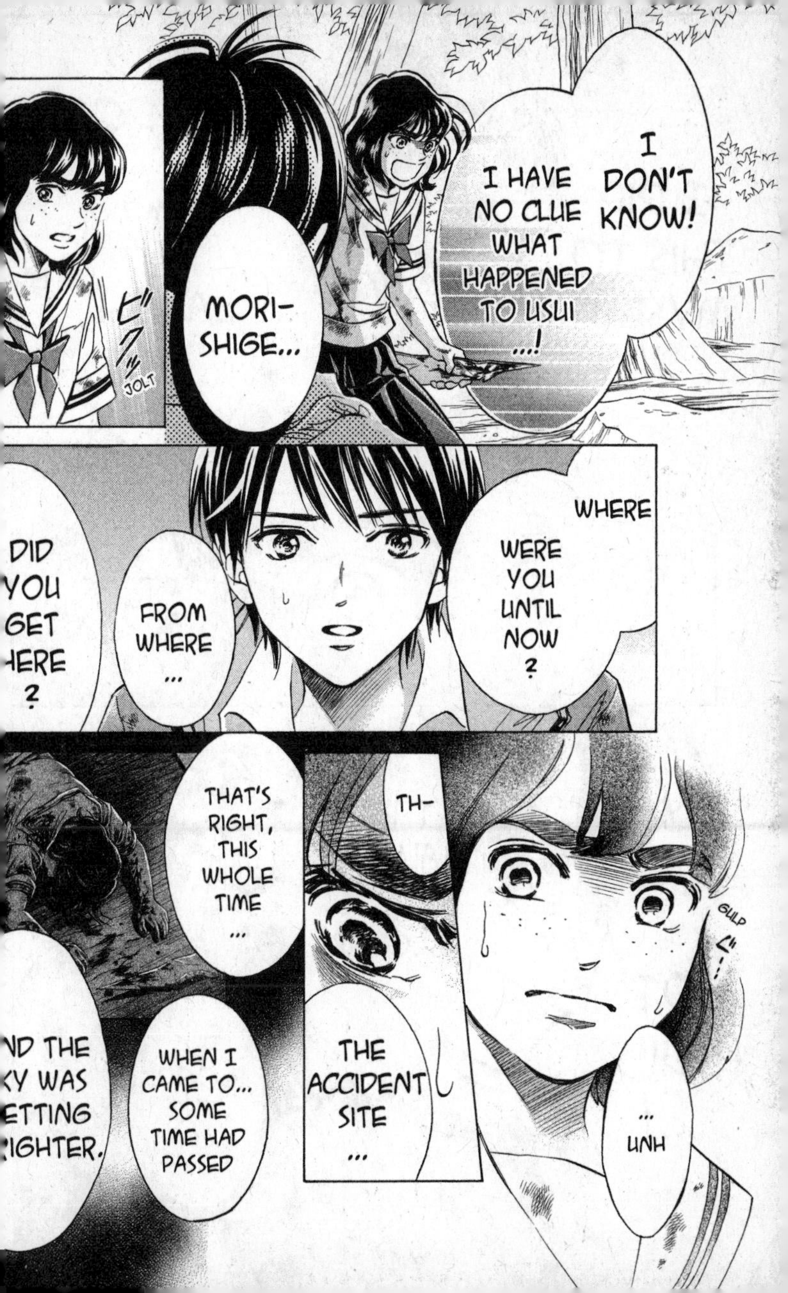
I DON'T KNOW!
I HAVE NO CLUE WHAT HAPPENED TO USUI ...!
MORI-SHIGE...
ビクッ
JOLT
WHERE WERE YOU UNTIL NOW?
FROM WHERE ...
DID YOU GET HERE?
GULP
... UNH
TH-
THE ACCIDENT SITE ...
THAT'S RIGHT, THIS WHOLE TIME ...
WHEN I CAME TO... SOME TIME HAD PASSED
ND THE KY WAS ETTING IGHTER.

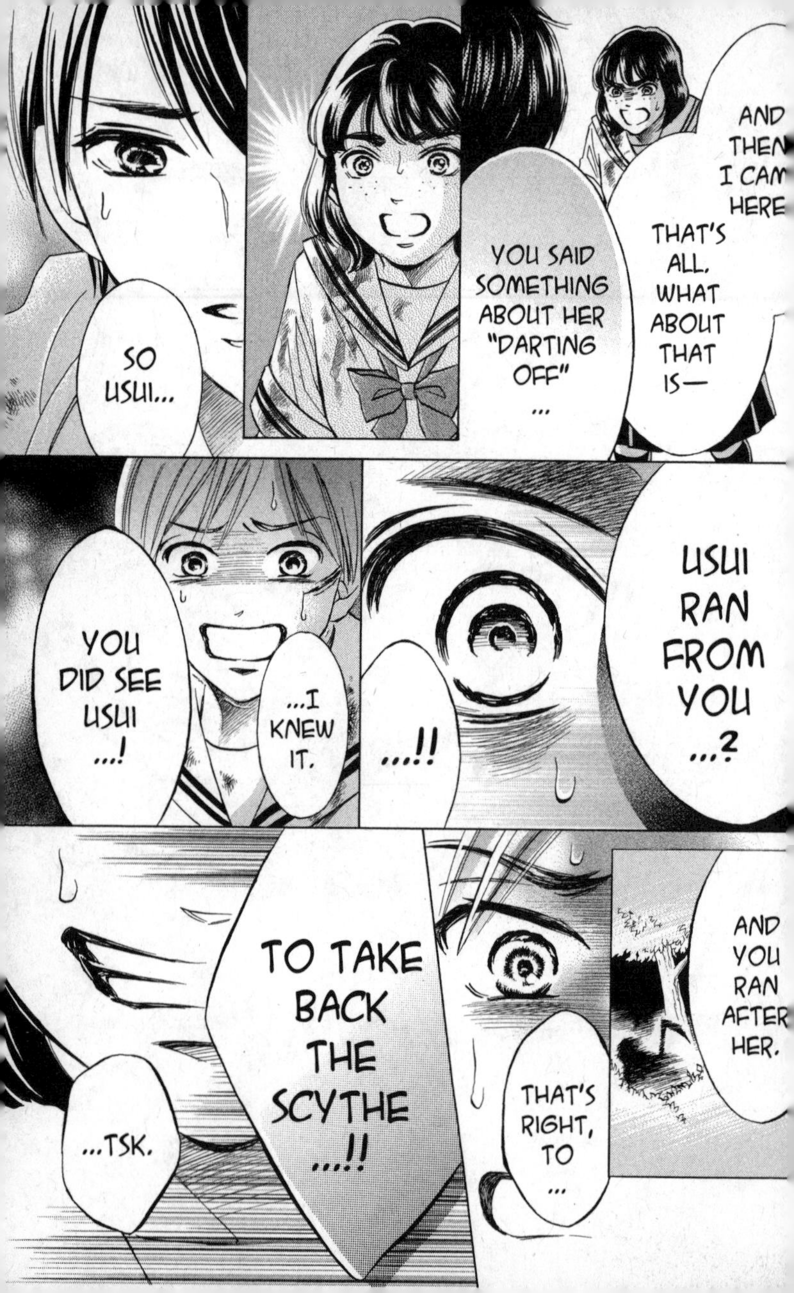
AND THEN I CAM HERE
THAT'S ALL. WHAT ABOUT THAT IS—
YOU SAID SOMETHING ABOUT HER "DARTING OFF" ...
SO USUI...
USUI RAN FROM YOU ...?
...!!
...I KNEW IT.
YOU DID SEE USUI ...!
AND YOU RAN AFTER HER.
THAT'S RIGHT, TO ...
TO TAKE BACK THE SCYTHE ...!!
...TSK.

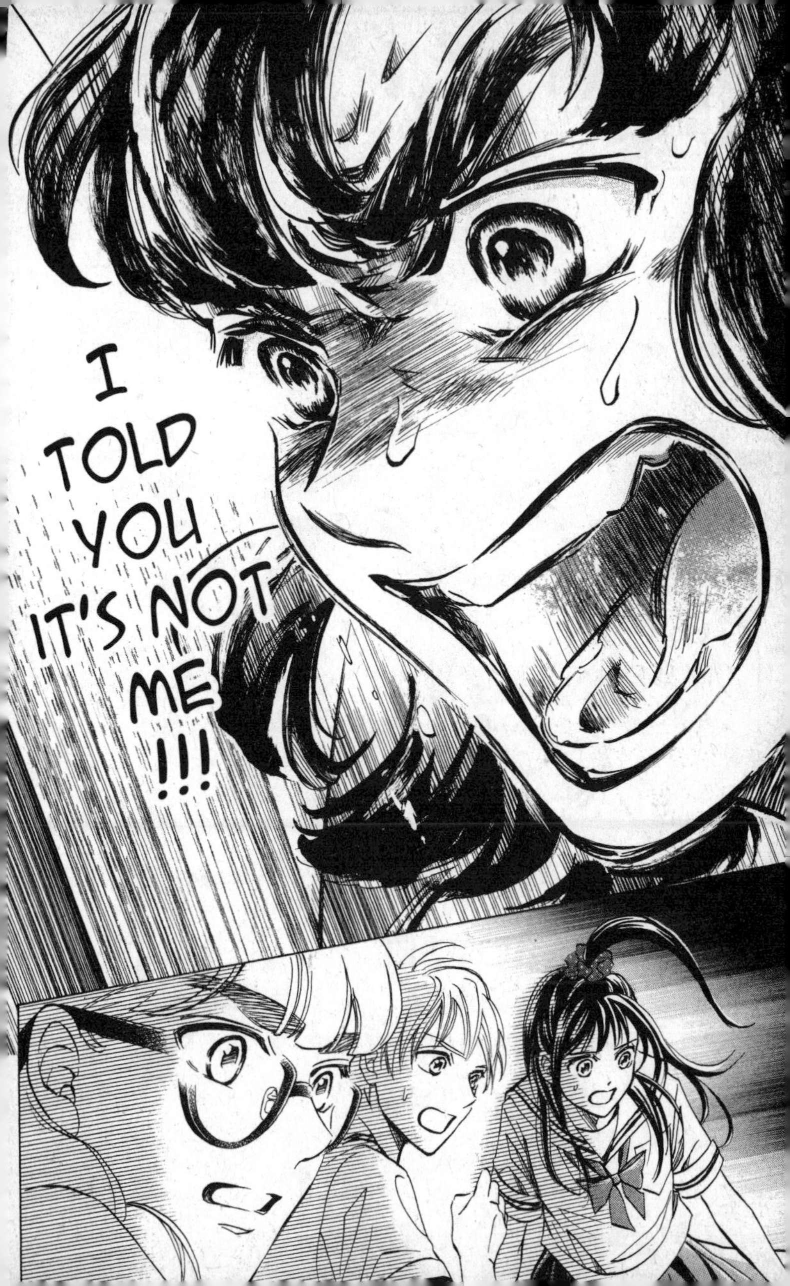
I TOLD YOU IT'S NOT ME!!!

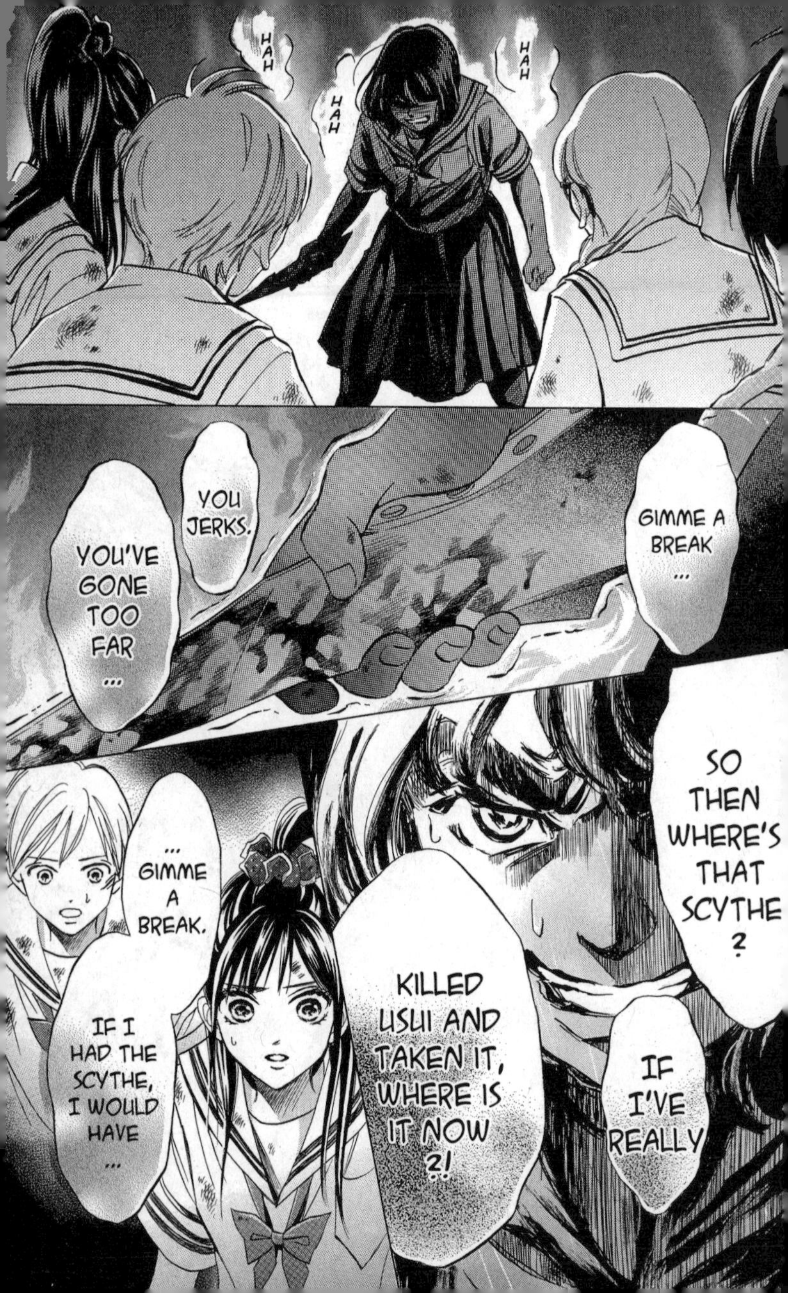
HAH
HAH
HAH
GIMME A BREAK ...
YOU JERKS.
YOU'VE GONE TOO FAR ...
SO THEN WHERE'S THAT SCYTHE?
IF I'VE REALLY
KILLED USUI AND TAKEN IT, WHERE IS IT NOW?!
... GIMME A BREAK.
IF I HAD THE SCYTHE, I WOULD HAVE ...

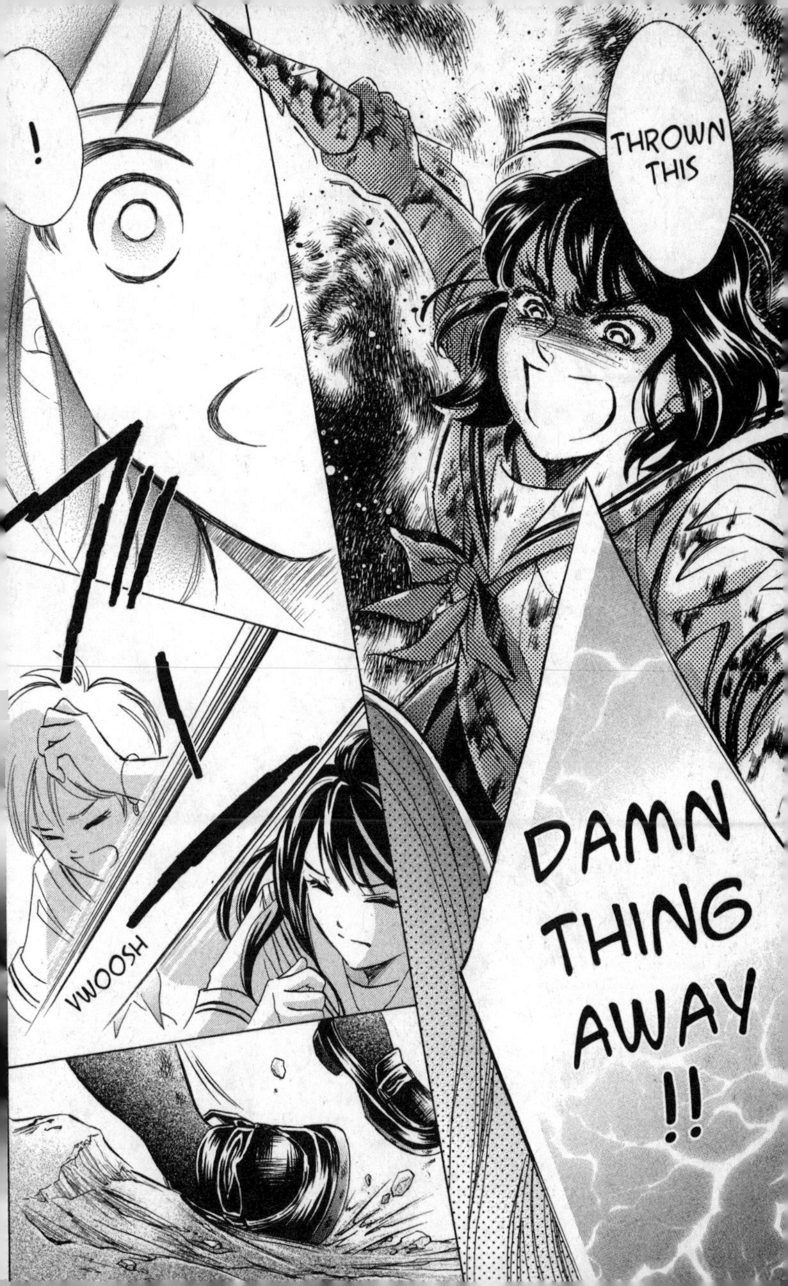
THROWN THIS
DAMN THING AWAY !!
!
VWOOSH

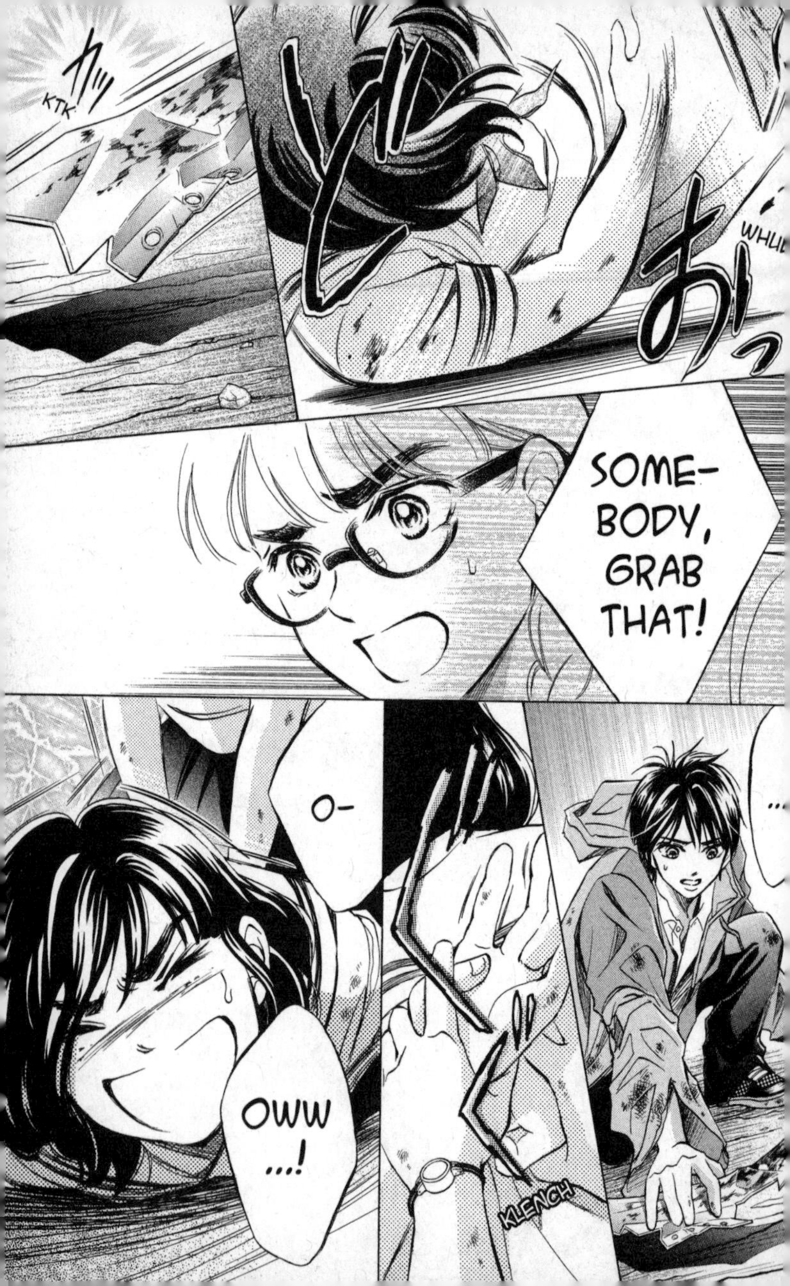
KTK
SOMEBODY, GRAB THAT!
...
KLENCH
O-
OWW ...!

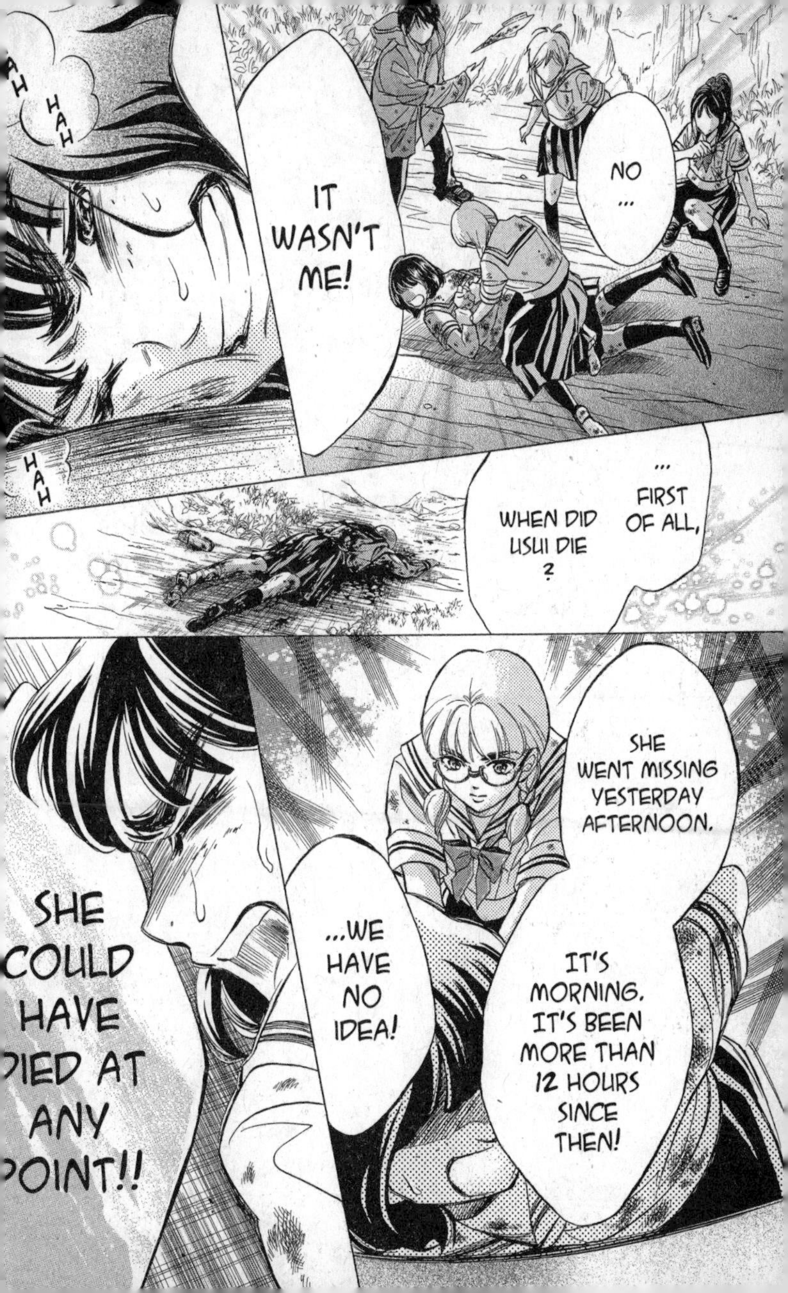
NO ...
IT WASN'T ME!
HAH HAH
HAH
... FIRST OF ALL,
WHEN DID USUI DIE ?
SHE WENT MISSING YESTERDAY AFTERNOON.
IT'S MORNING. IT'S BEEN MORE THAN 12 HOURS SINCE THEN!
...WE HAVE NO IDEA!
SHE COULD HAVE DIED AT ANY POINT!!

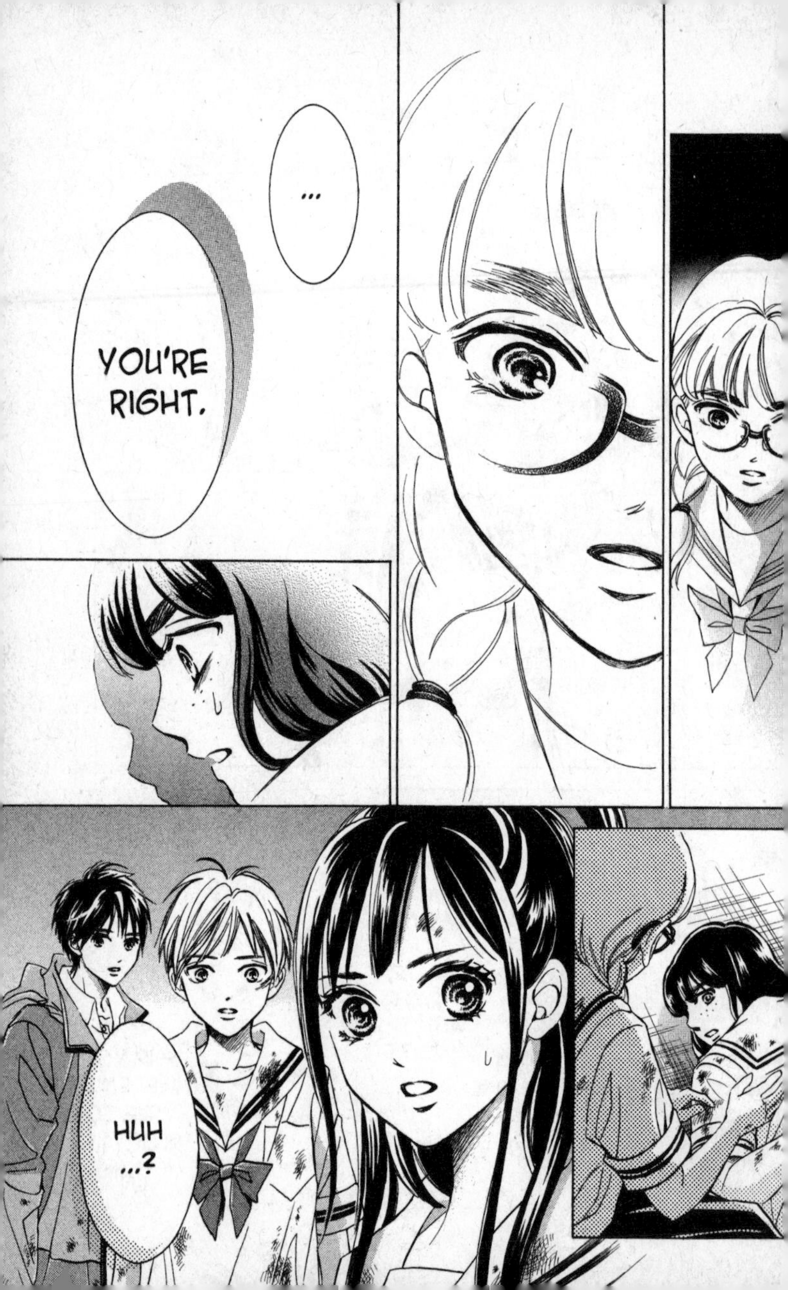
...
YOU'RE RIGHT.
HUH ...?

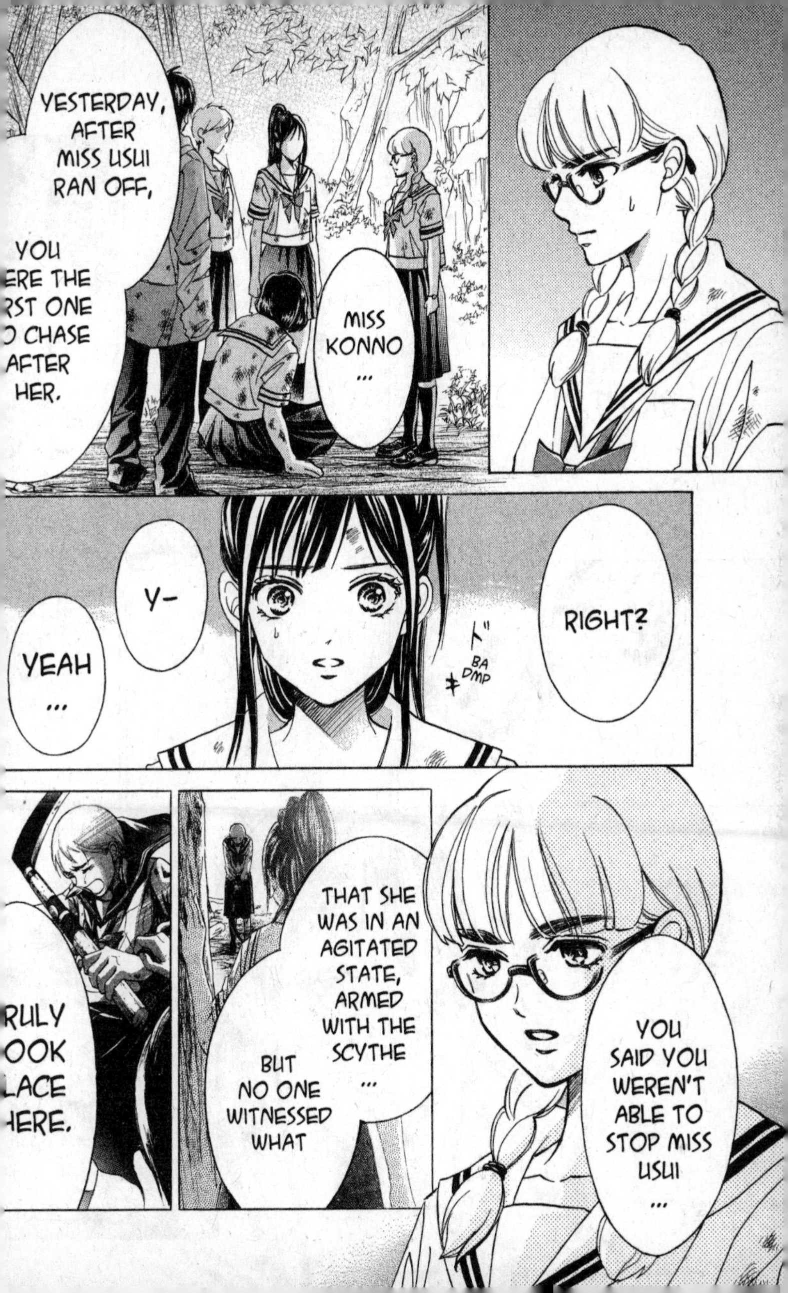
MISS KONNO ...
YESTERDAY, AFTER MISS USUI RAN OFF,
YOU ERE THE RST ONE O CHASE AFTER HER.
RIGHT?
ドキ BA DMP
Y-
YEAH ...
YOU SAID YOU WEREN'T ABLE TO STOP MISS USUI ...
THAT SHE WAS IN AN AGITATED STATE, ARMED WITH THE SCYTHE ...
BUT NO ONE WITNESSED WHAT
RULY OOK LACE HERE.

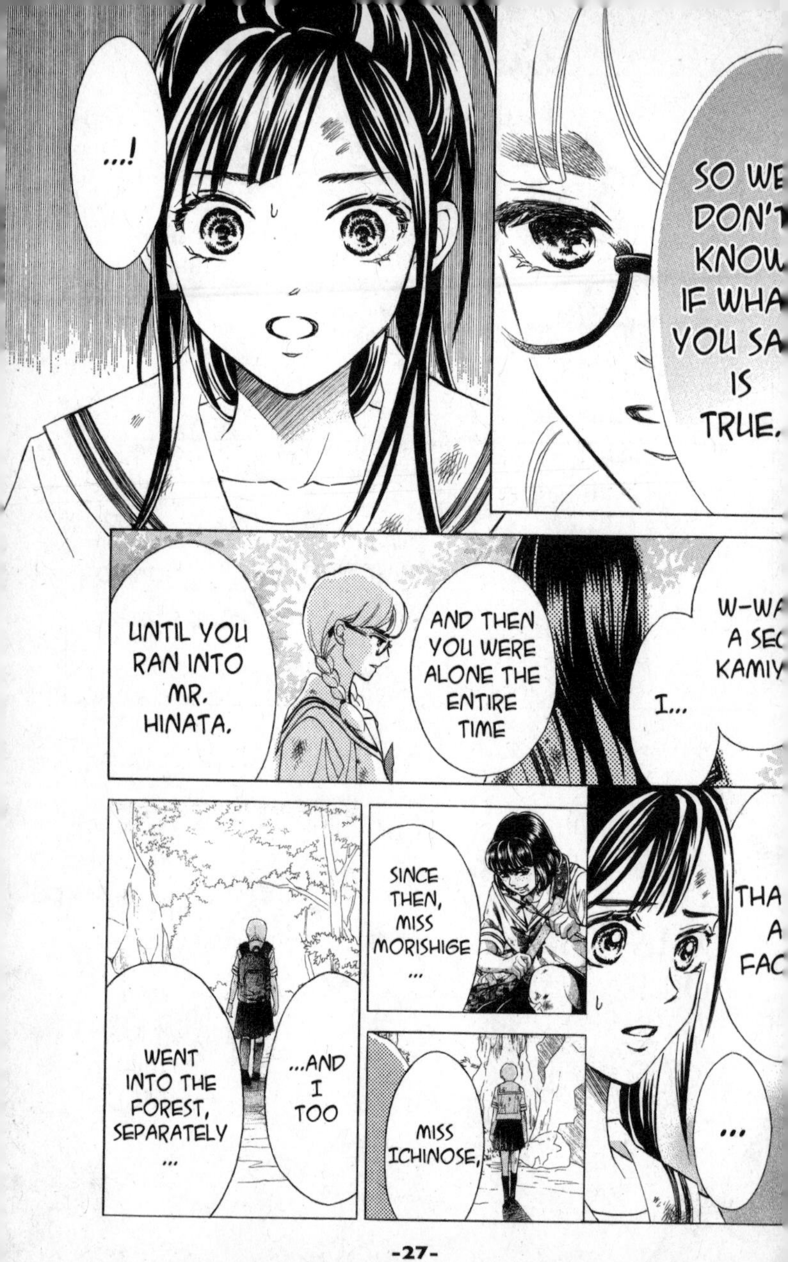
SO WE DON'T KNOW IF WHA YOU SA IS TRUE.
...!
W-WA A SEC KAMIY
I...
AND THEN YOU WERE ALONE THE ENTIRE TIME
UNTIL YOU RAN INTO MR. HINATA.
THA A FAC
...
SINCE THEN, MISS MORISHIGE ...
MISS ICHINOSE,
...AND I TOO
WENT INTO THE FOREST, SEPARATELY ...

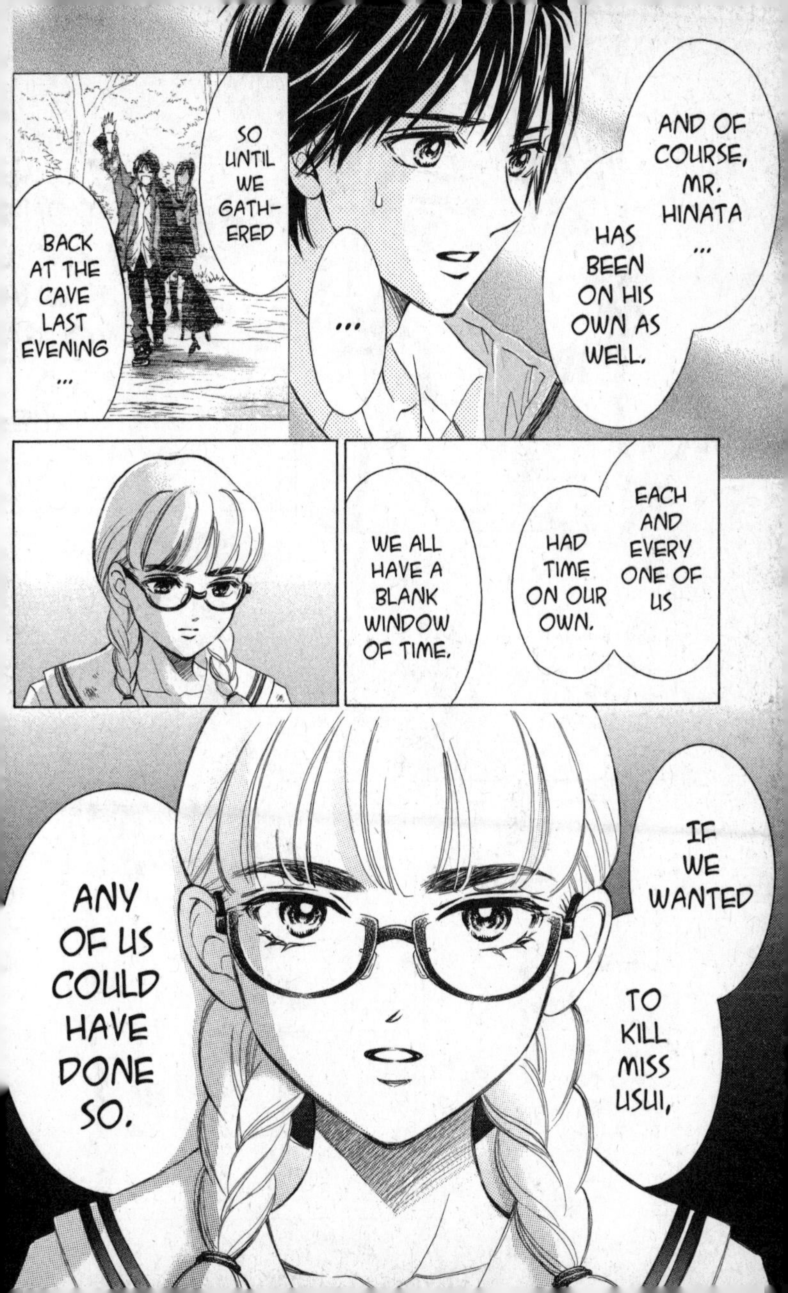
AND OF COURSE, MR. HINATA ...
HAS BEEN ON HIS OWN AS WELL.
...
SO UNTIL WE GATH-ERED
BACK AT THE CAVE LAST EVENING ...
EACH AND EVERY ONE OF US
HAD TIME ON OUR OWN.
WE ALL HAVE A BLANK WINDOW OF TIME.
IF WE WANTED
TO KILL MISS USUI,
ANY OF US COULD HAVE DONE SO.

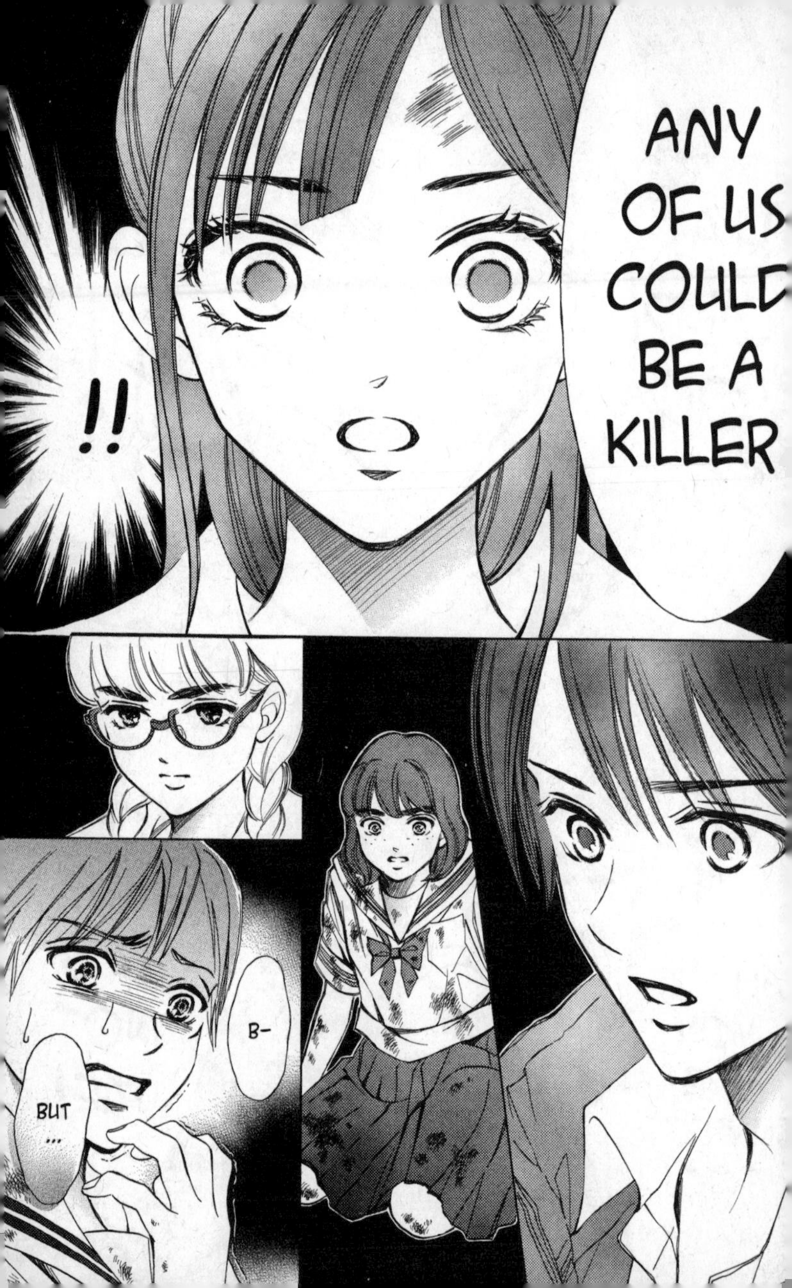
ANY OF US COULD BE A KILLER
!!
B-
BUT ...

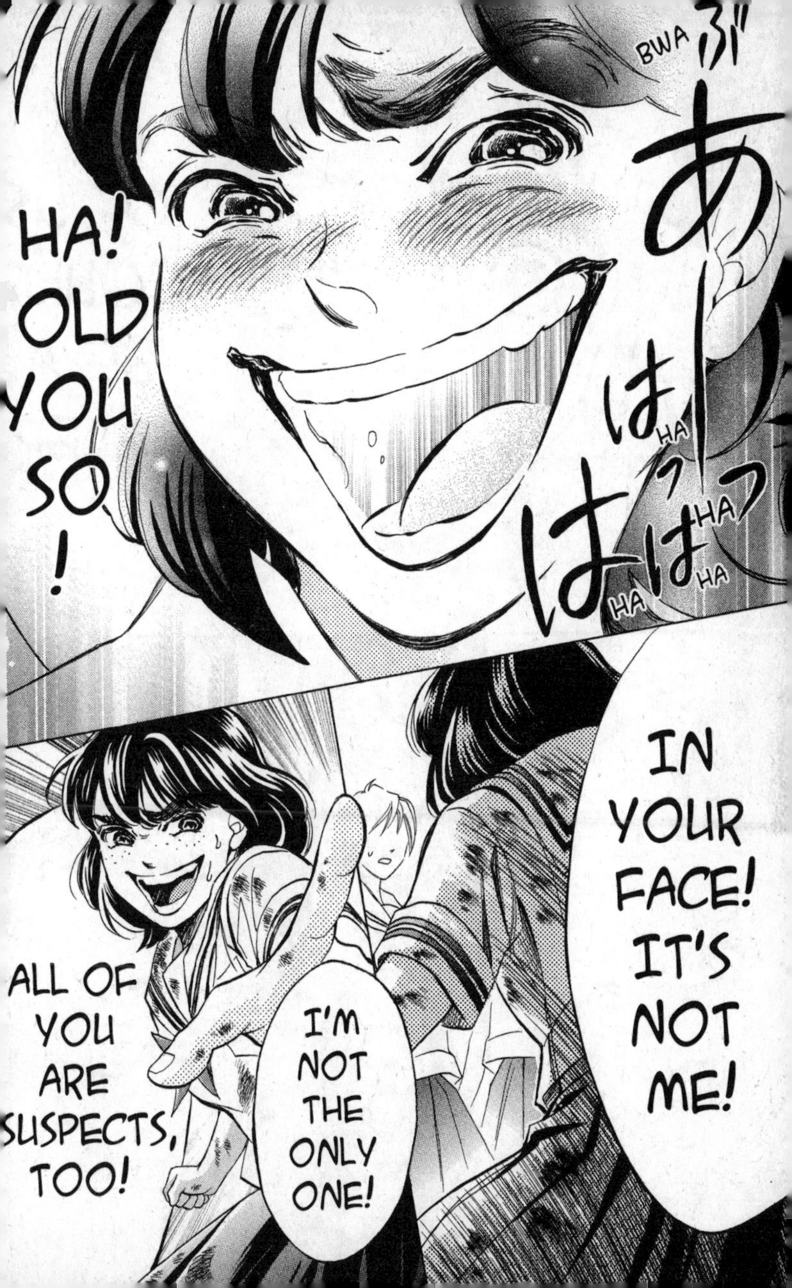

BWA ぶ
あーはっはっ
HA HA HA HA
HA! OLD YOU SO!
IN YOUR FACE! IT'S NOT ME!
I'M NOT THE ONLY ONE!
ALL OF YOU ARE SUSPECTS, TOO!

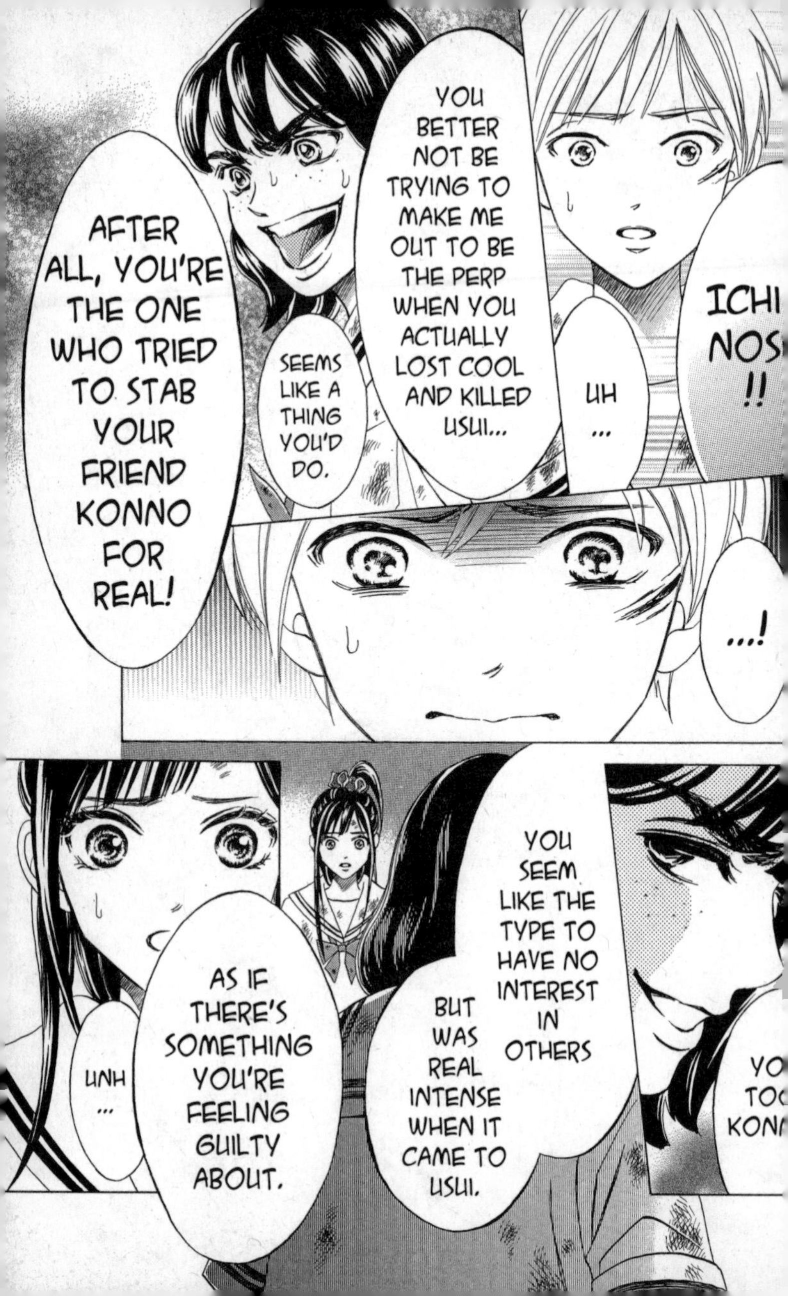
ICHI NOS !!
UH ...
YOU BETTER NOT BE TRYING TO MAKE ME OUT TO BE THE PERP WHEN YOU ACTUALLY LOST COOL AND KILLED USUI...
SEEMS LIKE A THING YOU'D DO.
AFTER ALL, YOU'RE THE ONE WHO TRIED TO STAB YOUR FRIEND KONNO FOR REAL!
...!
YO TOO KON
YOU SEEM LIKE THE TYPE TO HAVE NO INTEREST IN OTHERS
BUT WAS REAL INTENSE WHEN IT CAME TO USUI.
AS IF THERE'S SOMETHING YOU'RE FEELING GUILTY ABOUT.
UNH ...

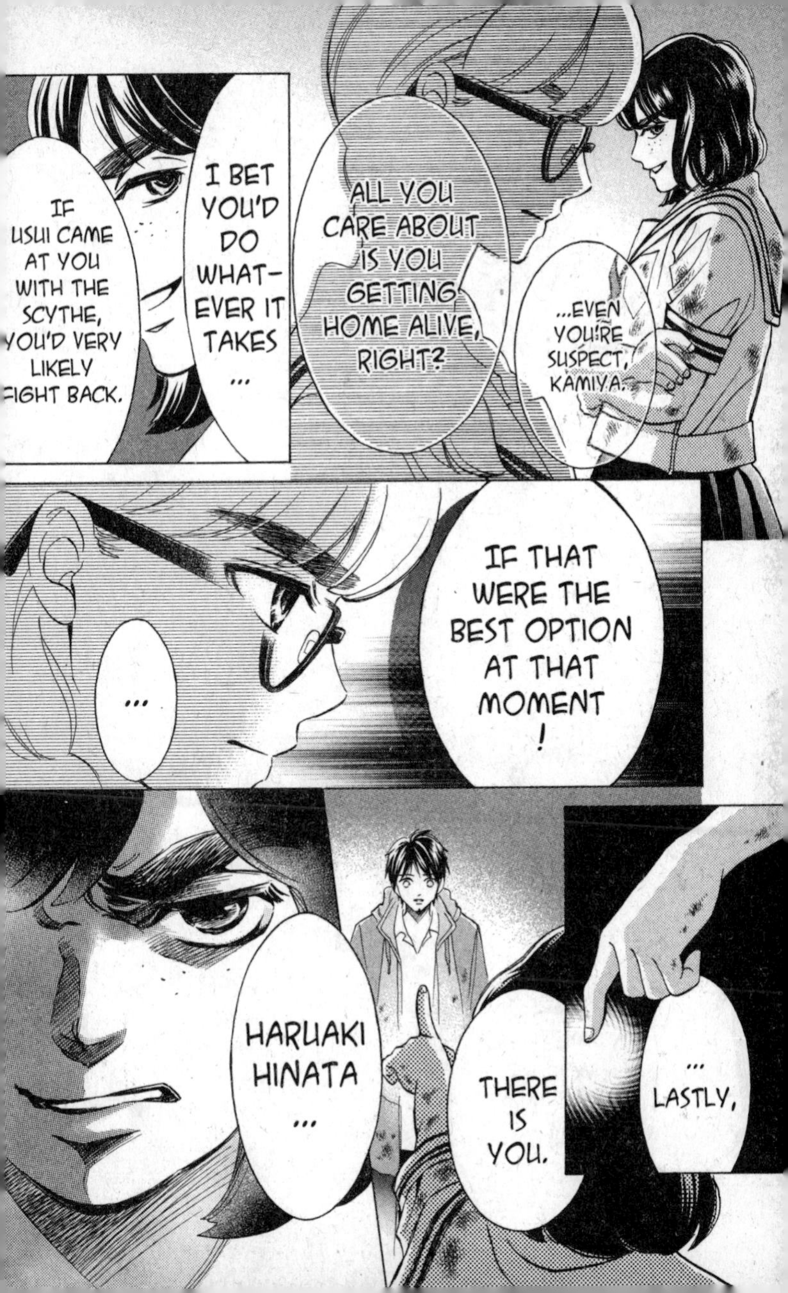
...EVEN YOU'RE SUSPECT, KAMIYA.
ALL YOU CARE ABOUT IS YOU GETTING HOME ALIVE, RIGHT?
I BET YOU'D DO WHATEVER IT TAKES...
IF USUI CAME AT YOU WITH THE SCYTHE, YOU'D VERY LIKELY FIGHT BACK.
IF THAT WERE THE BEST OPTION AT THAT MOMENT!
...
...LASTLY,
THERE IS YOU.
HARUAKI HINATA...

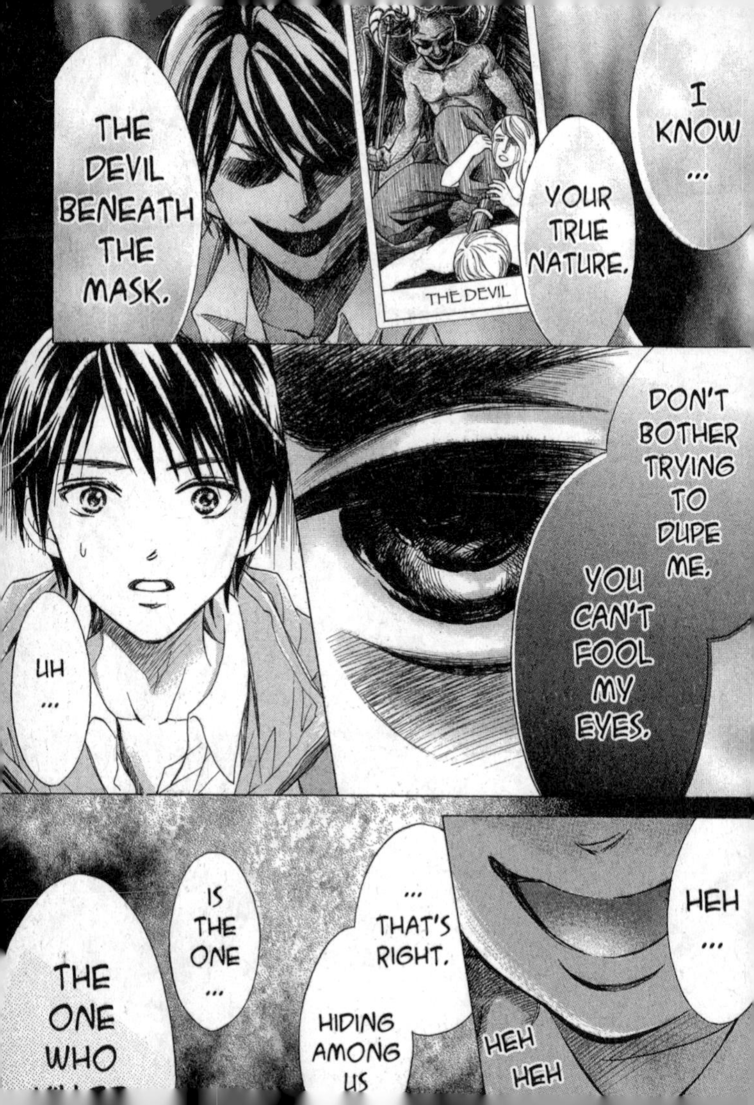
I KNOW ...
YOUR TRUE NATURE.
THE DEVIL
THE DEVIL BENEATH THE MASK.
DON'T BOTHER TRYING TO DUPE ME.
YOU CAN'T FOOL MY EYES.
UH ...
HEH ...
HEH HEH
... THAT'S RIGHT.
HIDING AMONG US
IS THE ONE ...
THE ONE WHO

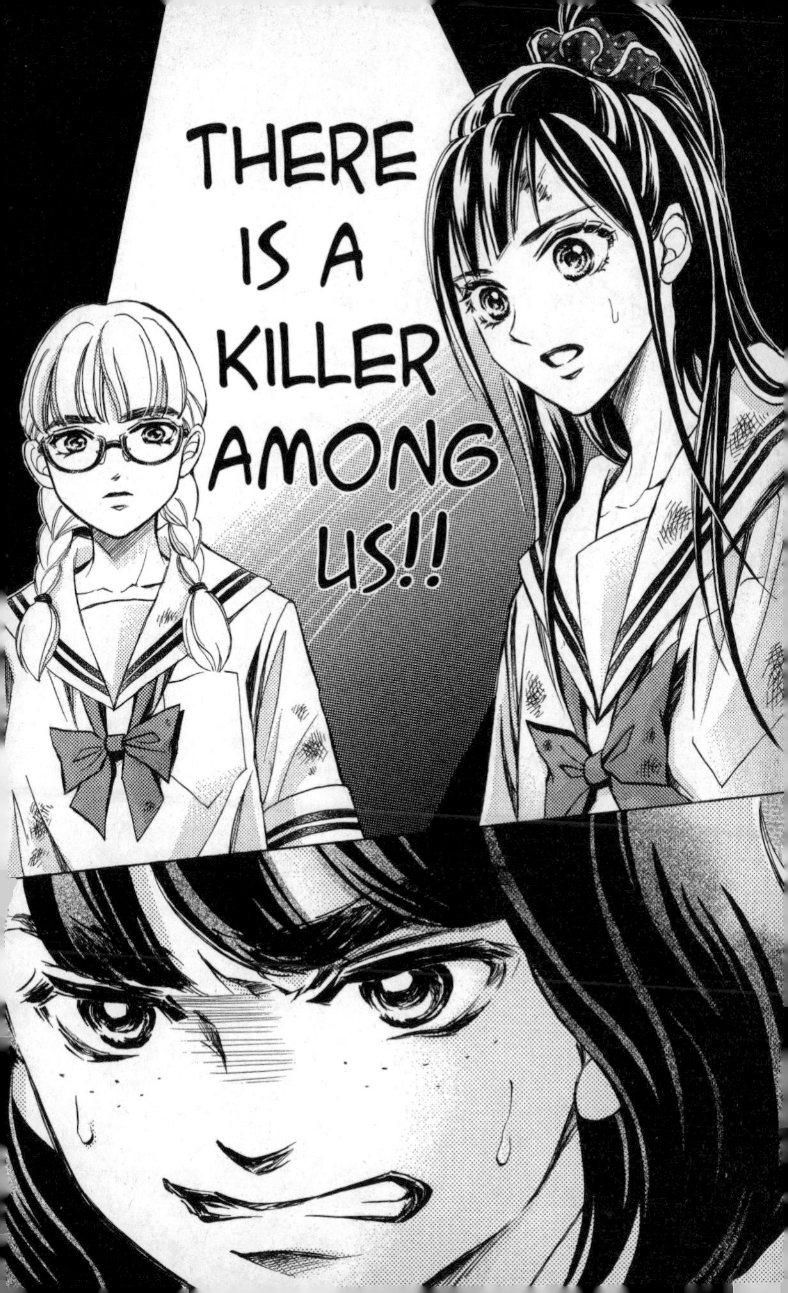
THERE IS A KILLER AMONG US!!

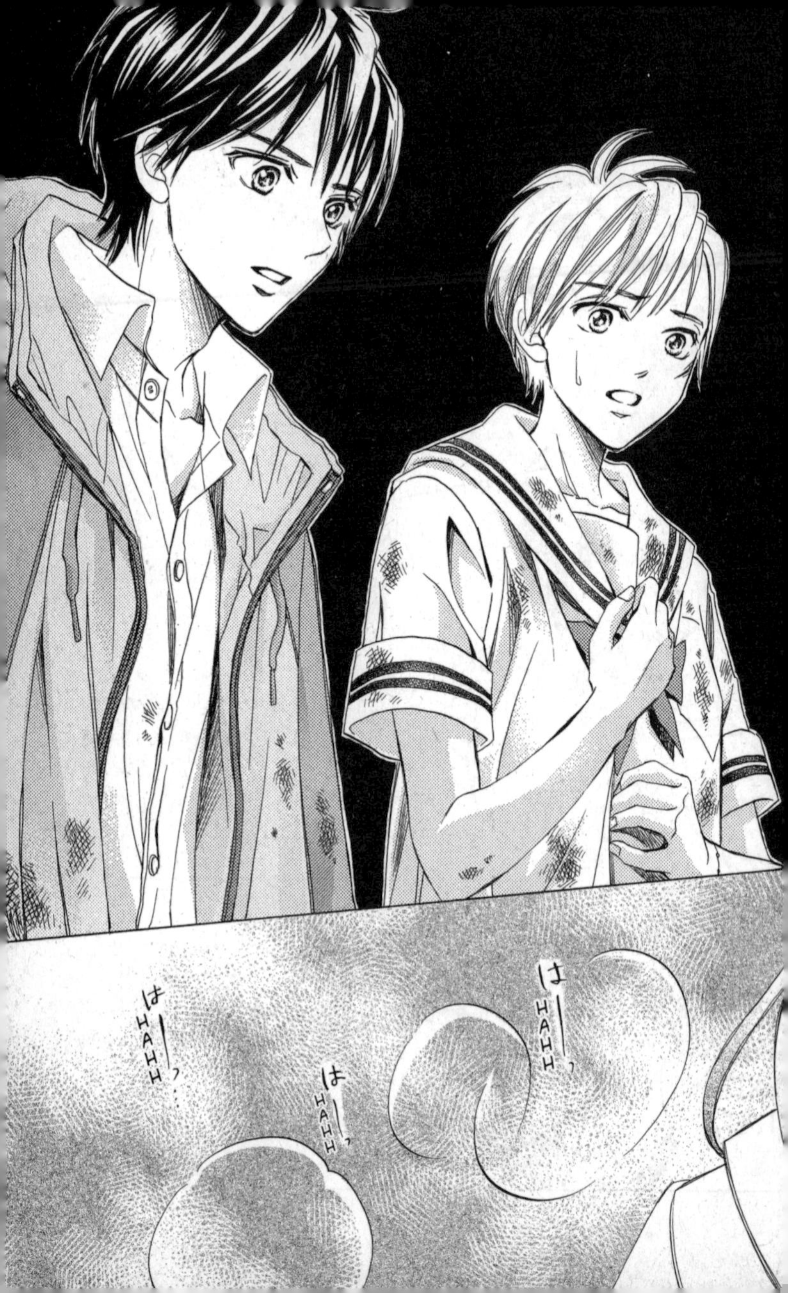

は―、
HAHH
は―、
HAHH
は―っ…
HAHH

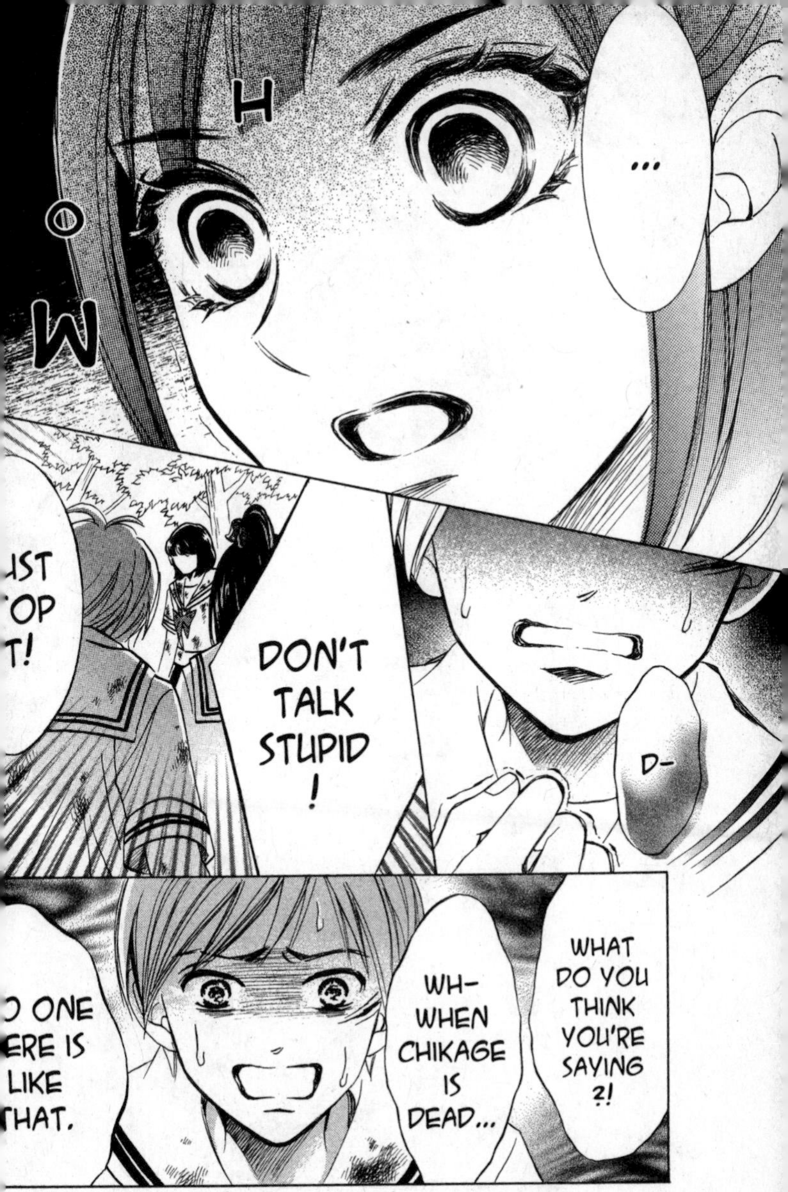
...
H O W
D-
DON'T TALK STUPID!
ST OP T!
WHAT DO YOU THINK YOU'RE SAYING?!
WH-WHEN CHIKAGE IS DEAD...
O ONE ERE IS LIKE THAT.

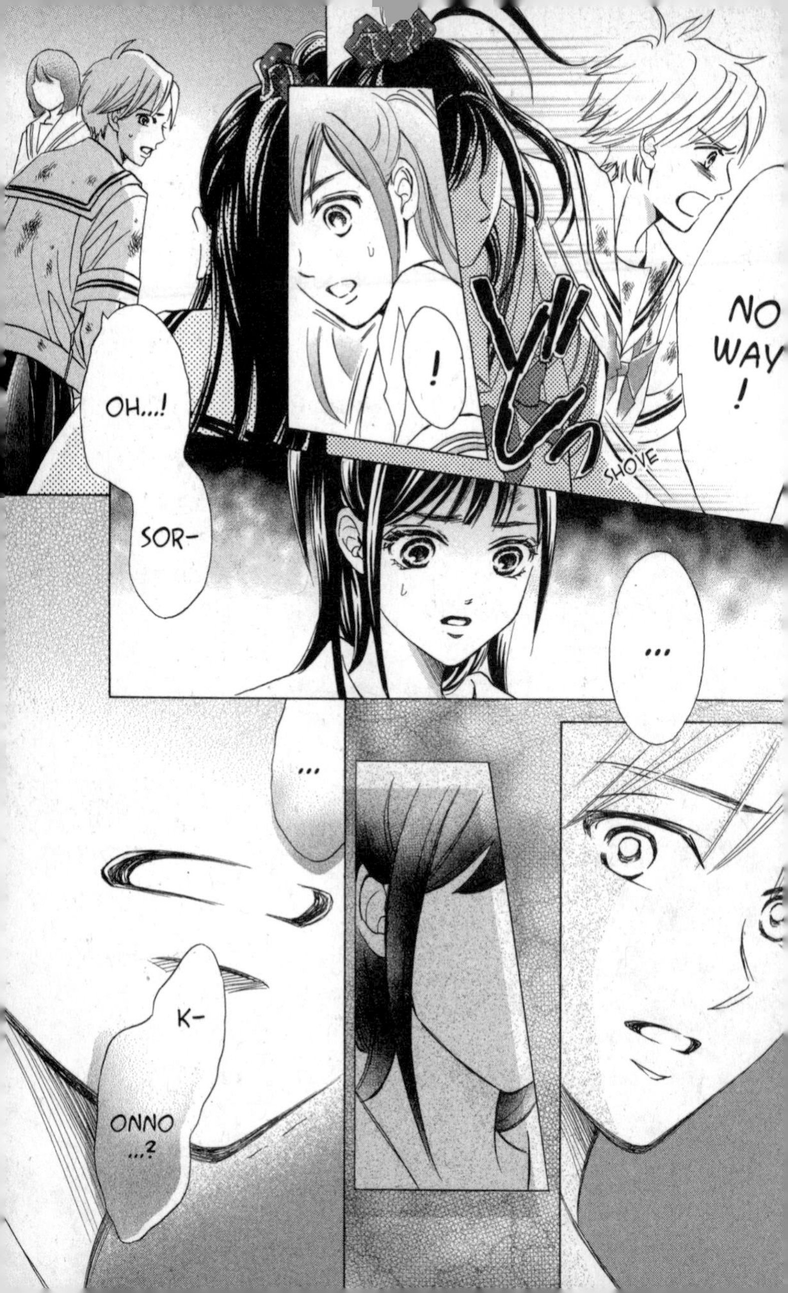
NO WAY!
SHOVE
!
OH...! SOR-
...
...
K- ONNO ...?

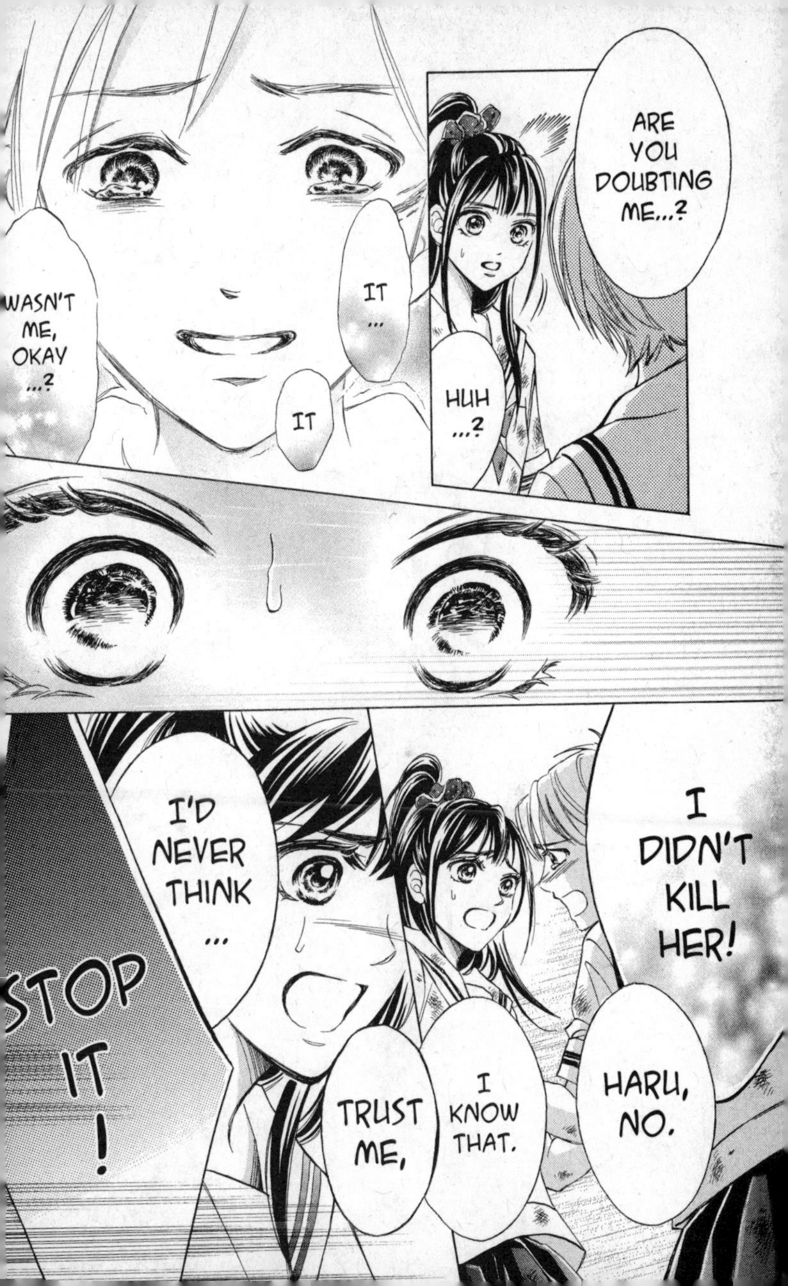
ARE YOU DOUBTING ME...?
HUH ...?
IT ...
IT
WASN'T ME, OKAY ...?
I DIDN'T KILL HER!
HARU, NO.
I KNOW THAT.
TRUST ME,
I'D NEVER THINK ...
STOP IT!

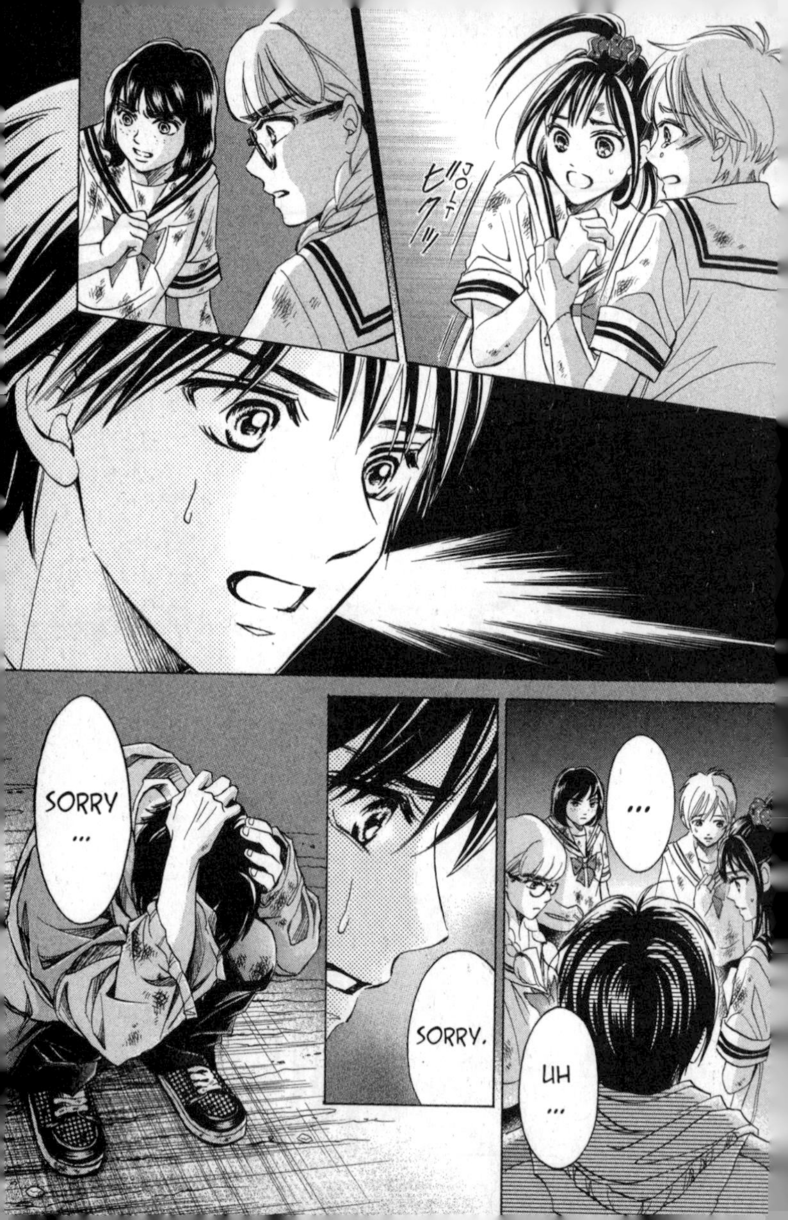
JOLT
ビクッ
...
UH ...
SORRY.
SORRY ...

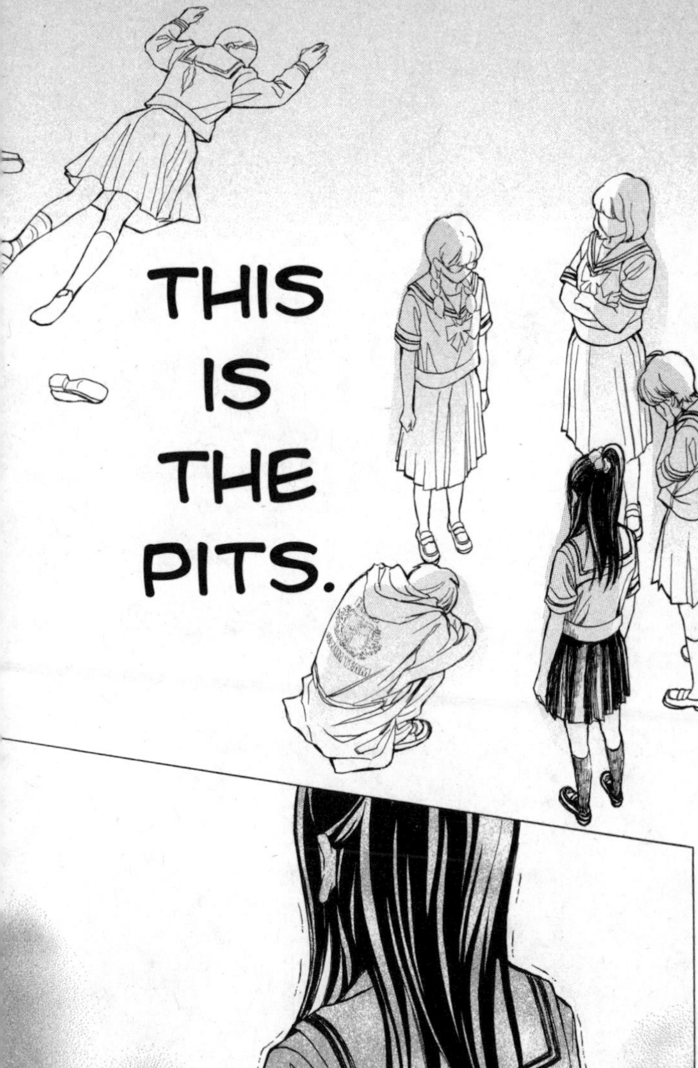
THIS IS THE PITS.

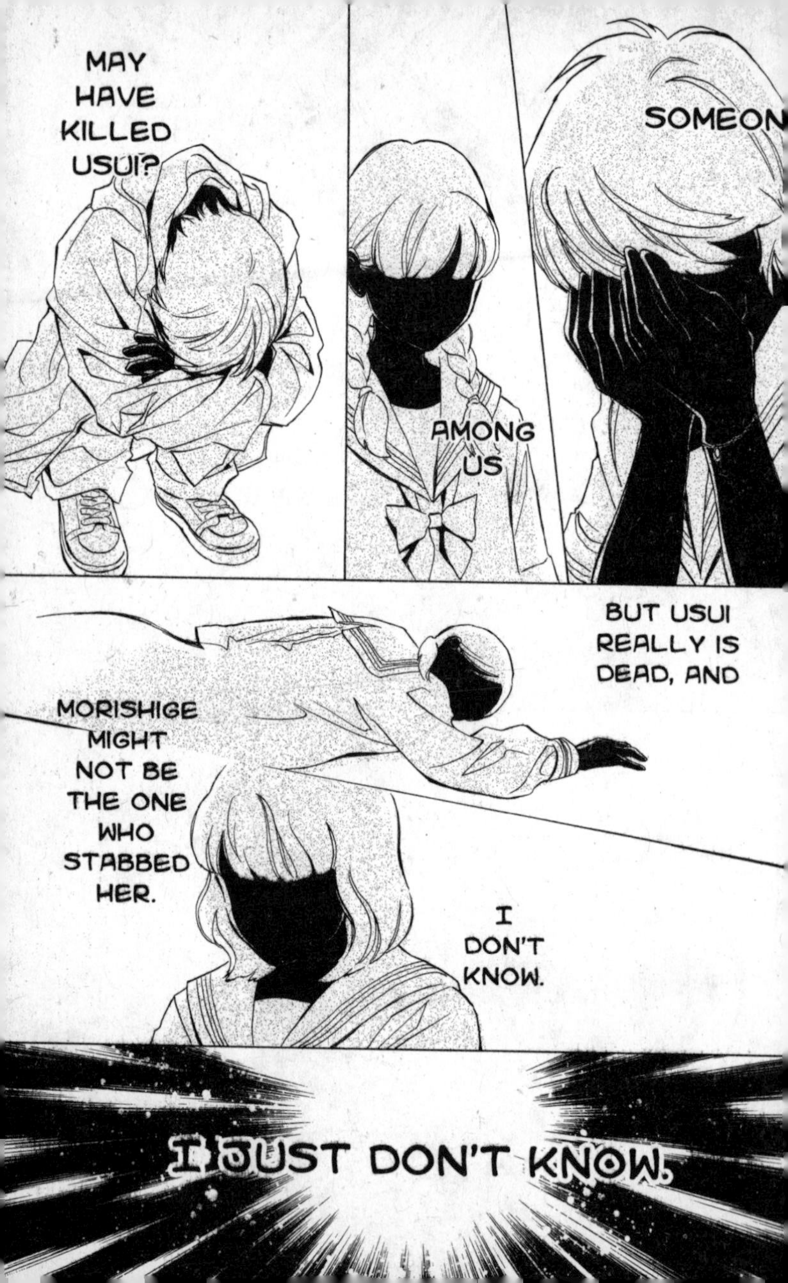

SOMEON
AMONG US
MAY HAVE KILLED USUI?
BUT USUI REALLY IS DEAD, AND
MORISHIGE MIGHT NOT BE THE ONE WHO STABBED HER.
I DON'T KNOW.
I JUST DON'T KNOW.

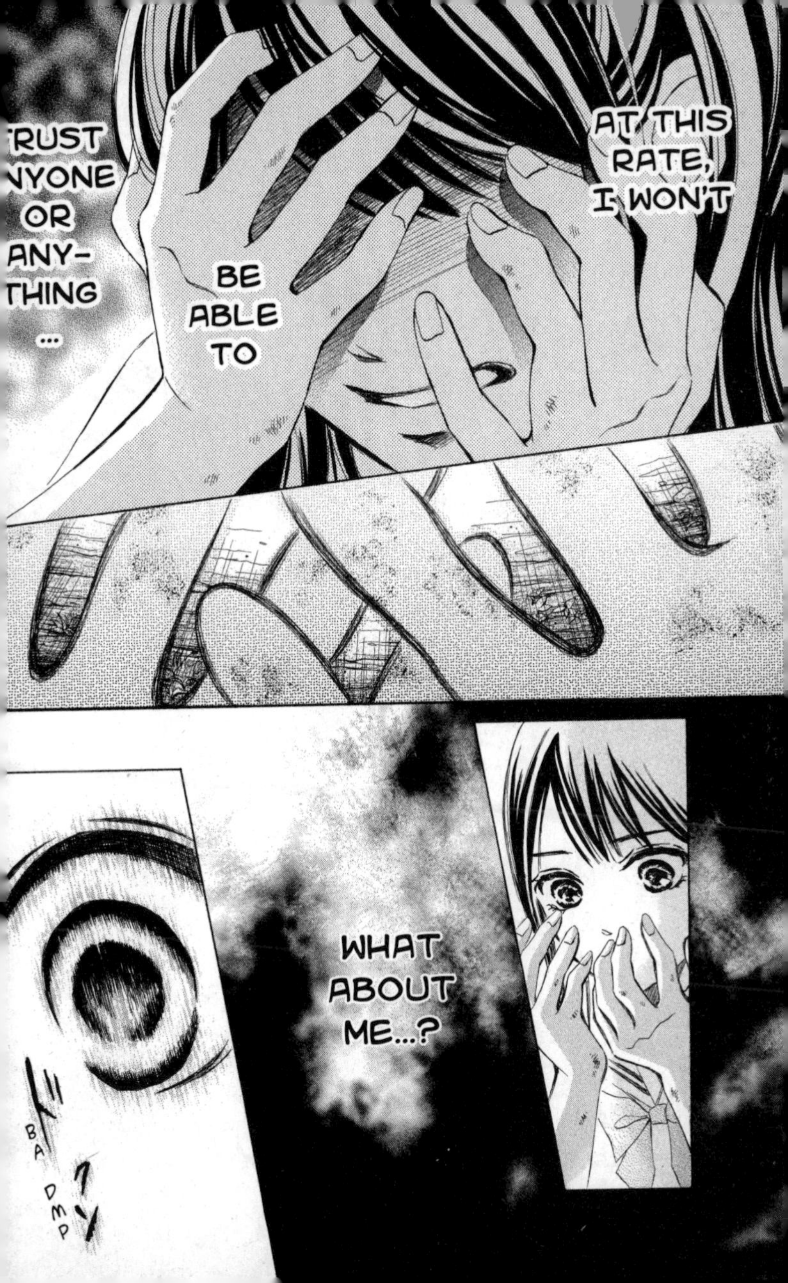

AT THIS RATE, I WON'T
BE ABLE TO
RUST NYONE OR ANY-THING ...
WHAT ABOUT ME...?
BA DMP

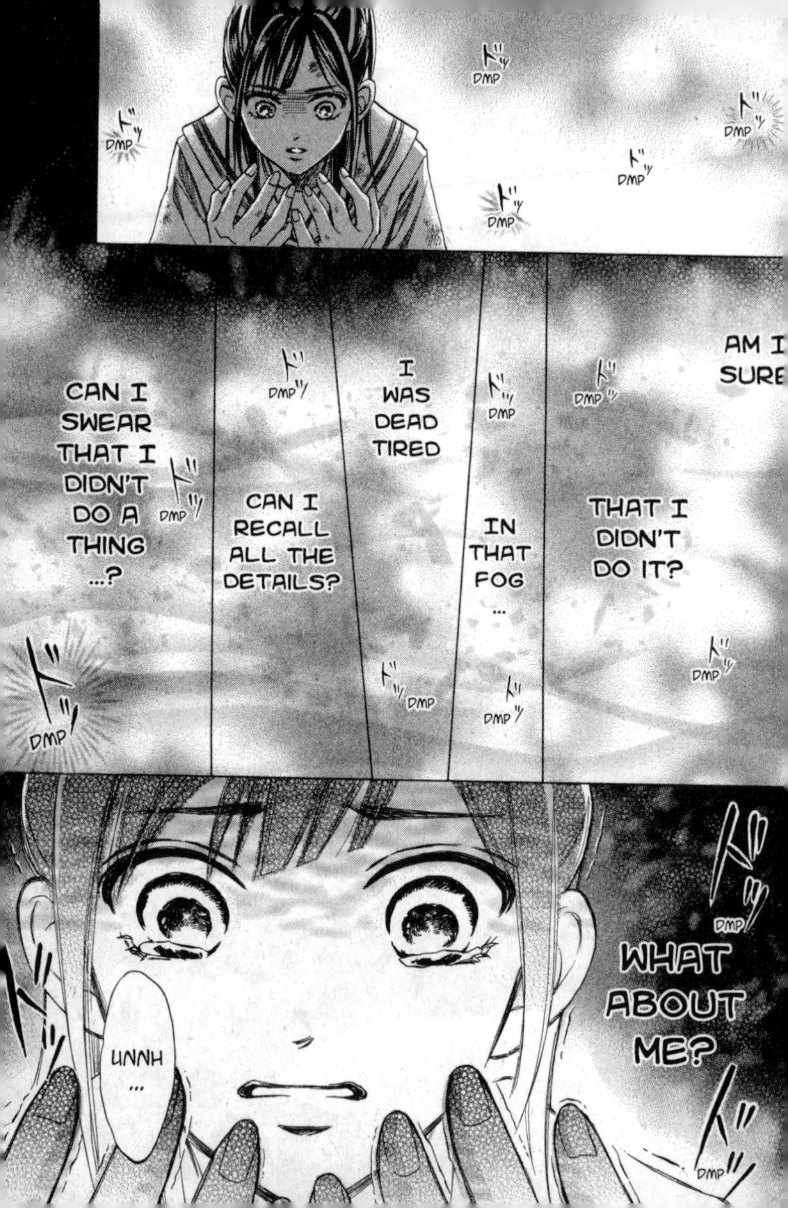

DMP
DMP
DMP
DMP
DMP
AM I SURE
THAT I DIDN'T DO IT?
DMP
DMP
IN THAT FOG ...
DMP
DMP
I WAS DEAD TIRED
DMP
DMP
CAN I RECALL ALL THE DETAILS?
DMP
CAN I SWEAR THAT I DIDN'T DO A THING ...?
DMP
DMP
WHAT ABOUT ME?
DMP
UNNH ...

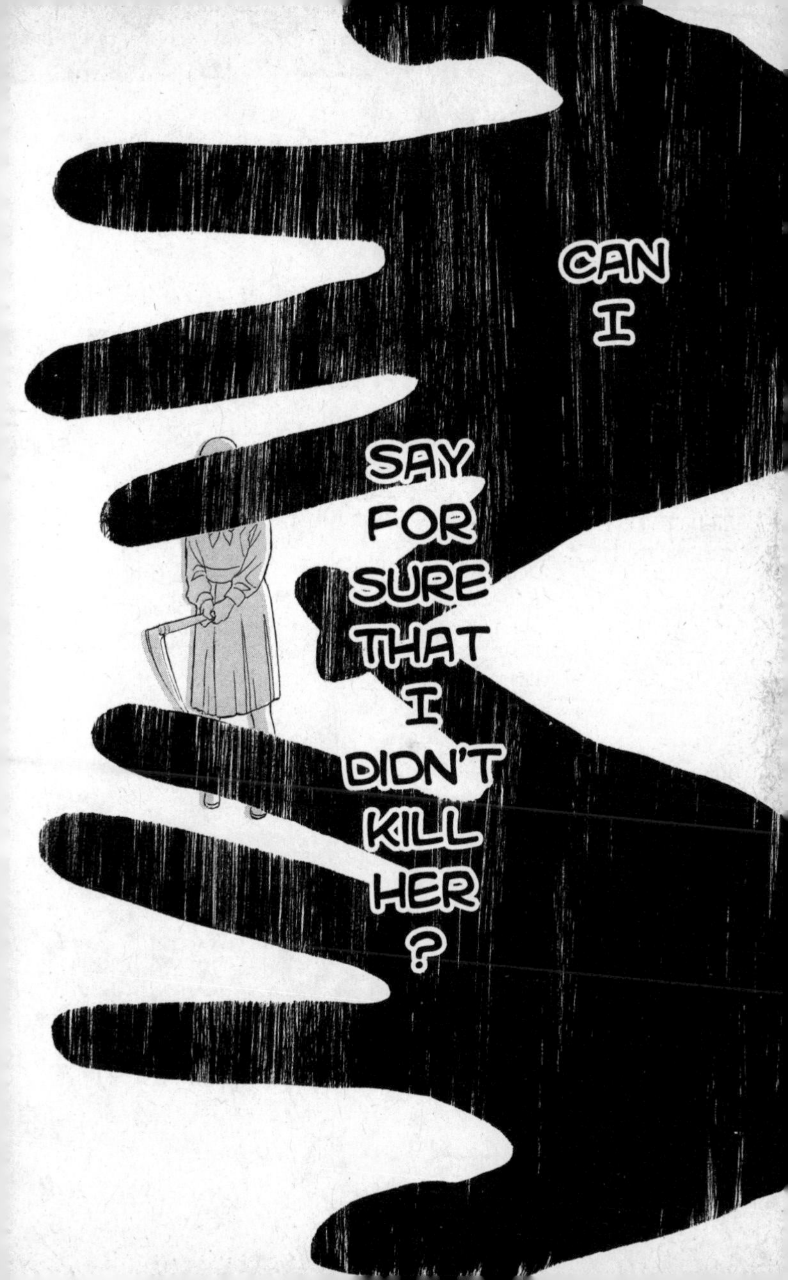
CAN I
SAY FOR SURE THAT I DIDN'T KILL HER?

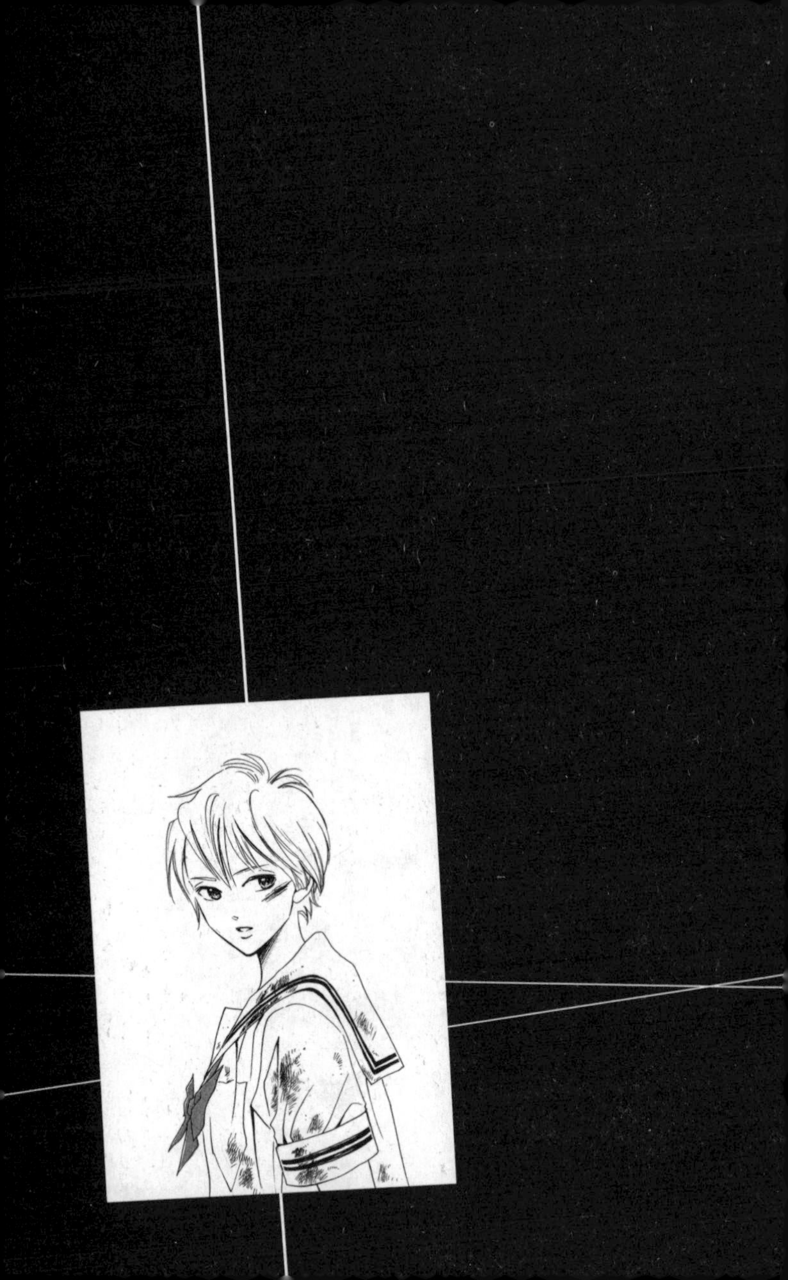

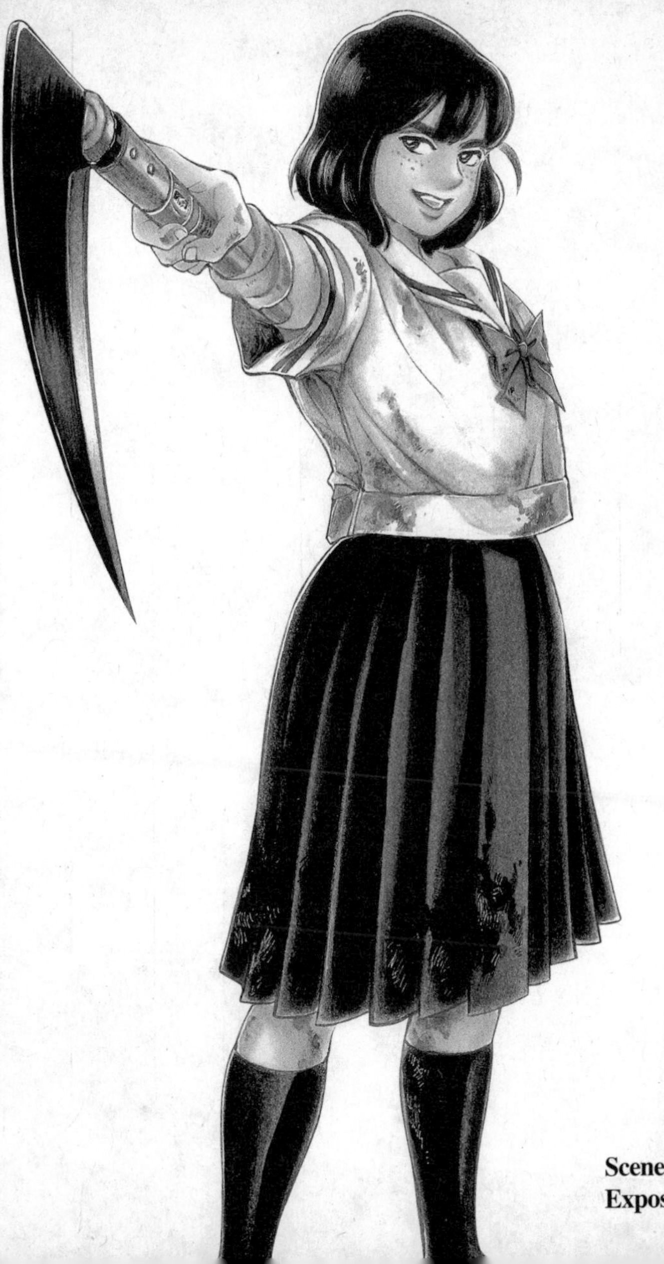

Scene.13
Exposure

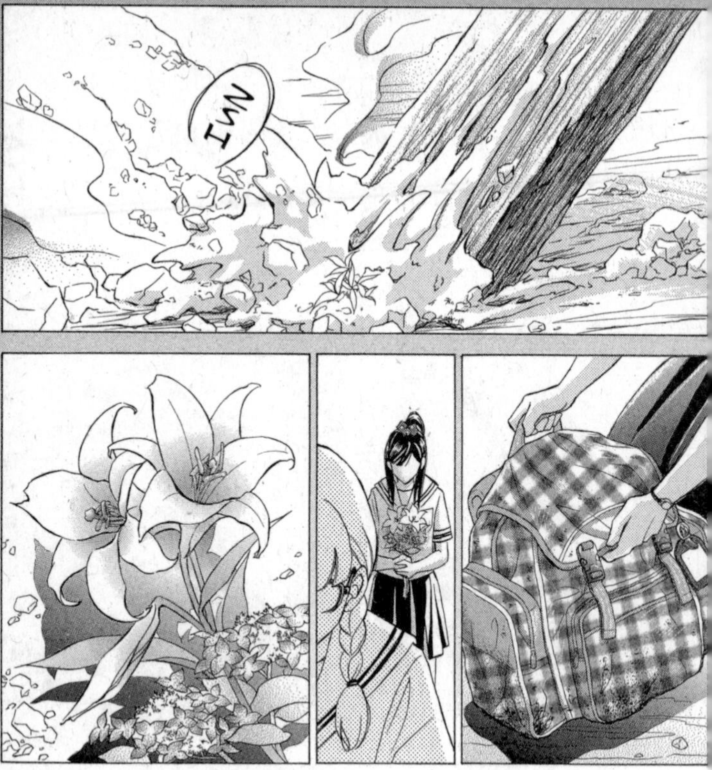

LIMIT

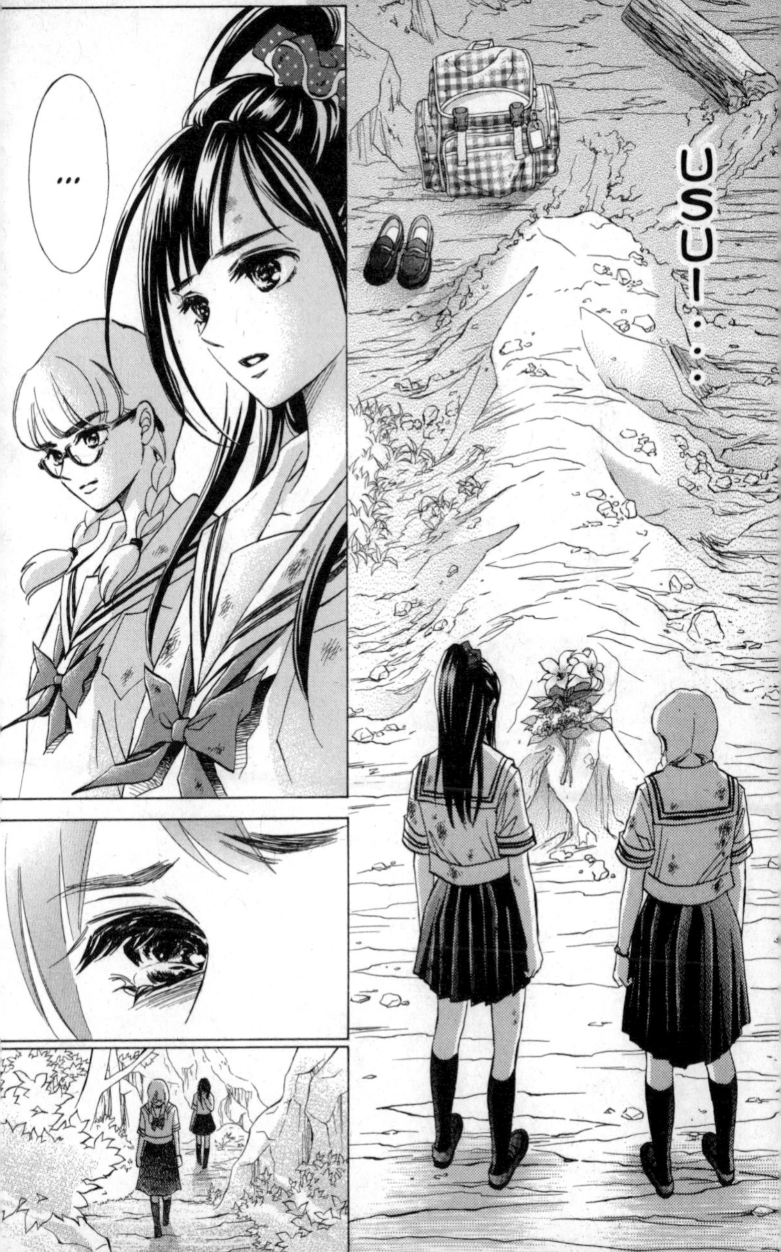
USUI . . .
...

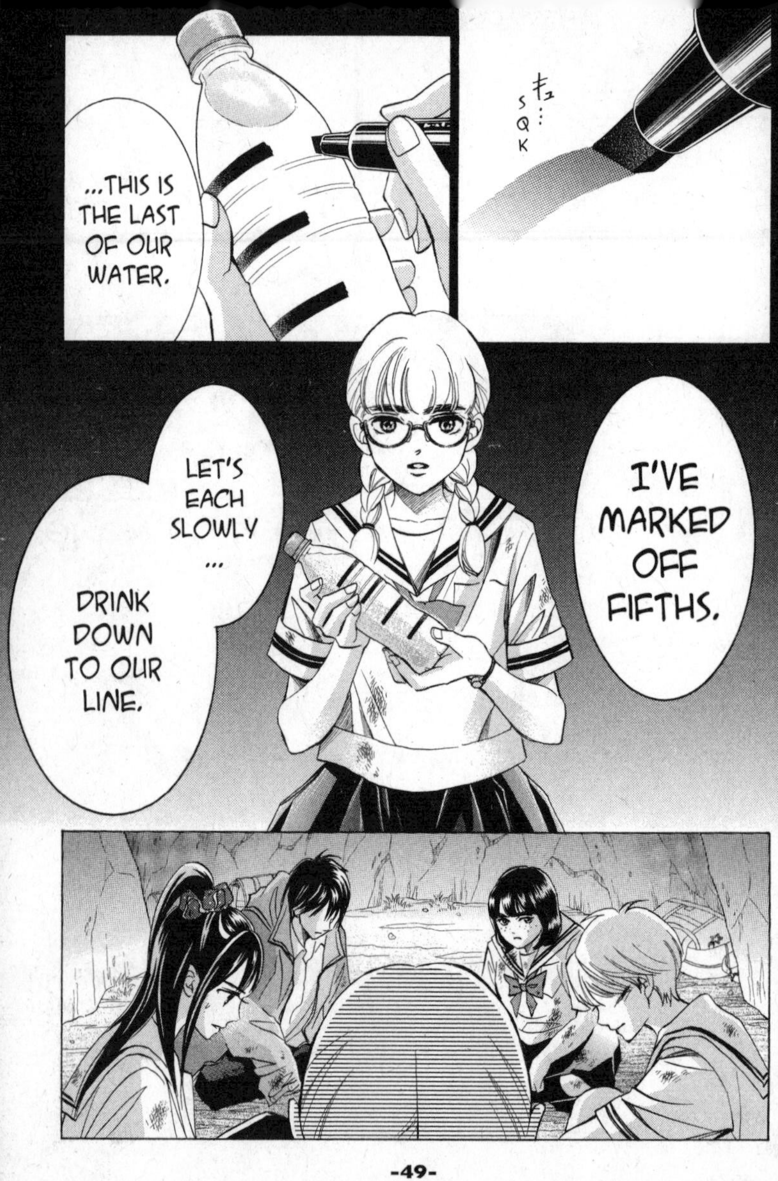
キュ… SQK
...THIS IS THE LAST OF OUR WATER.
I'VE MARKED OFF FIFTHS.
LET'S EACH SLOWLY ...
DRINK DOWN TO OUR LINE.

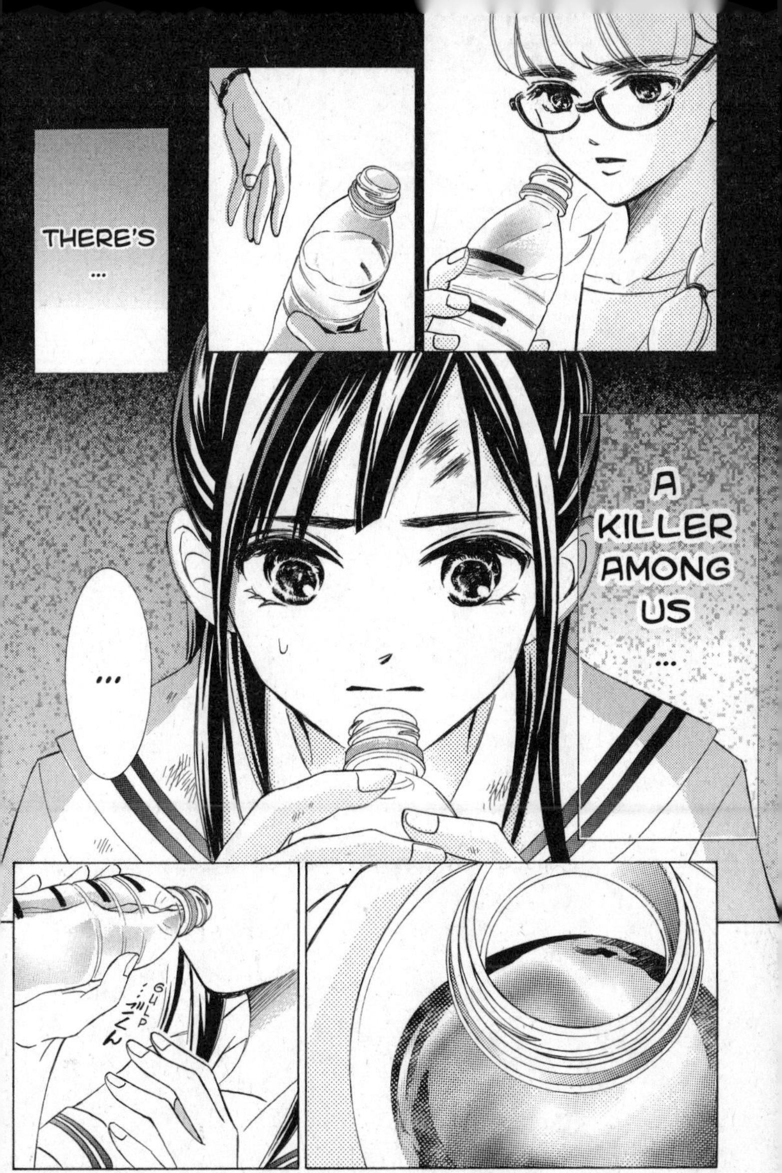
THERE'S ...
A KILLER AMONG US ...
...
GULP
...ゴクン

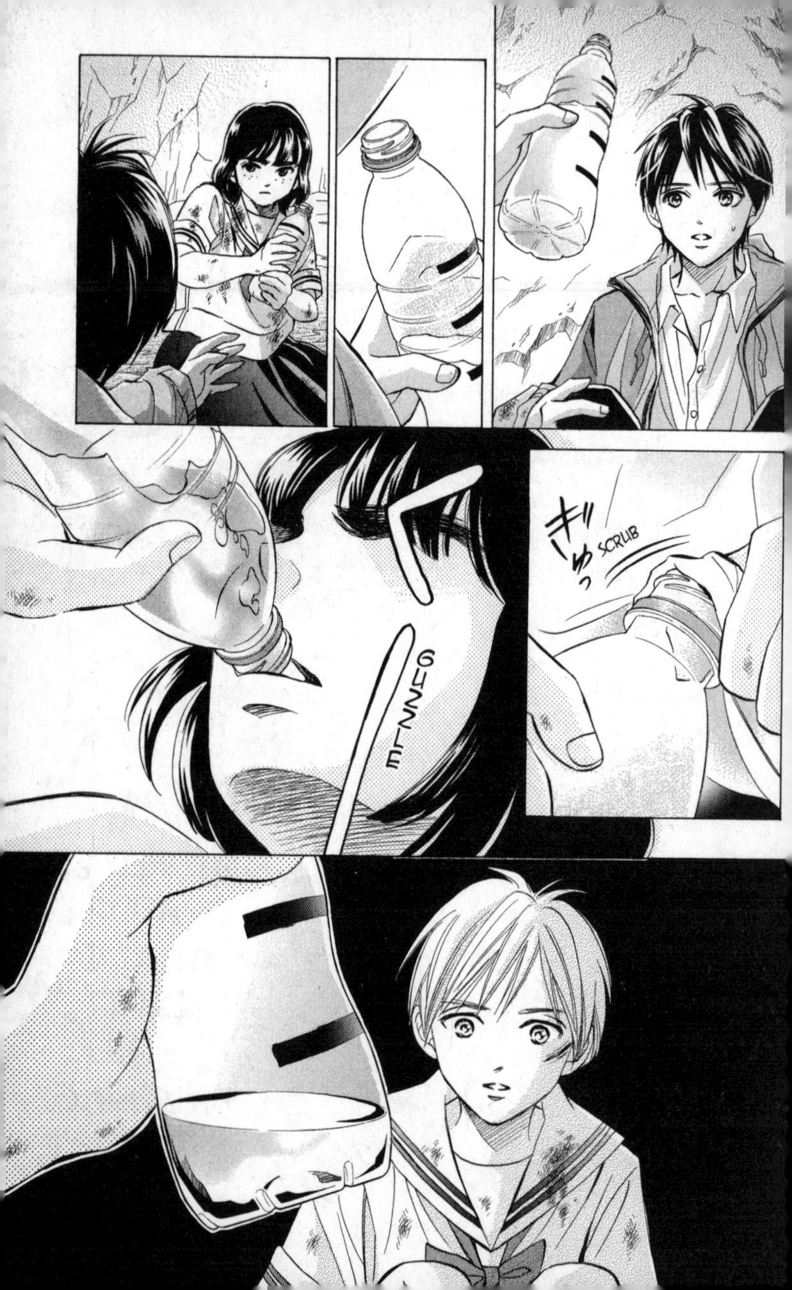
SCRUB
GUZZLE

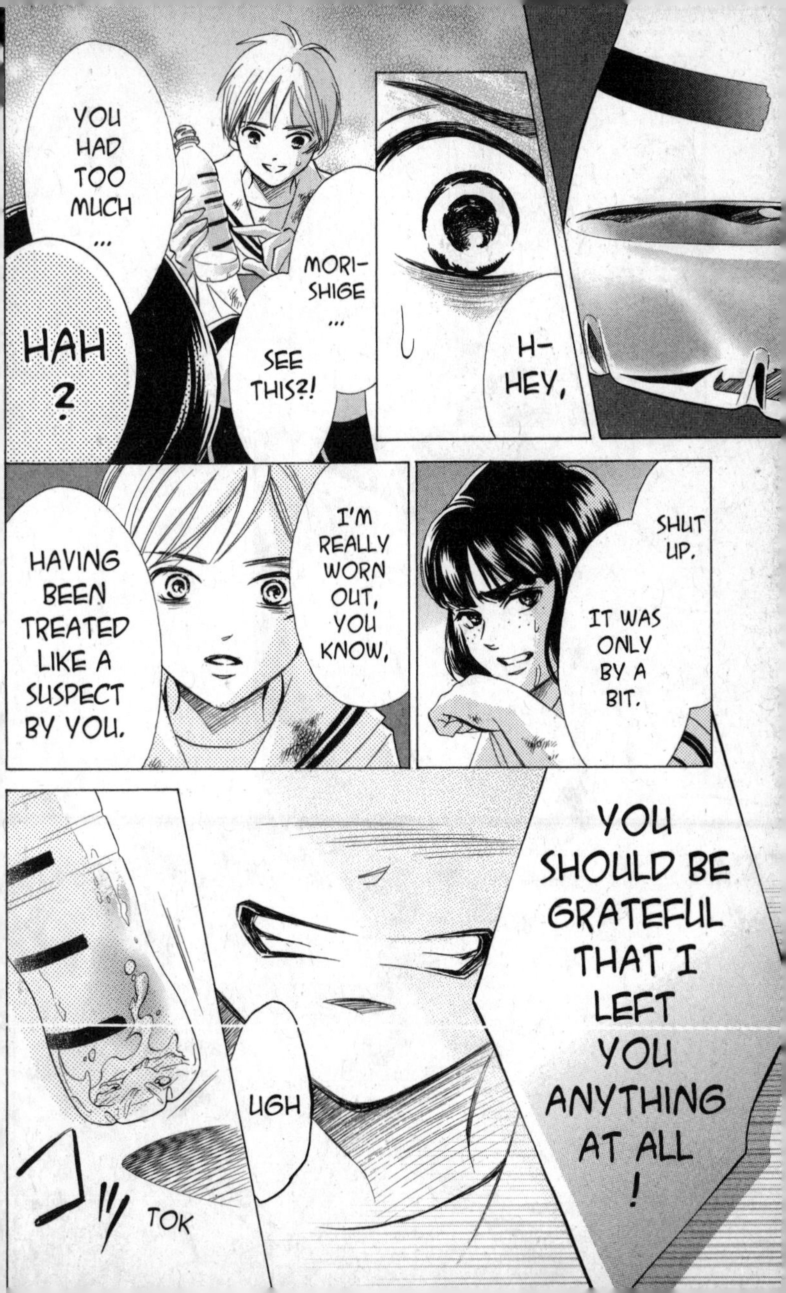
H-HEY,
MORI-SHIGE ... SEE THIS?!
YOU HAD TOO MUCH ...
HAH ?
SHUT UP.
IT WAS ONLY BY A BIT.
I'M REALLY WORN OUT, YOU KNOW,
HAVING BEEN TREATED LIKE A SUSPECT BY YOU.
YOU SHOULD BE GRATEFUL THAT I LEFT YOU ANYTHING AT ALL !
UGH
TOK

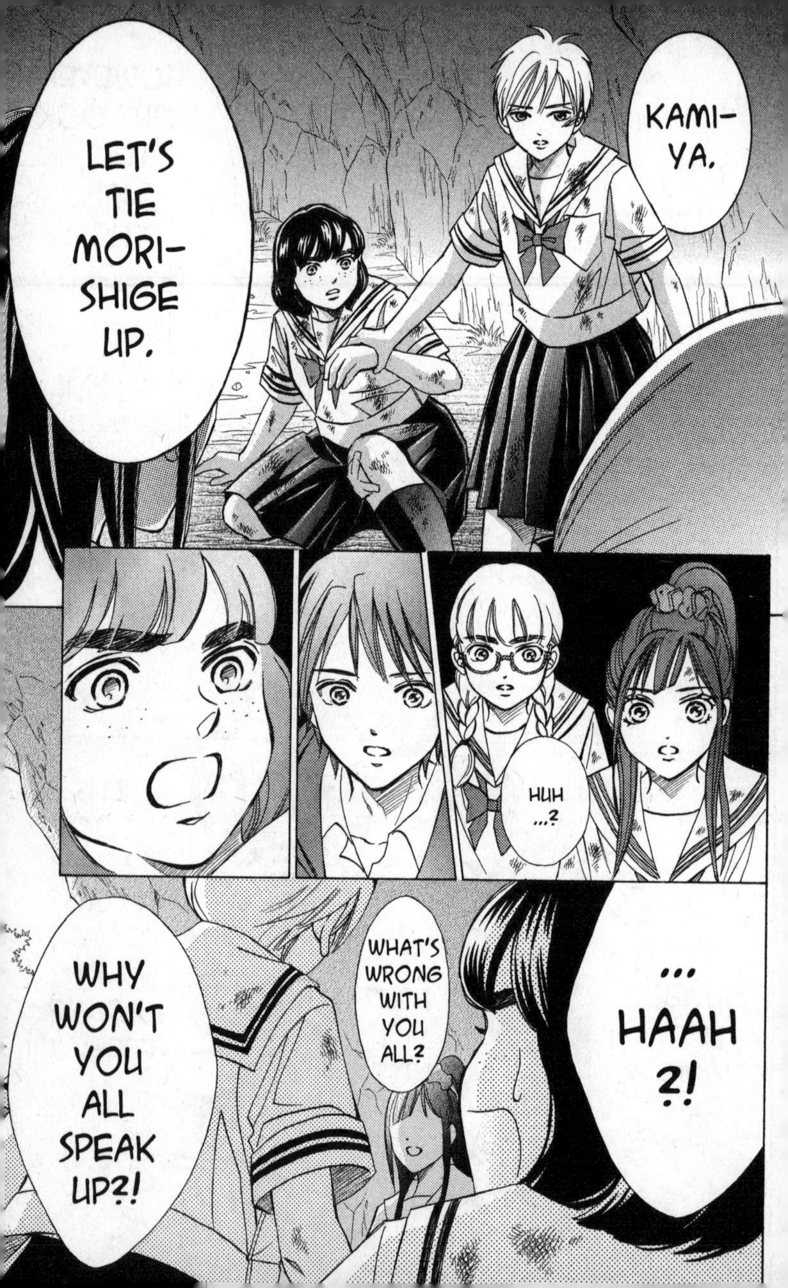
KAMI-YA.
LET'S TIE MORI-SHIGE UP.
HUH ...?
... HAAH ?!
WHAT'S WRONG WITH YOU ALL?
WHY WON'T YOU ALL SPEAK UP?!

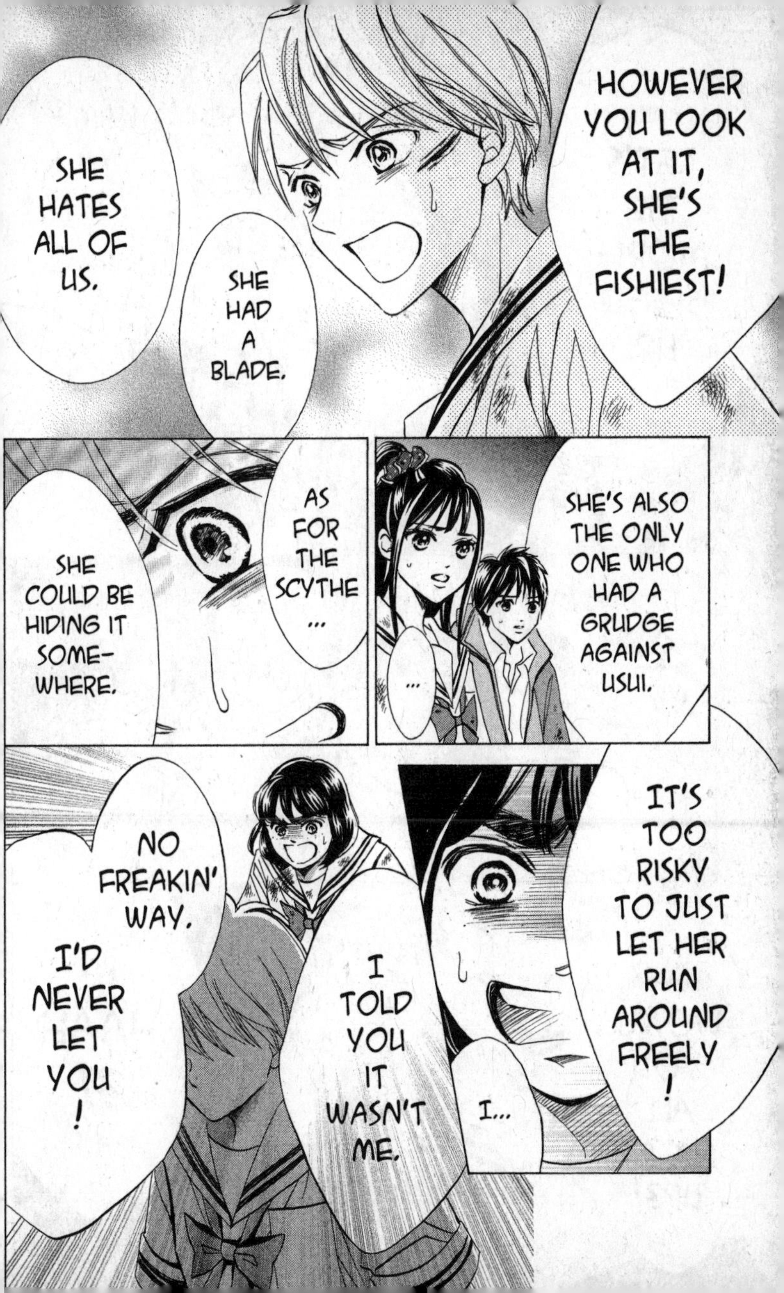
HOWEVER YOU LOOK AT IT, SHE'S THE FISHIEST!
SHE HAD A BLADE.
SHE HATES ALL OF US.
SHE'S ALSO THE ONLY ONE WHO HAD A GRUDGE AGAINST USUI.
...
AS FOR THE SCYTHE...
SHE COULD BE HIDING IT SOMEWHERE.
IT'S TOO RISKY TO JUST LET HER RUN AROUND FREELY!
I...
I TOLD YOU IT WASN'T ME.
NO FREAKIN' WAY.
I'D NEVER LET YOU!

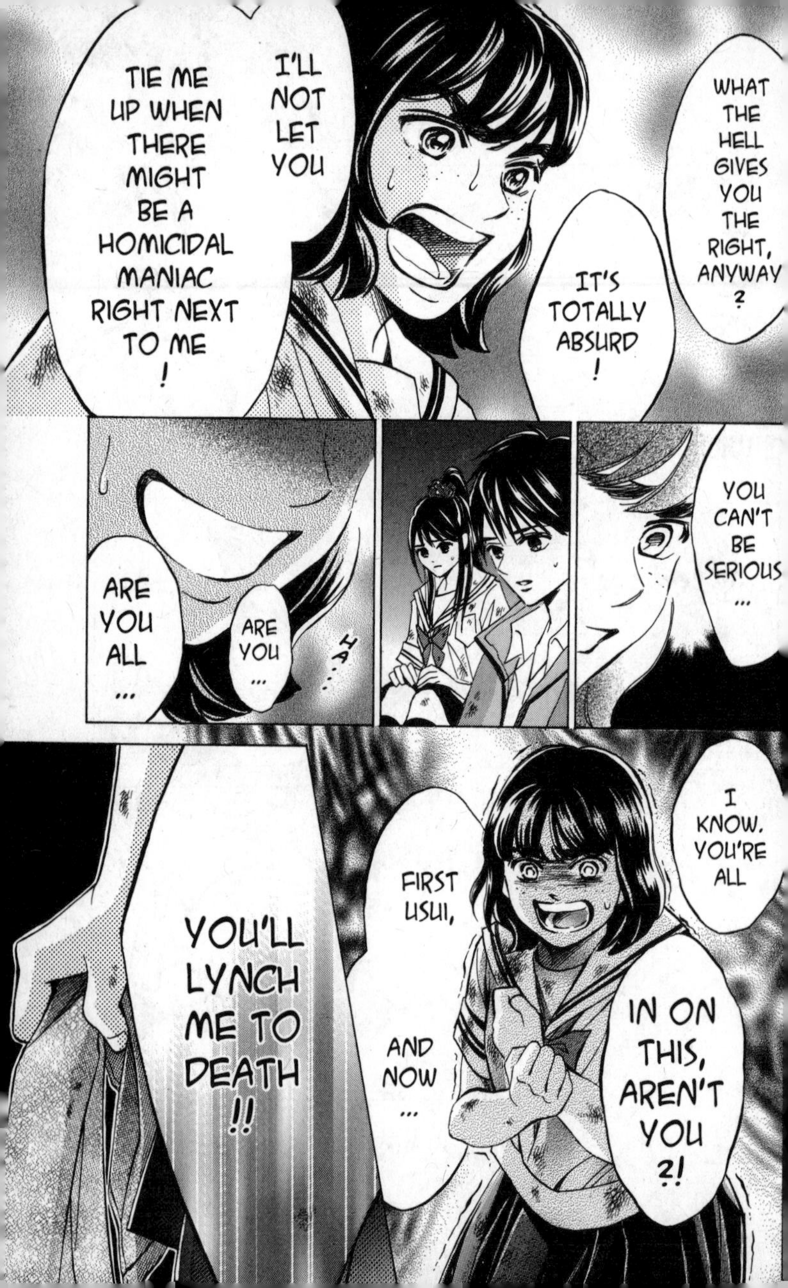
WHAT THE HELL GIVES YOU THE RIGHT, ANYWAY?
IT'S TOTALLY ABSURD!
I'LL NOT LET YOU
TIE ME UP WHEN THERE MIGHT BE A HOMICIDAL MANIAC RIGHT NEXT TO ME!
YOU CAN'T BE SERIOUS...
HA...
ARE YOU...
ARE YOU ALL...
I KNOW. YOU'RE ALL
IN ON THIS, AREN'T YOU?!
FIRST USUI,
AND NOW...
YOU'LL LYNCH ME TO DEATH!!

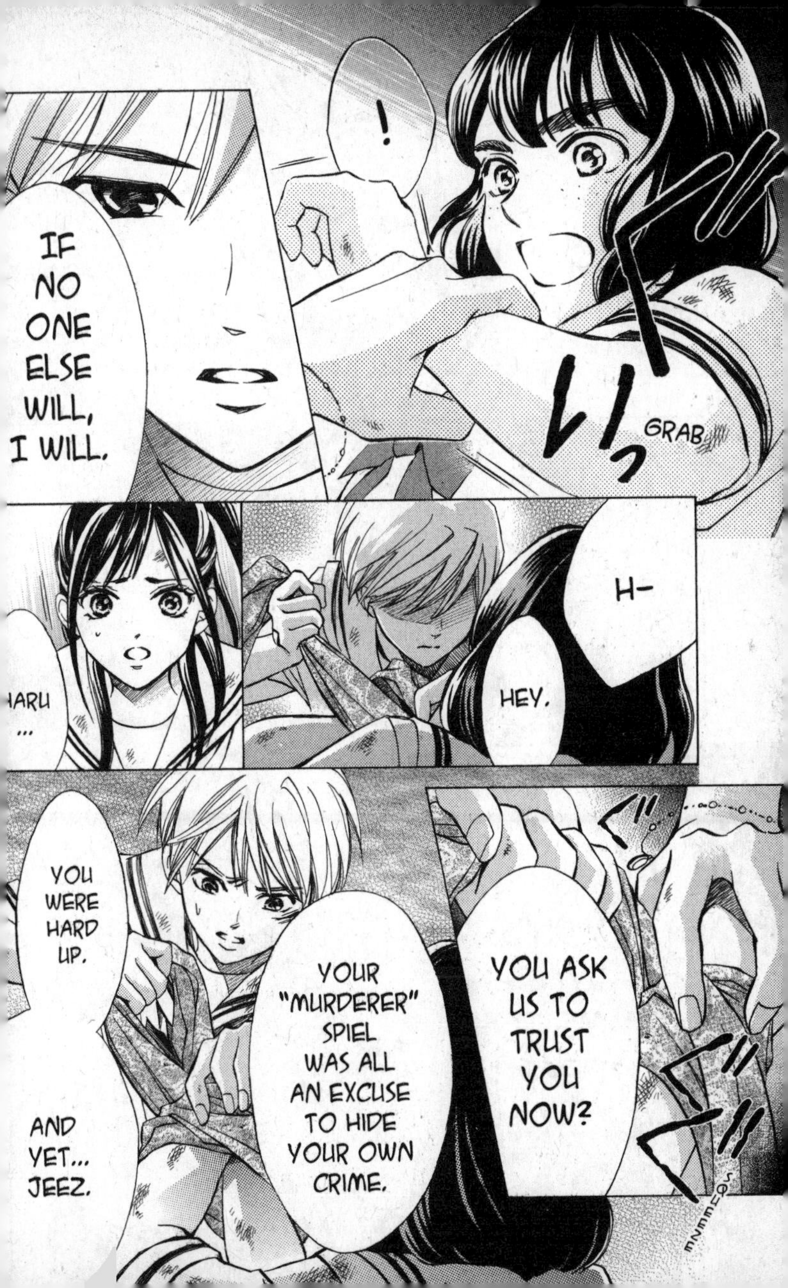
!
GRAB
IF NO ONE ELSE WILL, I WILL.
H-
HEY.
HARU ...
YOU ASK US TO TRUST YOU NOW?
SQUEEZE
YOUR "MURDERER" SPIEL WAS ALL AN EXCUSE TO HIDE YOUR OWN CRIME.
YOU WERE HARD UP.
AND YET... JEEZ.

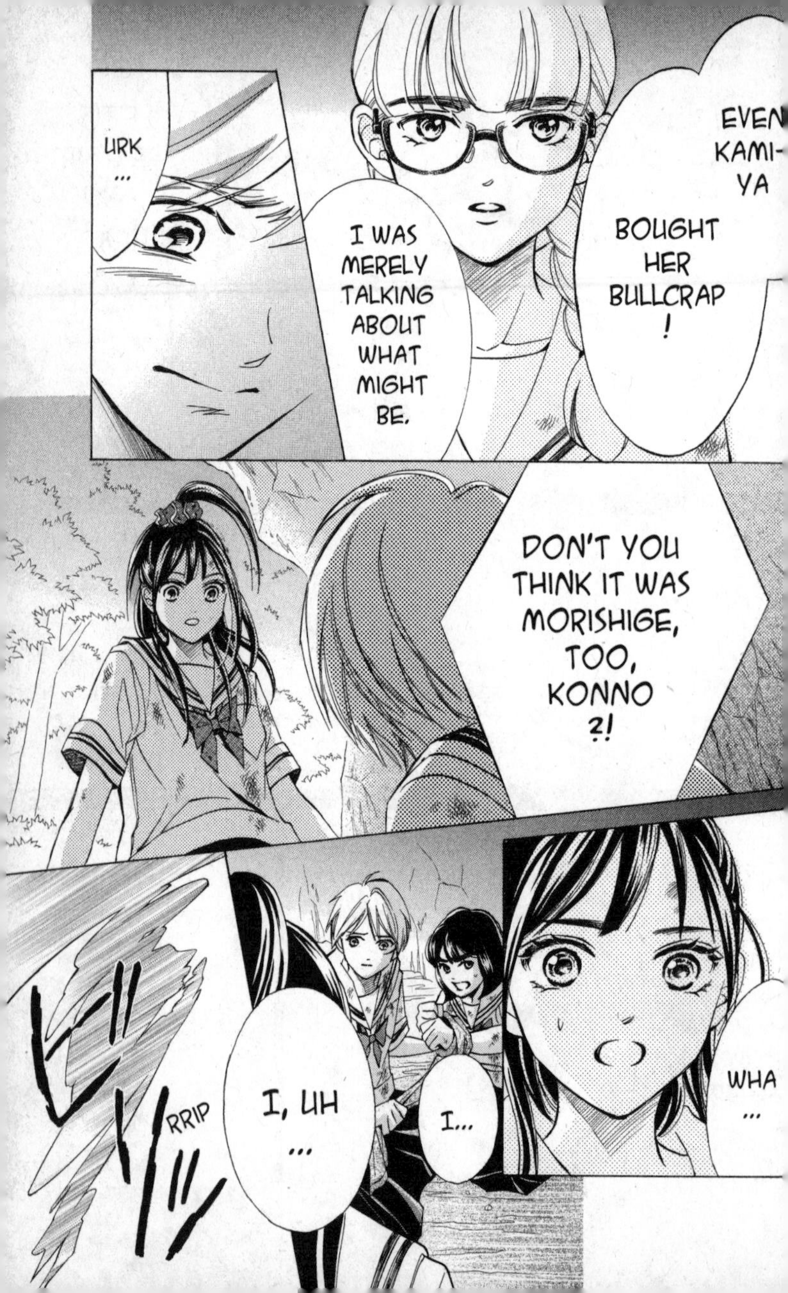
EVEN KAMIYA BOUGHT HER BULLCRAP!
I WAS MERELY TALKING ABOUT WHAT MIGHT BE.
URK ...
DON'T YOU THINK IT WAS MORISHIGE, TOO, KONNO ?!
WHA ...
I...
I, UH ...
RRIP

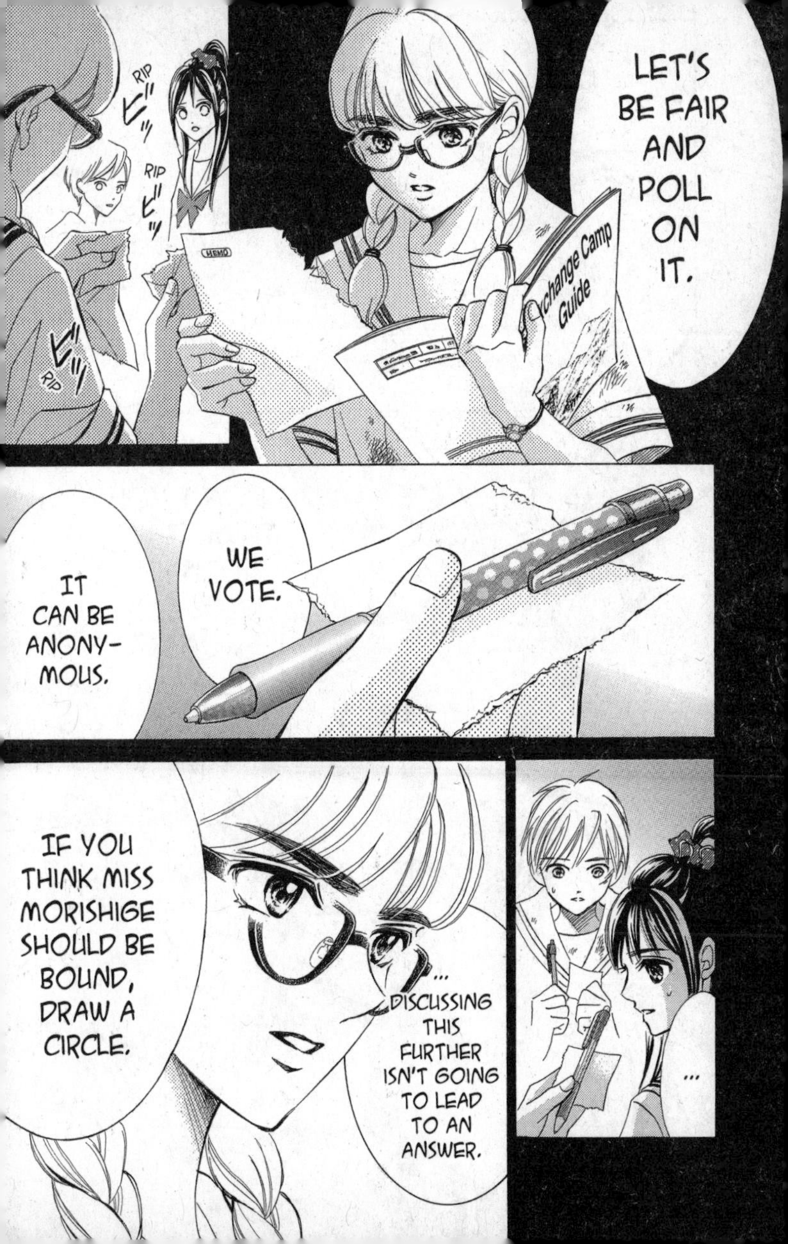
LET'S BE FAIR AND POLL ON IT.
xchange Camp Guide
MEMO
RIP
RIP
RIP
WE VOTE.
IT CAN BE ANONYMOUS.
...
... DISCUSSING THIS FURTHER ISN'T GOING TO LEAD TO AN ANSWER.
IF YOU THINK MISS MORISHIGE SHOULD BE BOUND, DRAW A CIRCLE.

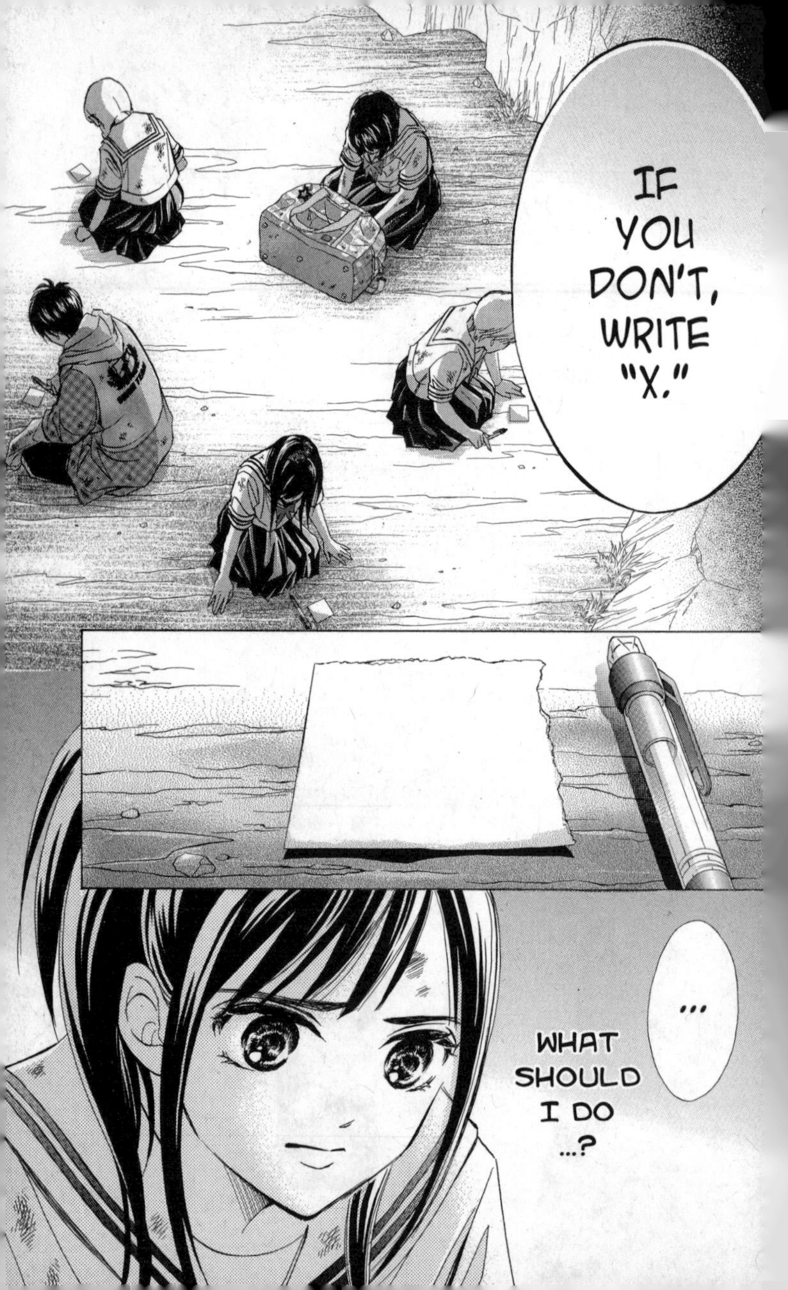
IF YOU DON'T, WRITE "X."
...
WHAT SHOULD I DO ...?

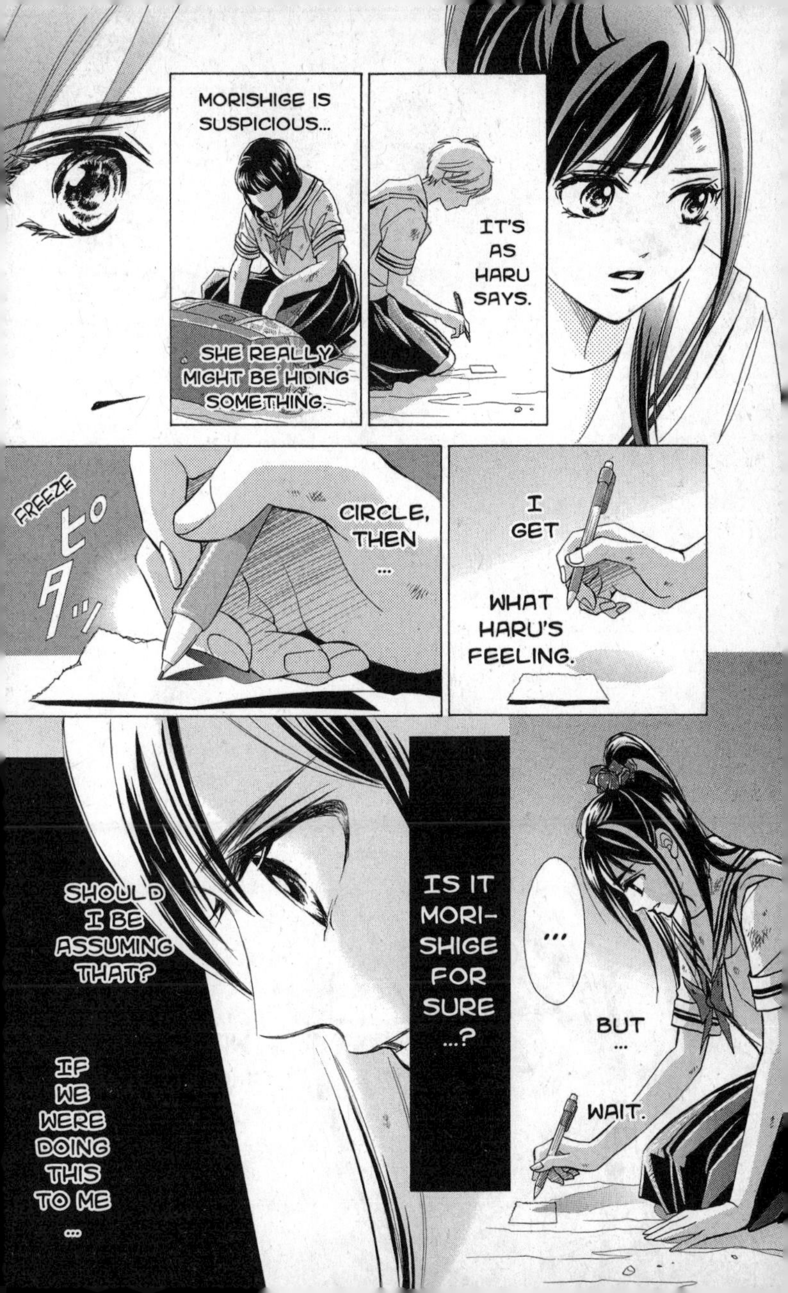
IT'S AS HARU SAYS.
MORISHIGE IS SUSPICIOUS...
SHE REALLY MIGHT BE HIDING SOMETHING.
I GET WHAT HARU'S FEELING.
CIRCLE, THEN ...
FREEZE
ピタッ
...
BUT ...
WAIT.
IS IT MORI-SHIGE FOR SURE ...?
SHOULD I BE ASSUMING THAT?
IF WE WERE DOING THIS TO ME ...

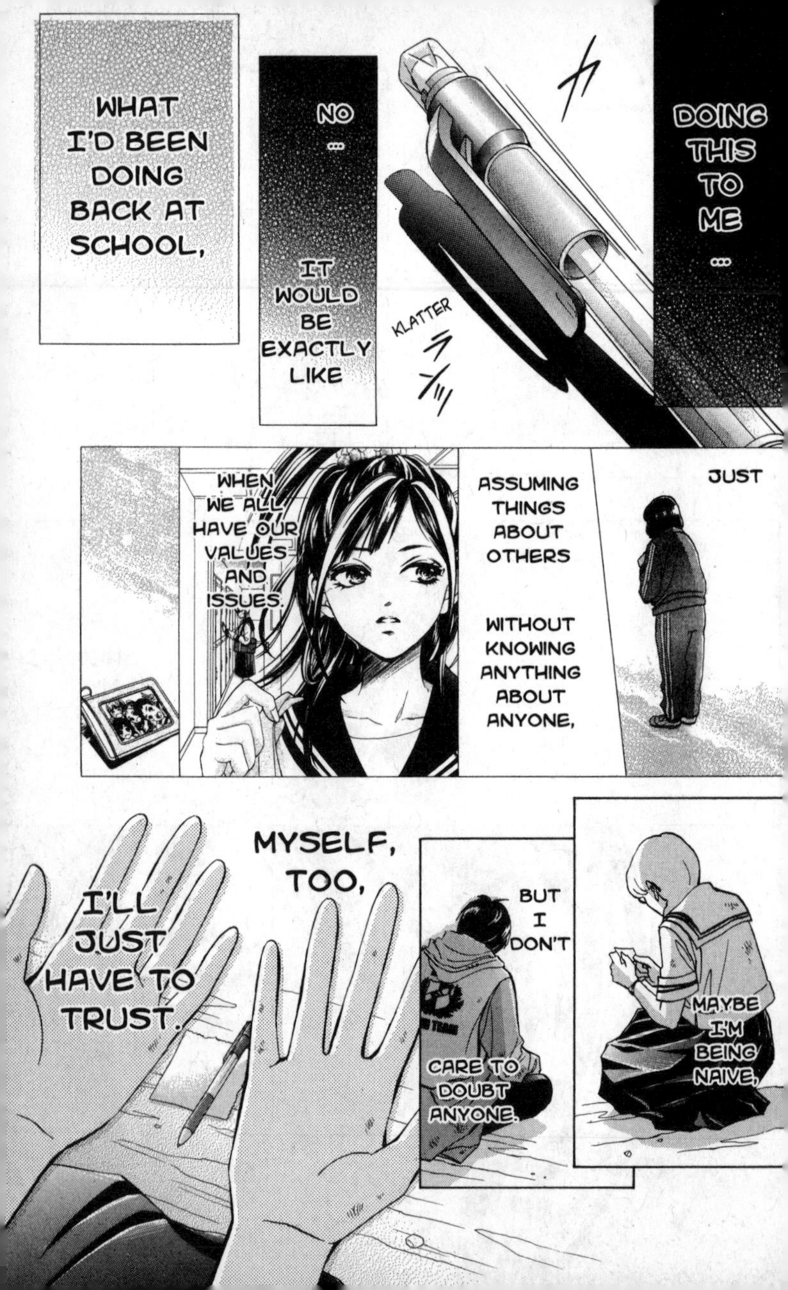
DOING THIS TO ME ...
KLATTER
NO ...
IT WOULD BE EXACTLY LIKE
WHAT I'D BEEN DOING BACK AT SCHOOL,
JUST
ASSUMING THINGS ABOUT OTHERS
WITHOUT KNOWING ANYTHING ABOUT ANYONE,
WHEN WE ALL HAVE OUR VALUES AND ISSUES.
MAYBE I'M BEING NAIVE,
BUT I DON'T
CARE TO DOUBT ANYONE.
MYSELF, TOO,
I'LL JUST HAVE TO TRUST.

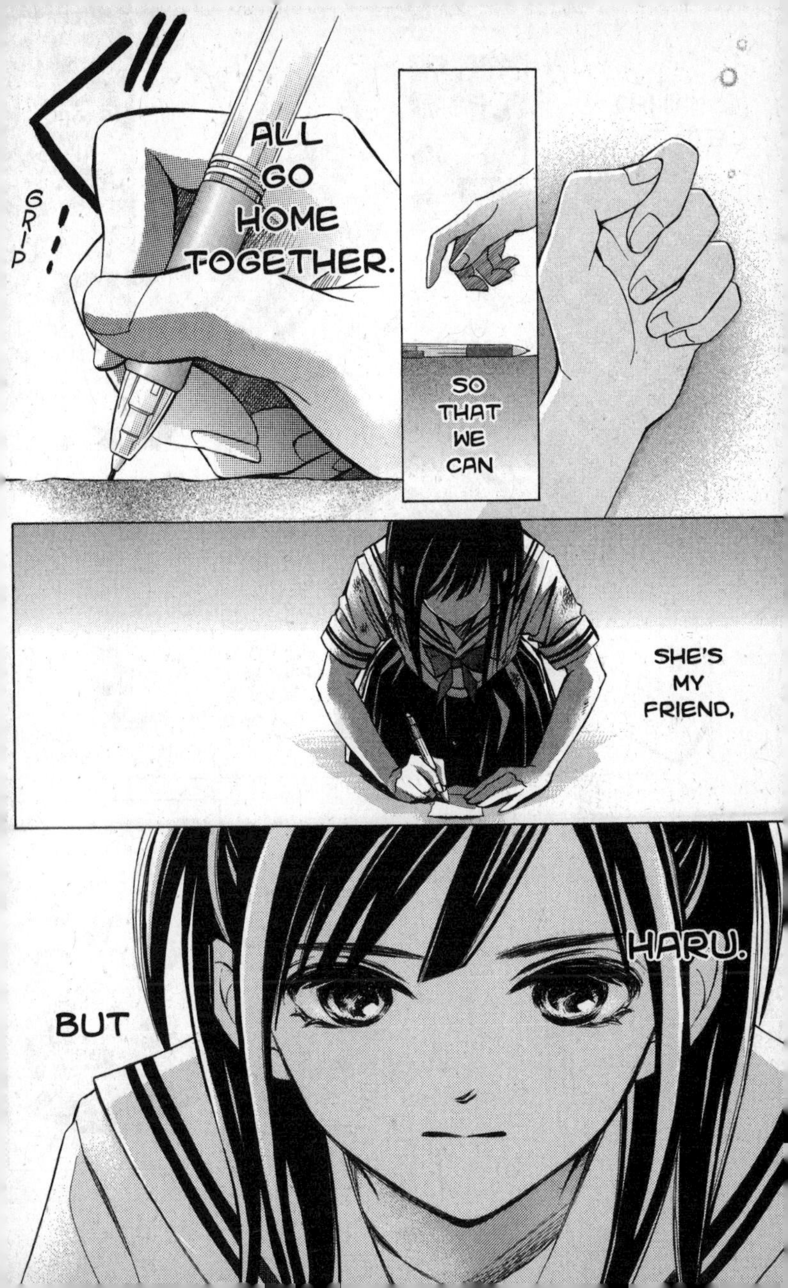
SO THAT WE CAN
ALL GO HOME TOGETHER.
GRIP
SHE'S MY FRIEND,
HARU.
BUT

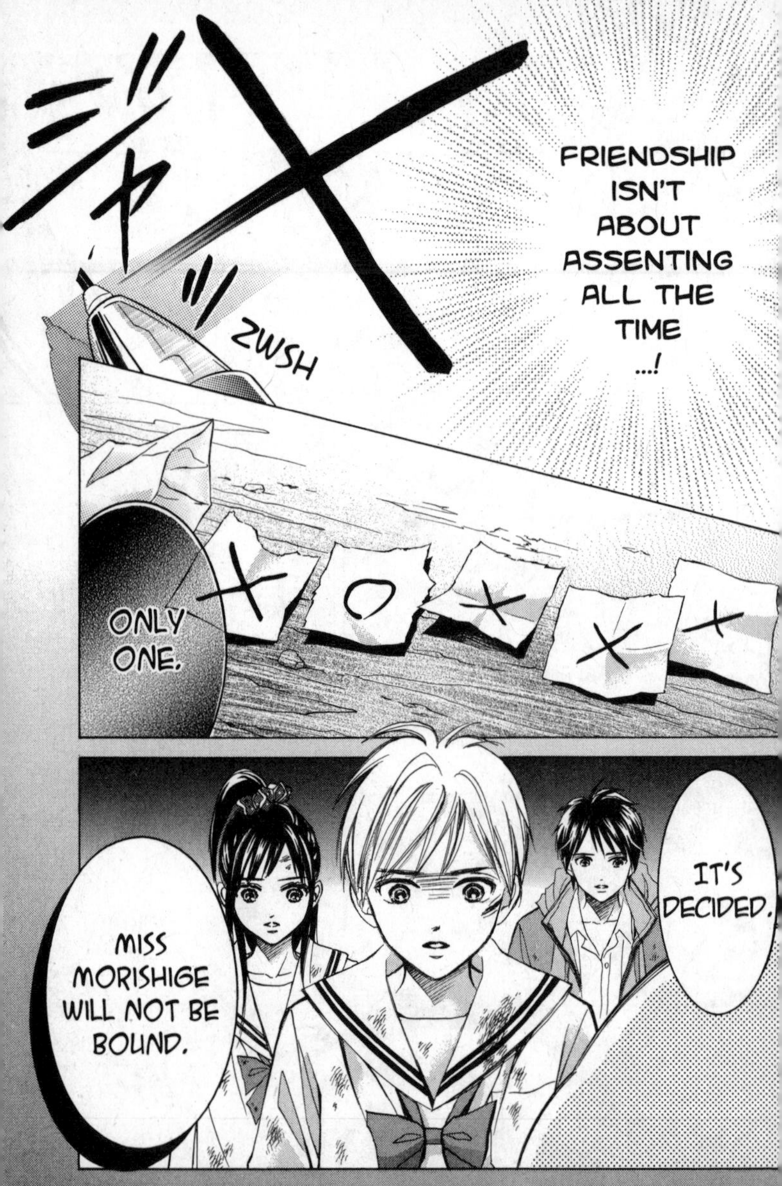
FRIENDSHIP ISN'T ABOUT ASSENTING ALL THE TIME ...!
ジャッ
ZWSH
ONLY ONE.
IT'S DECIDED.
MISS MORISHIGE WILL NOT BE BOUND.

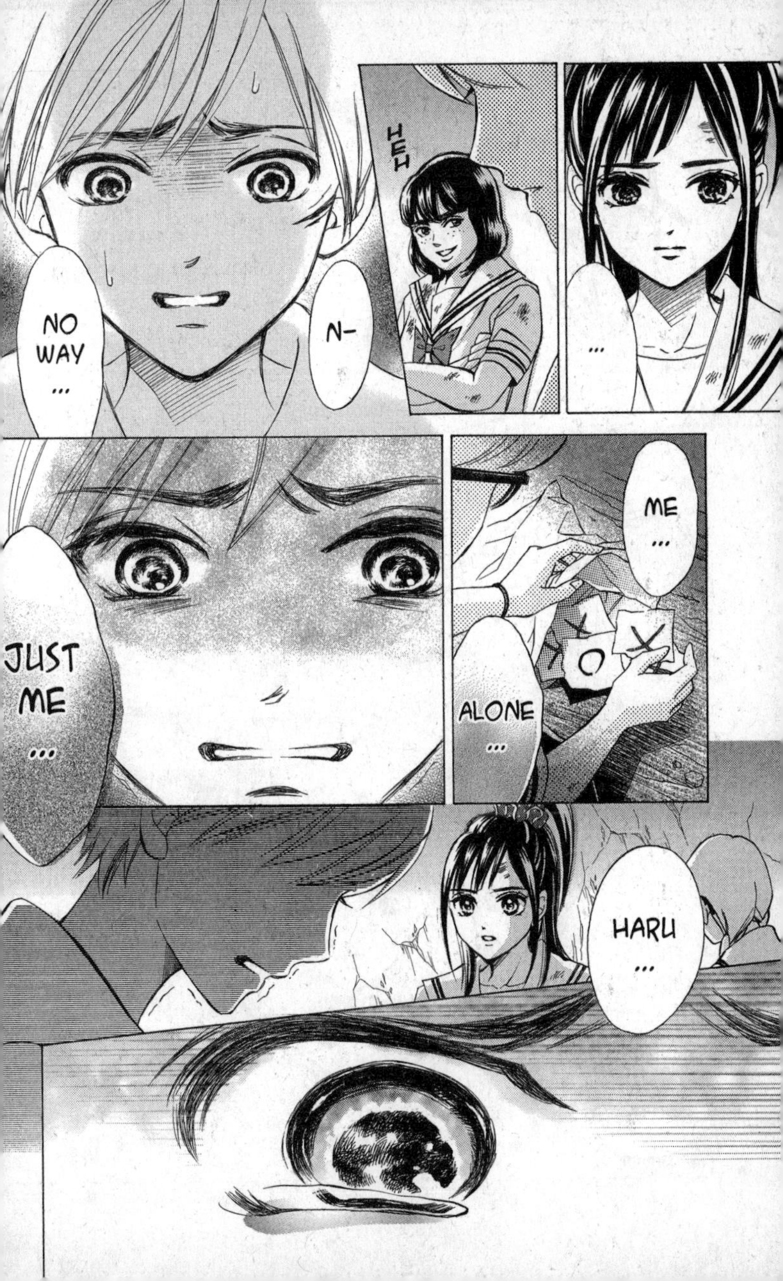
...
HEH
N-
NO WAY ...
ME ...
ALONE ...
JUST ME ...
HARU ...

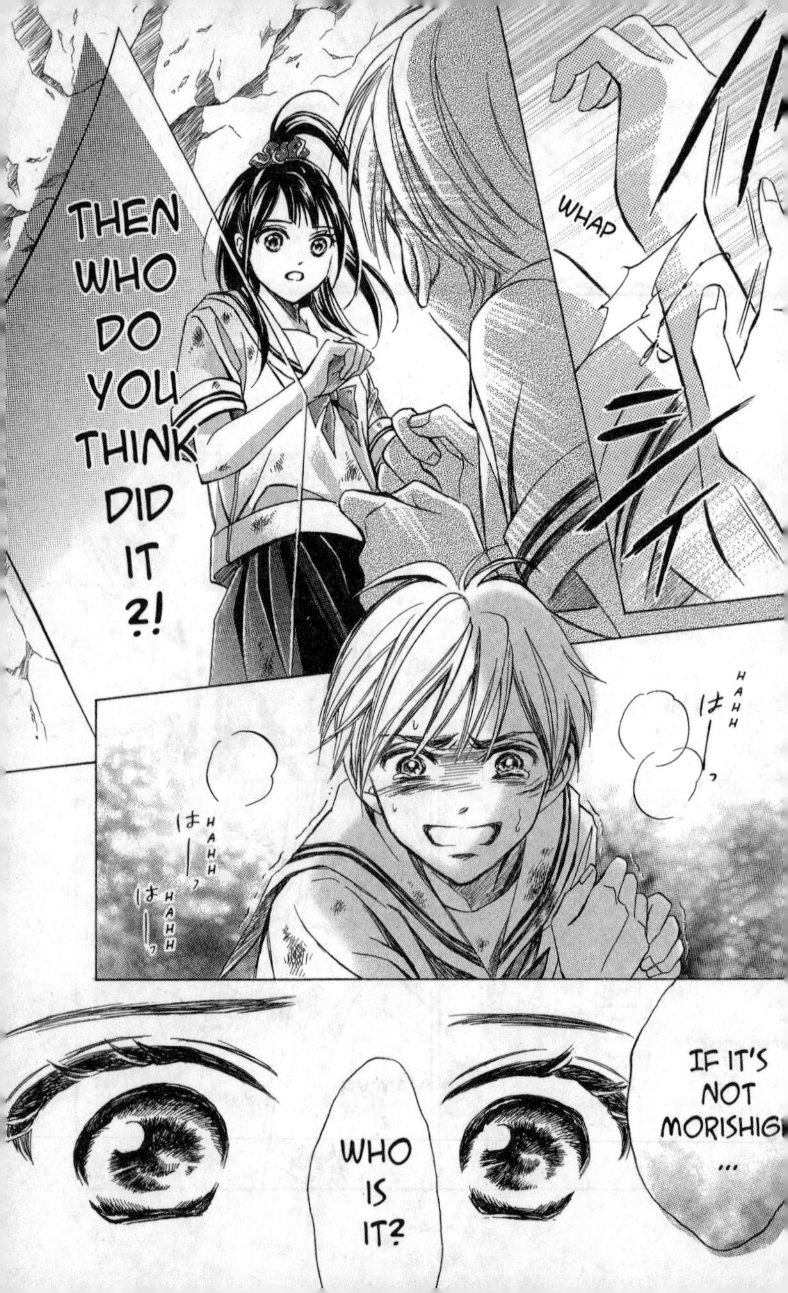
WHAP
THEN WHO DO YOU THINK DID IT?!
はーっ HAHH
はーっ HAHH
はーっ HAHH
IF IT'S NOT MORISHIG...
WHO IS IT?

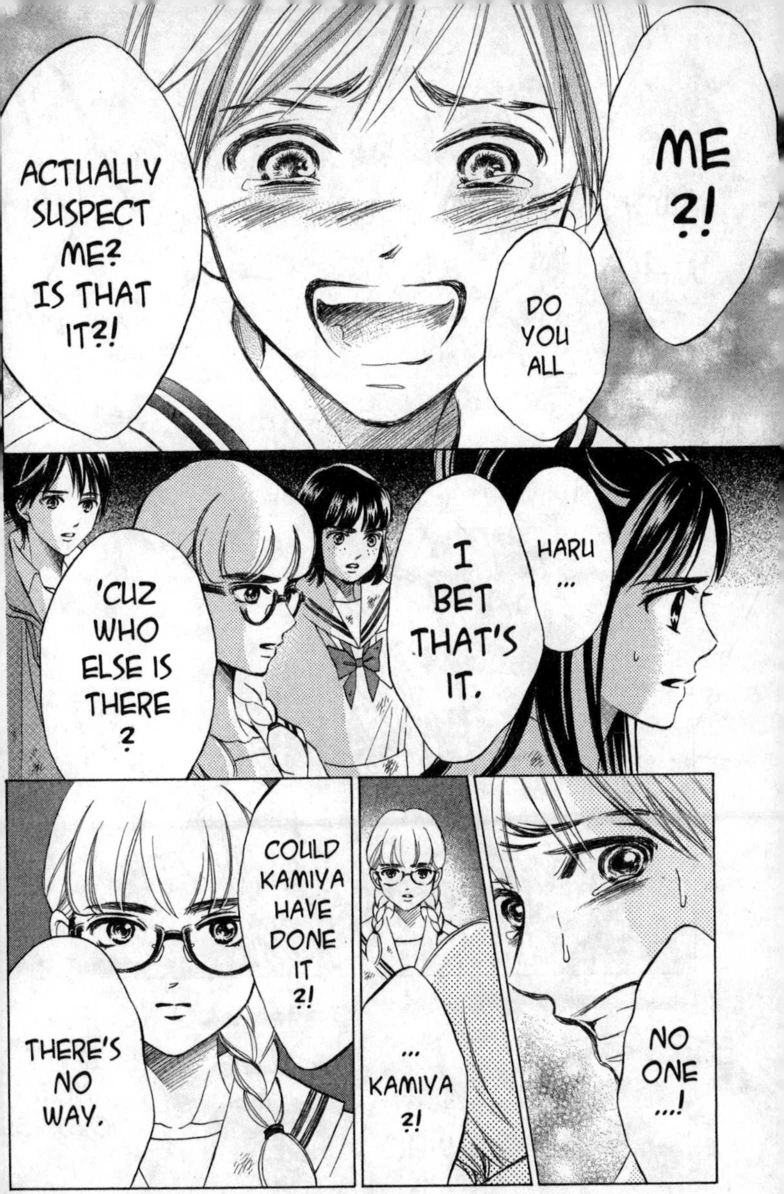
ME ?!
DO YOU ALL
ACTUALLY SUSPECT ME? IS THAT IT?!
HARU ...
I BET THAT'S IT.
'CUZ WHO ELSE IS THERE ?
NO ONE ...!
... KAMIYA ?!
COULD KAMIYA HAVE DONE IT ?!
THERE'S NO WAY.

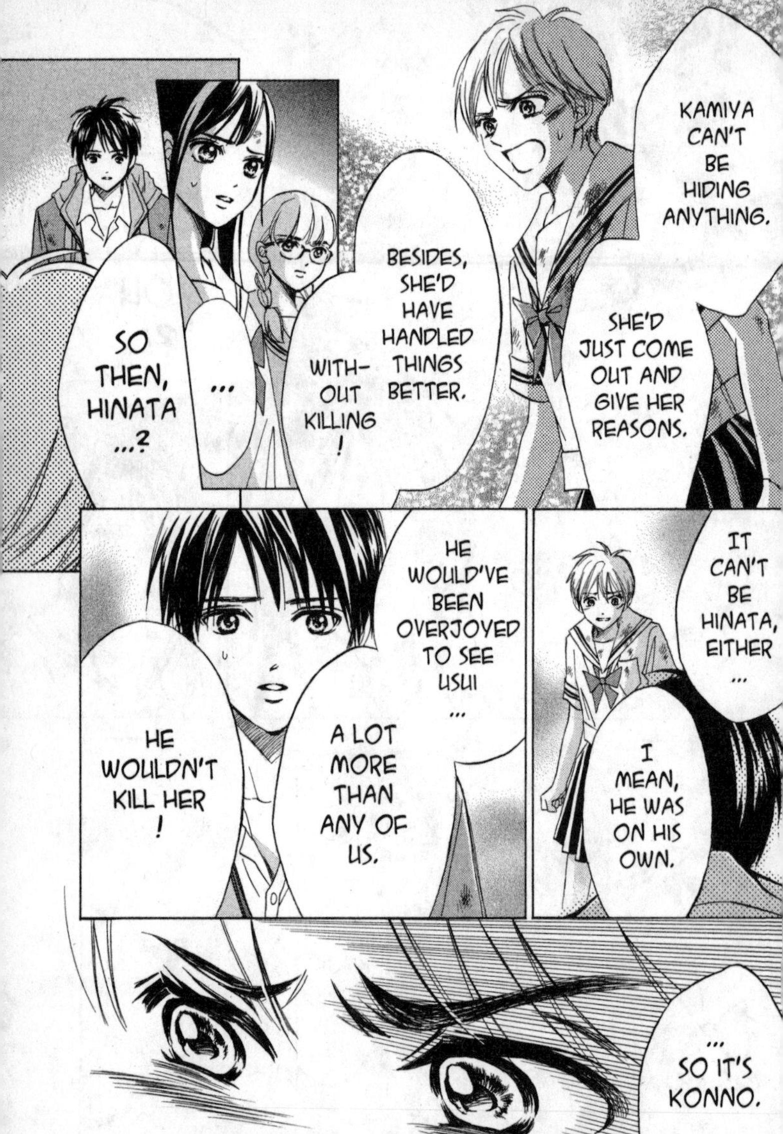
KAMIYA CAN'T BE HIDING ANYTHING.
SHE'D JUST COME OUT AND GIVE HER REASONS.
BESIDES, SHE'D HAVE HANDLED THINGS BETTER.
WITH-OUT KILLING!
...
SO THEN, HINATA...?
IT CAN'T BE HINATA, EITHER...
I MEAN, HE WAS ON HIS OWN.
HE WOULD'VE BEEN OVERJOYED TO SEE USUI...
A LOT MORE THAN ANY OF US.
HE WOULDN'T KILL HER!
...SO IT'S KONNO.

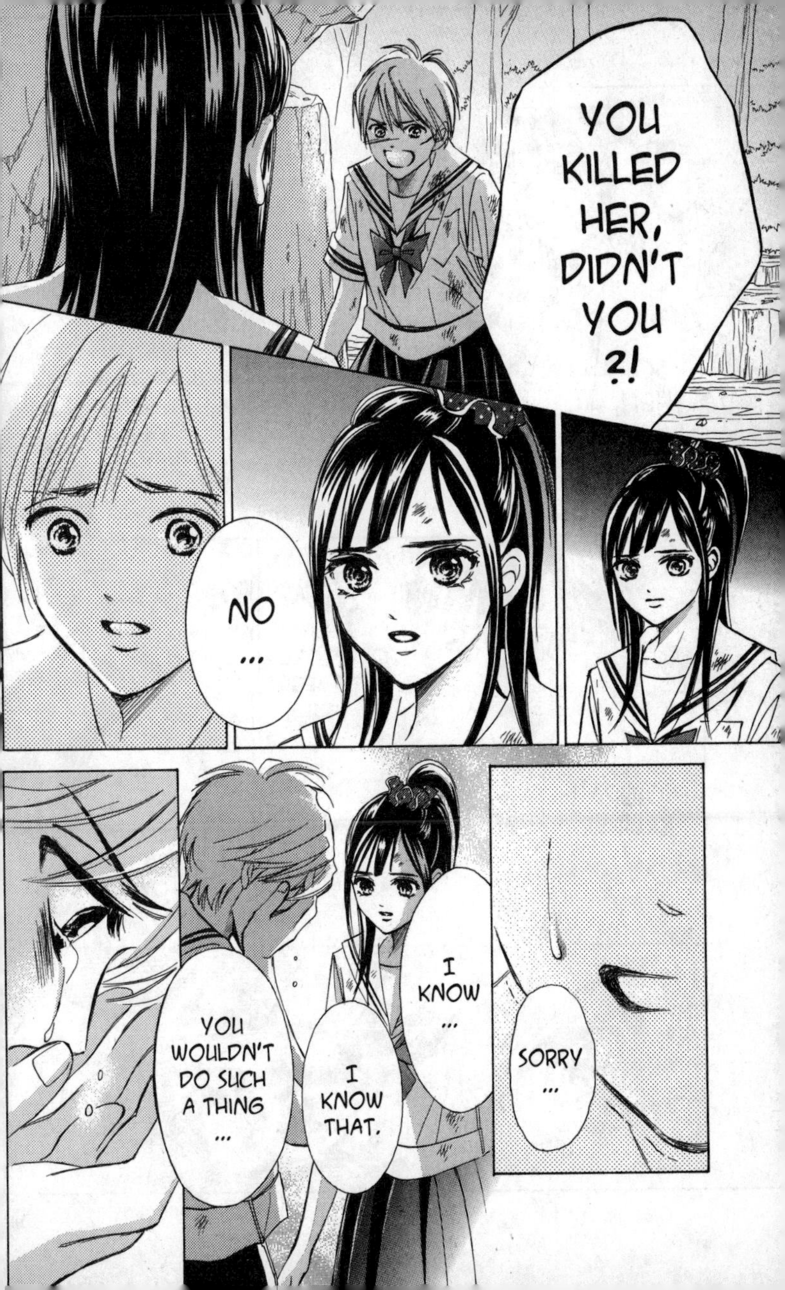
YOU KILLED HER, DIDN'T YOU?!
NO ...
SORRY ...
I KNOW ...
I KNOW THAT.
YOU WOULDN'T DO SUCH A THING ...

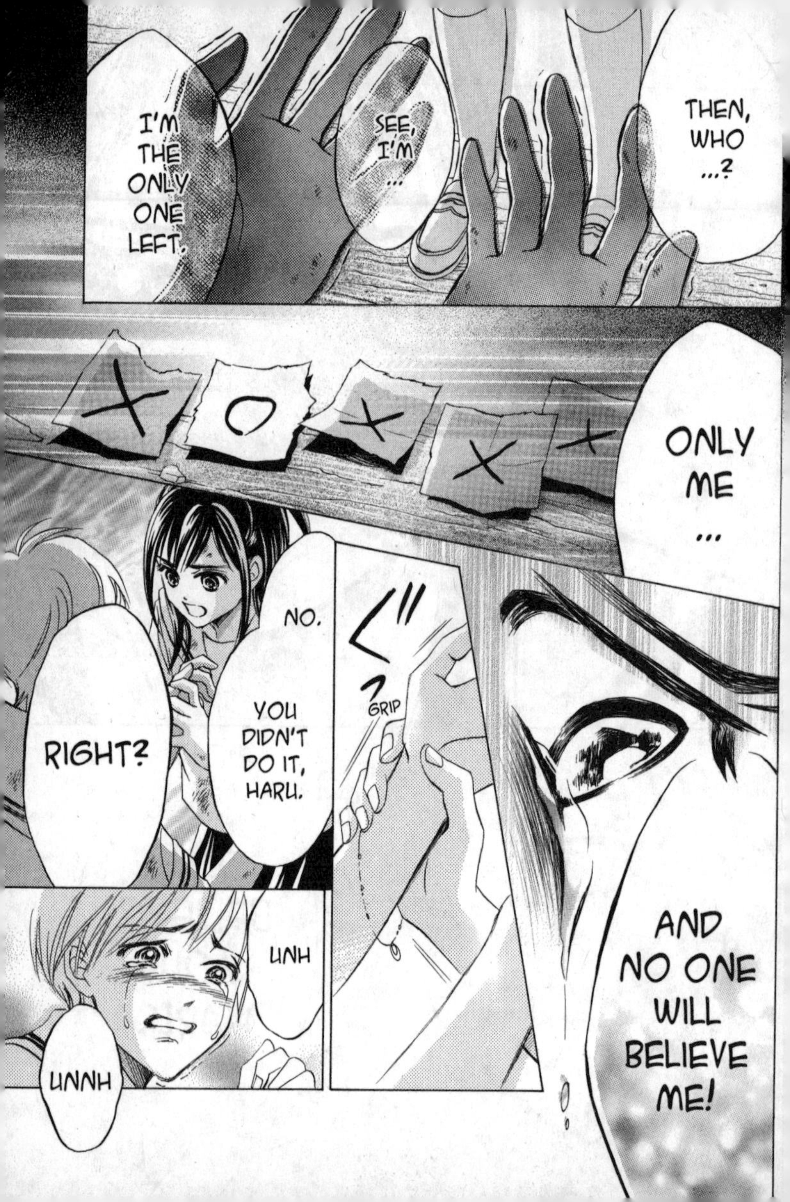
THEN, WHO ...?
SEE, I'M ...
I'M THE ONLY ONE LEFT.
ONLY ME ...
AND NO ONE WILL BELIEVE ME!
GRIP
NO.
YOU DIDN'T DO IT, HARU.
RIGHT?
UNH
UNNH

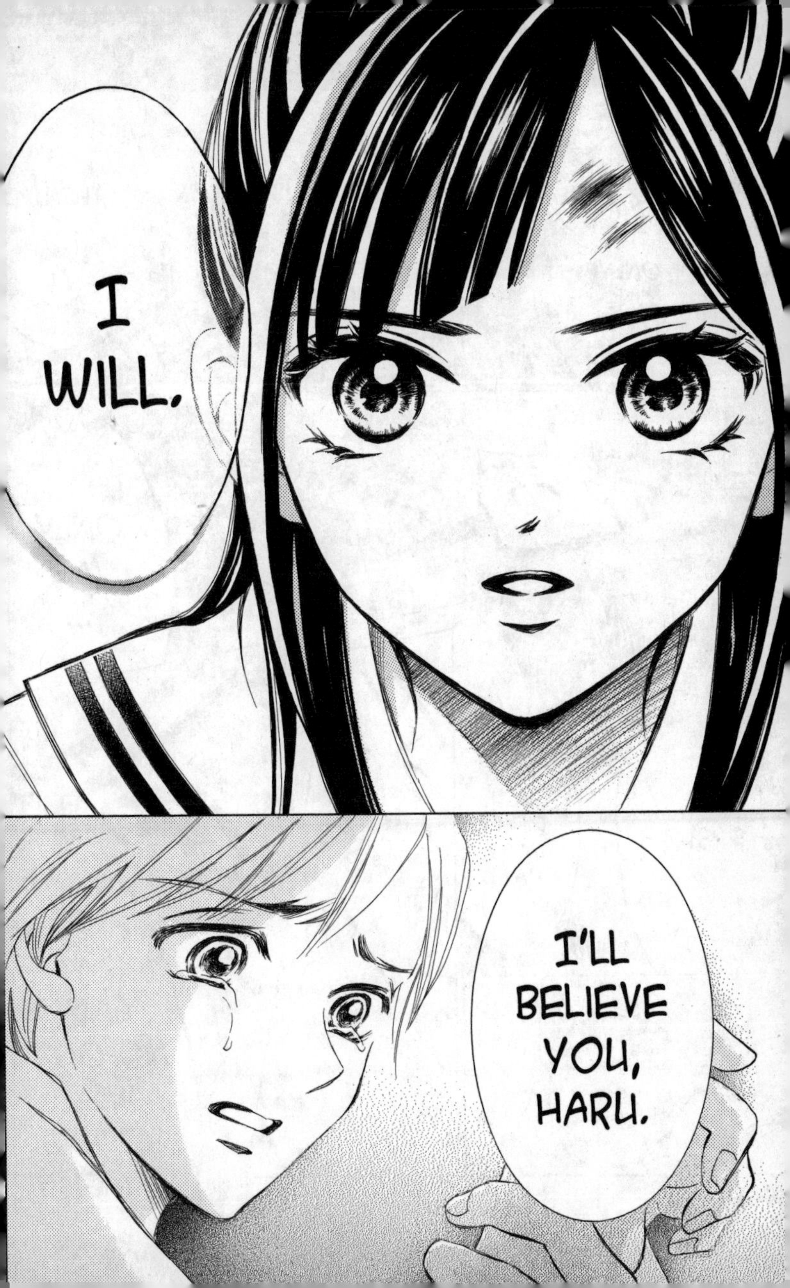
I WILL.
I'LL BELIEVE YOU, HARU.

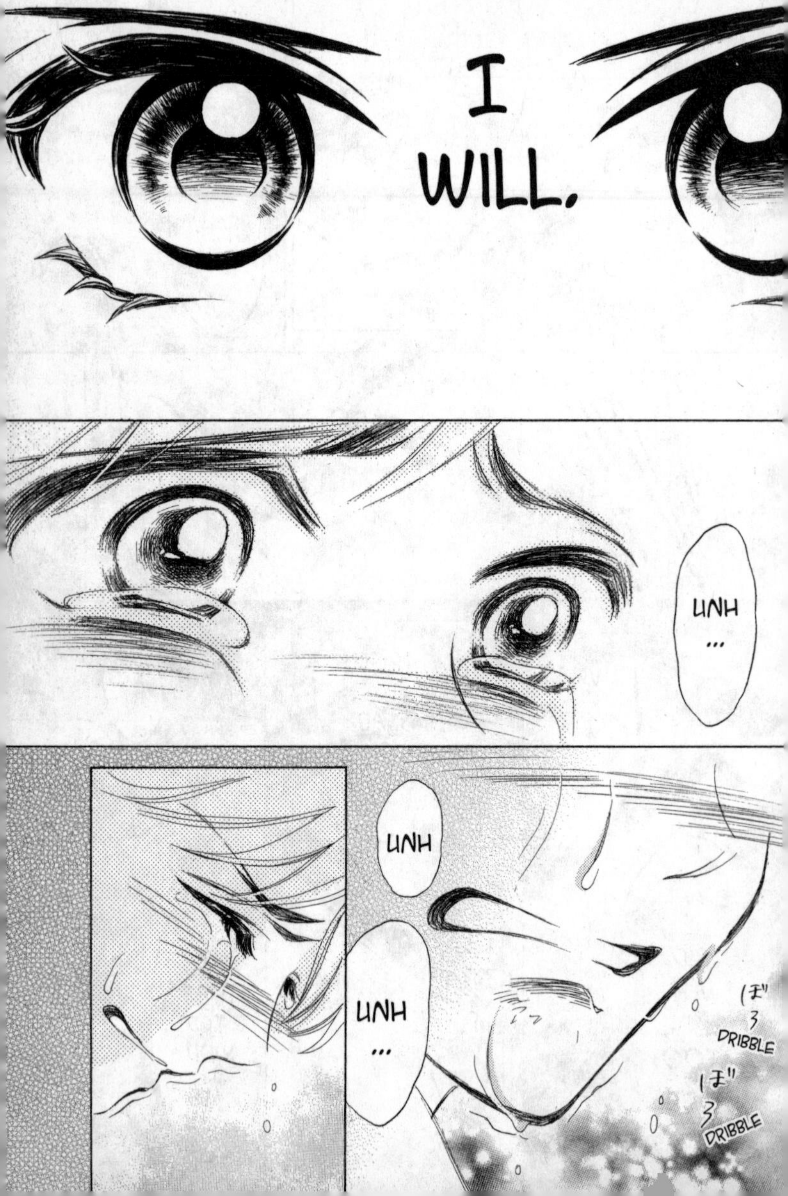
I WILL.
UNH ...
ぼろ DRIBBLE
UNH
ぼろ DRIBBLE
UNH ...

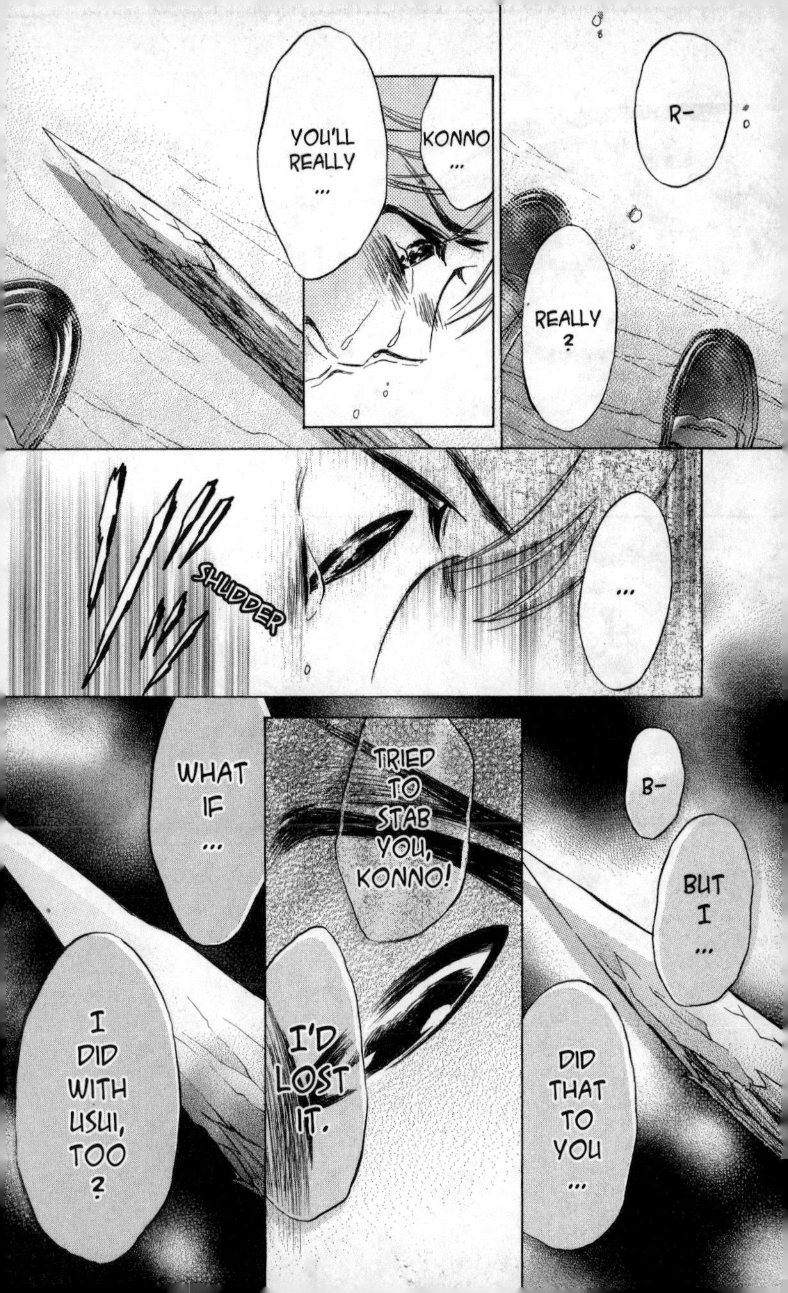
R-
REALLY?
KONNO...
YOU'LL REALLY...
...
SHUDDER
B-
BUT I...
DID THAT TO YOU...
TRIED TO STAB YOU, KONNO!
I'D LOST IT.
WHAT IF...
I DID WITH USUI, TOO?

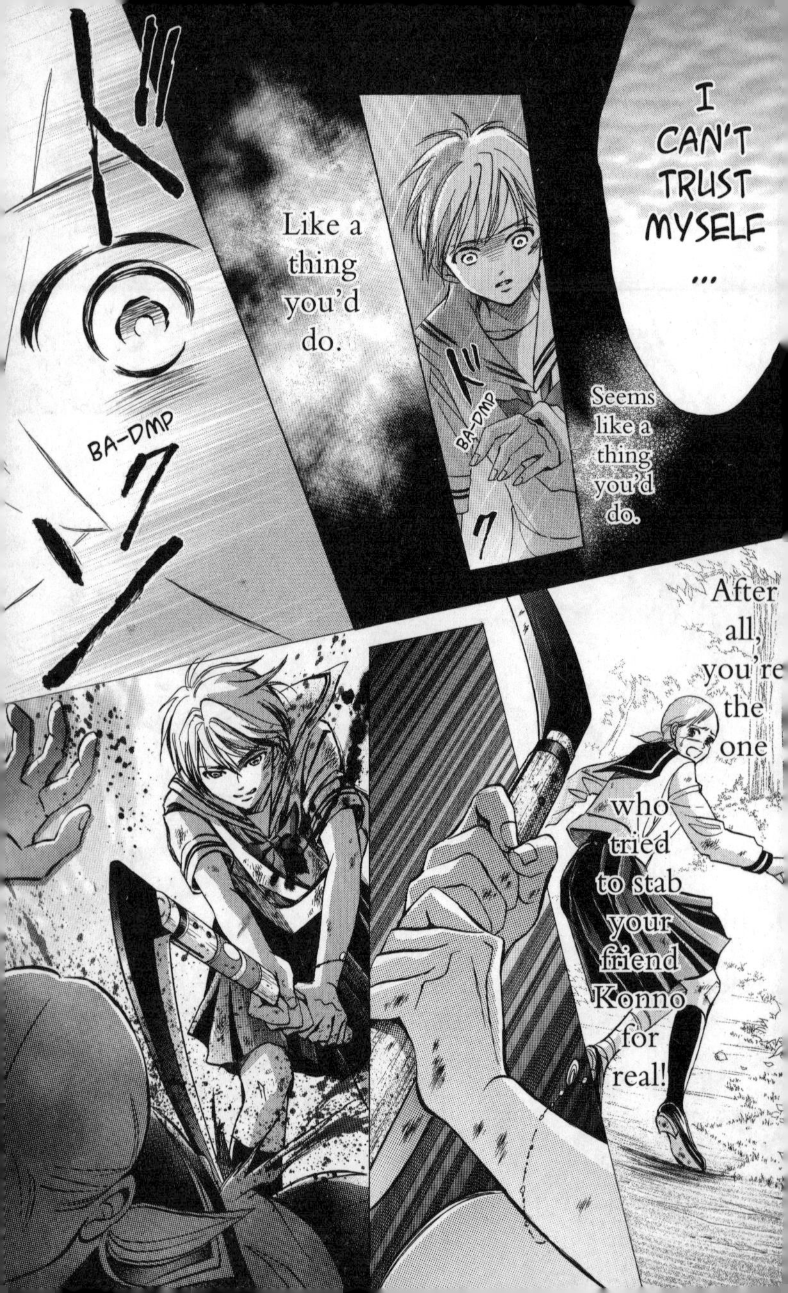
I CAN'T TRUST MYSELF ...
BA-DMP
Seems like a thing you'd do.
Like a thing you'd do.
BA-DMP
After all, you're the one who tried to stab your friend Konno for real!

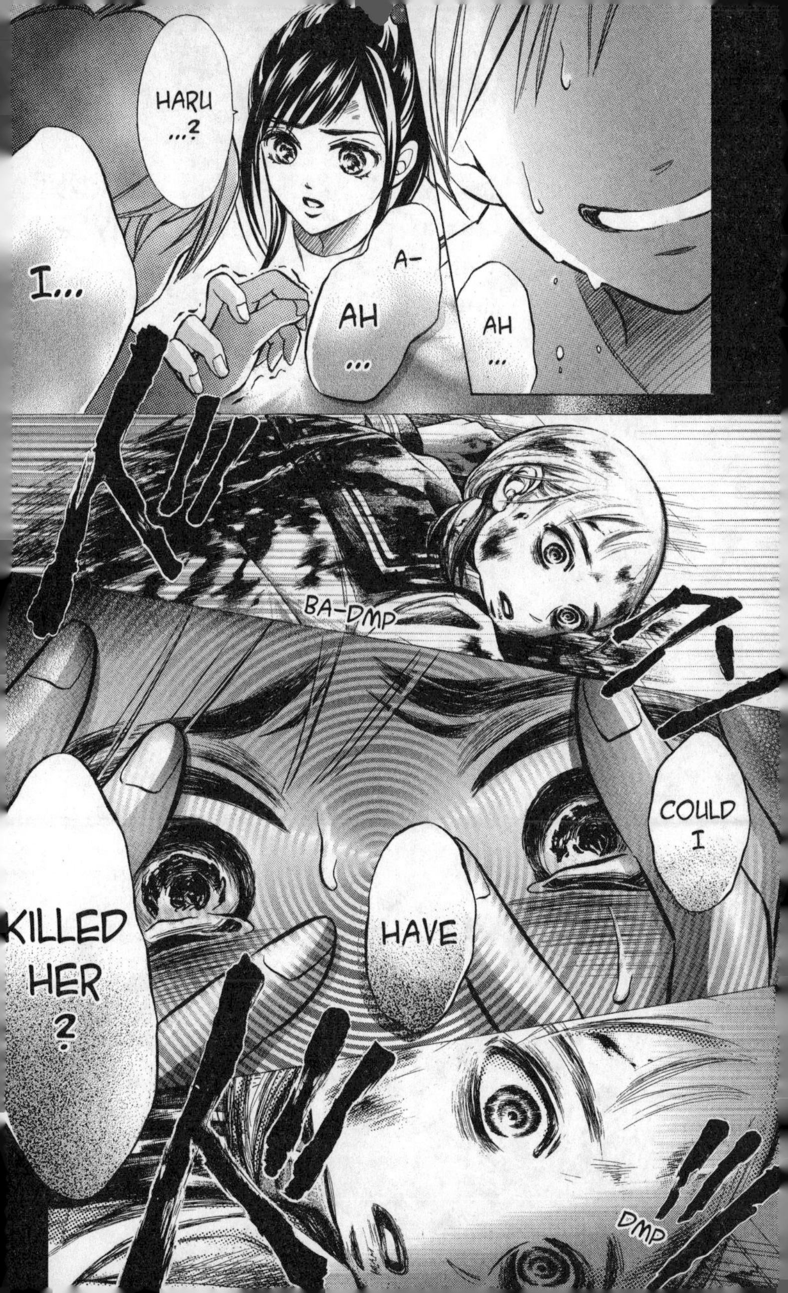
HARU ...?
AH ...
A- AH ...
I...
BA-DMP
COULD I
HAVE
KILLED HER?
DMP

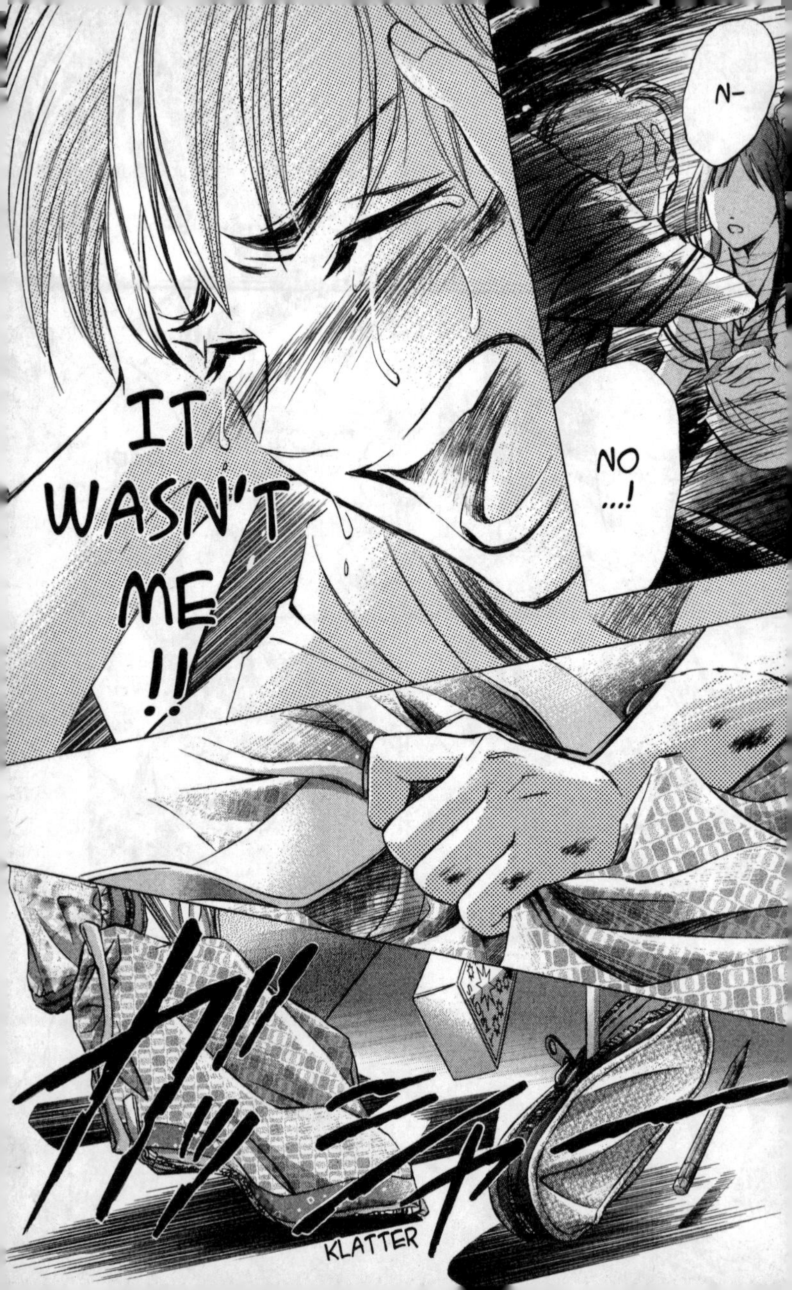
N-
NO ...!
IT WASN'T ME !!
KLATTER

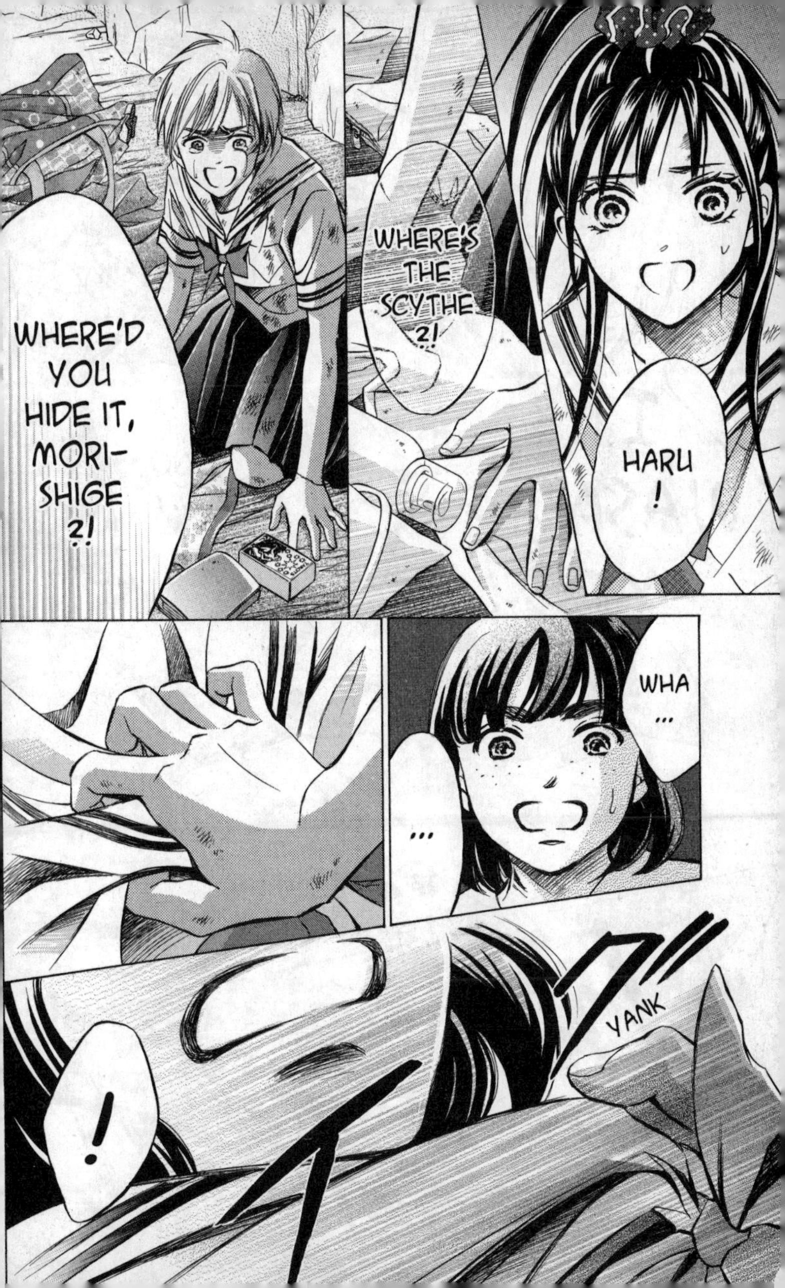
HARU!
WHERE'S THE SCYTHE?!
WHERE'D YOU HIDE IT, MORI-SHIGE?!
WHA...
...
YANK
!

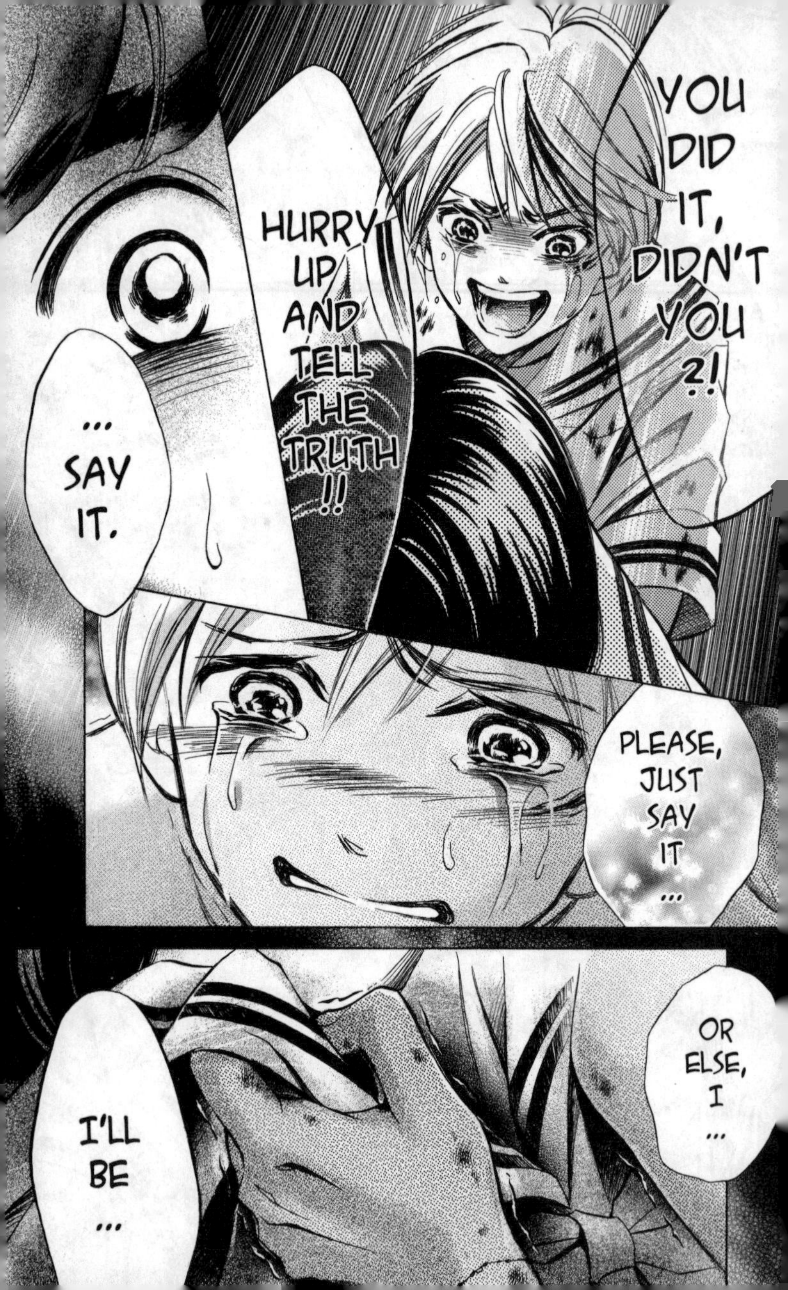
YOU DID IT, DIDN'T YOU ?!
HURRY UP AND TELL THE TRUTH !!
... SAY IT.
PLEASE, JUST SAY IT ...
OR ELSE, I ...
I'LL BE ...

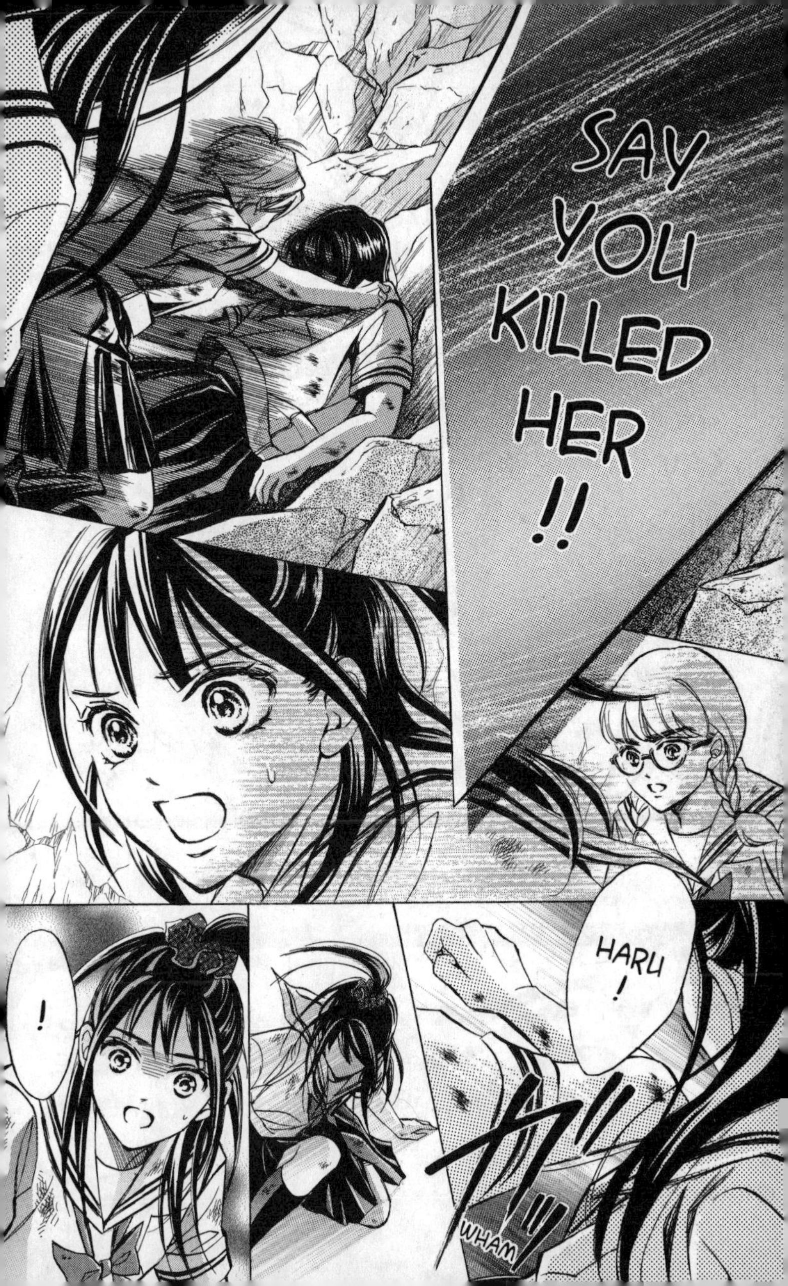
SAY YOU KILLED HER !!
HARU !
WHAM
!

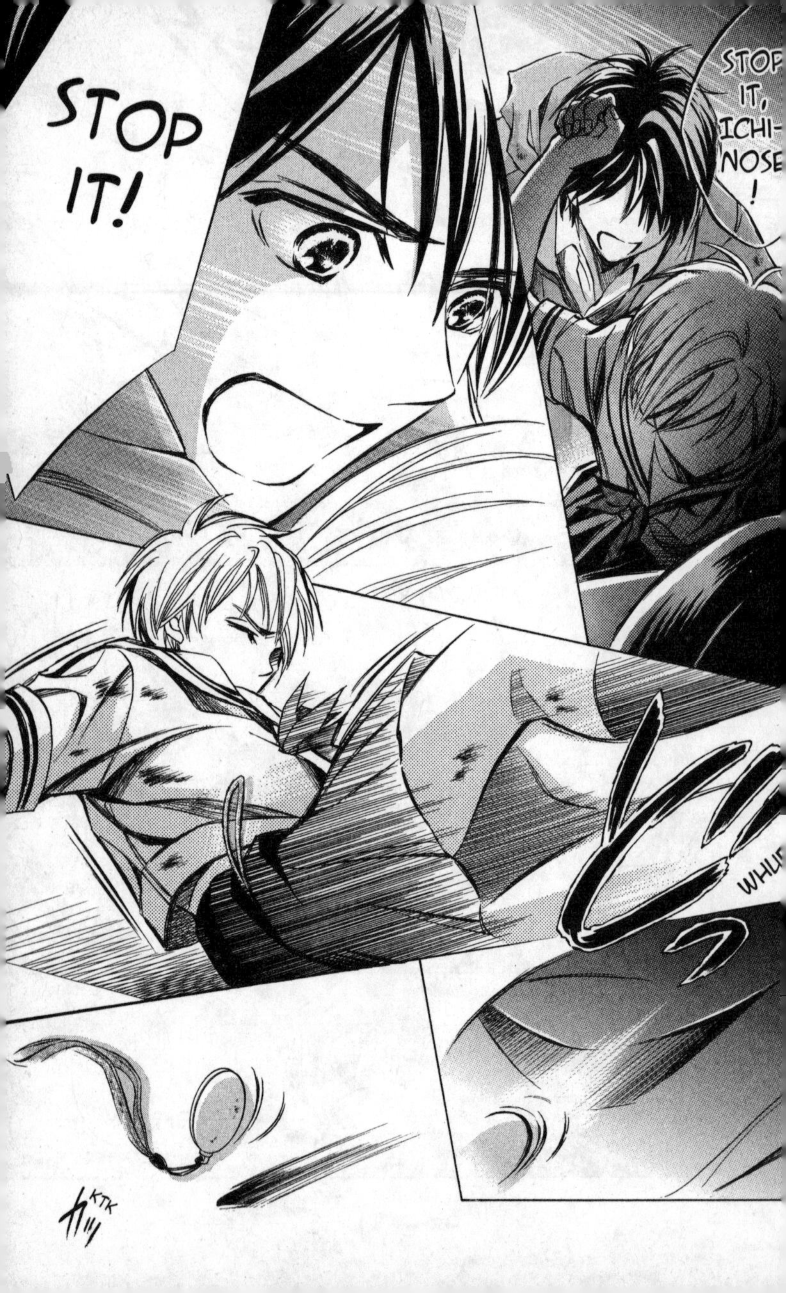
STOP IT, ICHI-NOSE!
STOP IT!
WHU
KTK

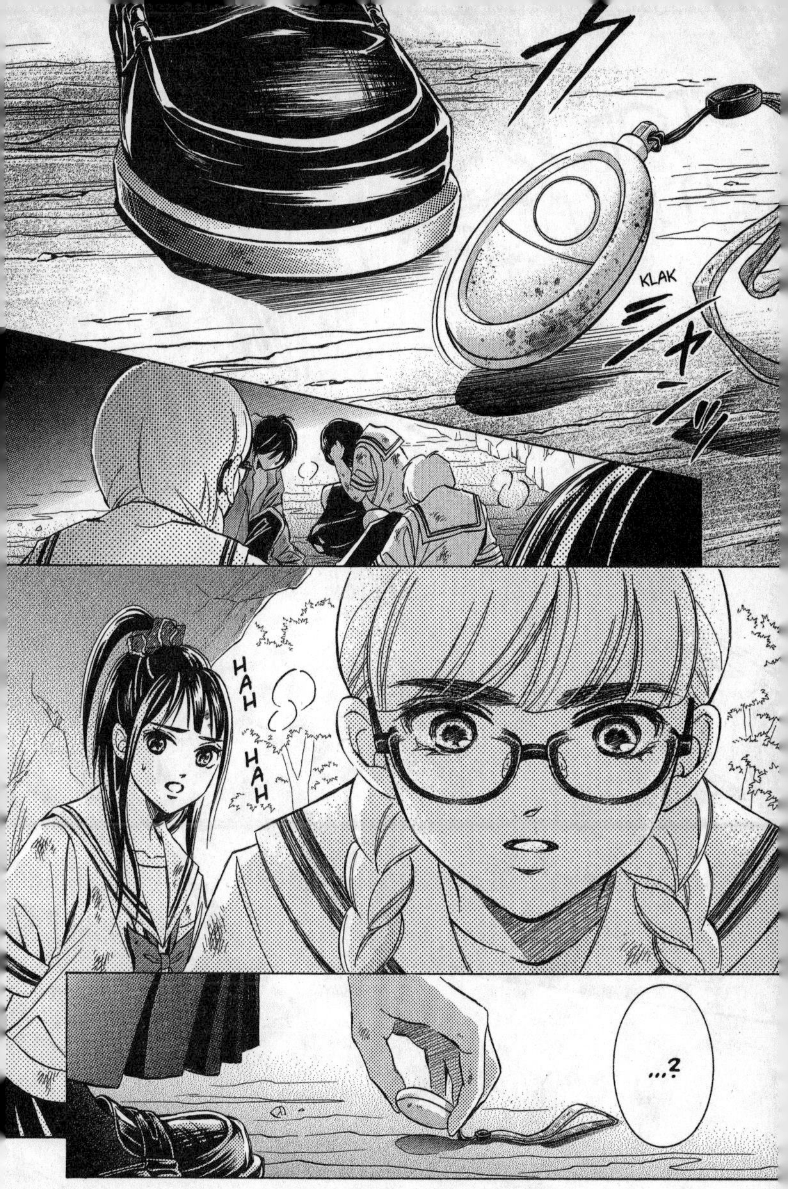
KLAK
HAH HAH
...?

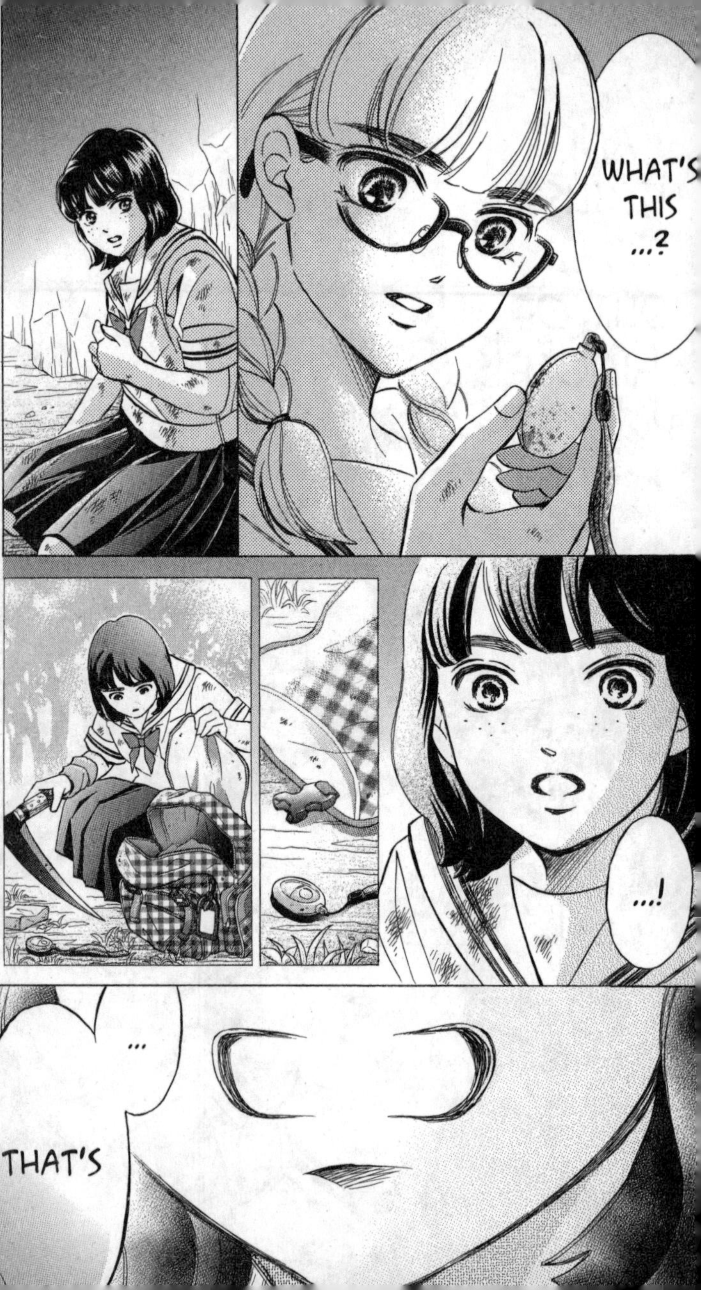
WHAT'S THIS ...?
...!
...
THAT'S

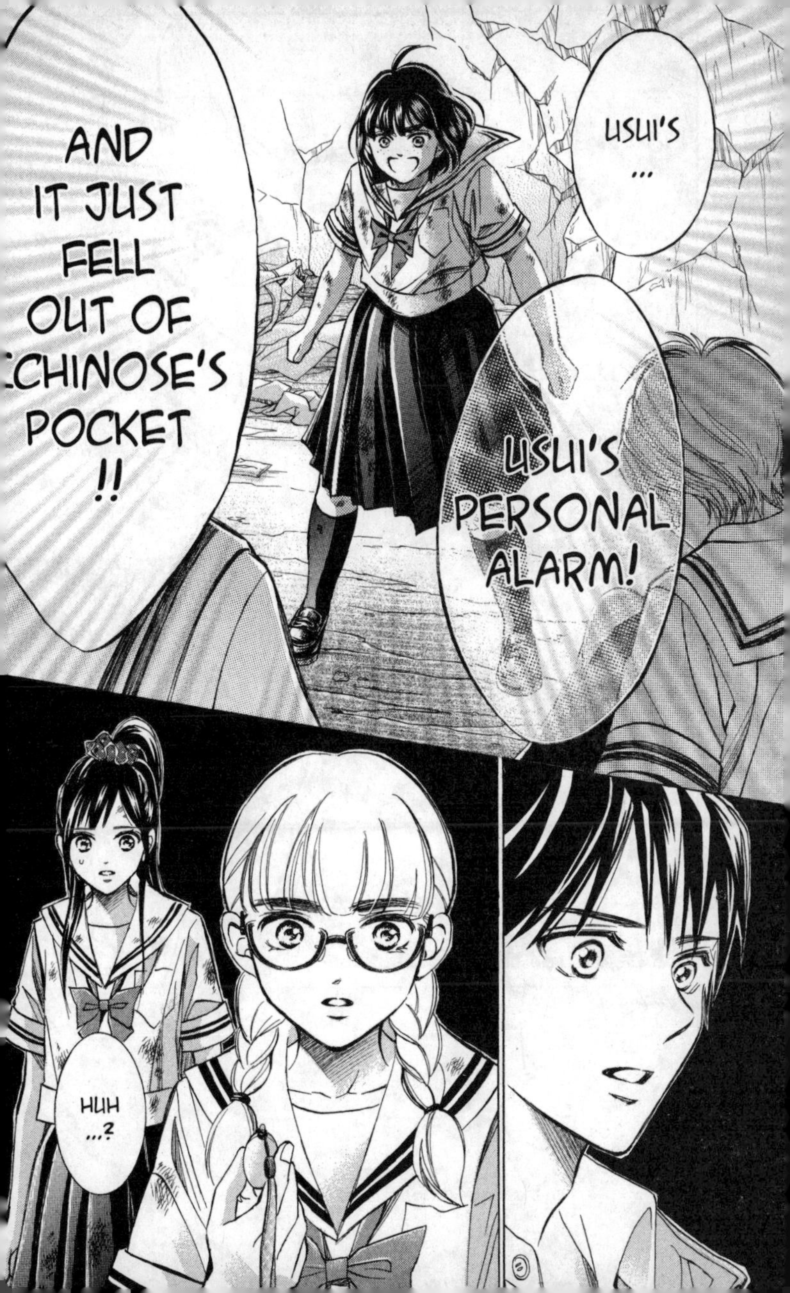
USUI'S ...
USUI'S PERSONAL ALARM!
AND IT JUST FELL OUT OF CHINOSE'S POCKET !!
HUH ...?

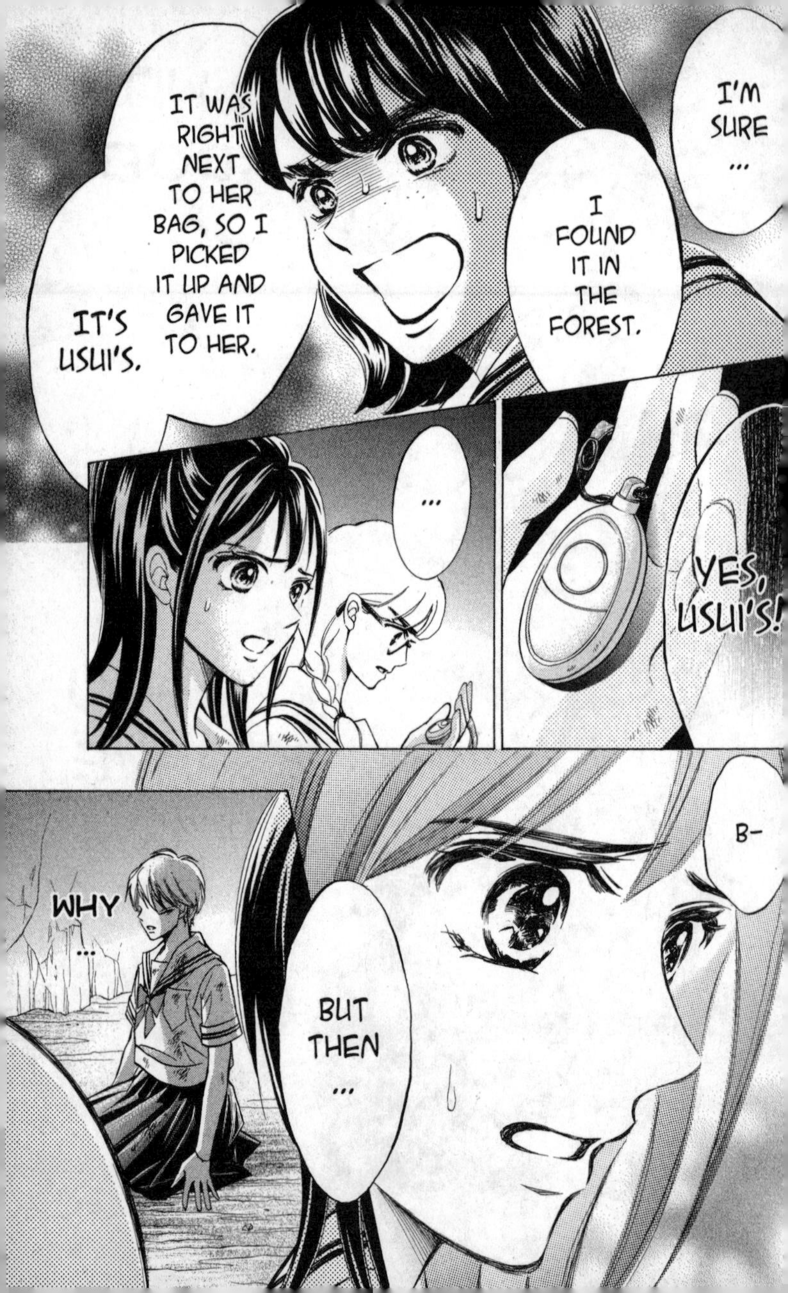
I'M SURE ...
I FOUND IT IN THE FOREST.
IT WAS RIGHT NEXT TO HER BAG, SO I PICKED IT UP AND GAVE IT TO HER.
IT'S USUI'S.
YES, USUI'S!
...
B-
BUT THEN ...
WHY ...

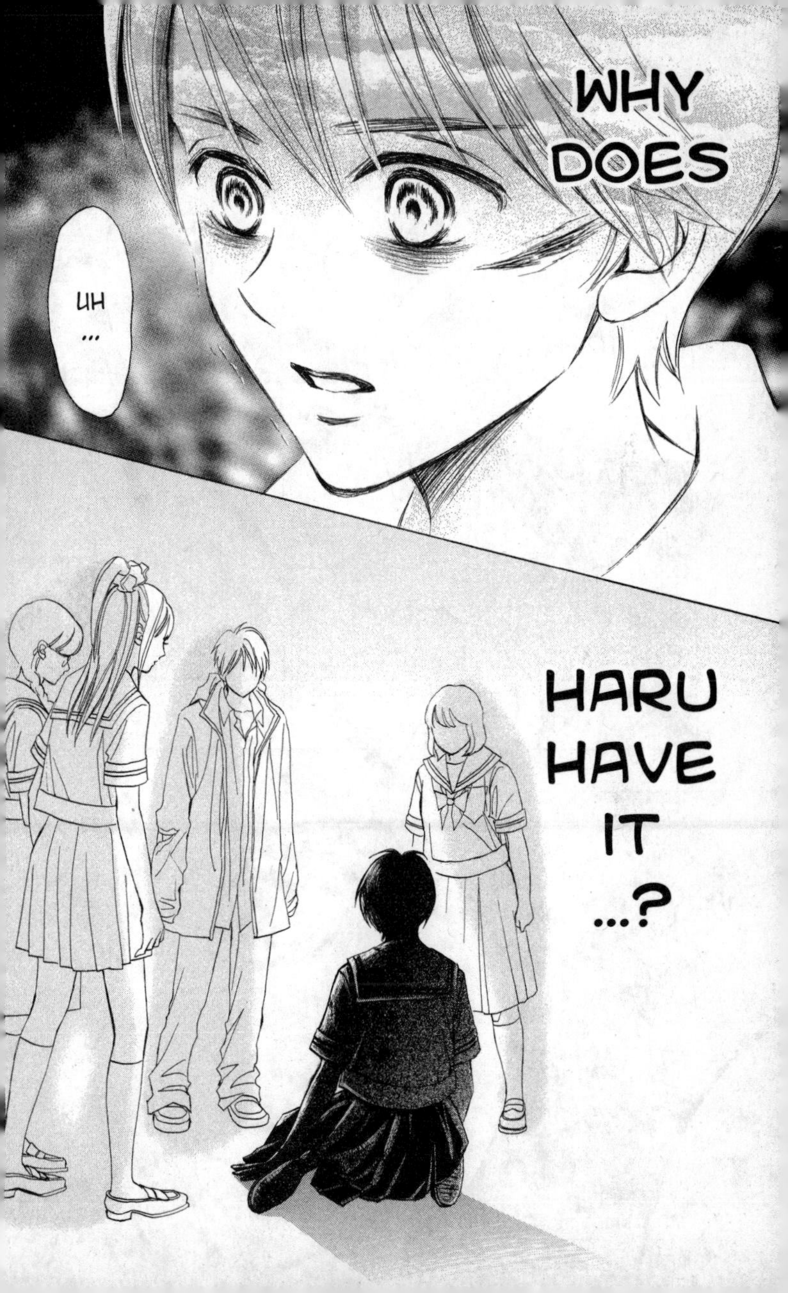
WHY DOES
UH ...
HARU HAVE IT ...?

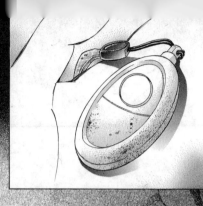

HOW DID

USUI'S PERSONAL ALARM

END UP IN HARU'S POCKET?

Scene.14 Limit

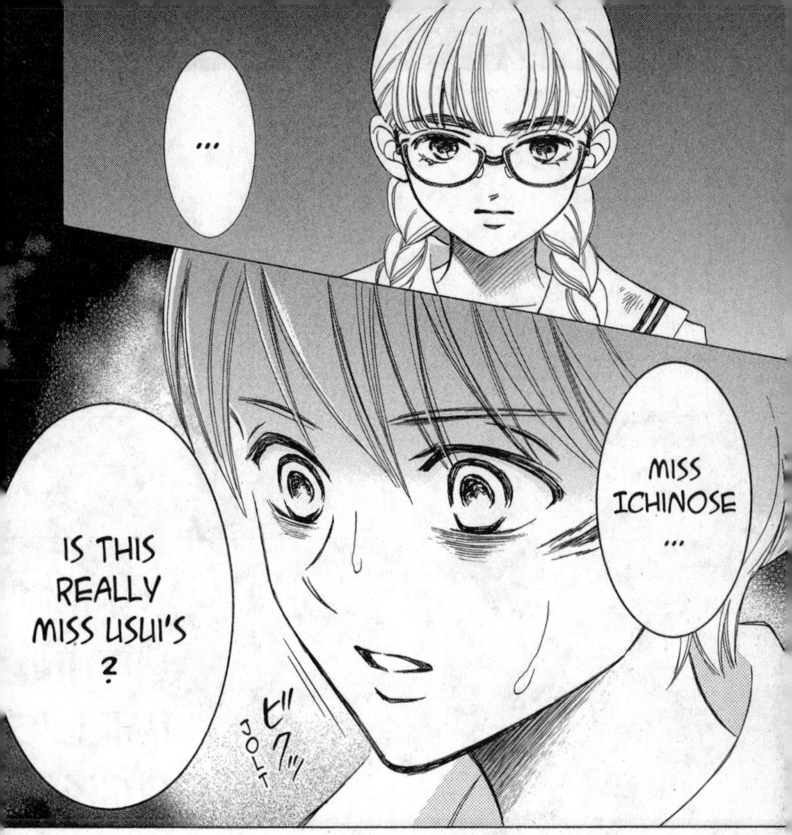
...
MISS ICHINOSE ...
IS THIS REALLY MISS USUI'S?
ビクッ
JOLT

LIMIT

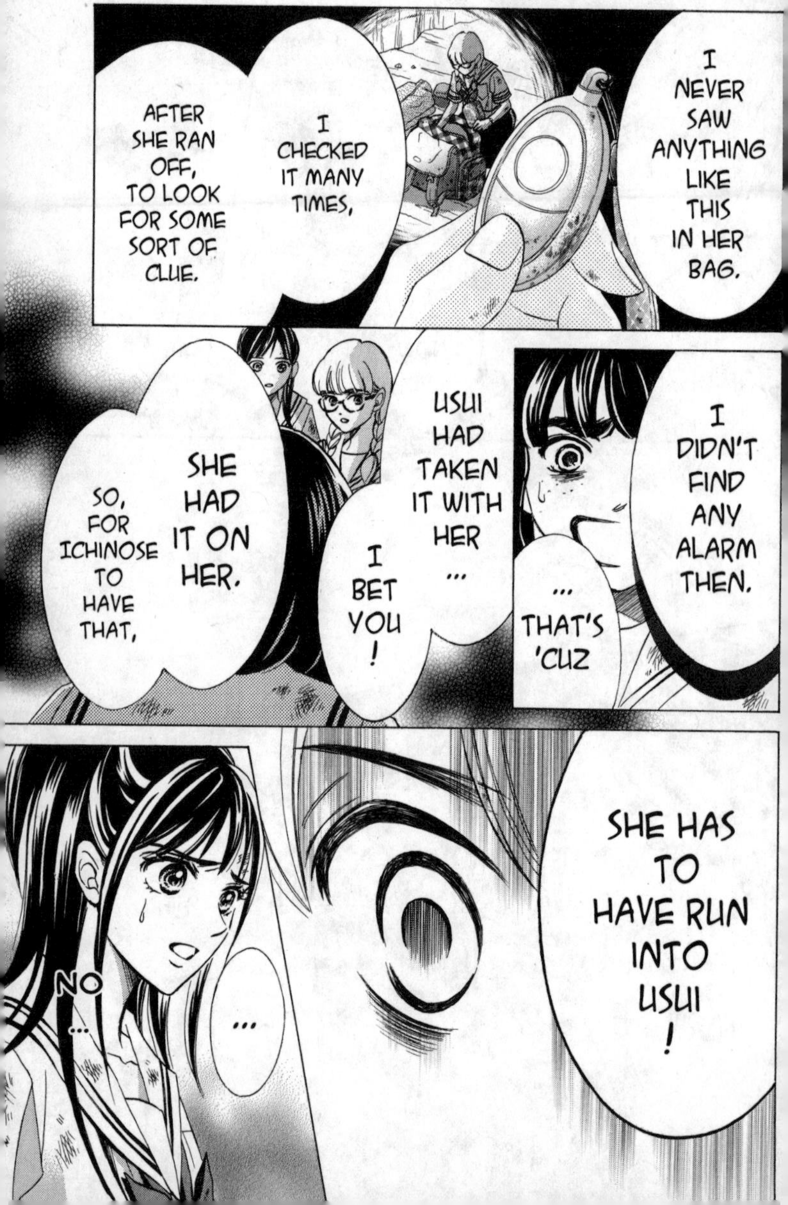
I NEVER SAW ANYTHING LIKE THIS IN HER BAG.
I CHECKED IT MANY TIMES,
AFTER SHE RAN OFF, TO LOOK FOR SOME SORT OF CLUE.
I DIDN'T FIND ANY ALARM THEN.
... THAT'S 'CUZ
USUI HAD TAKEN IT WITH HER ...
I BET YOU!
SHE HAD IT ON HER.
SO, FOR ICHINOSE TO HAVE THAT,
SHE HAS TO HAVE RUN INTO USUI!
...
NO ...

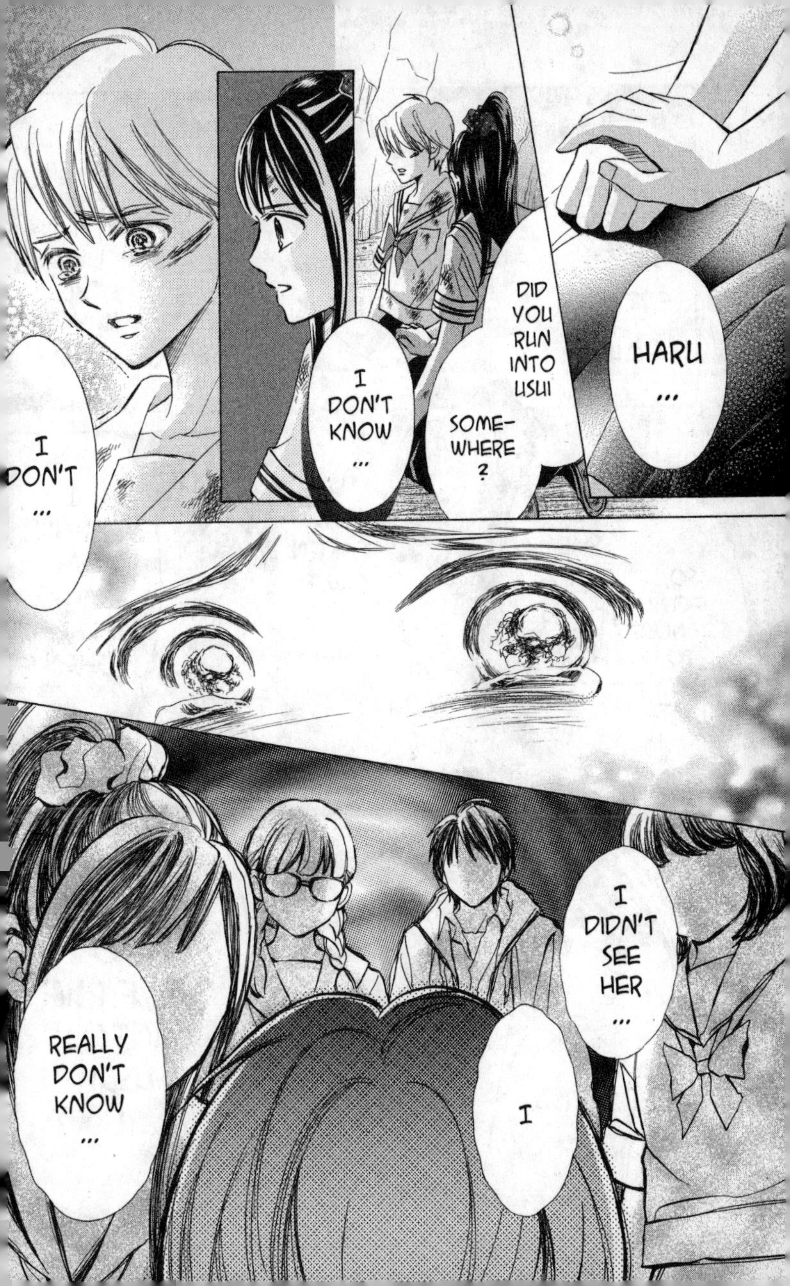
HARU ...
DID YOU RUN INTO USUI SOME-WHERE?
I DON'T KNOW ...
I DON'T ...
I DIDN'T SEE HER ...
I
REALLY DON'T KNOW ...

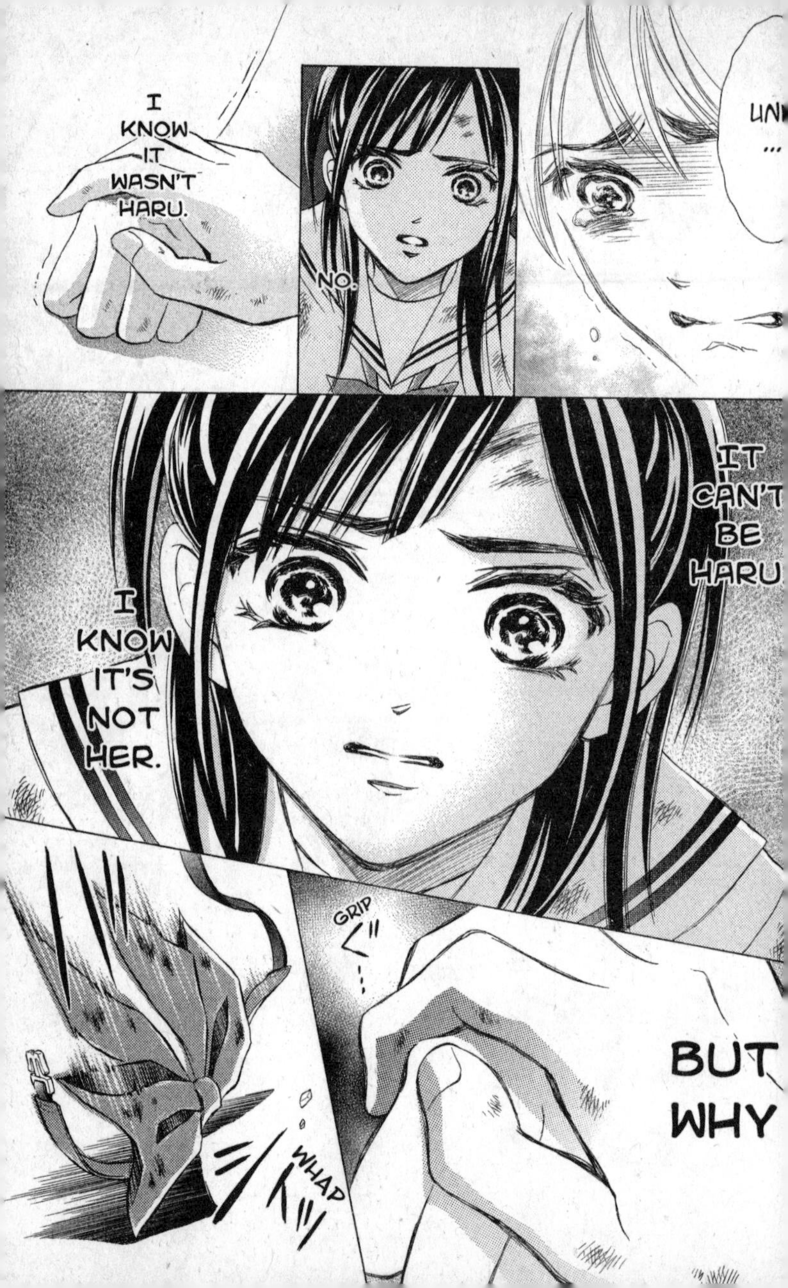
UN
...
NO.
I KNOW IT WASN'T HARU.
IT CAN'T BE HARU.
I KNOW IT'S NOT HER.
GRIP
BUT WHY
WHAP

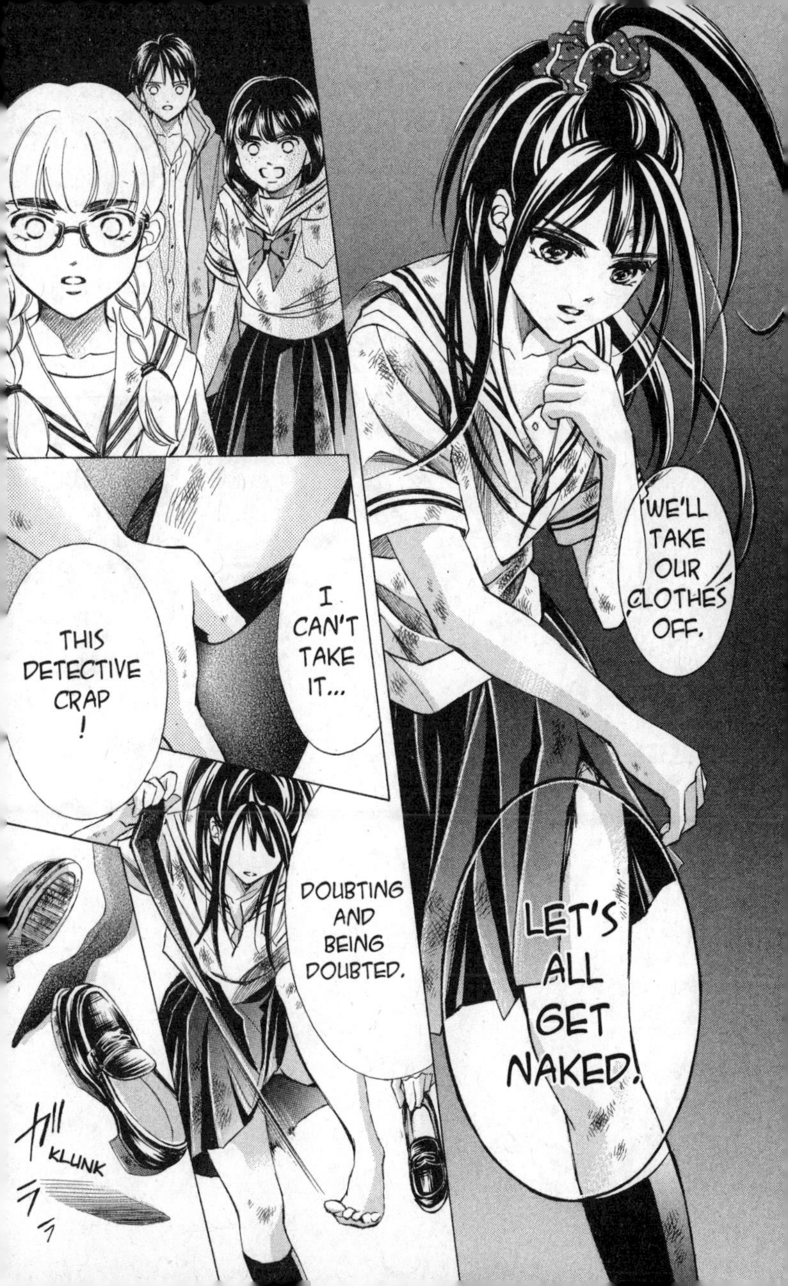
WE'LL TAKE OUR CLOTHES OFF.
LET'S ALL GET NAKED!
I CAN'T TAKE IT...
THIS DETECTIVE CRAP!
DOUBTING AND BEING DOUBTED.
KLUNK

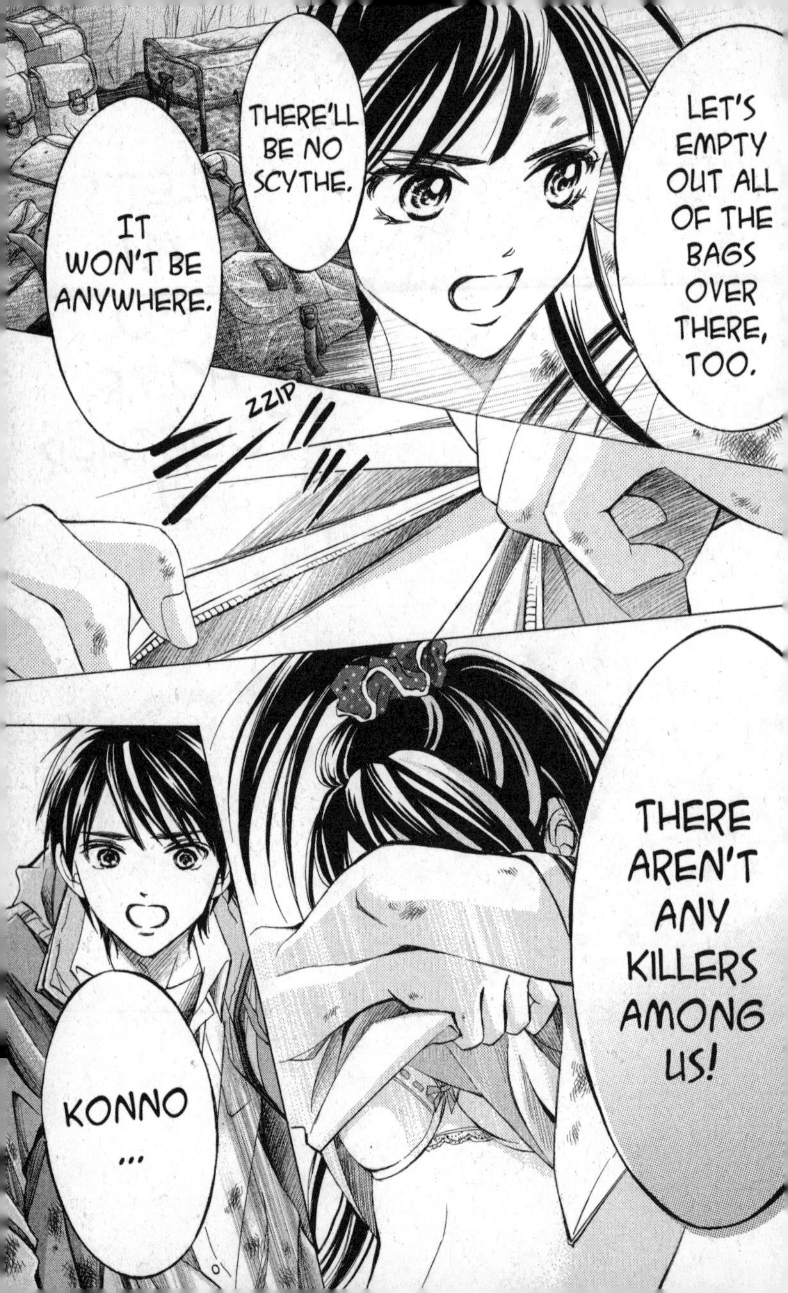
LET'S EMPTY OUT ALL OF THE BAGS OVER THERE, TOO.
THERE'LL BE NO SCYTHE.
IT WON'T BE ANYWHERE.
ZZIP
THERE AREN'T ANY KILLERS AMONG US!
KONNO ...

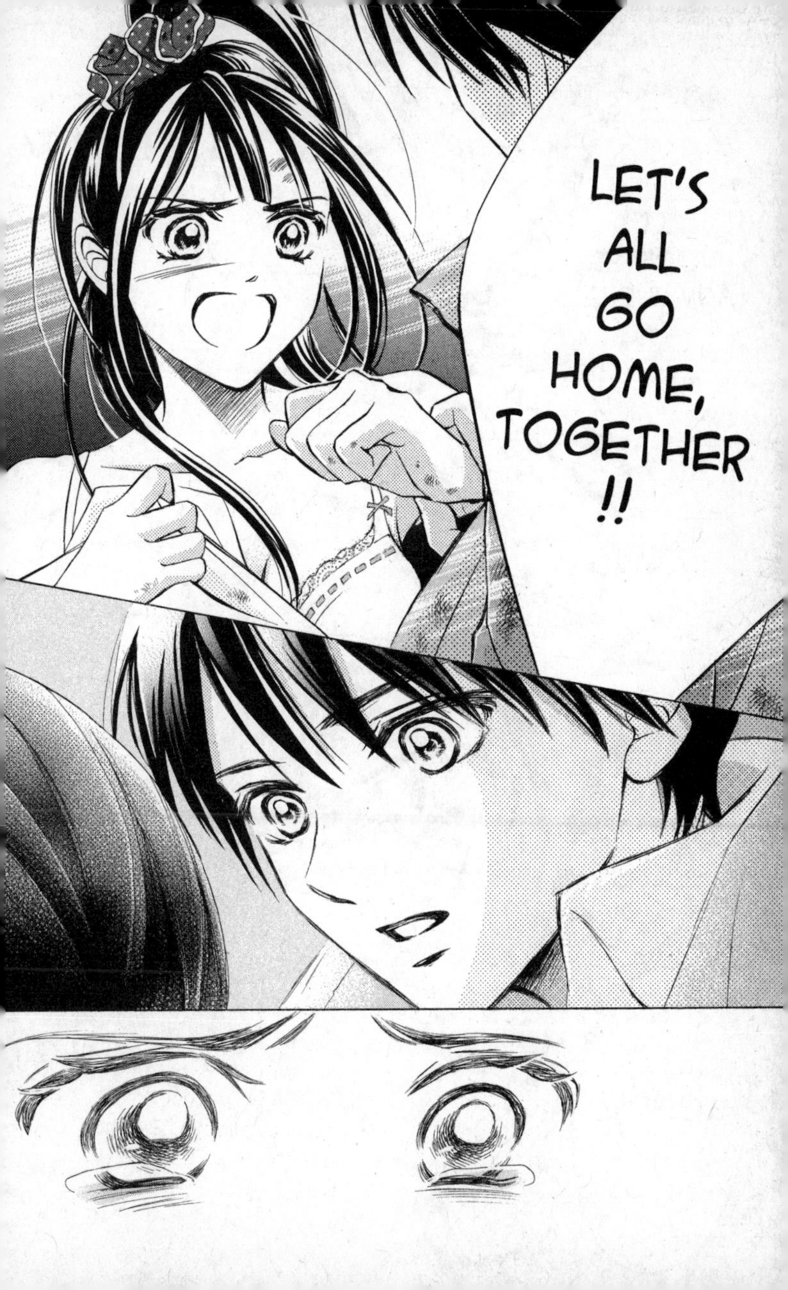
LET'S ALL GO HOME, TOGETHER!!

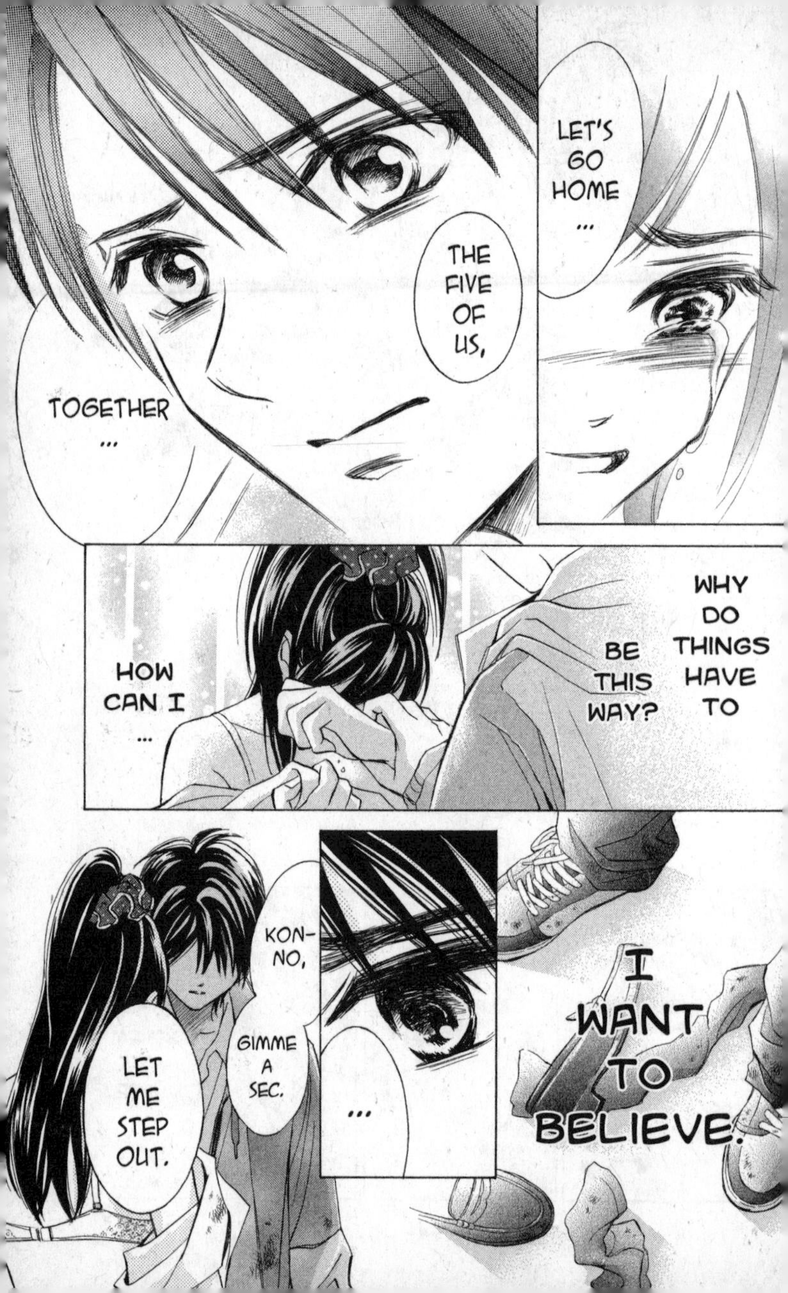
LET'S GO HOME ...
THE FIVE OF US,
TOGETHER ...
WHY DO THINGS HAVE TO BE THIS WAY?
HOW CAN I ...
I WANT TO BELIEVE.
KON-NO,
...
GIMME A SEC.
LET ME STEP OUT.

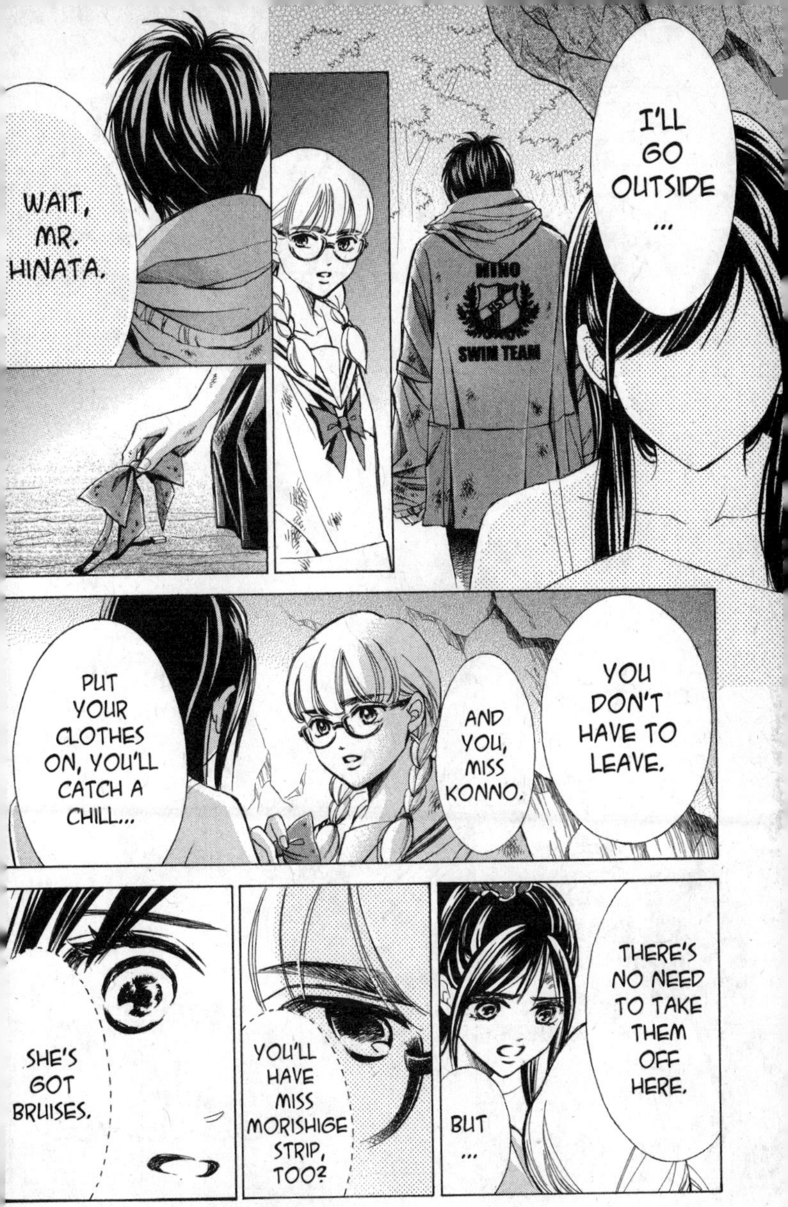
I'LL GO OUTSIDE ...
MINO
SWIM TEAM
WAIT, MR. HINATA.
YOU DON'T HAVE TO LEAVE.
AND YOU, MISS KONNO.
PUT YOUR CLOTHES ON, YOU'LL CATCH A CHILL...
THERE'S NO NEED TO TAKE THEM OFF HERE.
BUT ...
YOU'LL HAVE MISS MORISHIGE STRIP, TOO?
SHE'S GOT BRUISES.

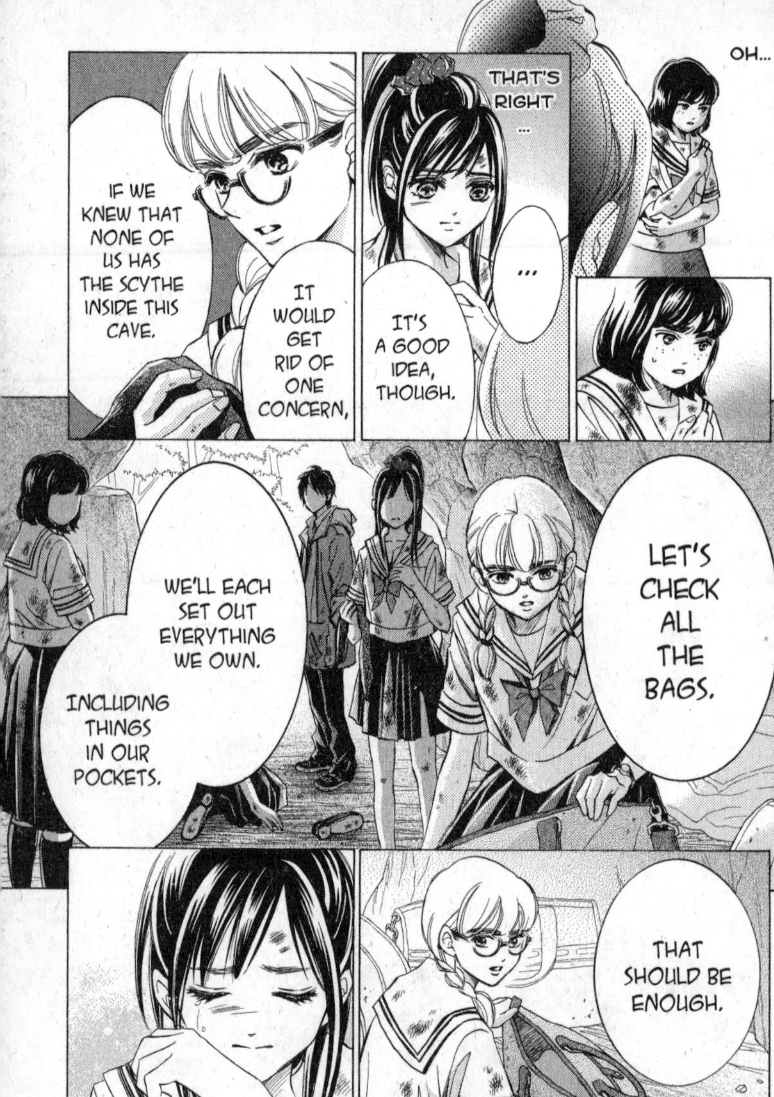
OH...
THAT'S RIGHT ...
...
IT'S A GOOD IDEA, THOUGH.
IT WOULD GET RID OF ONE CONCERN,
IF WE KNEW THAT NONE OF US HAS THE SCYTHE INSIDE THIS CAVE.
LET'S CHECK ALL THE BAGS.
WE'LL EACH SET OUT EVERYTHING WE OWN.
INCLUDING THINGS IN OUR POCKETS.
THAT SHOULD BE ENOUGH.

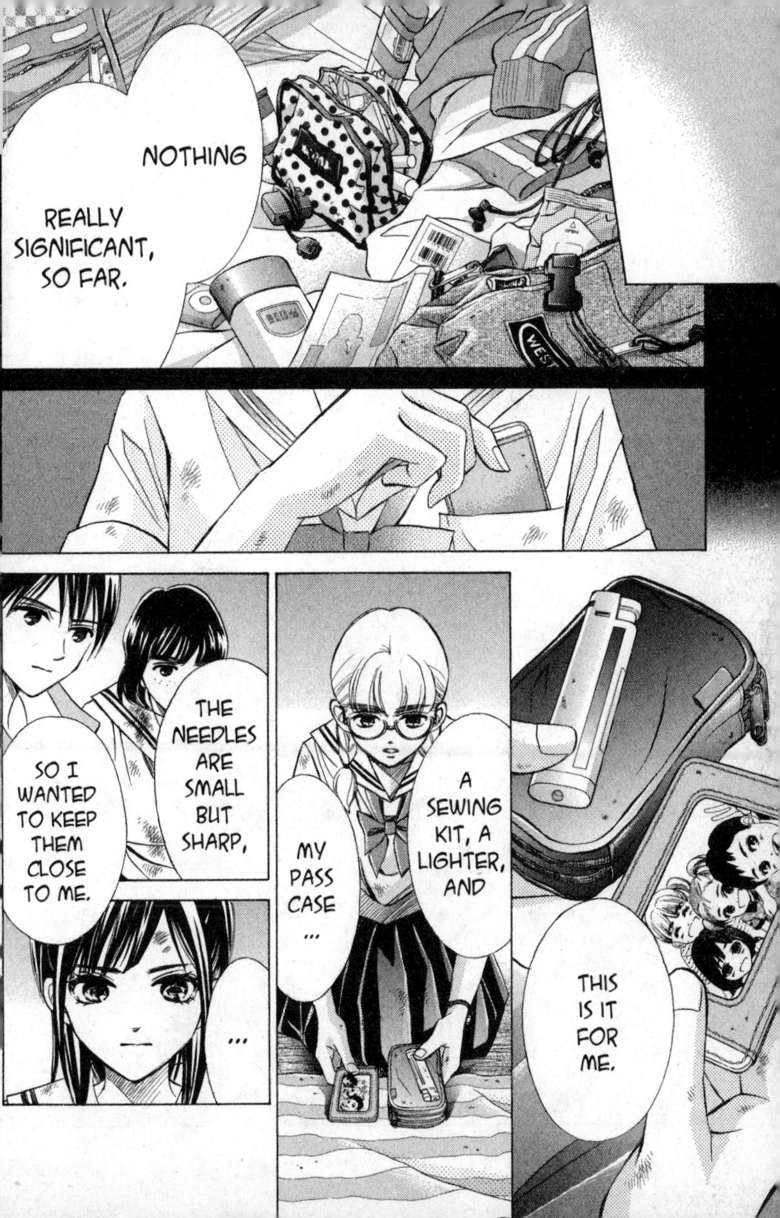
NOTHING
REALLY SIGNIFICANT, SO FAR.
THIS IS IT FOR ME.
A SEWING KIT, A LIGHTER, AND
MY PASS CASE ...
THE NEEDLES ARE SMALL BUT SHARP,
SO I WANTED TO KEEP THEM CLOSE TO ME.
...

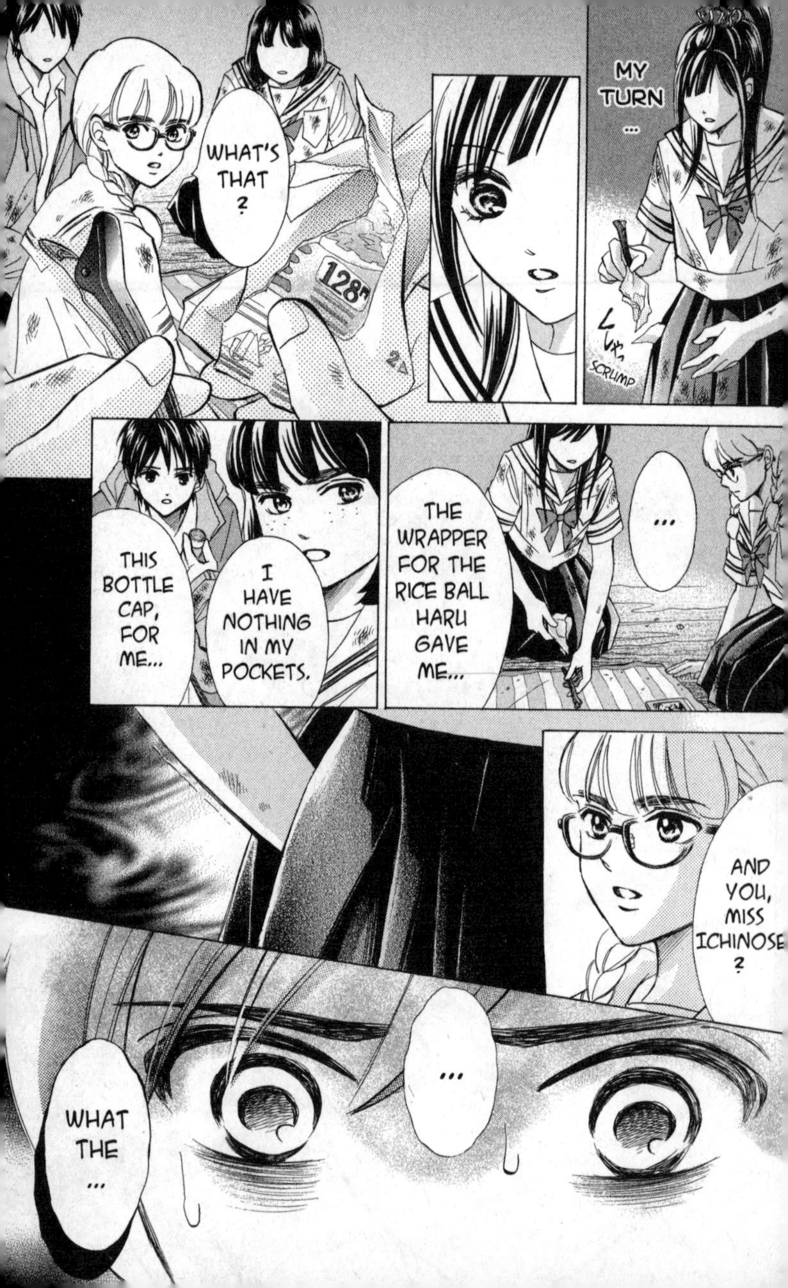
MY TURN ...
SCRUMP
WHAT'S THAT ?
128
...
THE WRAPPER FOR THE RICE BALL HARU GAVE ME...
I HAVE NOTHING IN MY POCKETS.
THIS BOTTLE CAP, FOR ME...
AND YOU, MISS ICHINOSE ?
...
WHAT THE ...

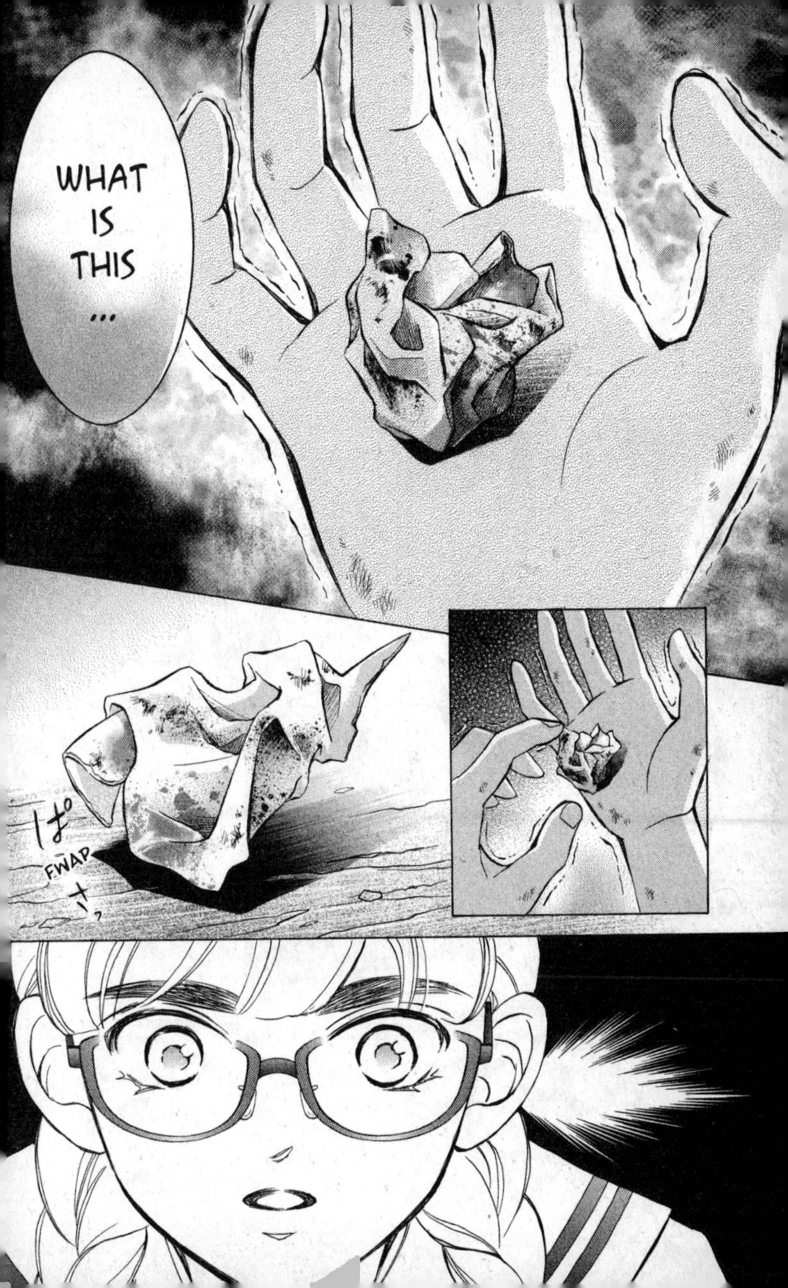
WHAT IS THIS ...
ぱっ
FWAP

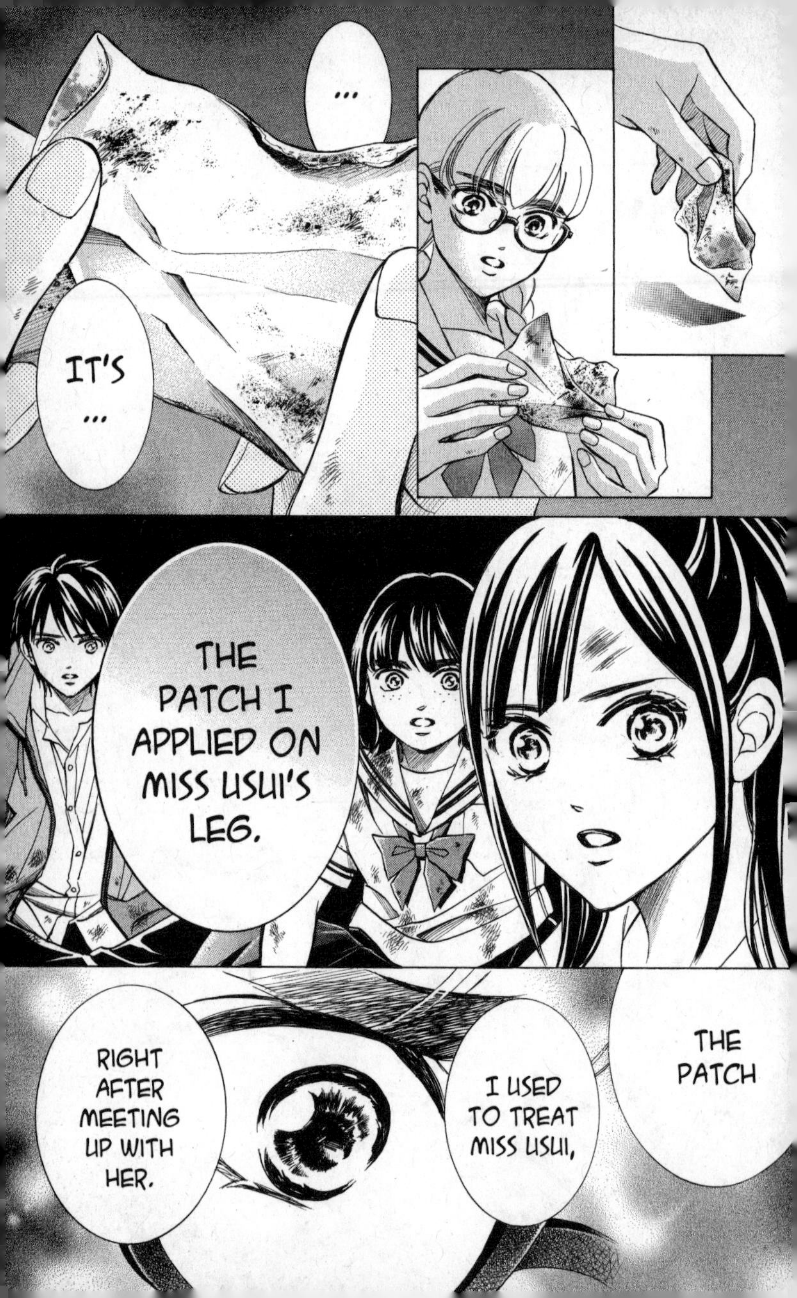
...
IT'S ...
THE PATCH I APPLIED ON MISS USUI'S LEG.
THE PATCH
I USED TO TREAT MISS USUI,
RIGHT AFTER MEETING UP WITH HER.

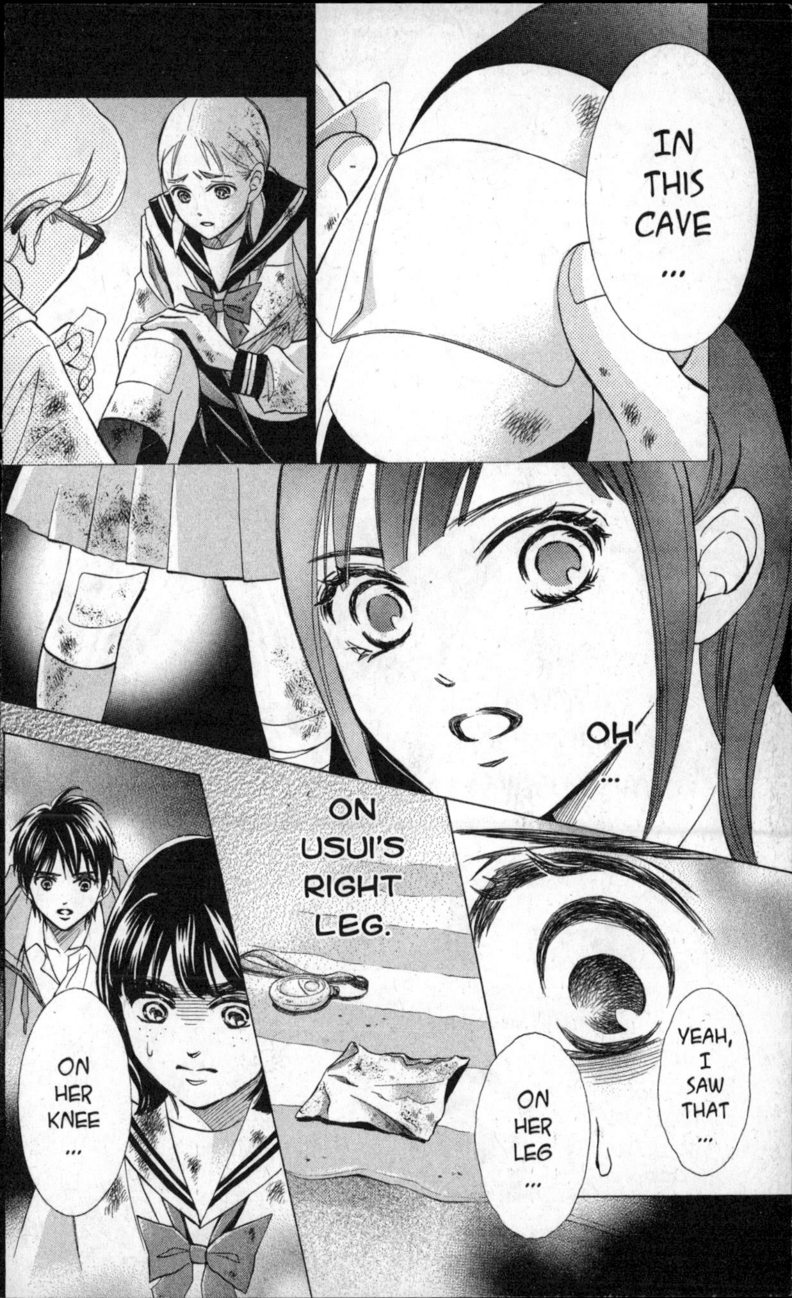
IN THIS CAVE ...
OH ...
YEAH, I SAW THAT ...
ON HER LEG ...
ON USUI'S RIGHT LEG.
ON HER KNEE ...

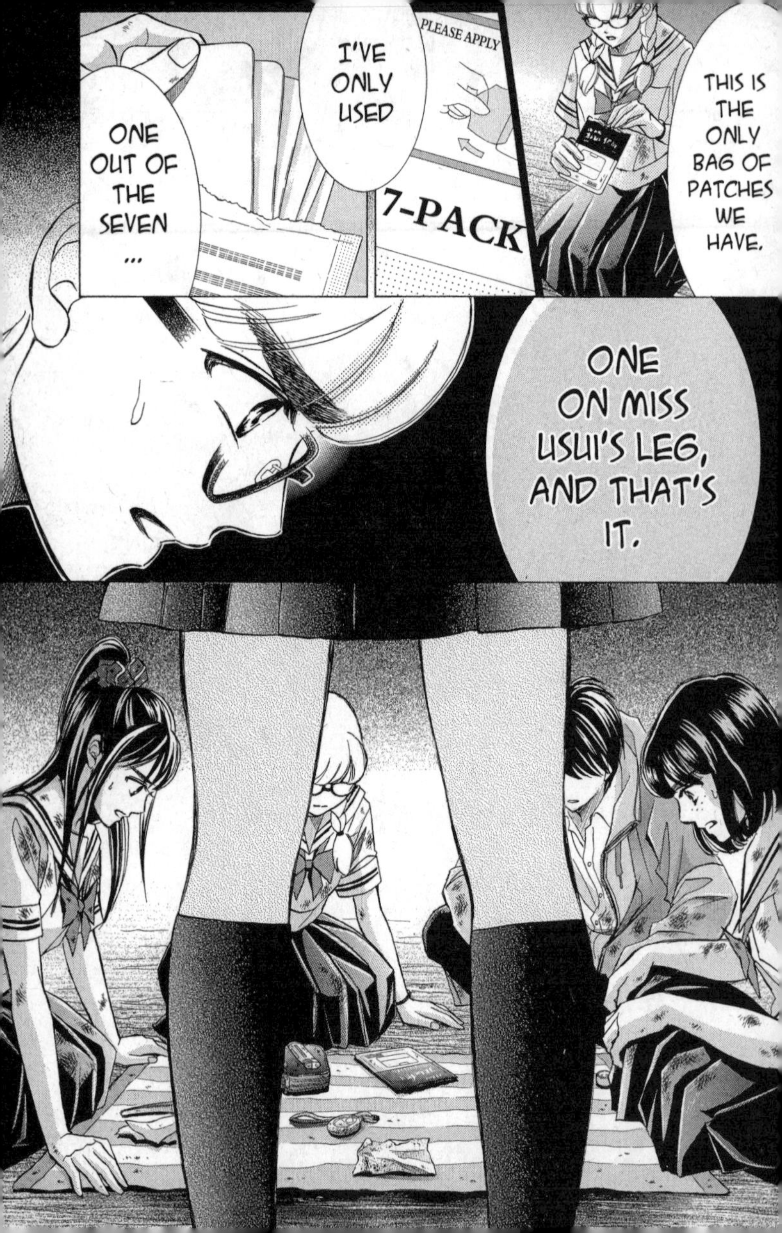
THIS IS THE ONLY BAG OF PATCHES WE HAVE.
PLEASE APPLY
I'VE ONLY USED
7-PACK
ONE OUT OF THE SEVEN ...
ONE ON MISS USUI'S LEG, AND THAT'S IT.

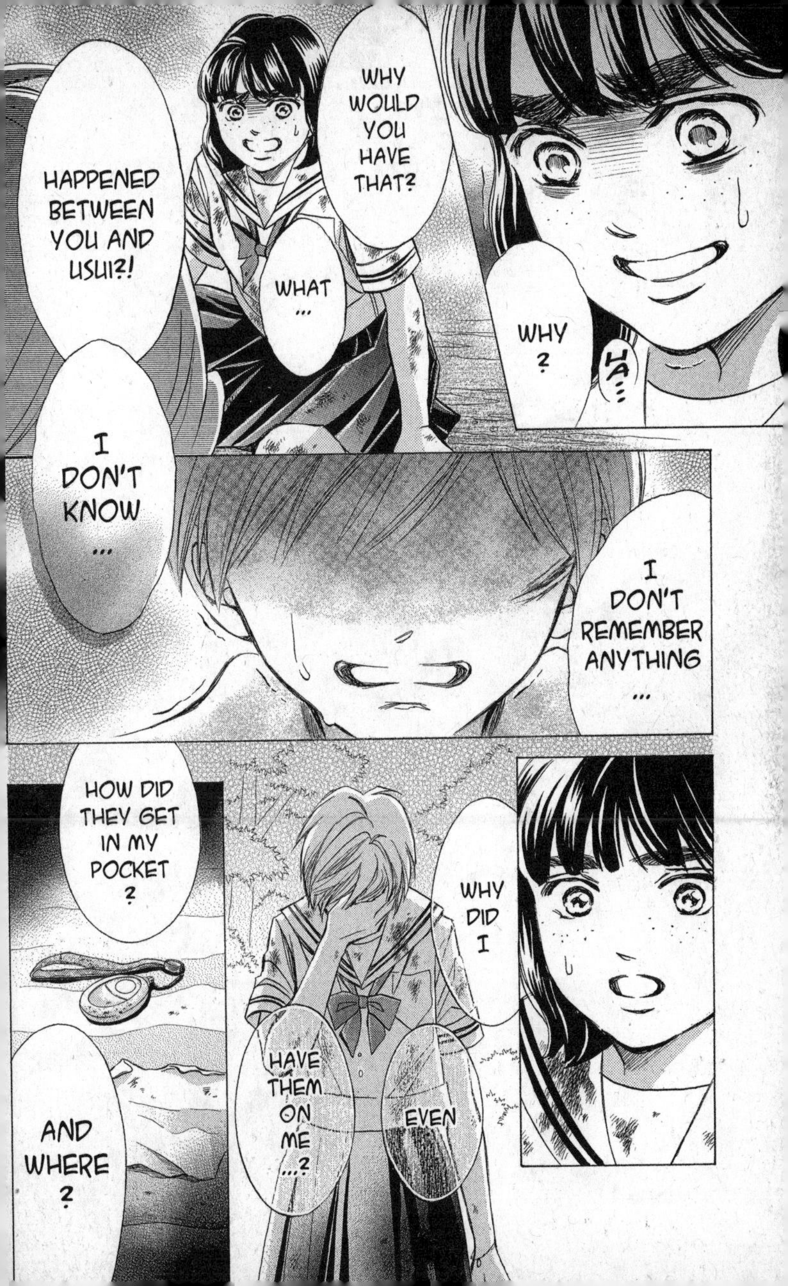
WHY ?
HA...
WHY WOULD YOU HAVE THAT?
WHAT ...
HAPPENED BETWEEN YOU AND USUI?!
I DON'T REMEMBER ANYTHING ...
I DON'T KNOW ...
WHY DID I
EVEN
HAVE THEM ON ME ...?
HOW DID THEY GET IN MY POCKET ?
AND WHERE ?

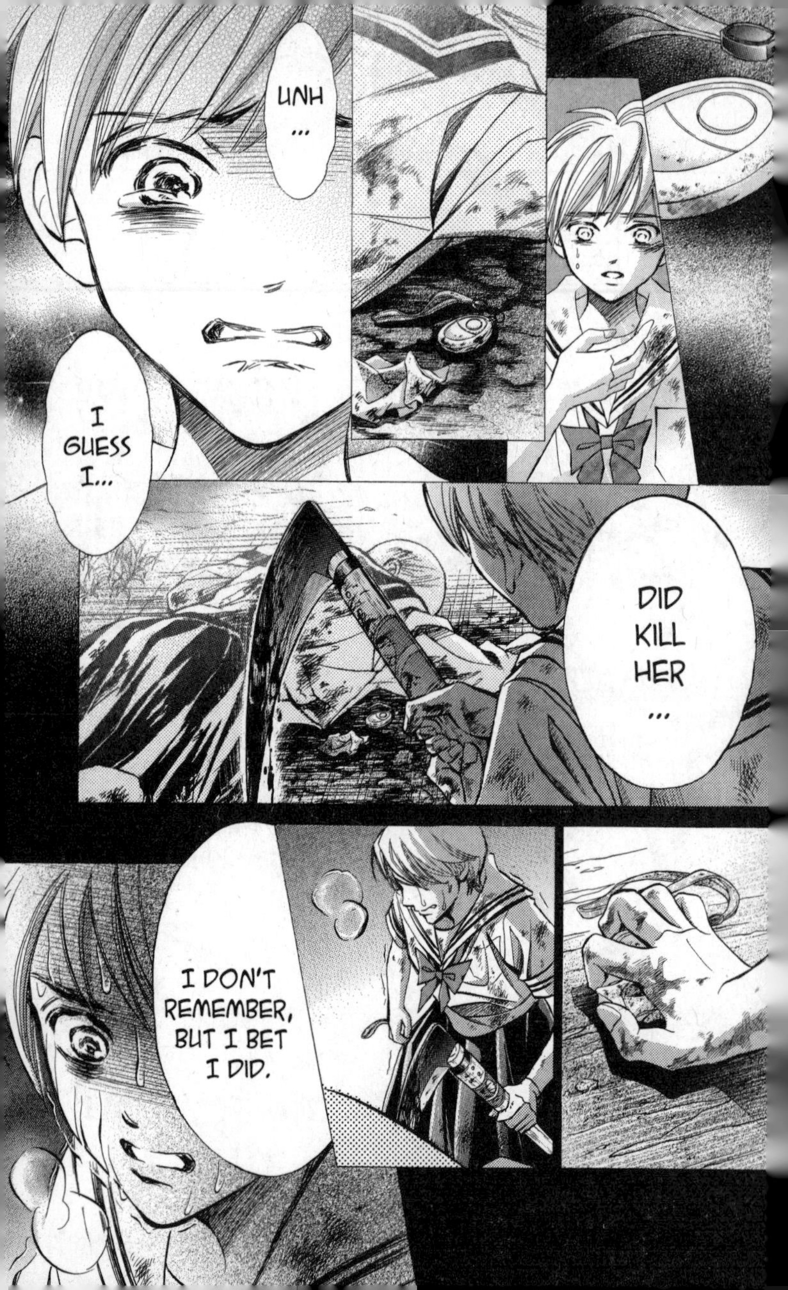
UNH ...
I GUESS I...
DID KILL HER ...
I DON'T REMEMBER, BUT I BET I DID.

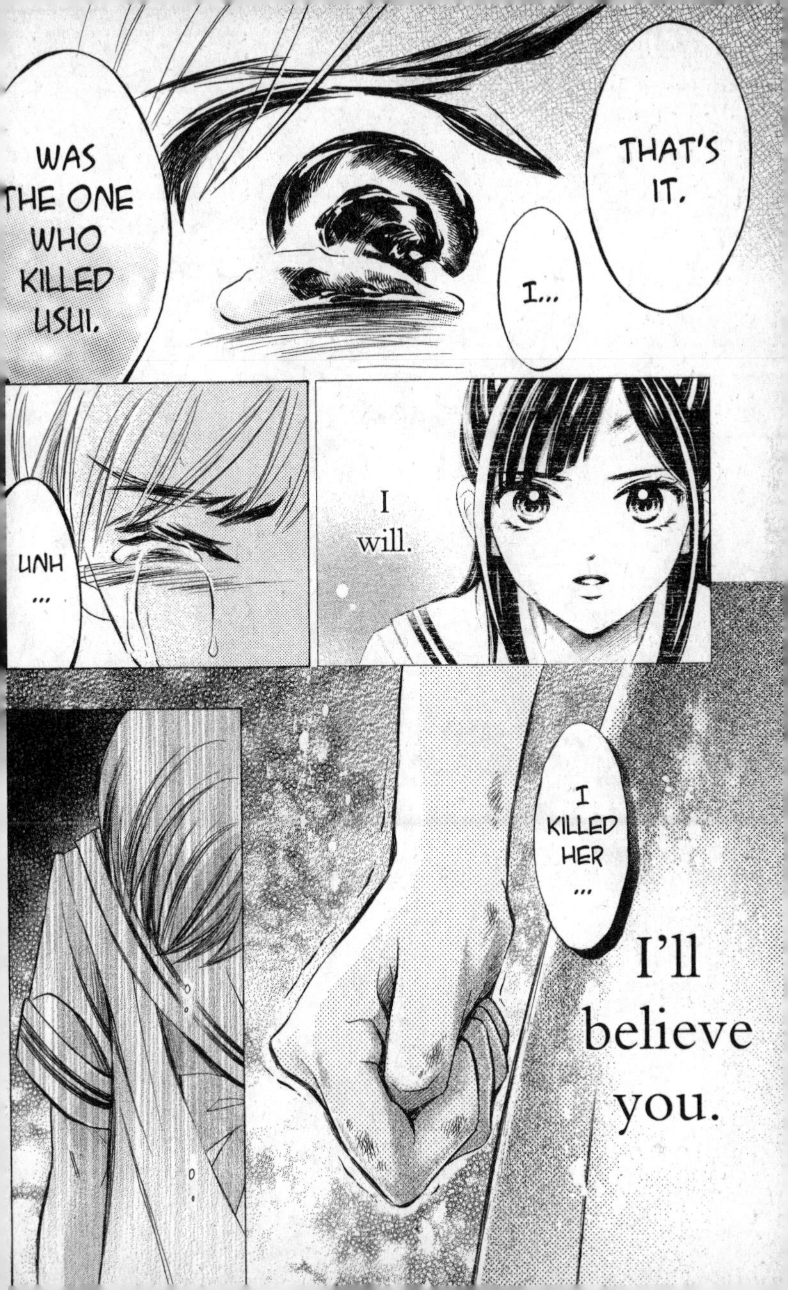
THAT'S IT.
I...
WAS THE ONE WHO KILLED USUI.
I will.
UNH ...
I KILLED HER ...
I'll believe you.

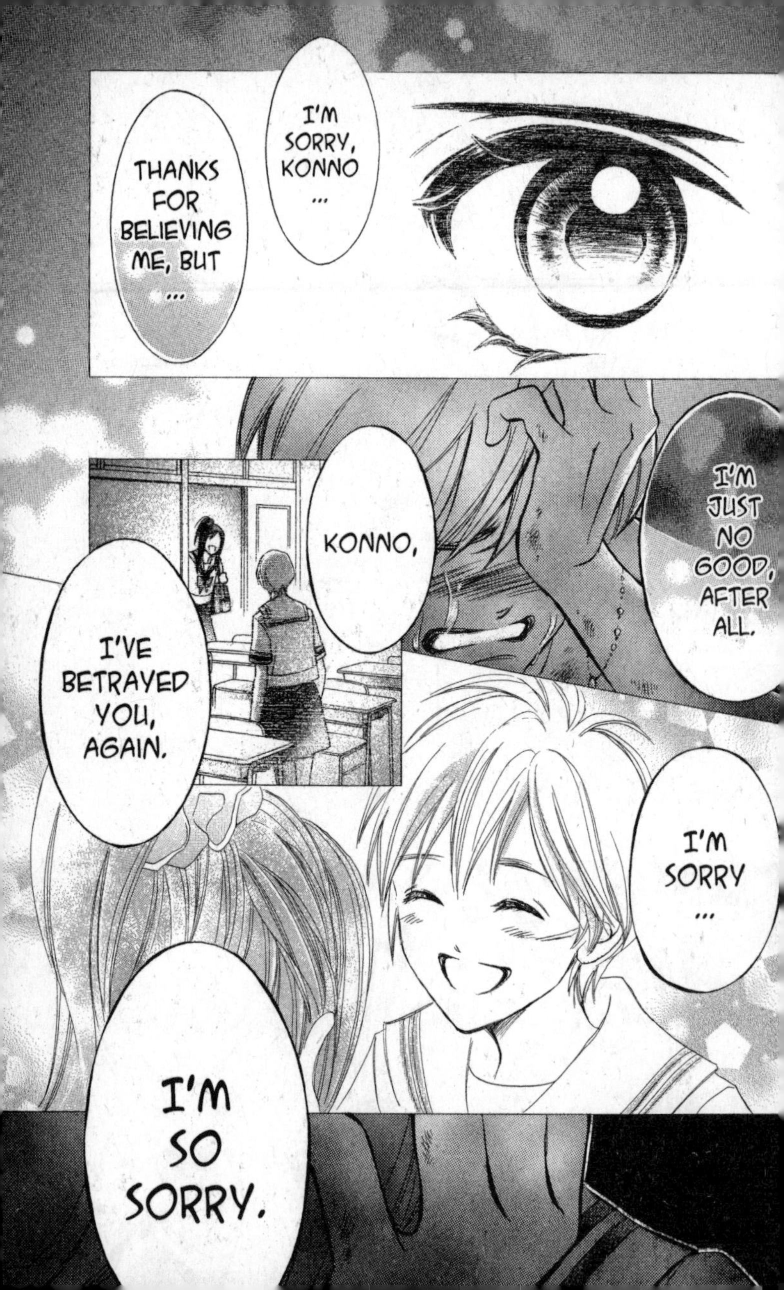
I'M SORRY, KONNO ...
THANKS FOR BELIEVING ME, BUT ...
I'M JUST NO GOOD, AFTER ALL.
KONNO,
I'VE BETRAYED YOU, AGAIN.
I'M SORRY ...
I'M SO SORRY.

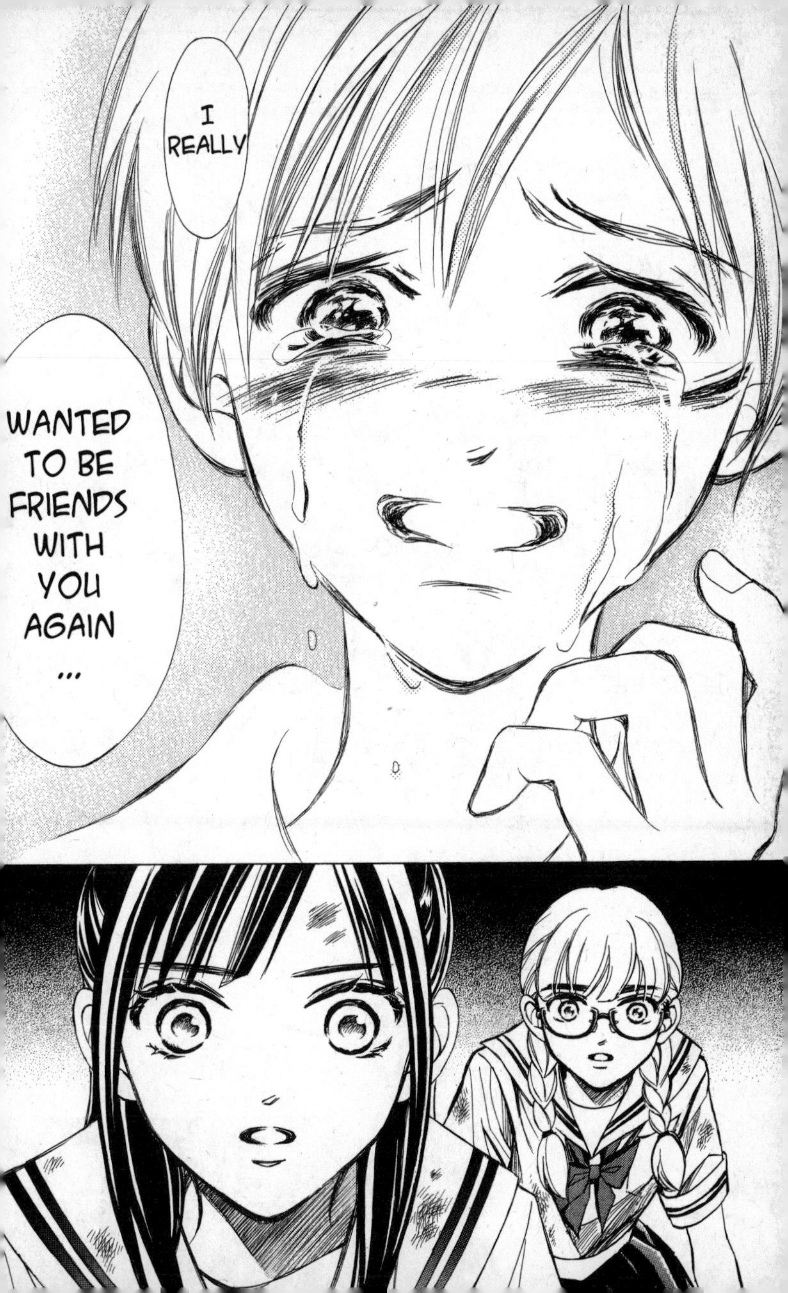
I REALLY
WANTED TO BE FRIENDS WITH YOU AGAIN ...

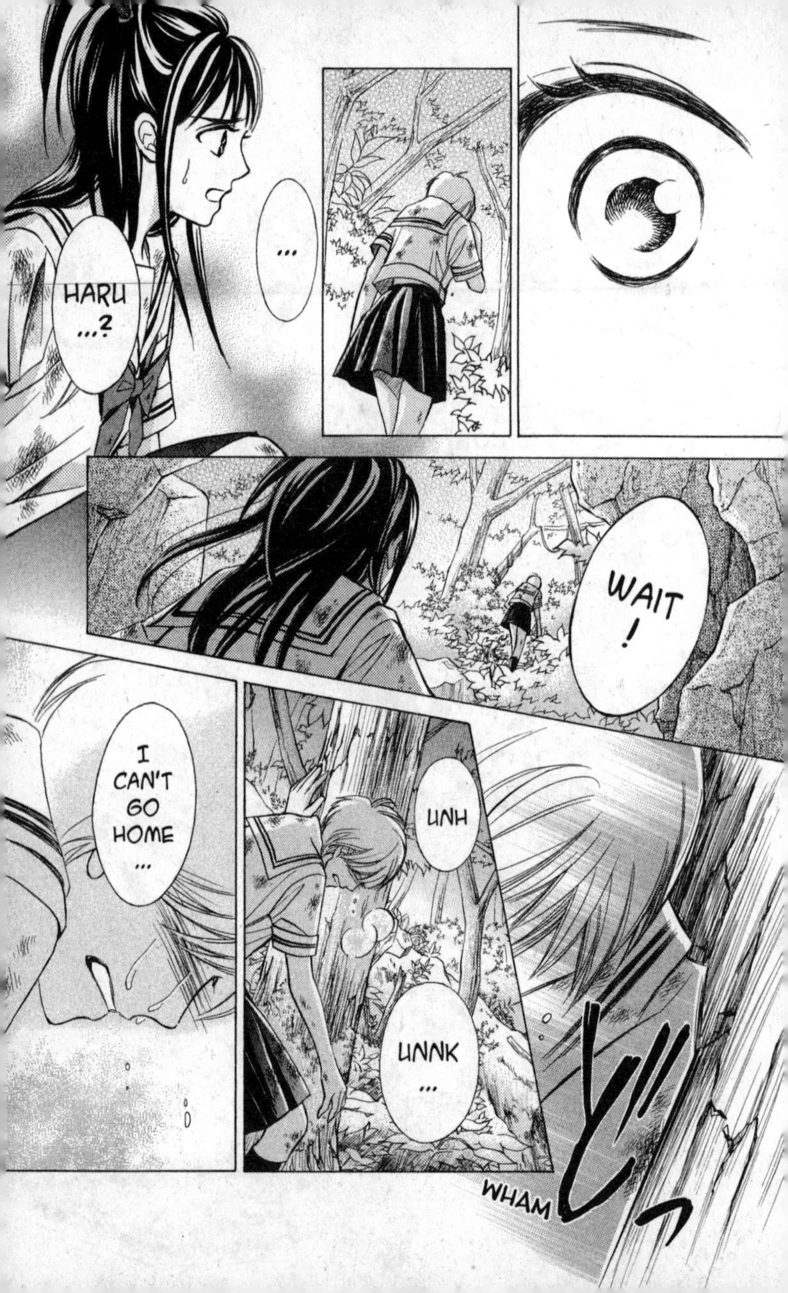
...
HARU ...?
WAIT!
WHAM
UNH
UNNK ...
I CAN'T GO HOME ...

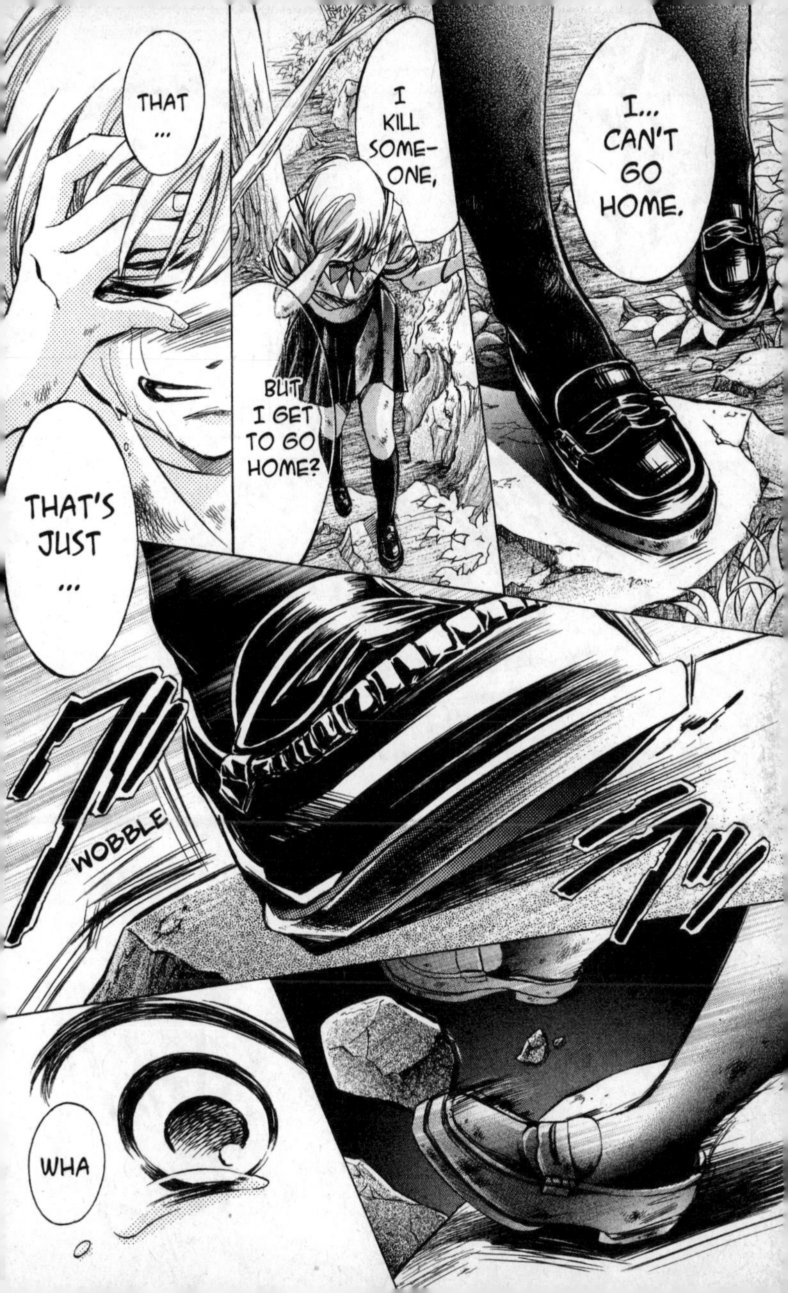
I... CAN'T GO HOME.
I KILL SOME-ONE,
BUT I GET TO GO HOME?
THAT ...
THAT'S JUST ...
WOBBLE
WHA

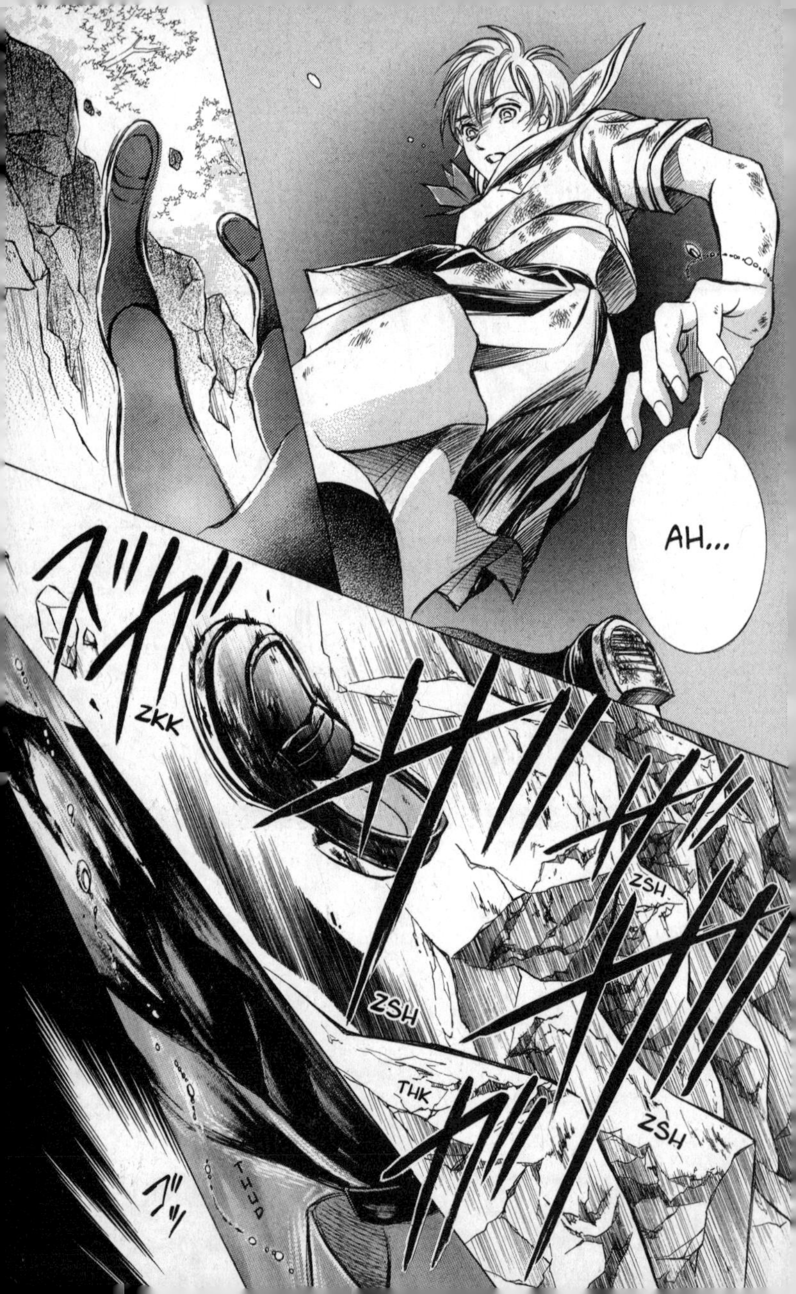
AH...
ZKK
ZSH
ZSH
ZSH
THK
THUD

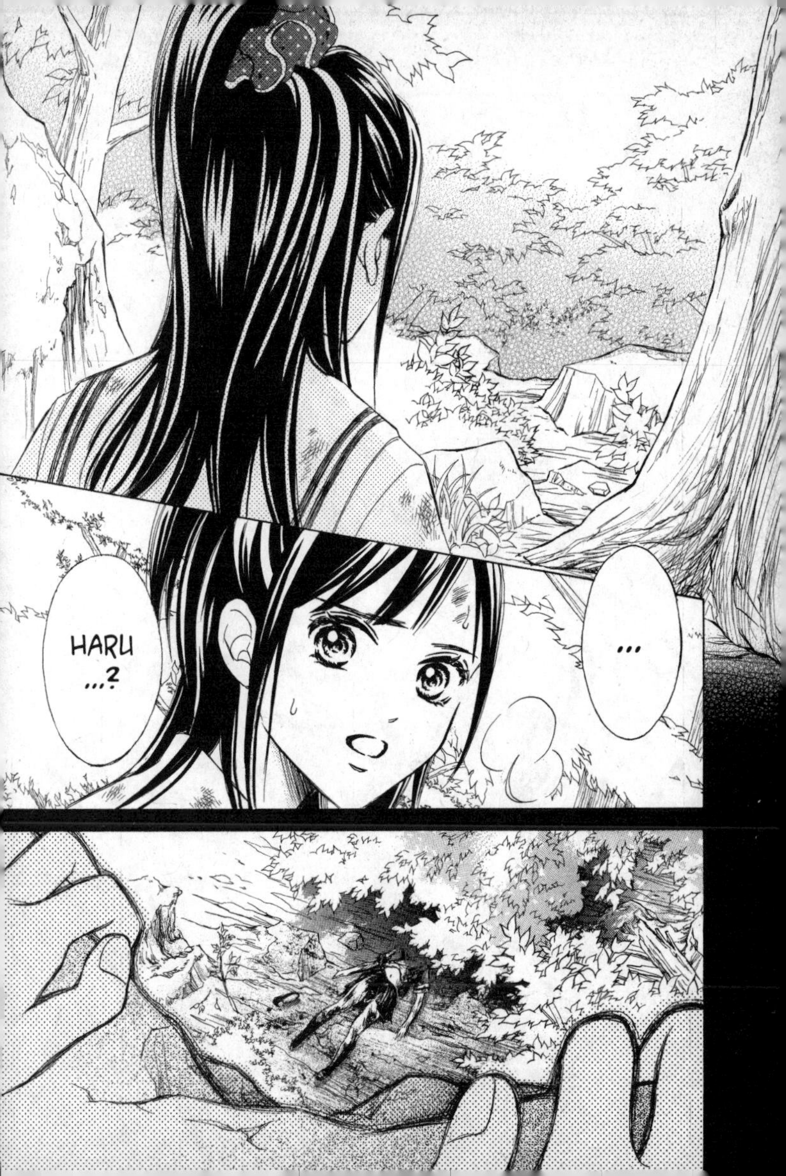
...
HARU ...?

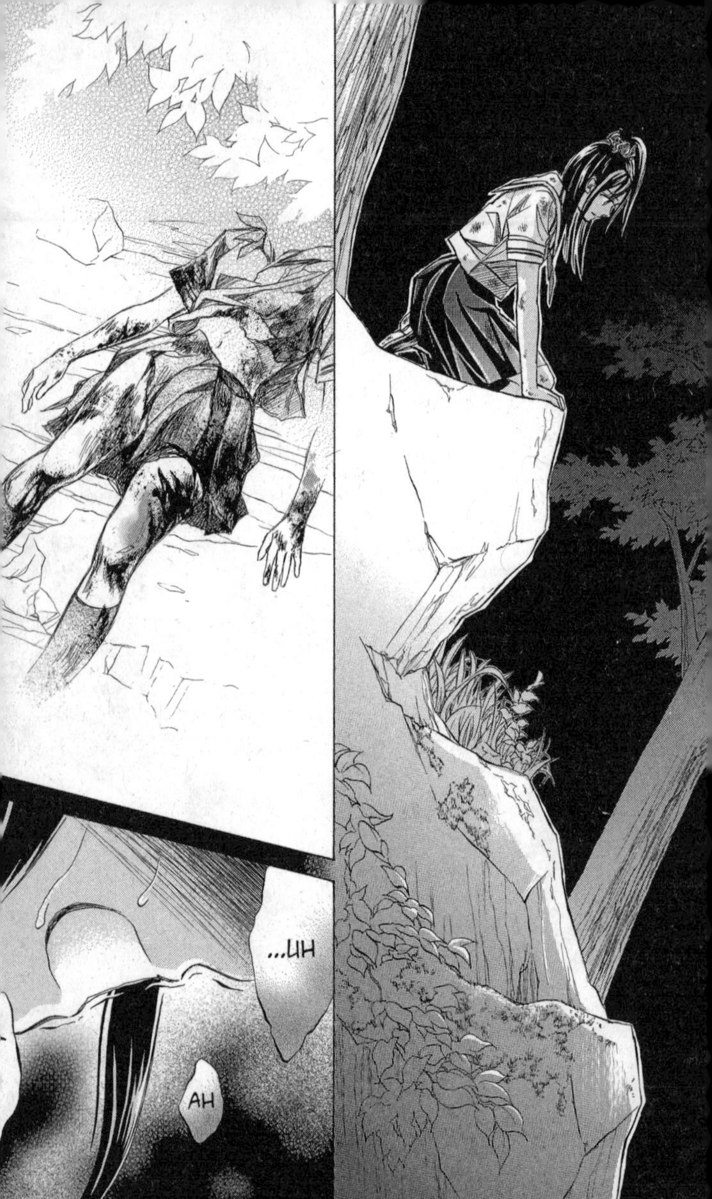
...UH
AH

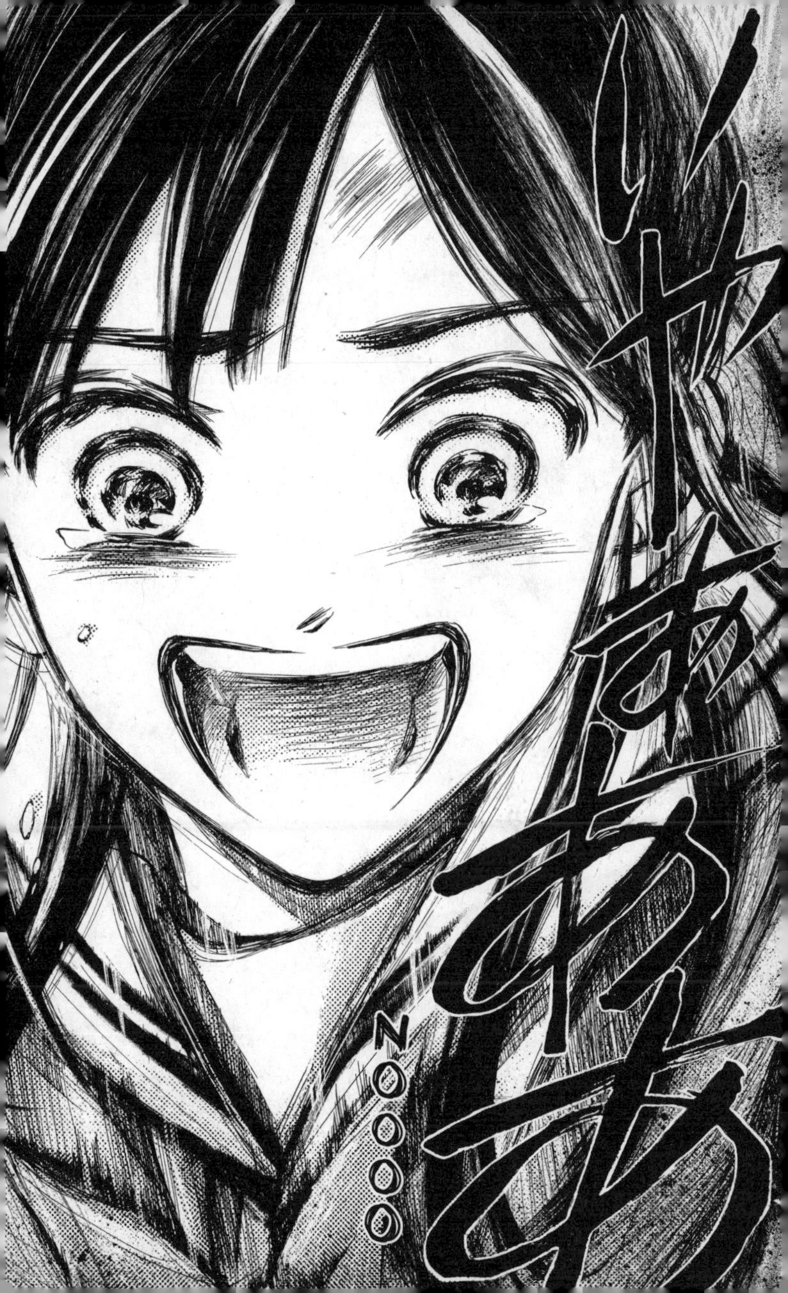
NOOOO

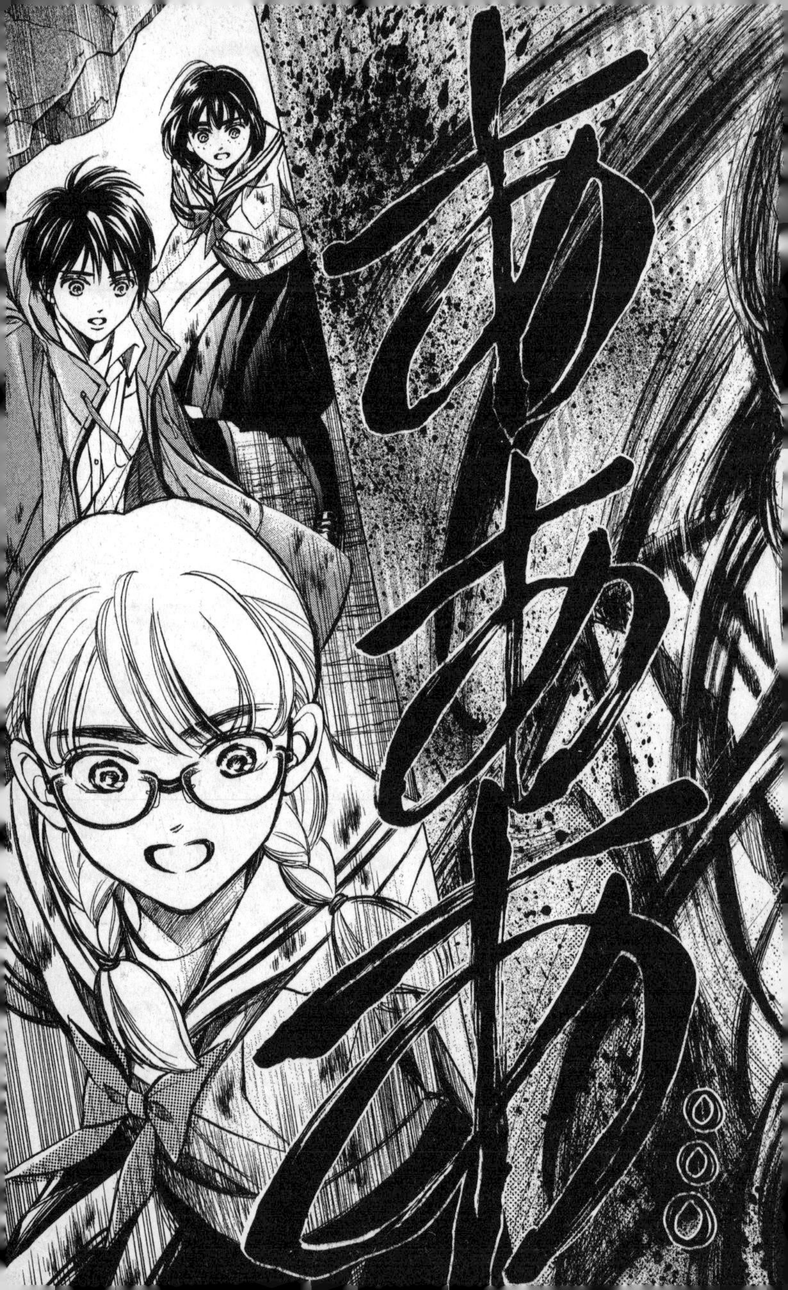
ああああ…

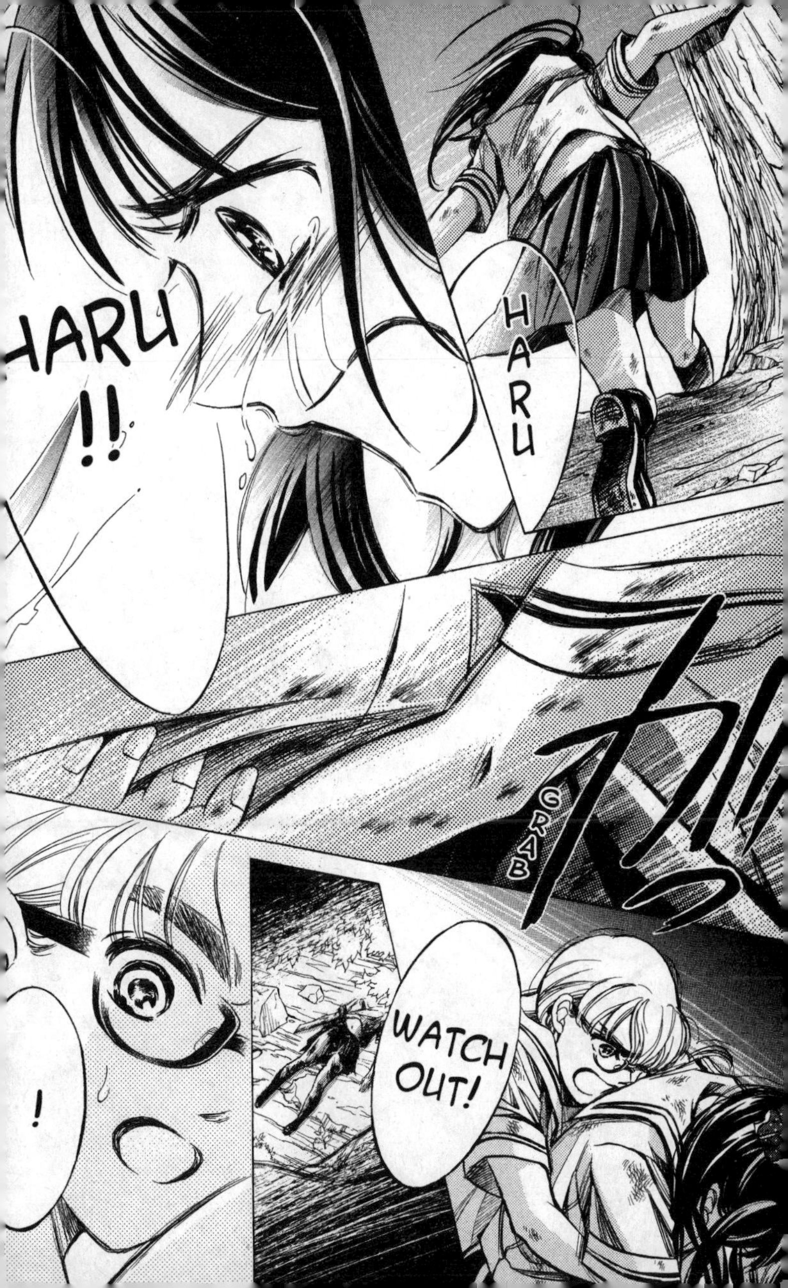
HARU
HARU !!
GRAB
WATCH OUT!
!

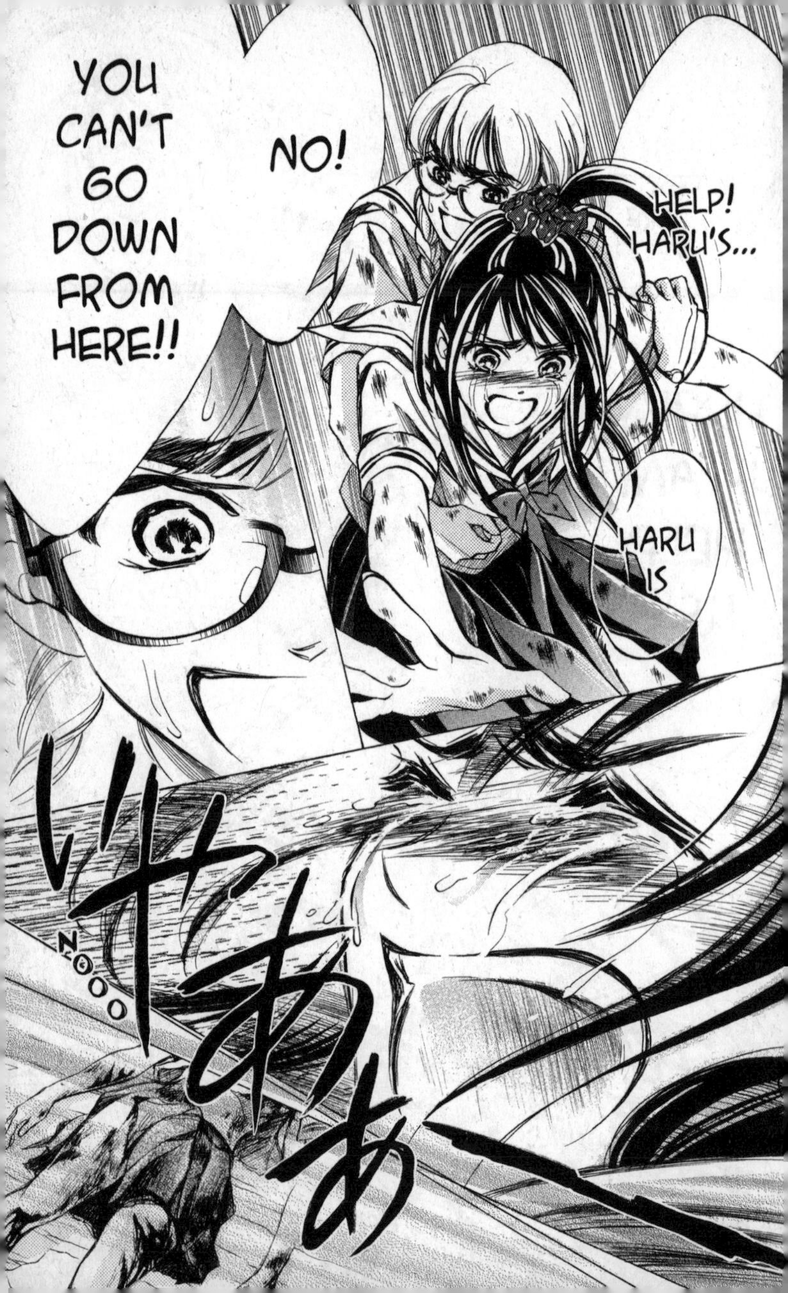
HELP! HARU'S...
HARU IS
NO!
YOU CAN'T GO DOWN FROM HERE!!
いやあぁ
NOOOO

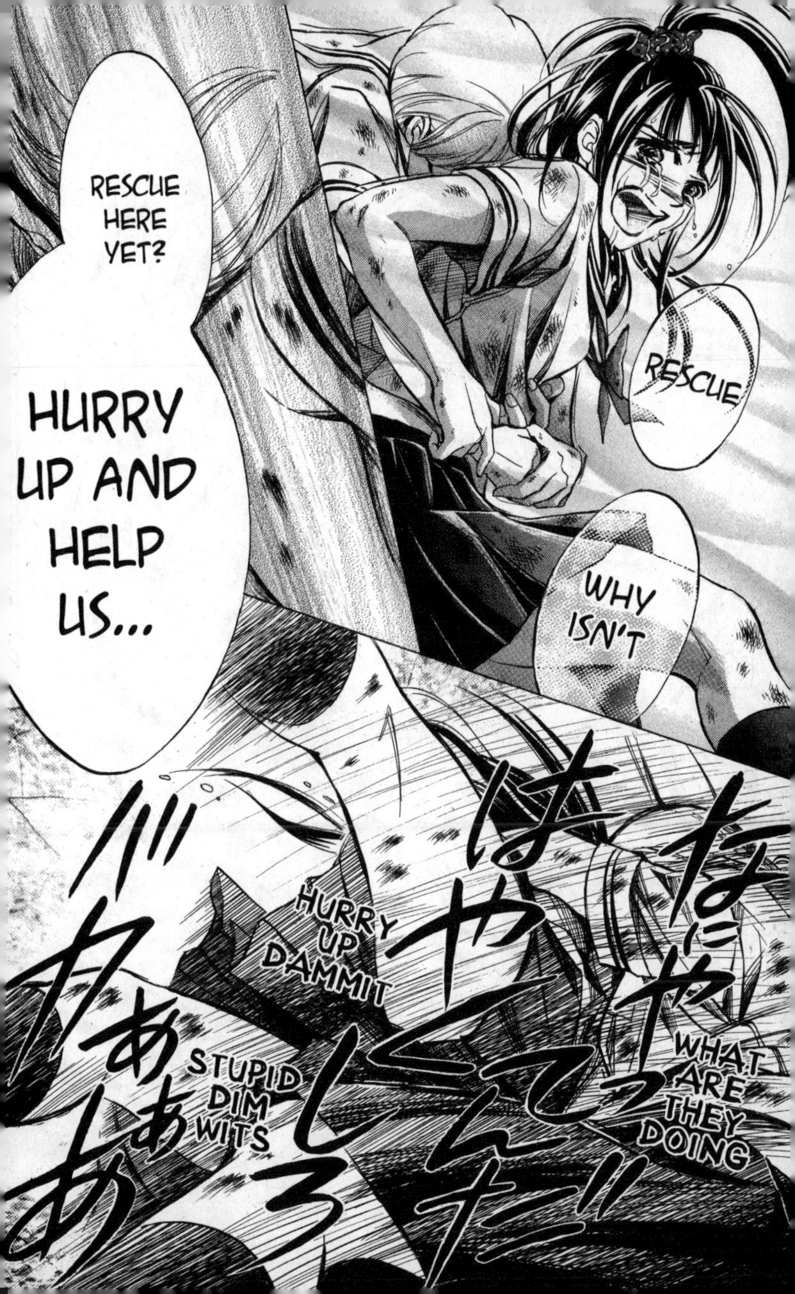
RESCUE
WHY ISN'T
RESCUE HERE YET?
HURRY UP AND HELP US...
なにやってんだ!!
WHAT ARE THEY DOING
はやくしろ
HURRY UP DAMMIT
バカあああ
STUPID DIM WITS

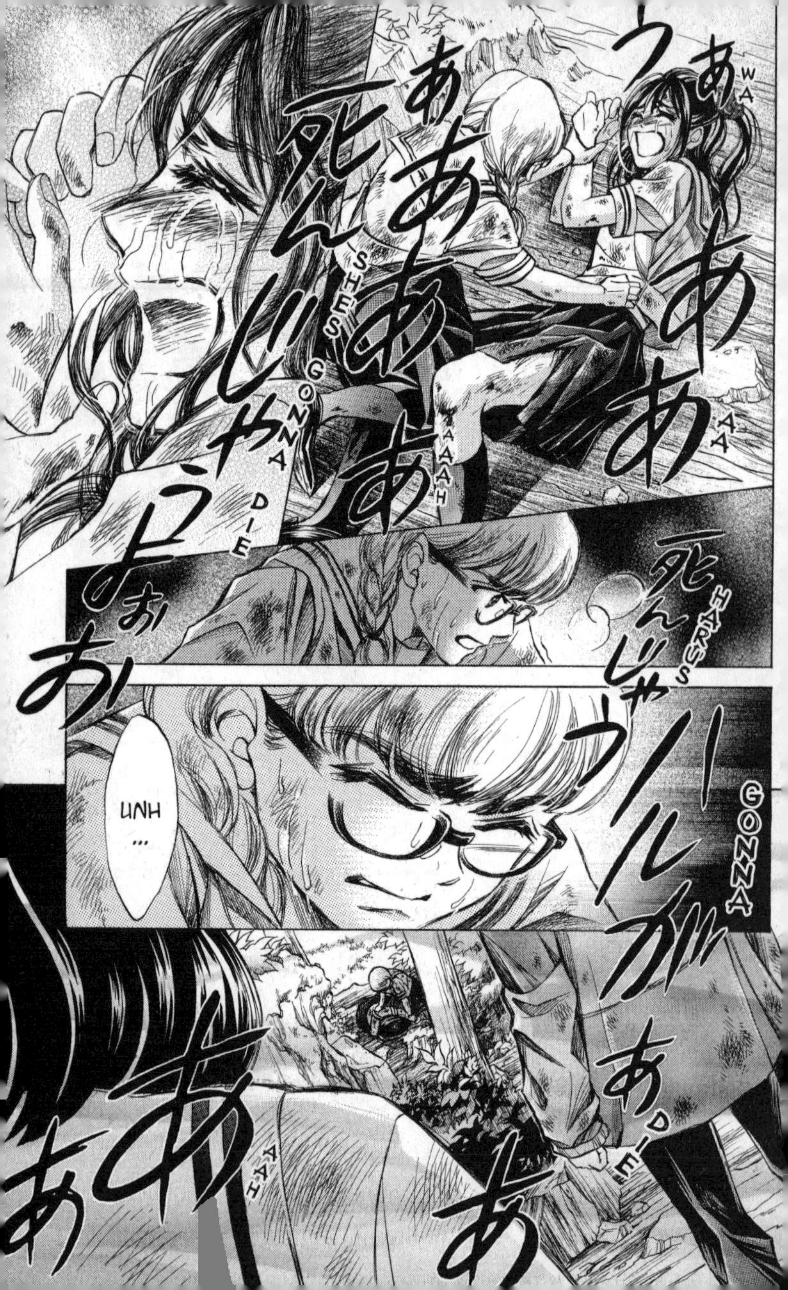
うああああああ
WA AA AAAH
死んじゃうよぉお
SHE'S GONNA DIE
死んじゃうーールがあ
HARU'S GONNA DIE
UNH ...
ああ
AAAH

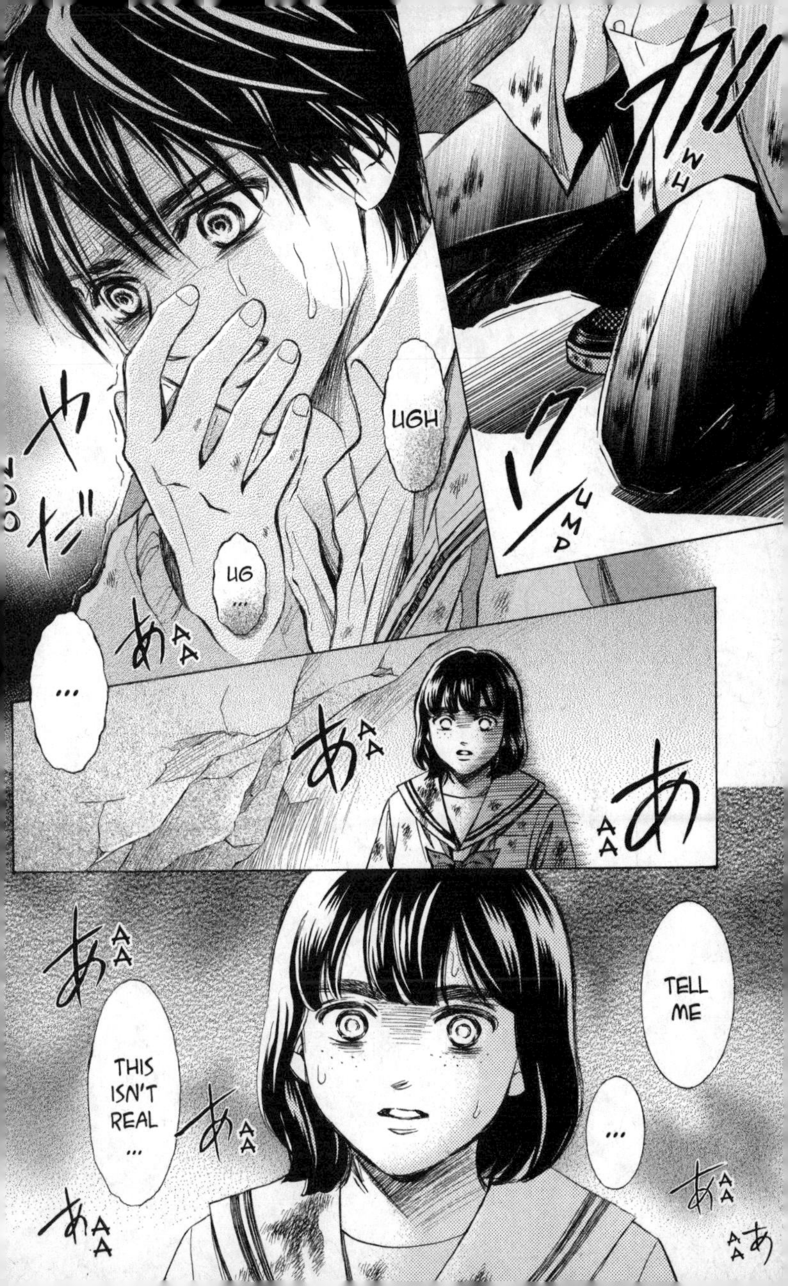
WH
UMP
UGH
UG...
NOO
AA
...
AA
AA
TELL ME
...
THIS ISN'T REAL ...
AA
AA
AA
AA
AA

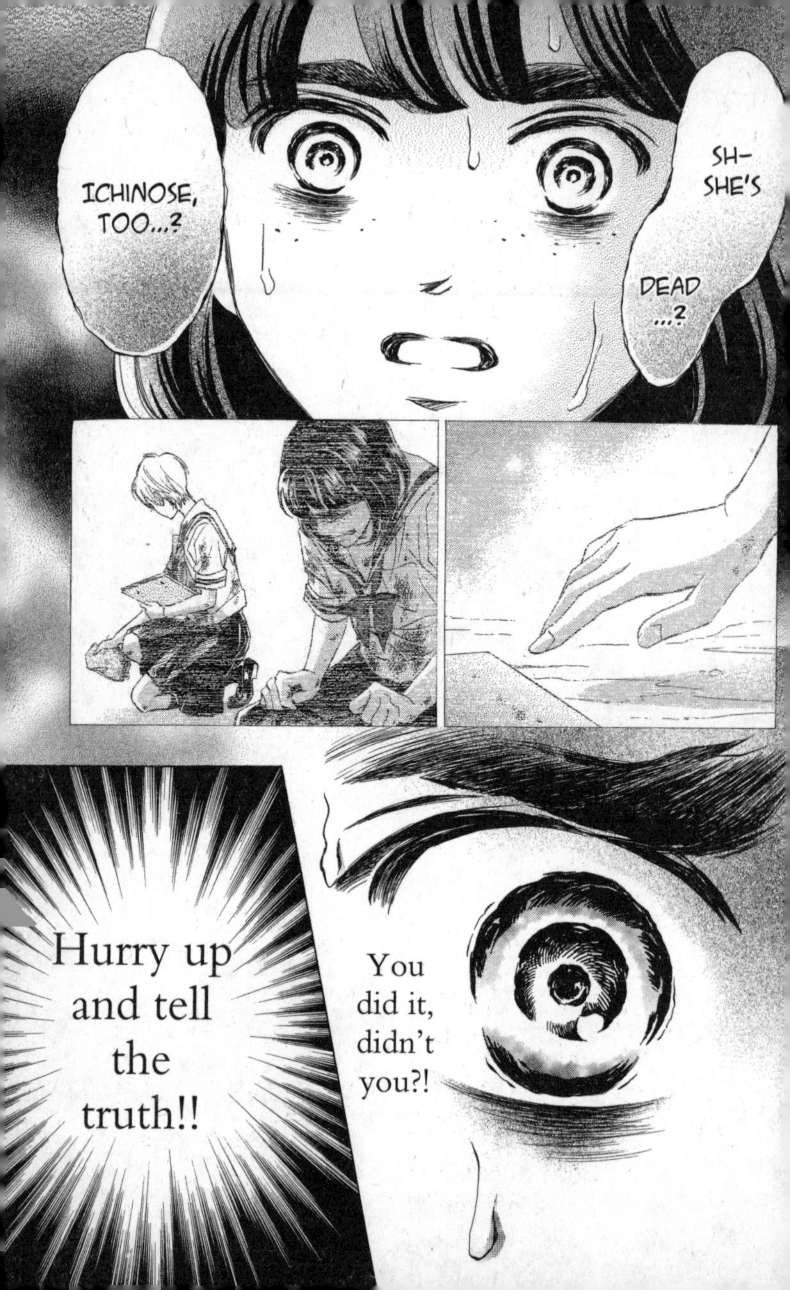
SH-SHE'S DEAD...?
ICHINOSE, TOO...?
You did it, didn't you?!
Hurry up and tell the truth!!

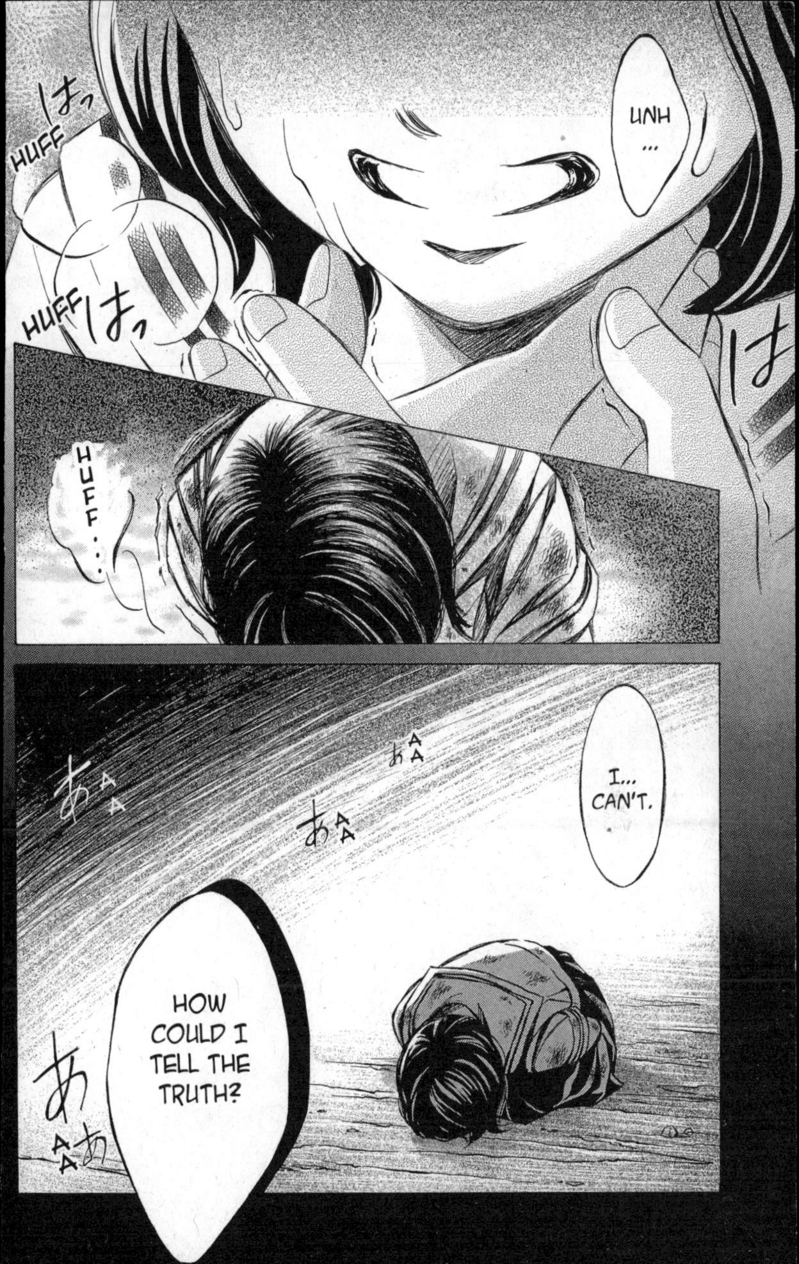
UNH ...
HUFF
HUFF
HUFF...
I... CAN'T.
A A
A A
A A
A A
HOW COULD I TELL THE TRUTH?

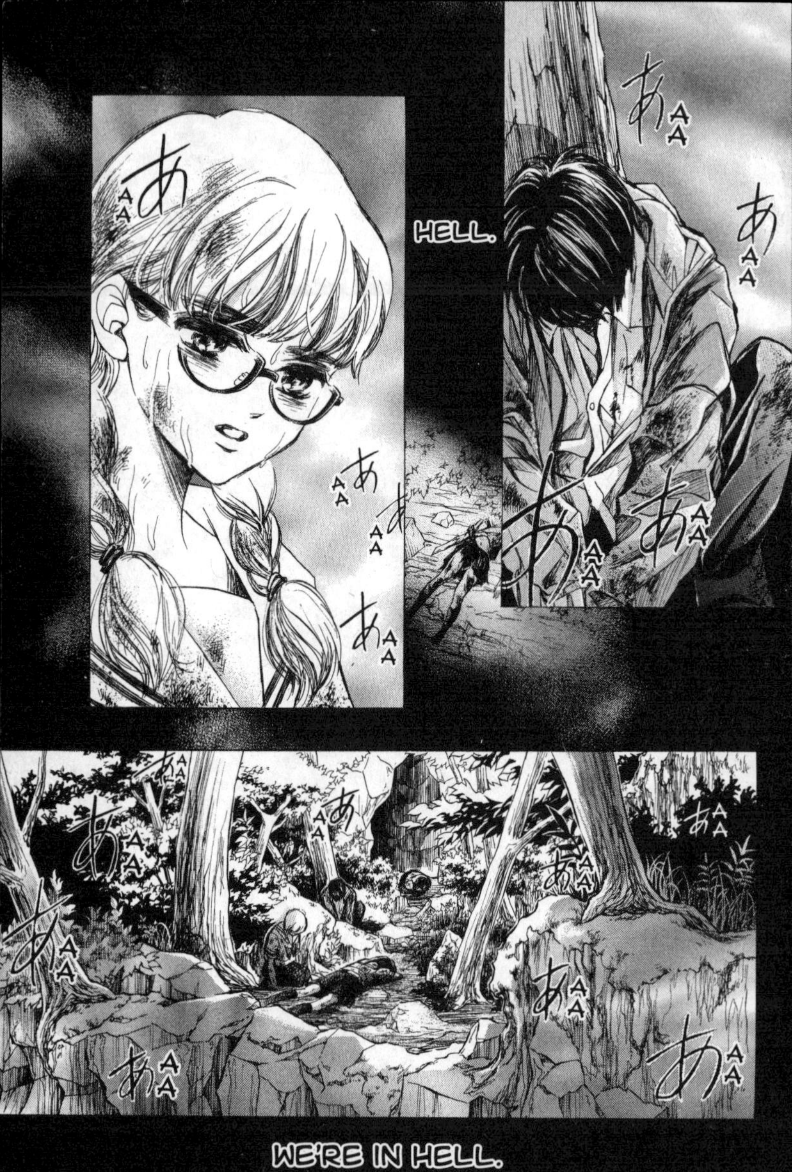

あAA
あAAA
あAA
あAA
HELL.
あAA
あAA
あAA
あAA
あAA
あAA
あAA
あAA
あAA
あAA
あAA
あAA
あAA
あAA
WE'RE IN HELL.

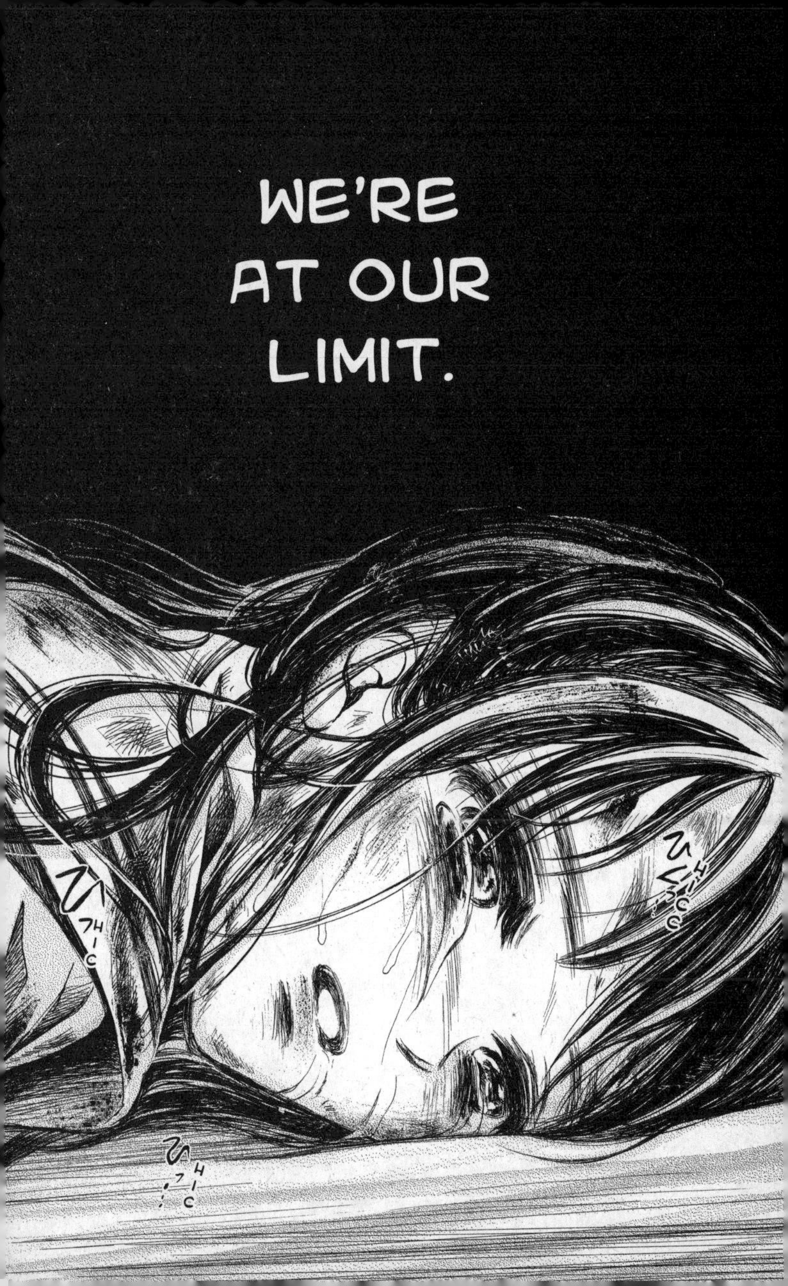
WE'RE AT OUR LIMIT.
HIC
HIC
HIC

L
I
M
I
T

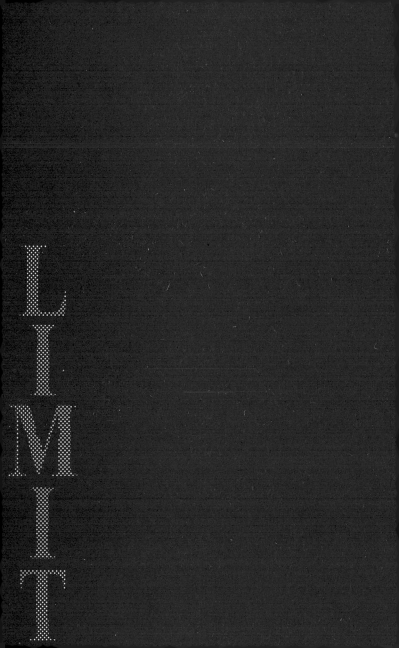

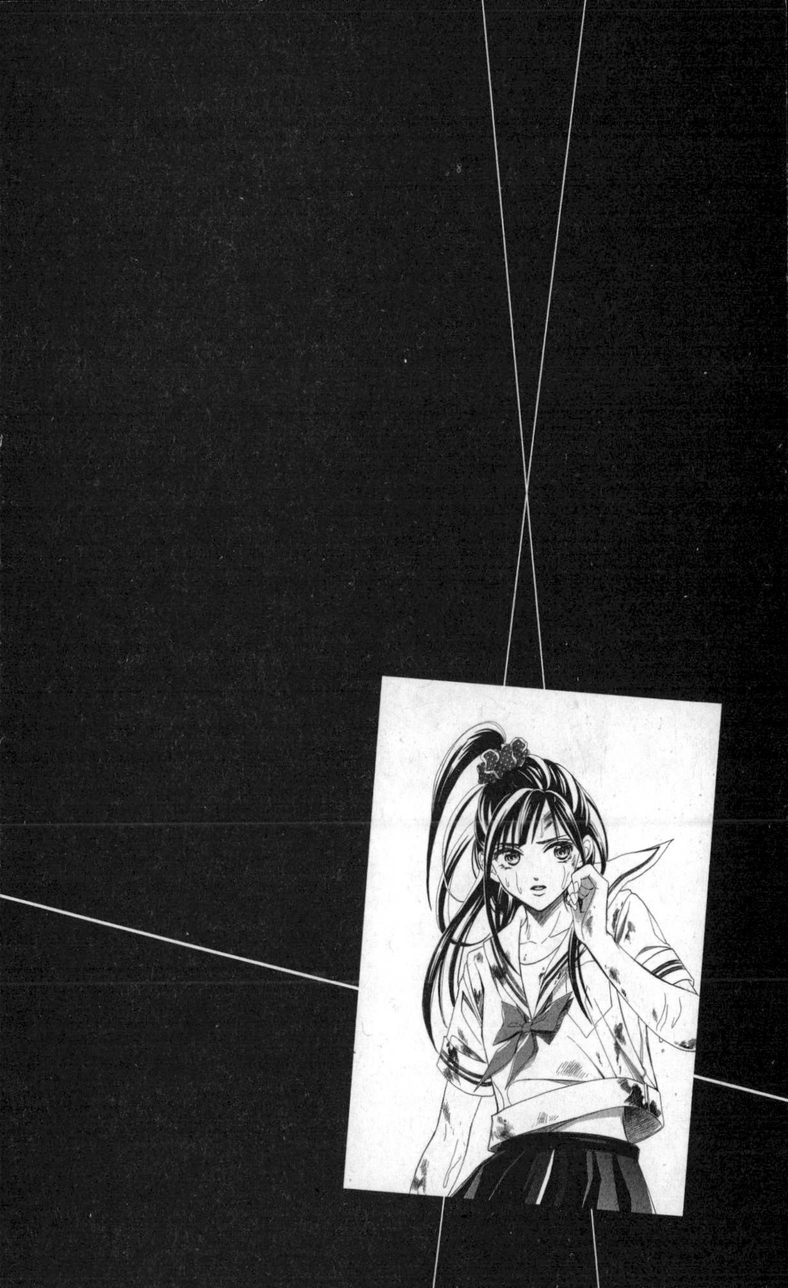

Scene.15 – The Concealment

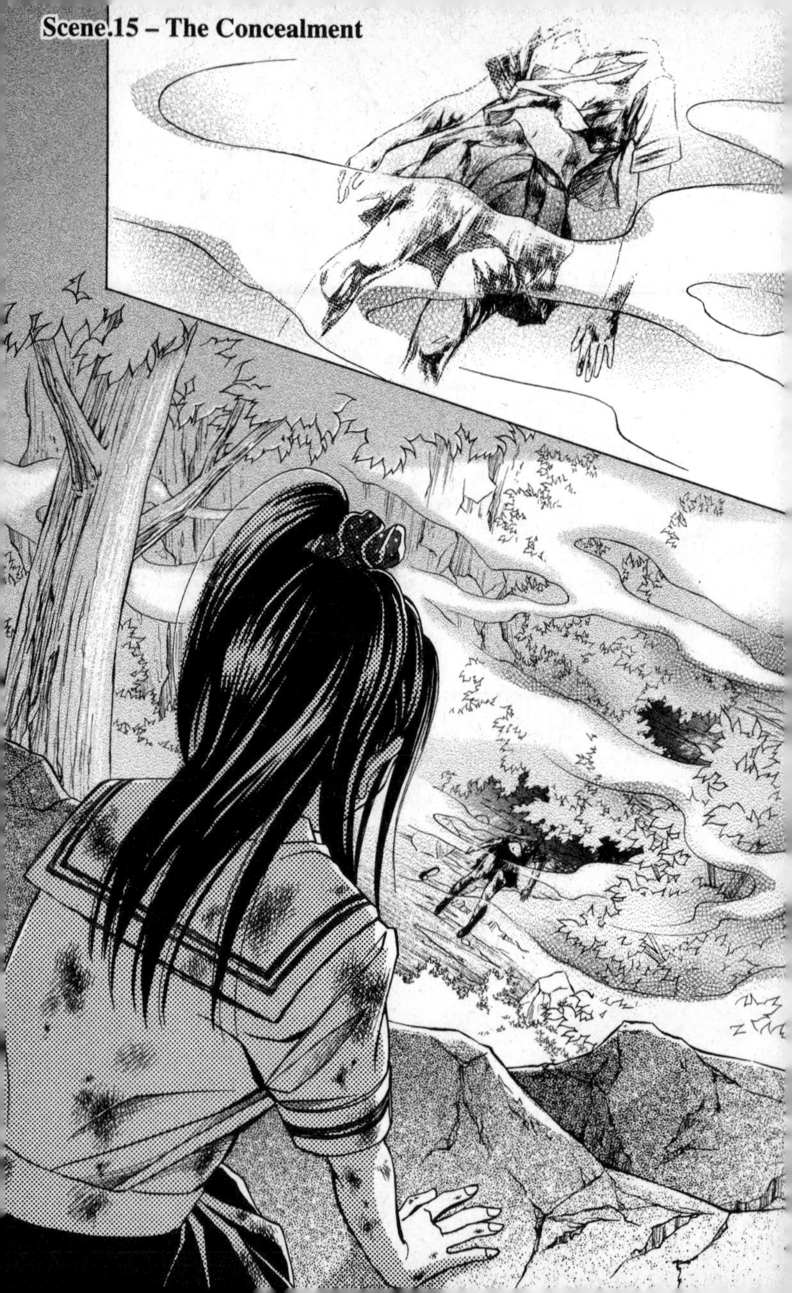

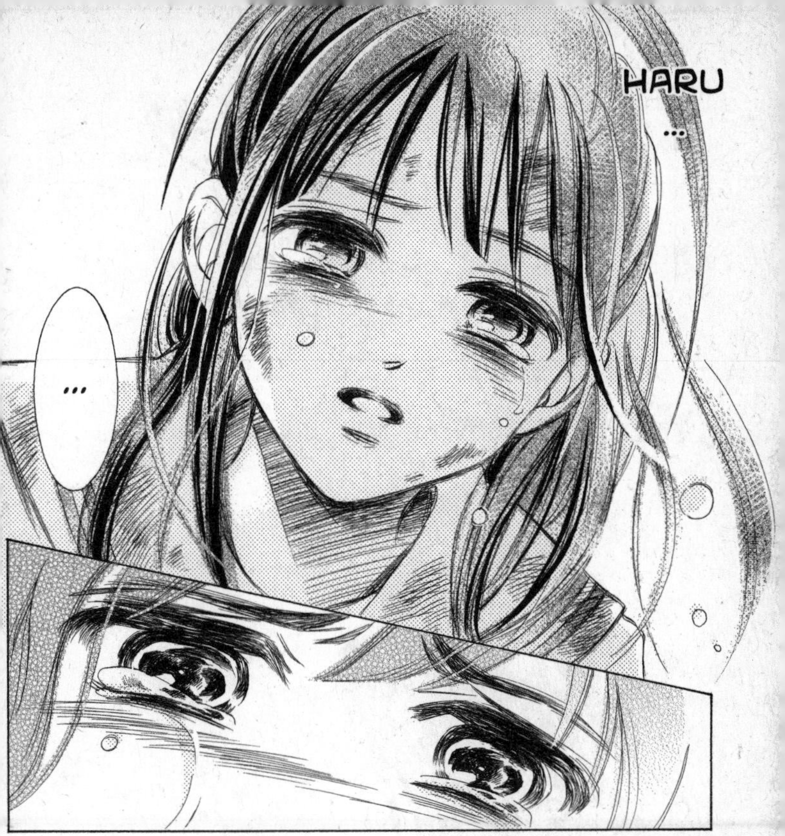
HARU
...
...

LIMIT

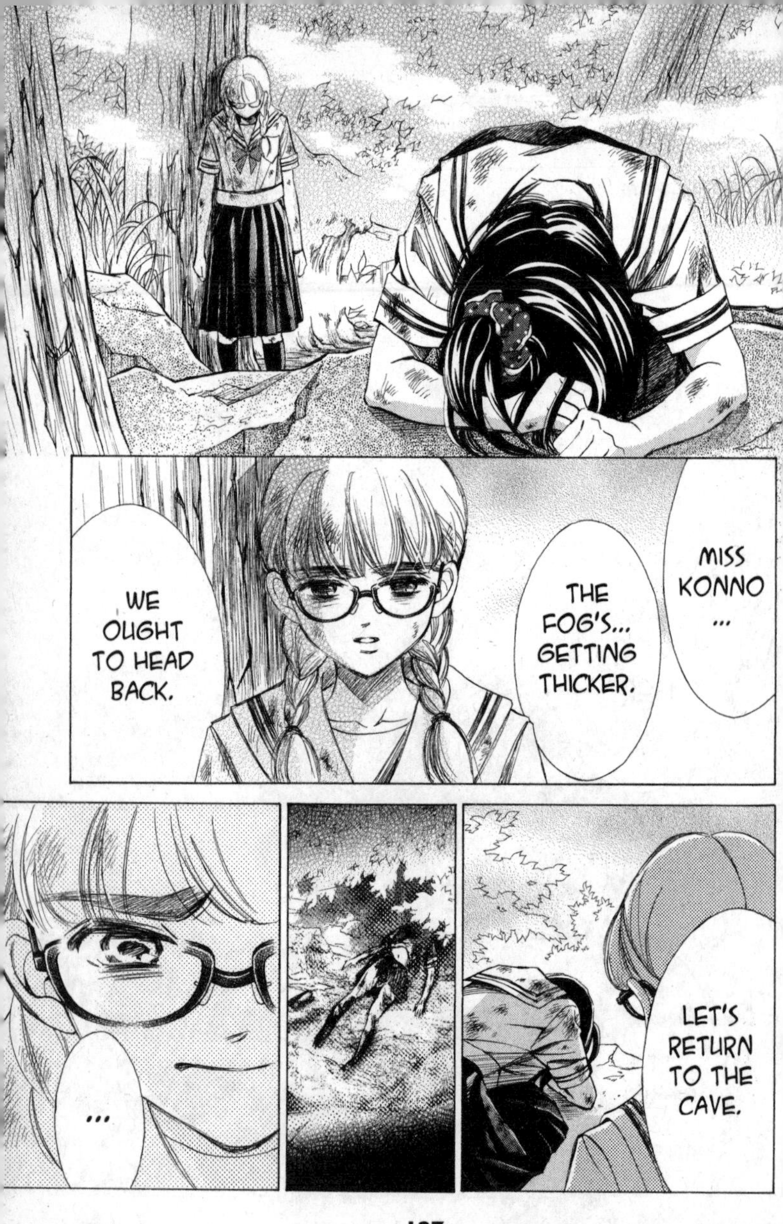
MISS KONNO ...
THE FOG'S... GETTING THICKER.
WE OUGHT TO HEAD BACK.
LET'S RETURN TO THE CAVE.
...

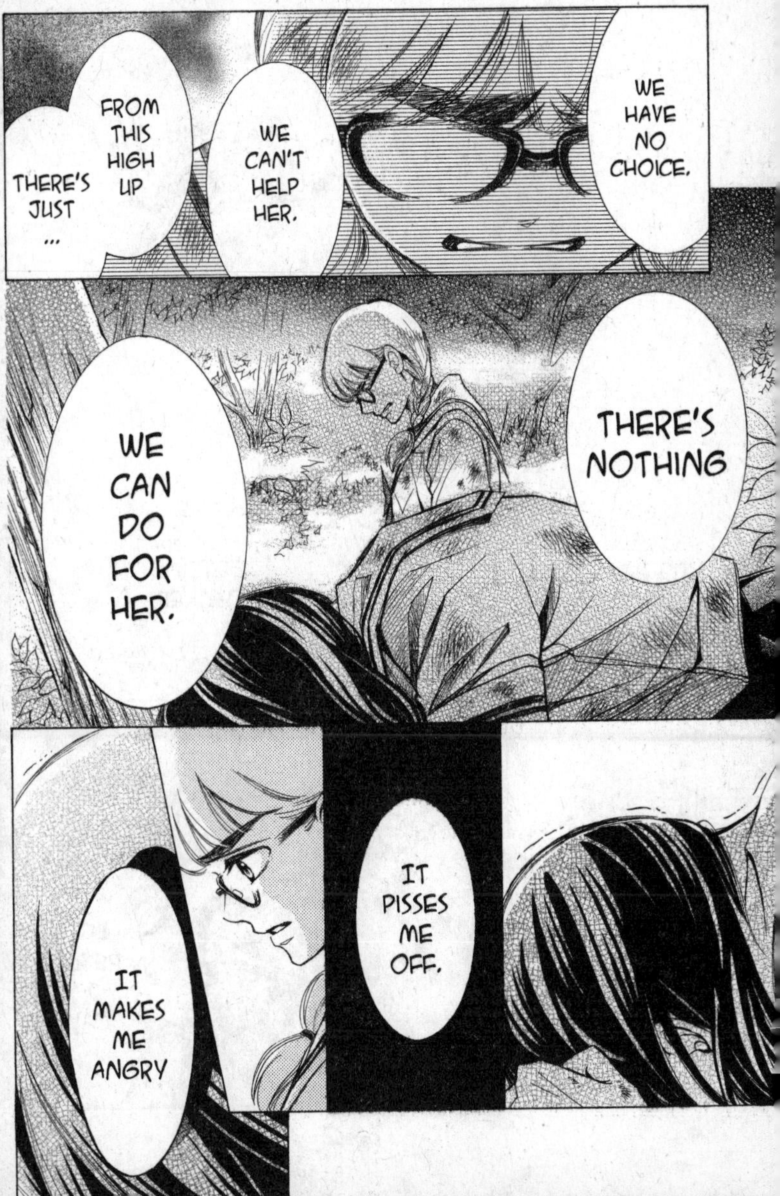
WE HAVE NO CHOICE.
WE CAN'T HELP HER.
FROM THIS HIGH UP
THERE'S JUST ...
THERE'S NOTHING
WE CAN DO FOR HER.
IT PISSES ME OFF.
IT MAKES ME ANGRY

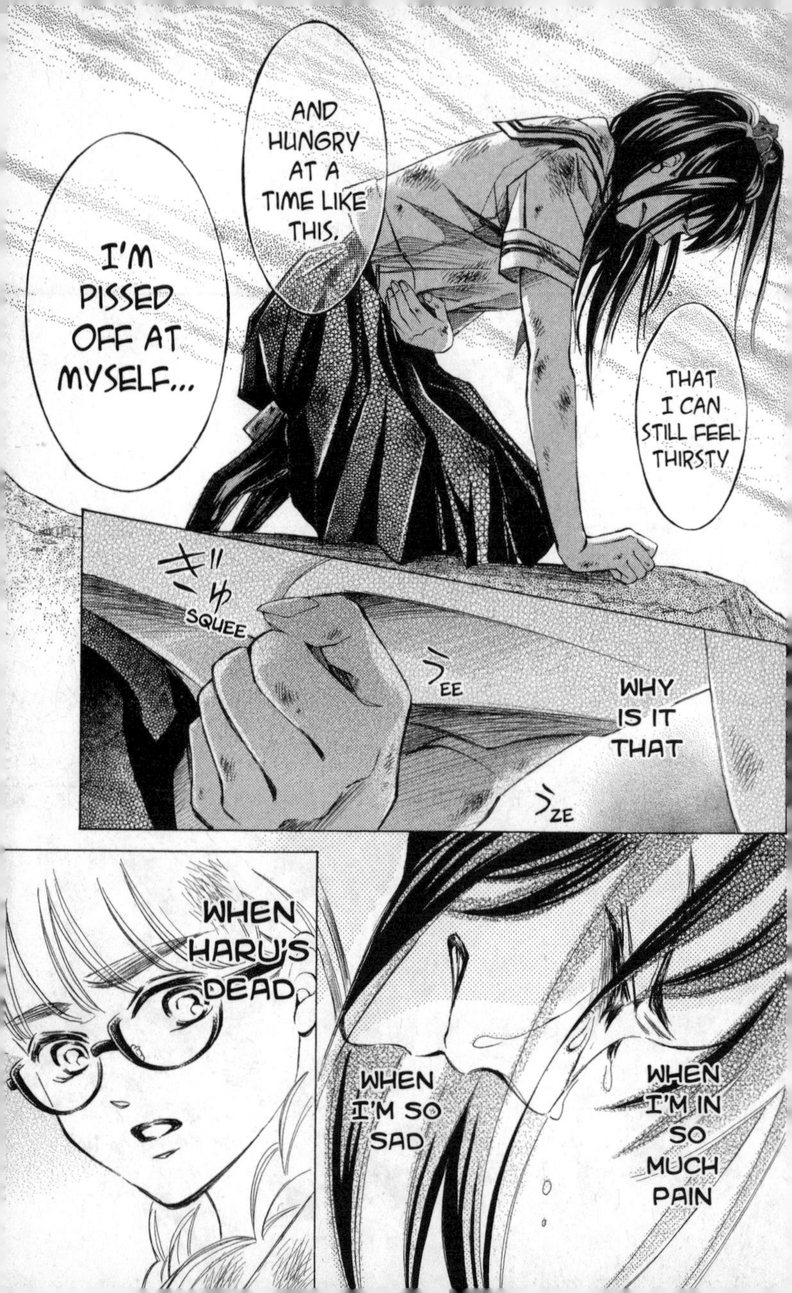
THAT I CAN STILL FEEL THIRSTY
AND HUNGRY AT A TIME LIKE THIS.
I'M PISSED OFF AT MYSELF...
WHY IS IT THAT
ぎゅ
SQUEE
う
EE
う
ZE
WHEN I'M IN SO MUCH PAIN
WHEN I'M SO SAD
WHEN HARU'S DEAD

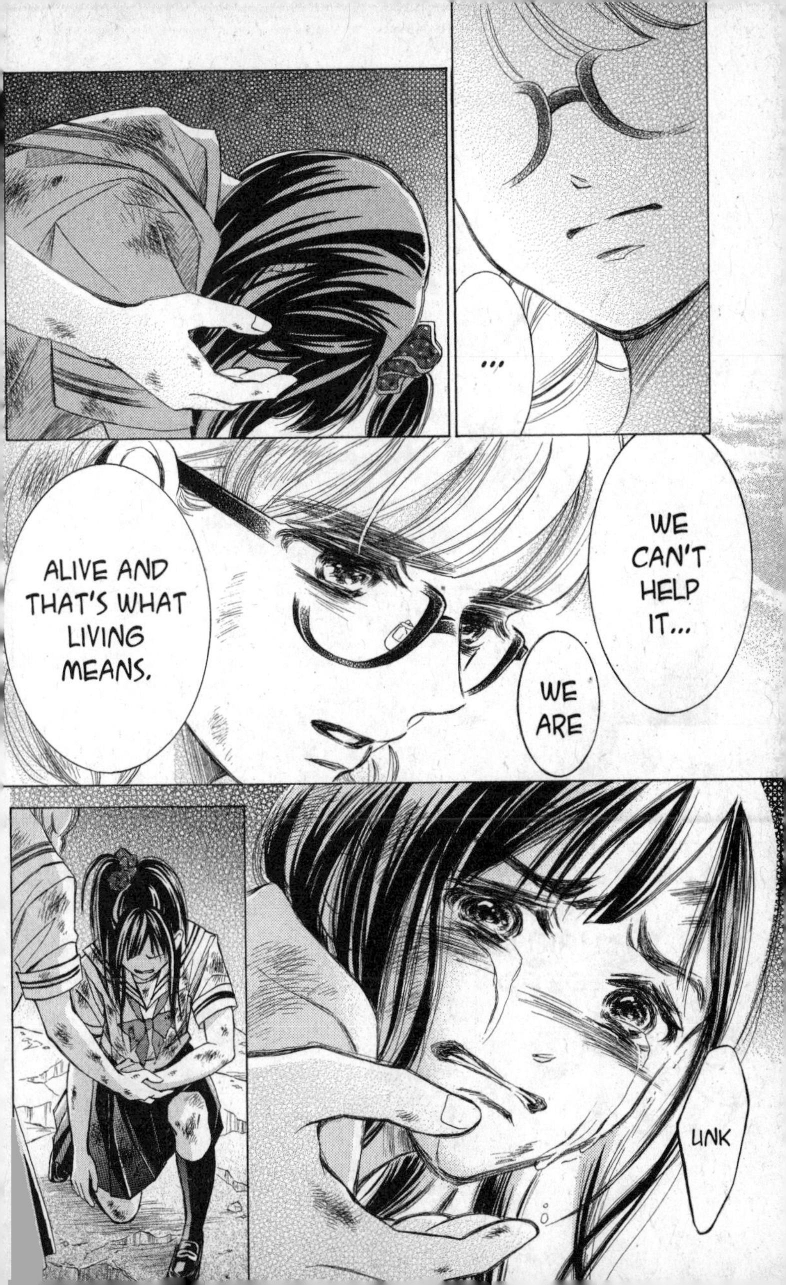
...
WE CAN'T HELP IT...
WE ARE
ALIVE AND THAT'S WHAT LIVING MEANS.
UNK

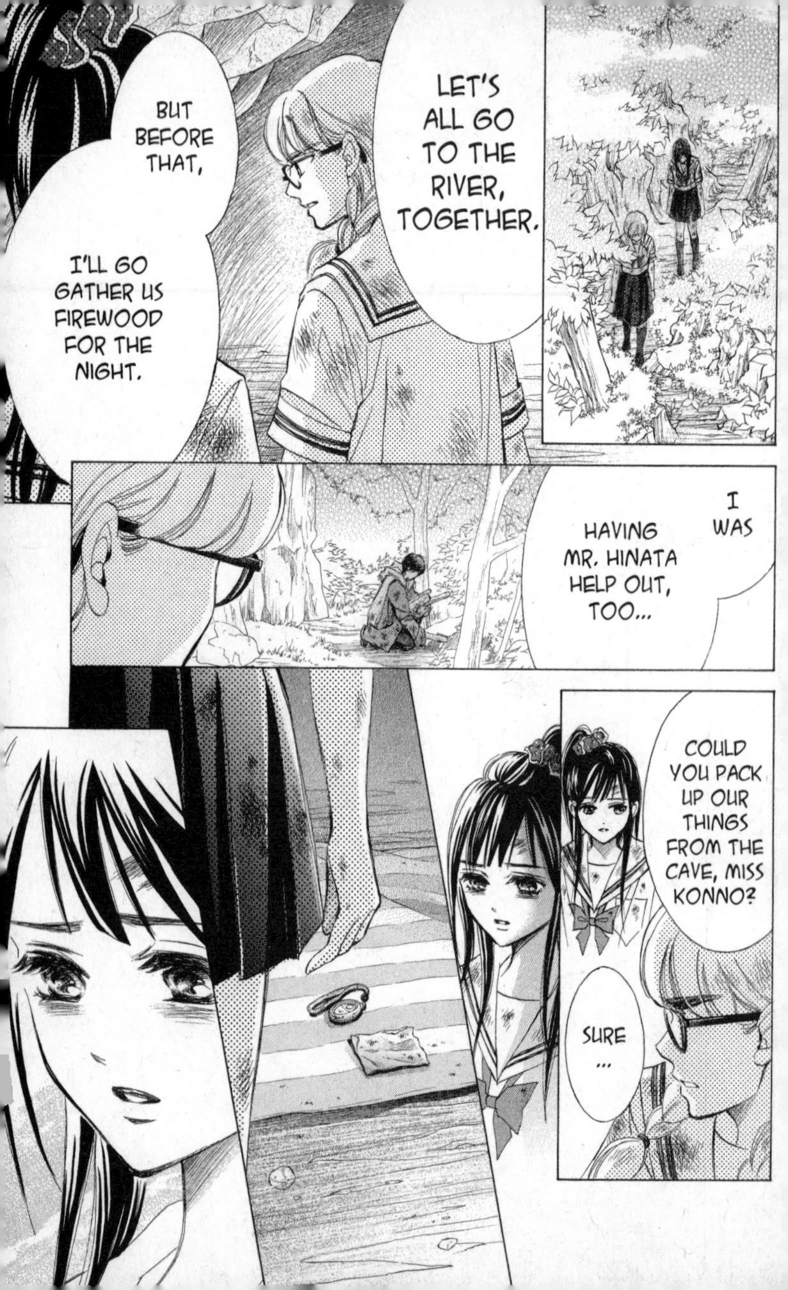
LET'S ALL GO TO THE RIVER, TOGETHER.
BUT BEFORE THAT,
I'LL GO GATHER US FIREWOOD FOR THE NIGHT.
I WAS HAVING MR. HINATA HELP OUT, TOO...
COULD YOU PACK UP OUR THINGS FROM THE CAVE, MISS KONNO?
SURE ...

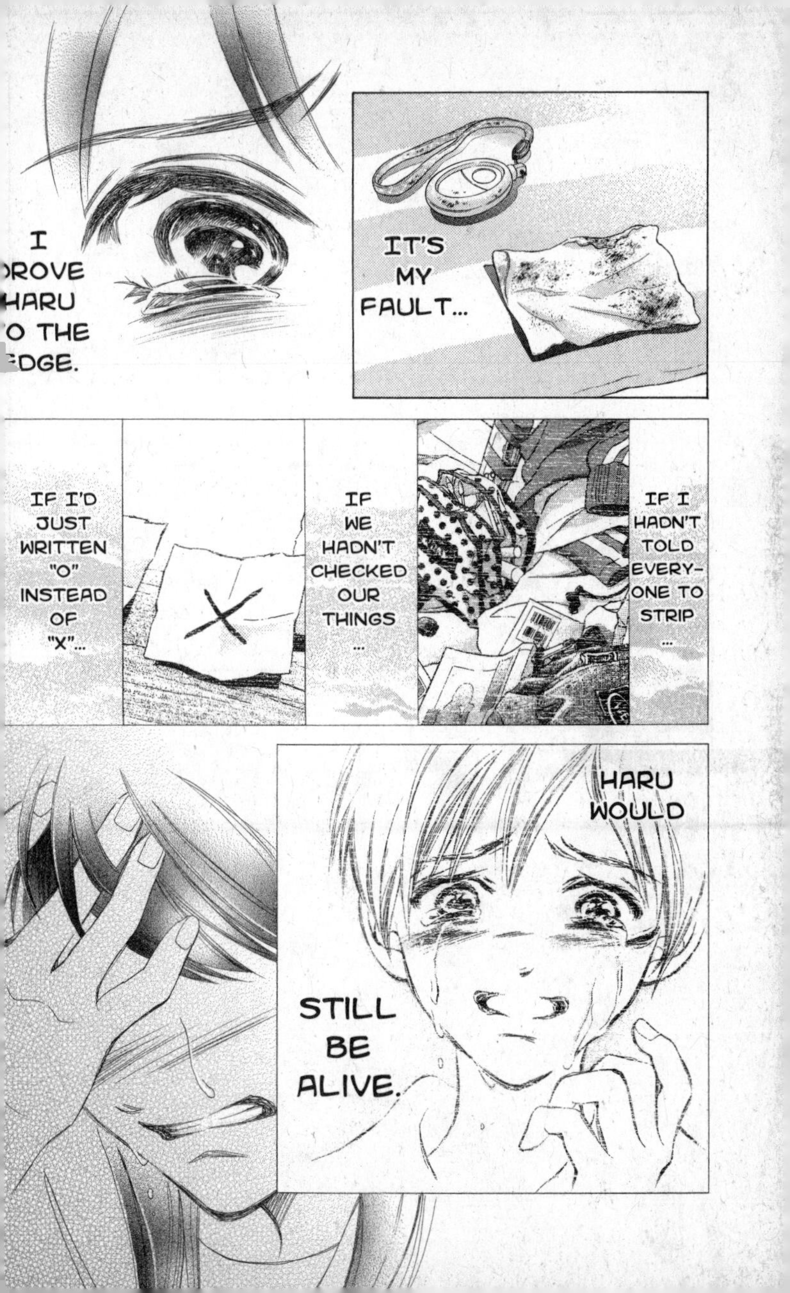

IT'S MY FAULT...
I DROVE HARU TO THE EDGE.
IF I HADN'T TOLD EVERY-ONE TO STRIP ...
IF WE HADN'T CHECKED OUR THINGS ...
IF I'D JUST WRITTEN "O" INSTEAD OF "X"...
HARU WOULD
STILL BE ALIVE.

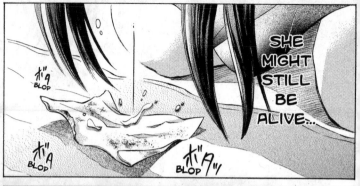

SHE MIGHT STILL BE ALIVE...

ボタ
BLOP

ボタ
BLOP

ボタ
BLOP

UHH ...

UNNH

UNKH ...

HOW ...?

DID THIS THING END UP

グ
GRIP

IN HARU'S POCKET?

WHY

-133-

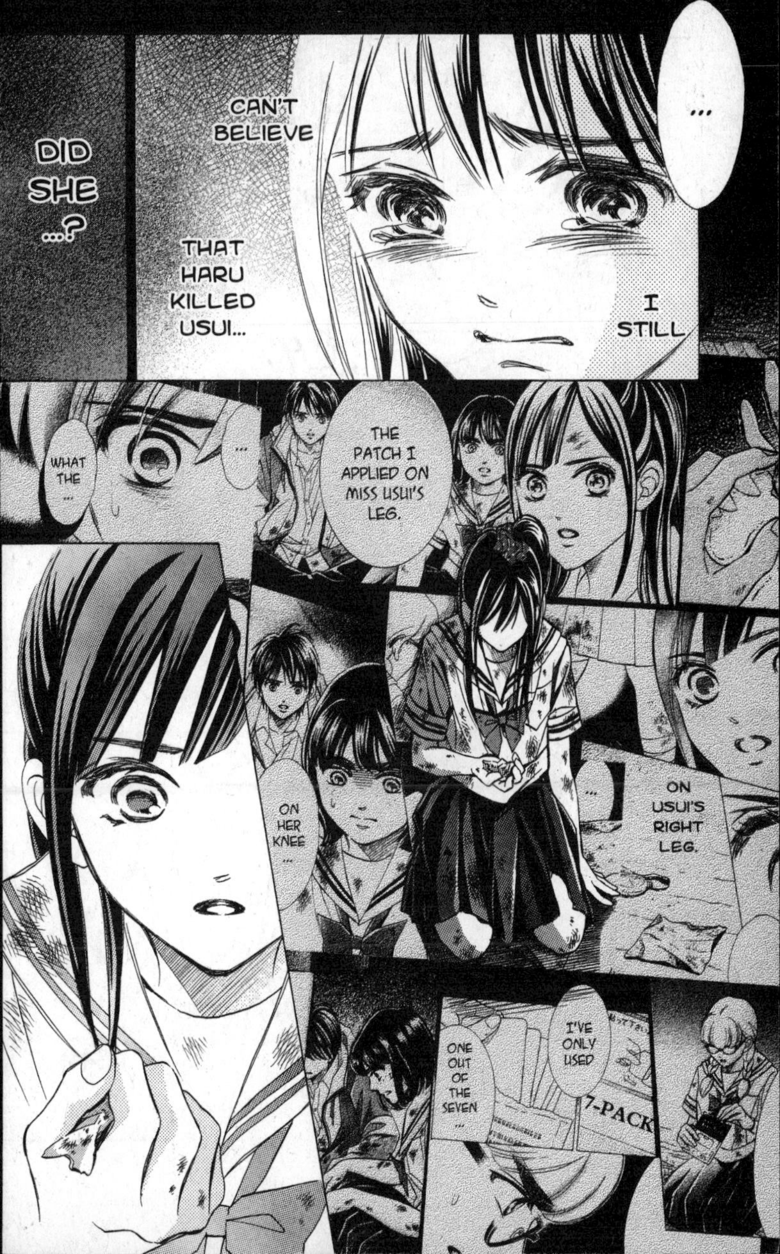
...
I STILL
CAN'T BELIEVE
THAT HARU KILLED USUI...
DID SHE ...?
THE PATCH I APPLIED ON MISS USUI'S LEG.
...
WHAT THE ...
ON USUI'S RIGHT LEG.
...
ON HER KNEE ...
I'VE ONLY USED
ONE OUT OF THE SEVEN ...
7-PACK

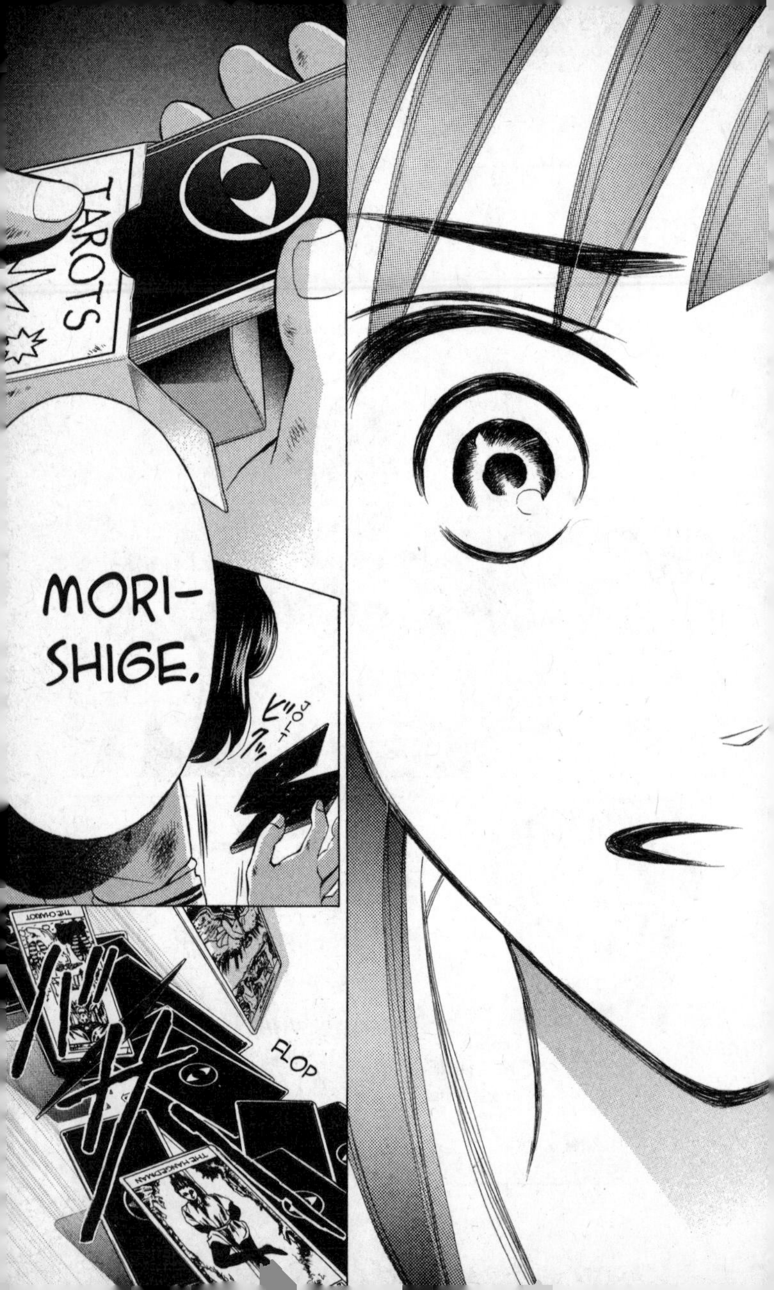
TAROTS
MORI-SHIGE.
ビクッ JOLT
FLOP

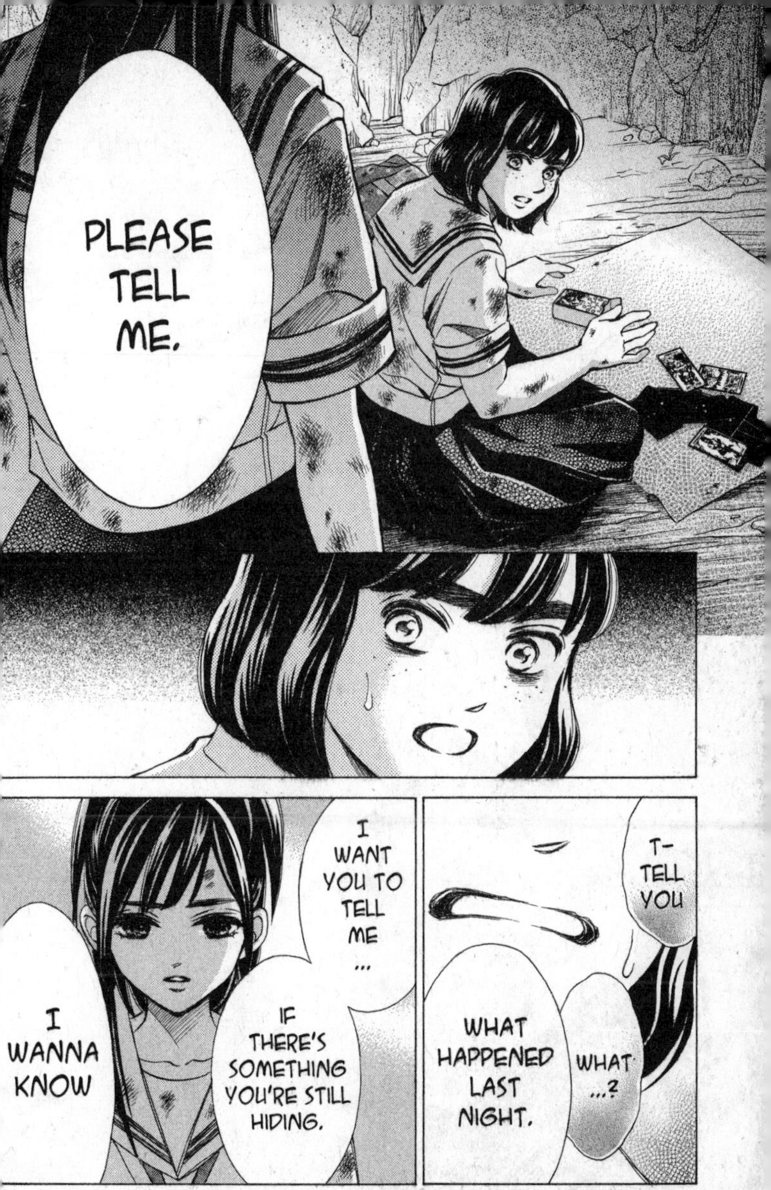
PLEASE TELL ME.
T-TELL YOU
WHAT ...?
WHAT HAPPENED LAST NIGHT.
I WANT YOU TO TELL ME ...
IF THERE'S SOMETHING YOU'RE STILL HIDING.
I WANNA KNOW

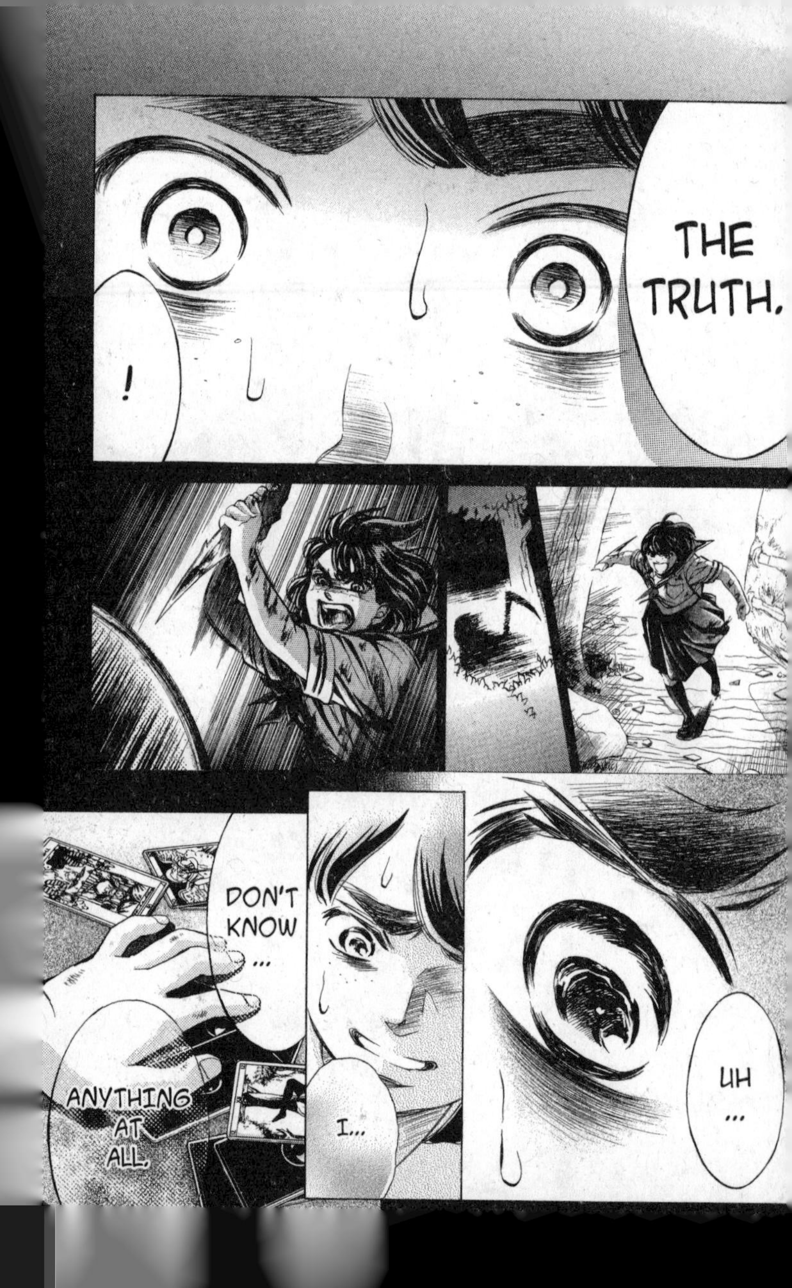
THE TRUTH.
!
UH ...
I...
DON'T KNOW ...
ANYTHING AT ALL.

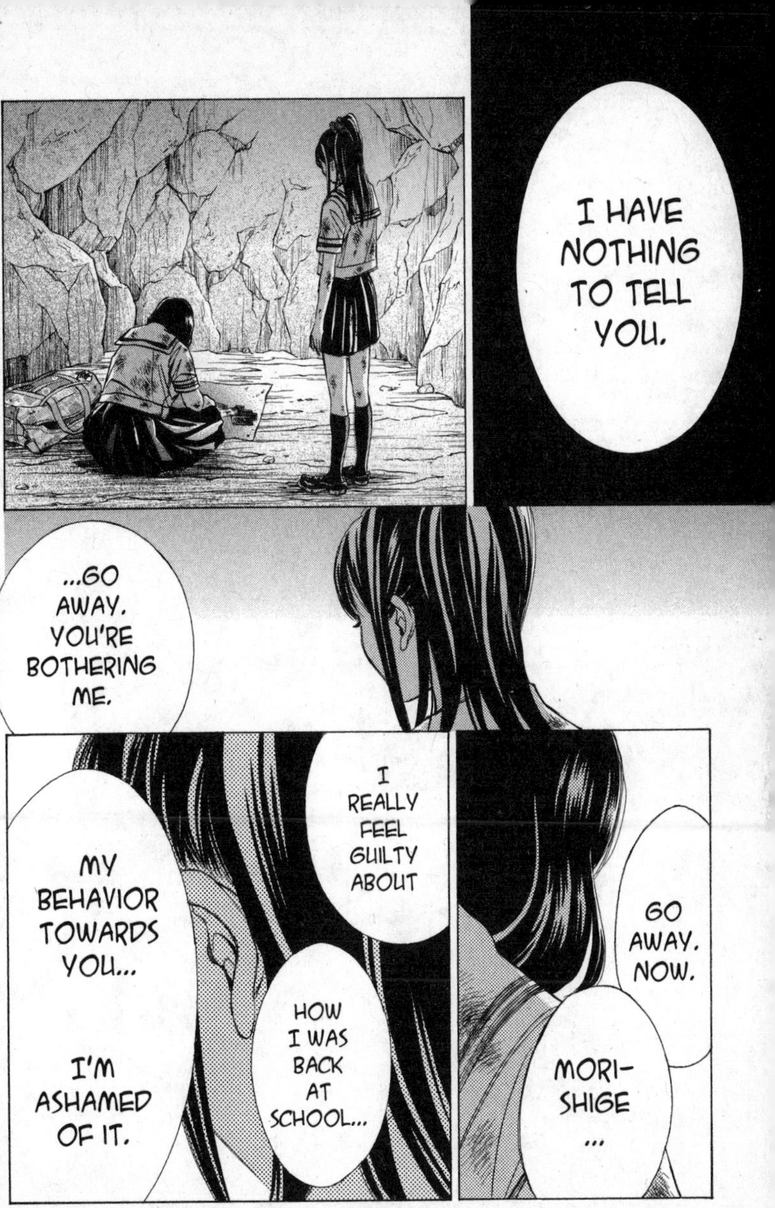
I HAVE NOTHING TO TELL YOU.
...GO AWAY. YOU'RE BOTHERING ME.
GO AWAY. NOW.
MORI-SHIGE ...
I REALLY FEEL GUILTY ABOUT
MY BEHAVIOR TOWARDS YOU...
HOW I WAS BACK AT SCHOOL...
I'M ASHAMED OF IT.

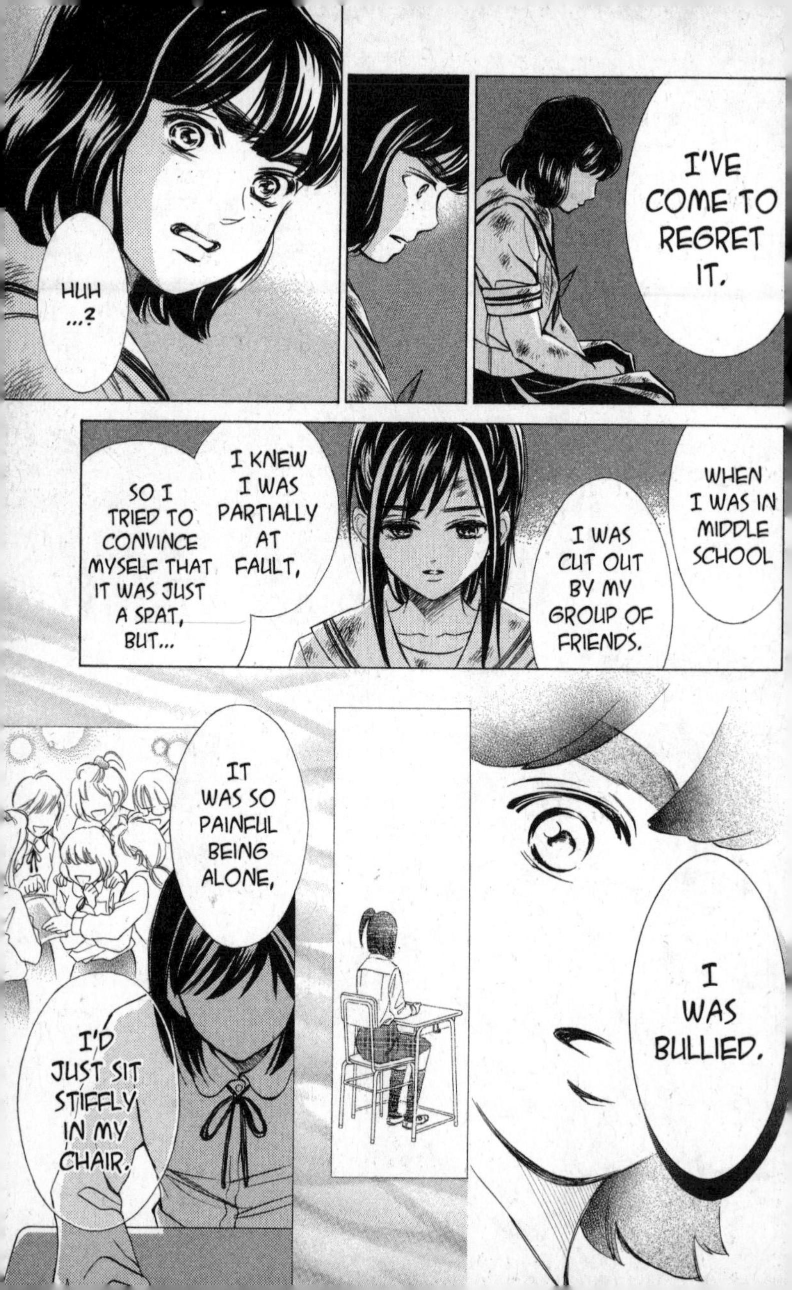
I'VE COME TO REGRET IT.
HUH ...?
WHEN I WAS IN MIDDLE SCHOOL
I WAS CUT OUT BY MY GROUP OF FRIENDS.
I KNEW I WAS PARTIALLY AT FAULT,
SO I TRIED TO CONVINCE MYSELF THAT IT WAS JUST A SPAT, BUT...
I WAS BULLIED.
IT WAS SO PAINFUL BEING ALONE,
I'D JUST SIT STIFFLY IN MY CHAIR.

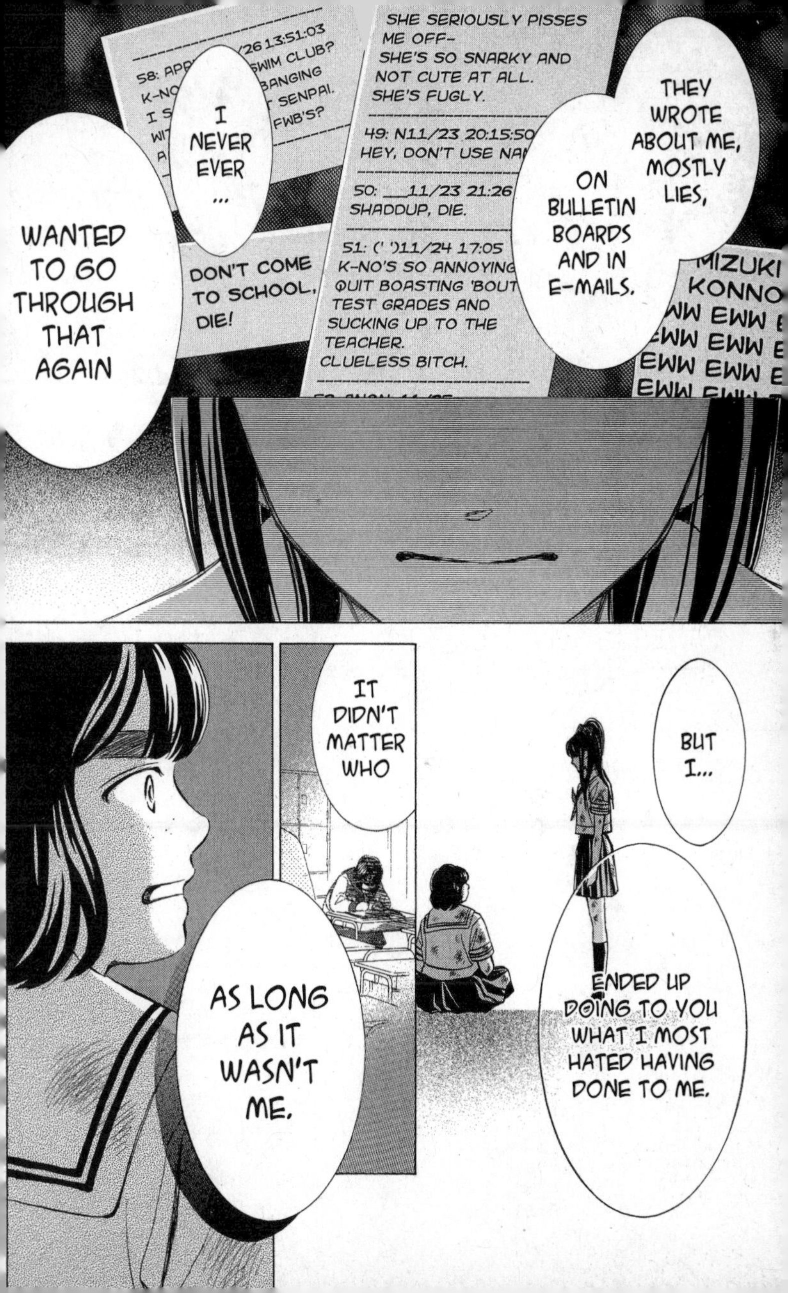
THEY WROTE ABOUT ME, MOSTLY LIES,
ON BULLETIN BOARDS AND IN E-MAILS.
MIZUKI KONNO
EWW EWW
EWW EWW
EWW EWW
SHE SERIOUSLY PISSES ME OFF- SHE'S SO SNARKY AND NOT CUTE AT ALL. SHE'S FUGLY.
49: N11/23 20:15:50
50: __11/23 21:26
SHADDUP, DIE.
51: (' ')11/24 17:05
K-NO'S SO ANNOYING QUIT BOASTING 'BOUT TEST GRADES AND SUCKING UP TO THE TEACHER. CLUELESS BITCH.
SWIM CLUB?
BANGING
SENPAI.
FWB'S?
DON'T COME TO SCHOOL, DIE!
I NEVER EVER ...
WANTED TO GO THROUGH THAT AGAIN
BUT I...
ENDED UP DOING TO YOU WHAT I MOST HATED HAVING DONE TO ME.
IT DIDN'T MATTER WHO
AS LONG AS IT WASN'T ME.

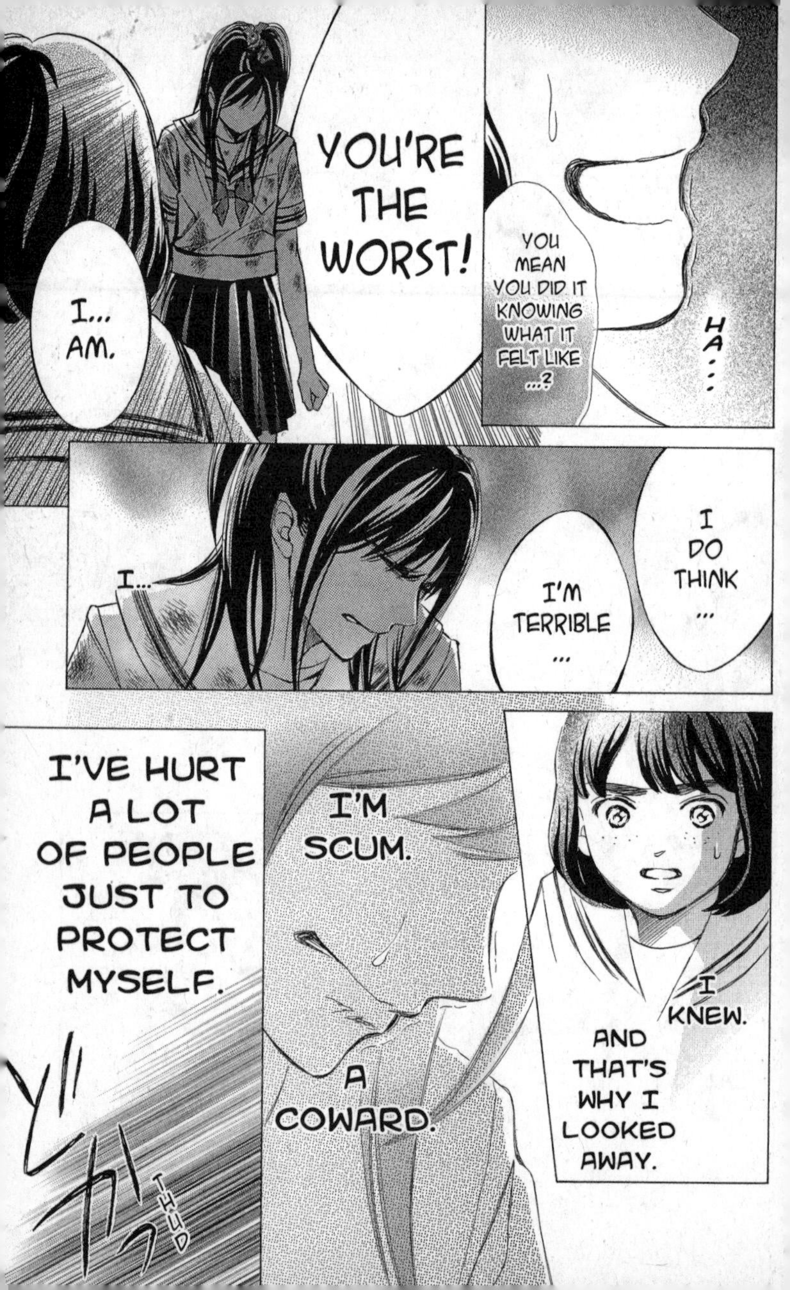

HA...
YOU MEAN YOU DID IT KNOWING WHAT IT FELT LIKE ...?
YOU'RE THE WORST!
I... AM.
I DO THINK...
I'M TERRIBLE...
I...
I KNEW.
AND THAT'S WHY I LOOKED AWAY.
I'M SCUM.
A COWARD.
I'VE HURT A LOT OF PEOPLE JUST TO PROTECT MYSELF.
THUD

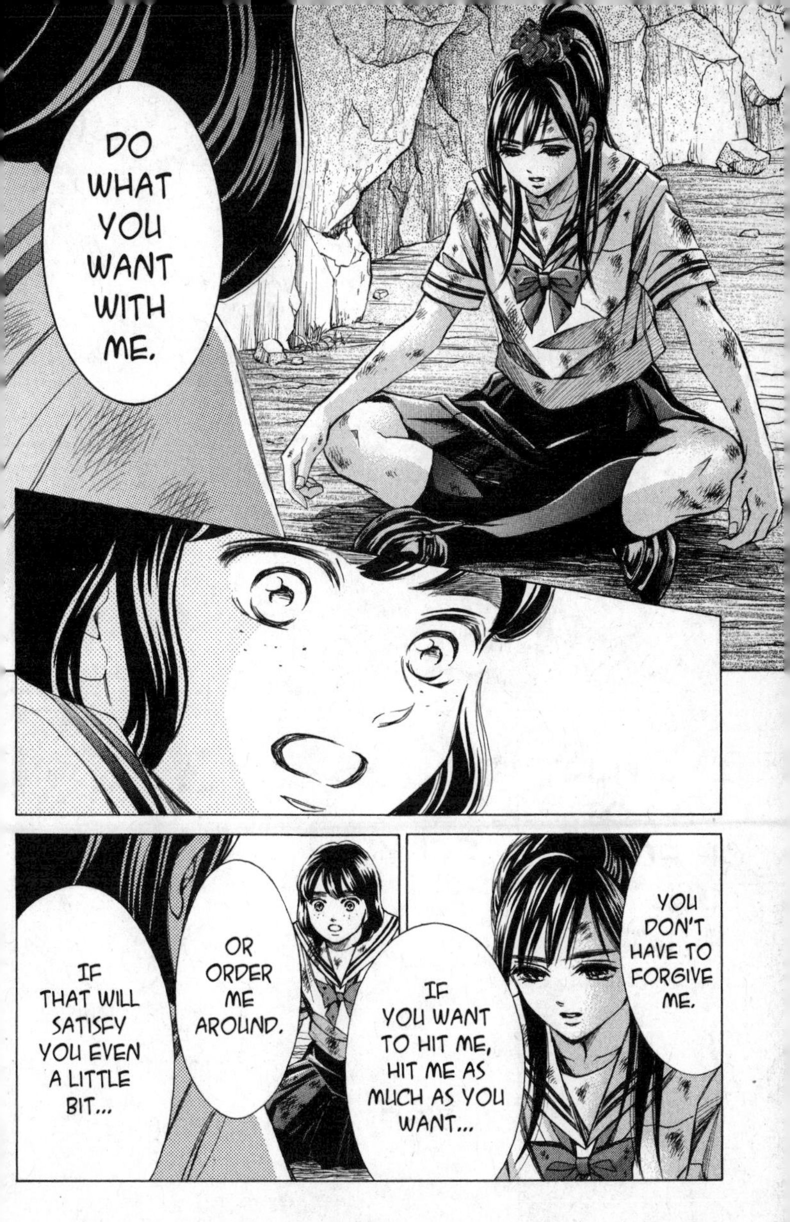
DO WHAT YOU WANT WITH ME.
YOU DON'T HAVE TO FORGIVE ME.
IF YOU WANT TO HIT ME, HIT ME AS MUCH AS YOU WANT...
OR ORDER ME AROUND.
IF THAT WILL SATISFY YOU EVEN A LITTLE BIT...

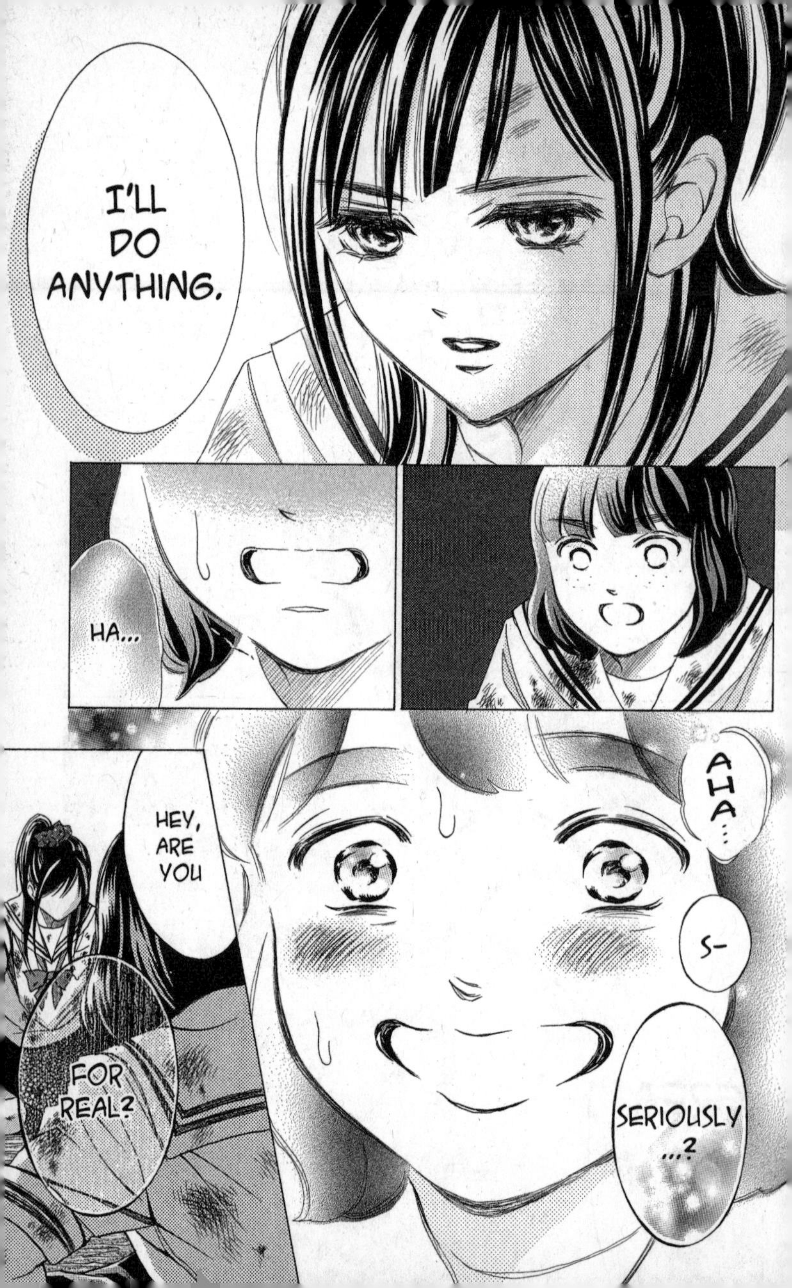
I'LL DO ANYTHING.
HA...
AHA...
S-
SERIOUSLY ...?
HEY, ARE YOU
FOR REAL?

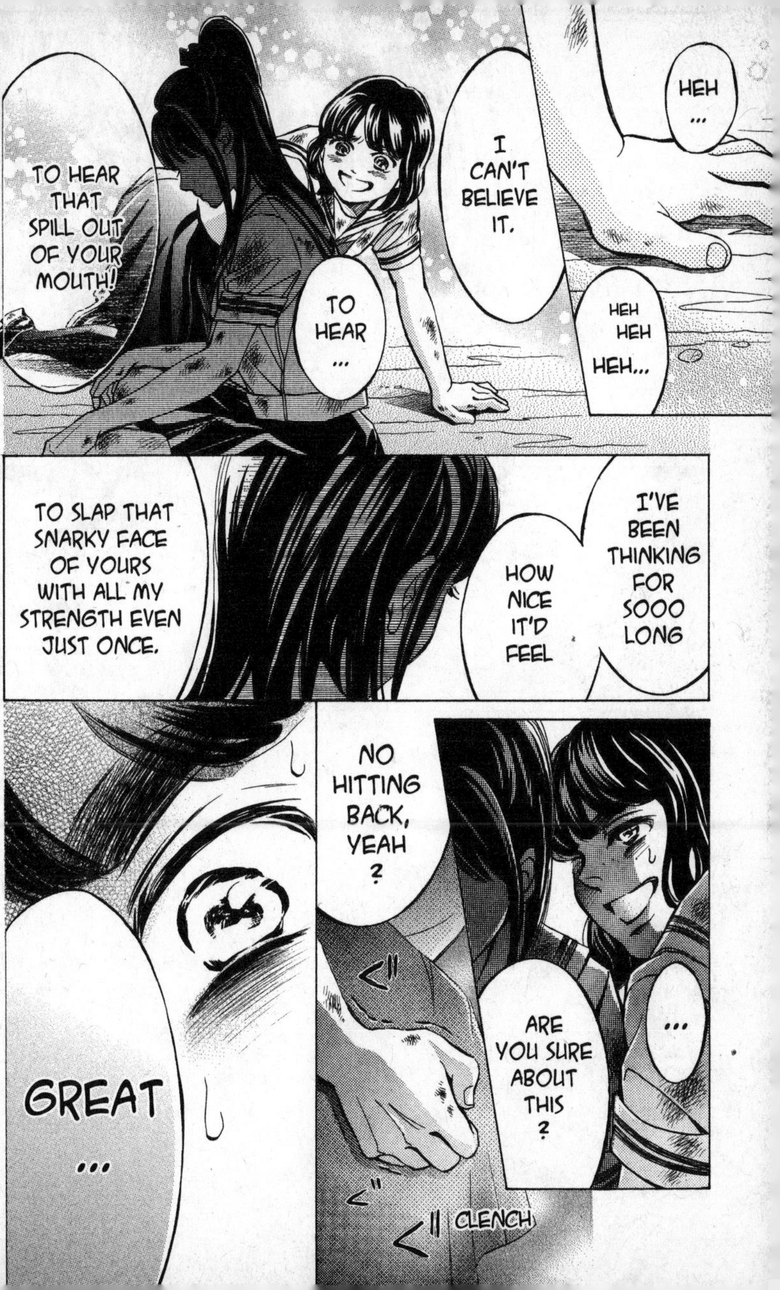
HEH ...
I CAN'T BELIEVE IT.
HEH HEH HEH...
TO HEAR ...
TO HEAR THAT SPILL OUT OF YOUR MOUTH!
I'VE BEEN THINKING FOR SOOO LONG
HOW NICE IT'D FEEL
TO SLAP THAT SNARKY FACE OF YOURS WITH ALL MY STRENGTH EVEN JUST ONCE.
NO HITTING BACK, YEAH?
...
ARE YOU SURE ABOUT THIS?
CLENCH
GREAT ...

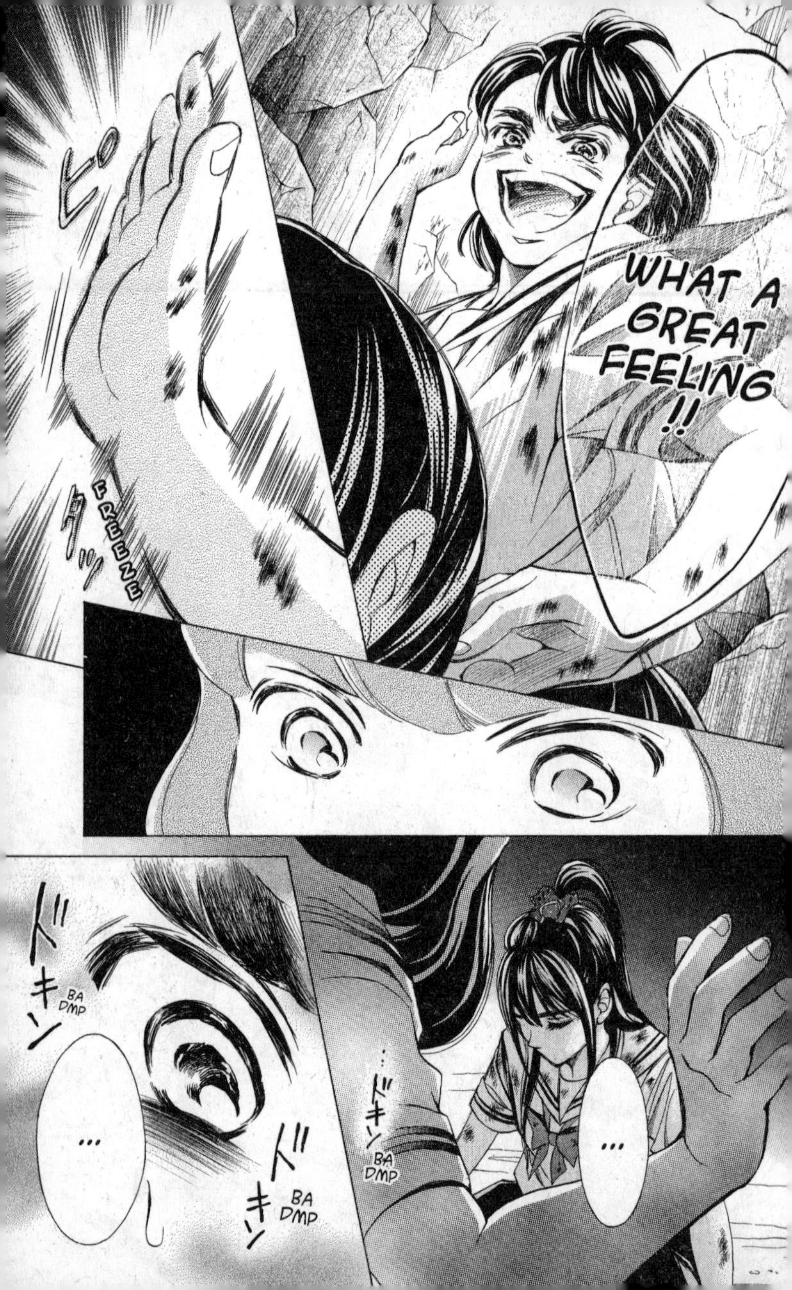
WHAT A GREAT FEELING!!
ピ
タッ
FREEZE
...
ドキン
BA DMP
ドキン
BA DMP
...
ドキン
BA DMP

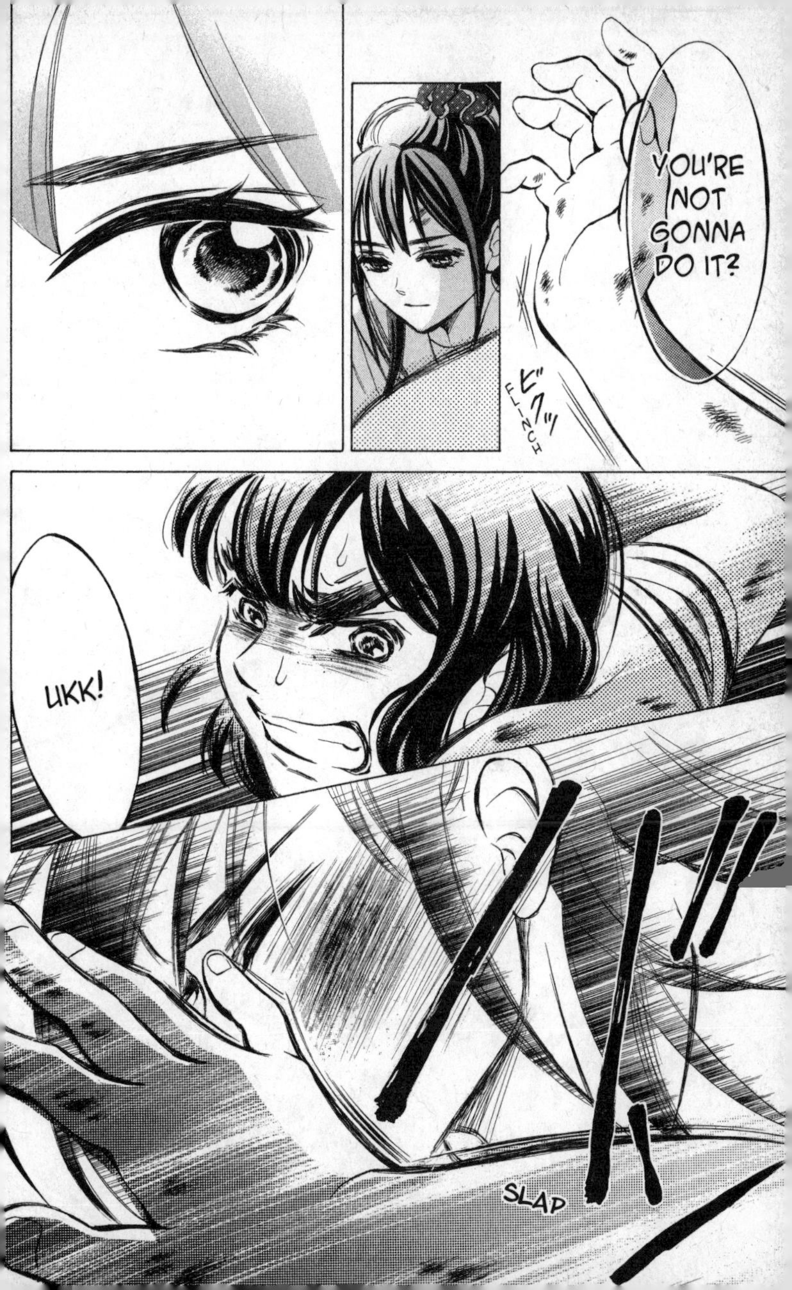
YOU'RE NOT GONNA DO IT?
ビクッ
FLINCH
UKK!
SLAP

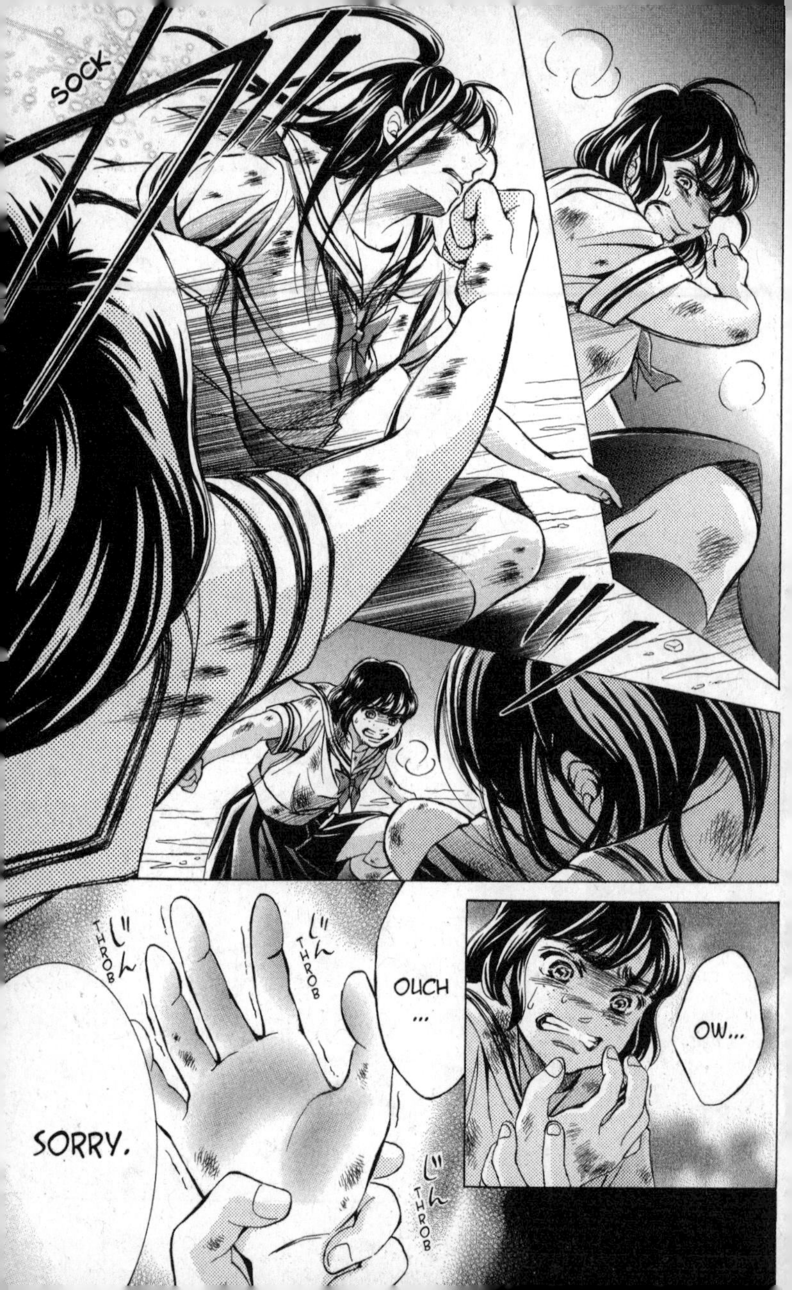
SOCK
OW...
じん THROB
OUCH ...
じん THROB
じん THROB
SORRY.

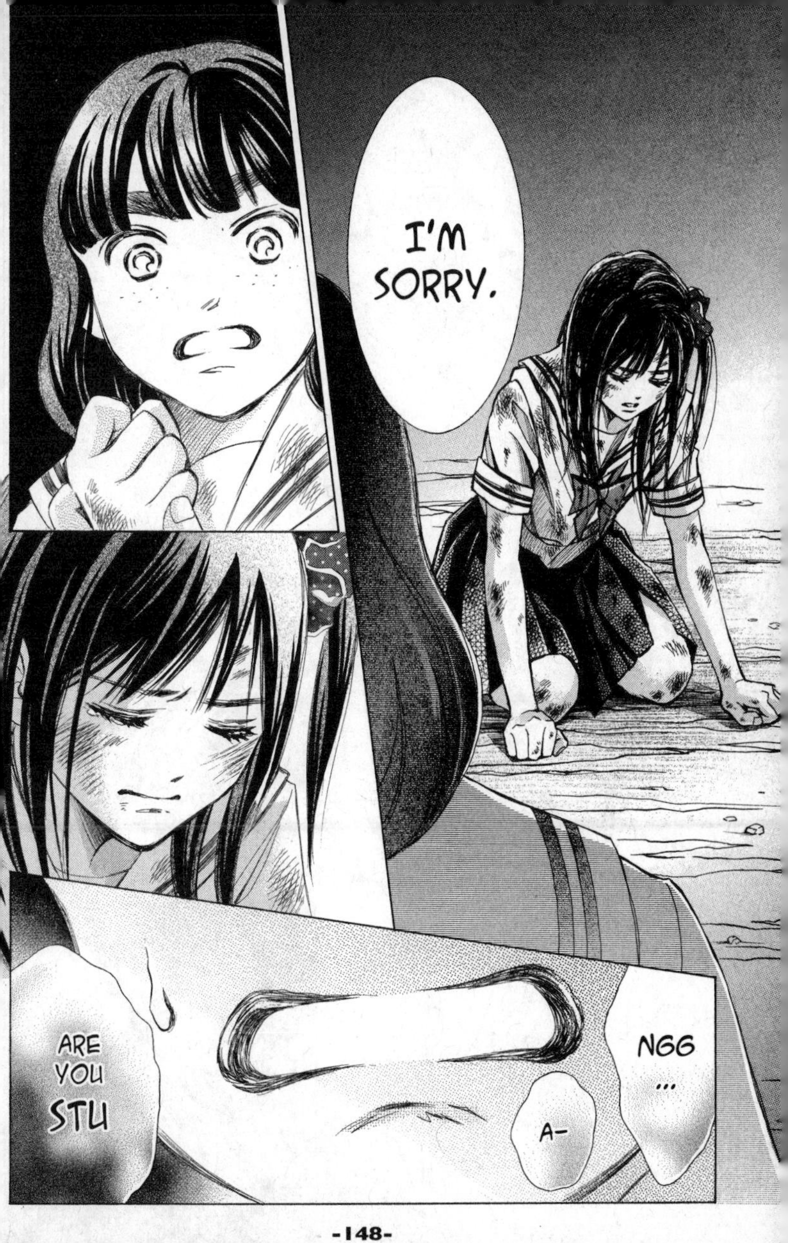
I'M SORRY.
NGG ...
A-
ARE YOU STU

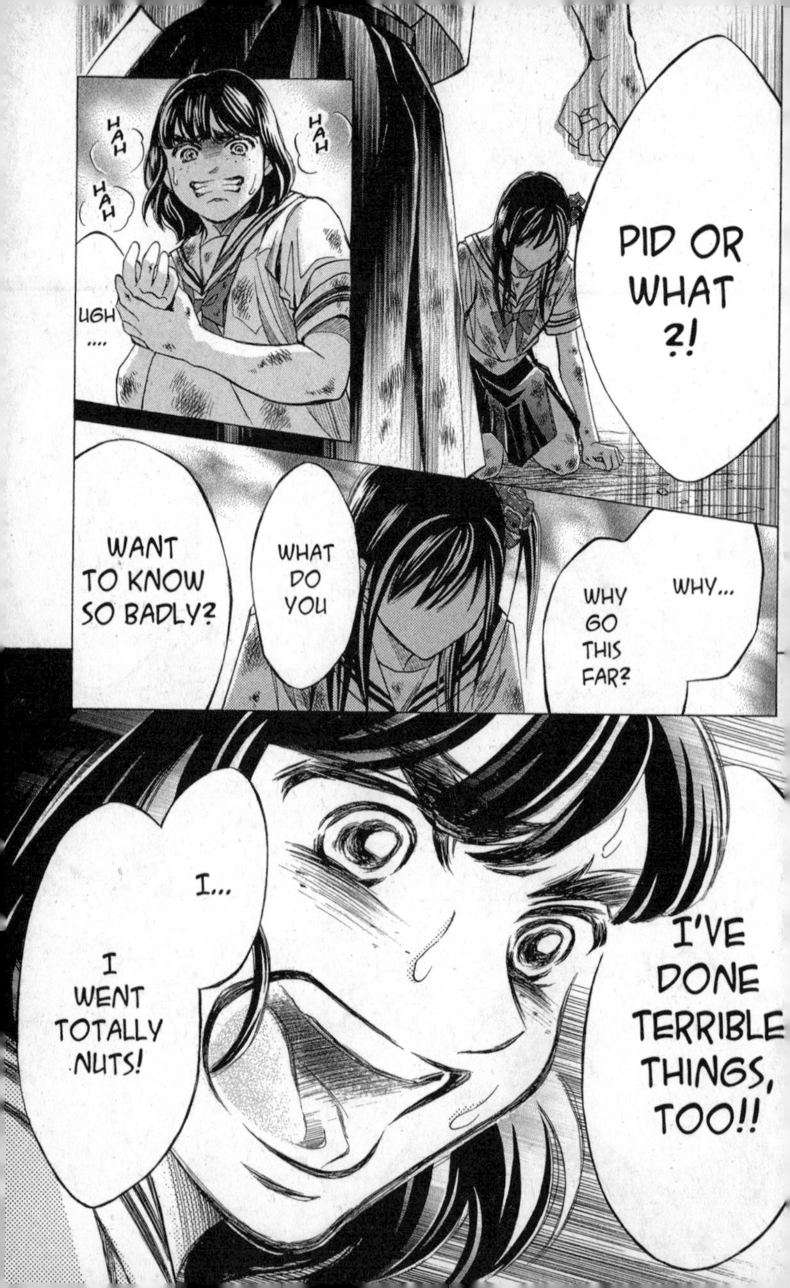
PID OR WHAT?!
HAH
HAH
HAH
UGH....
WHY...
WHY GO THIS FAR?
WHAT DO YOU
WANT TO KNOW SO BADLY?
I'VE DONE TERRIBLE THINGS, TOO!!
I...
I WENT TOTALLY NUTS!

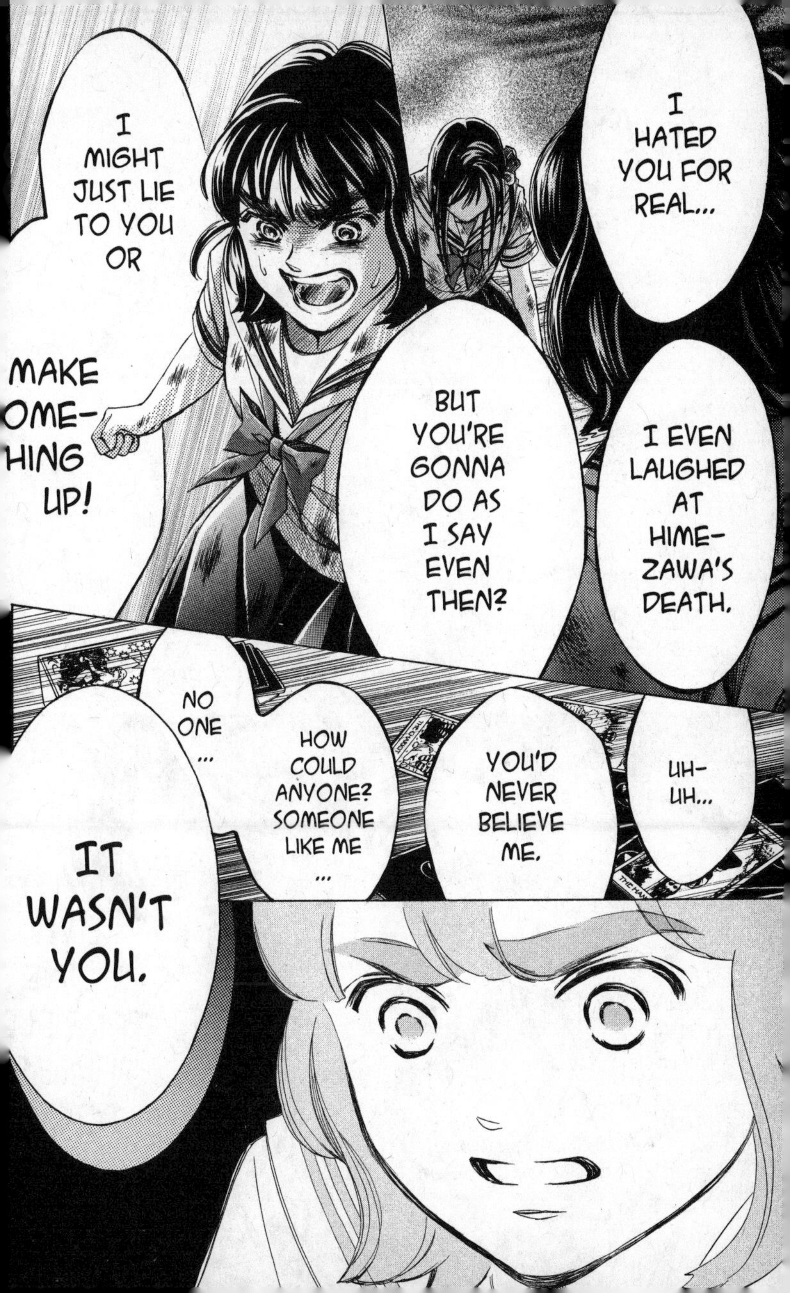
I HATED YOU FOR REAL...
I EVEN LAUGHED AT HIME-ZAWA'S DEATH.
BUT YOU'RE GONNA DO AS I SAY EVEN THEN?
I MIGHT JUST LIE TO YOU OR
MAKE OME-HING UP!
UH-UH...
YOU'D NEVER BELIEVE ME.
HOW COULD ANYONE? SOMEONE LIKE ME...
NO ONE...
IT WASN'T YOU.

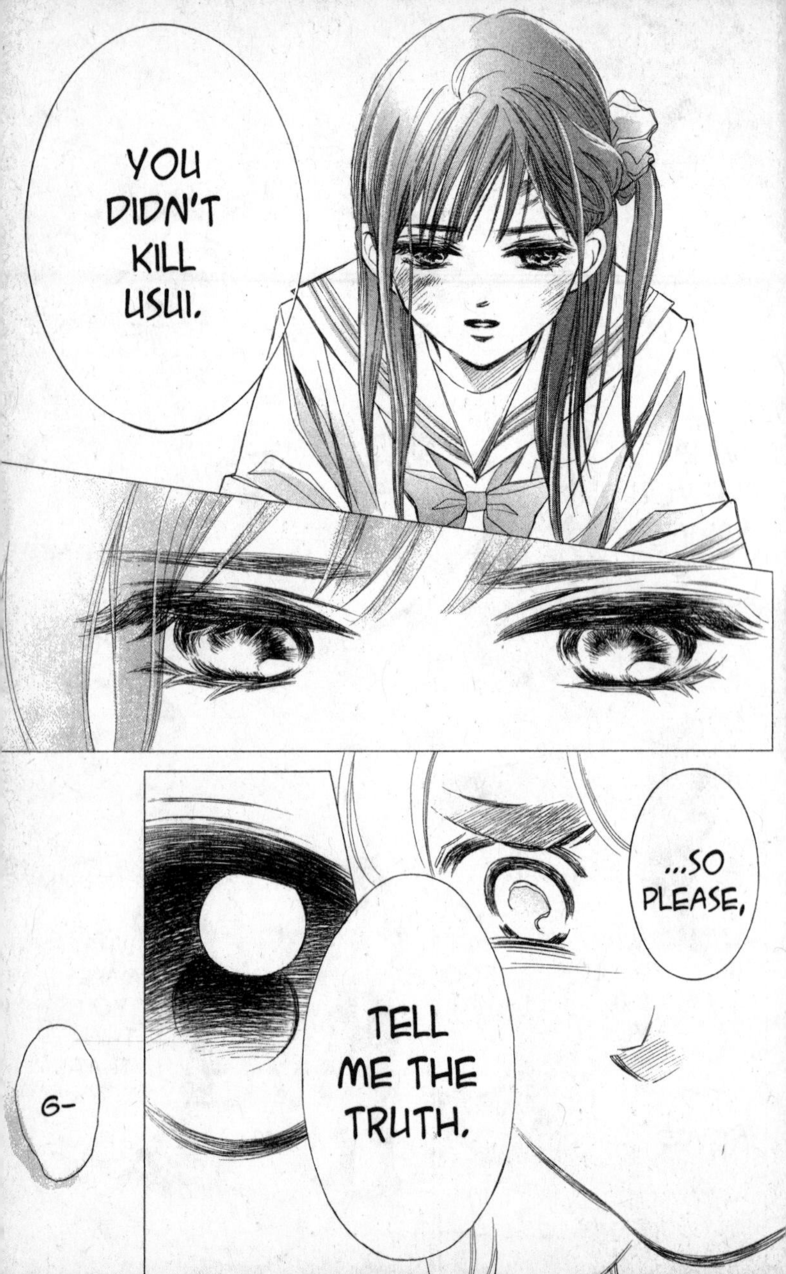
YOU DIDN'T KILL USUI.
...SO PLEASE,
TELL ME THE TRUTH.
G-

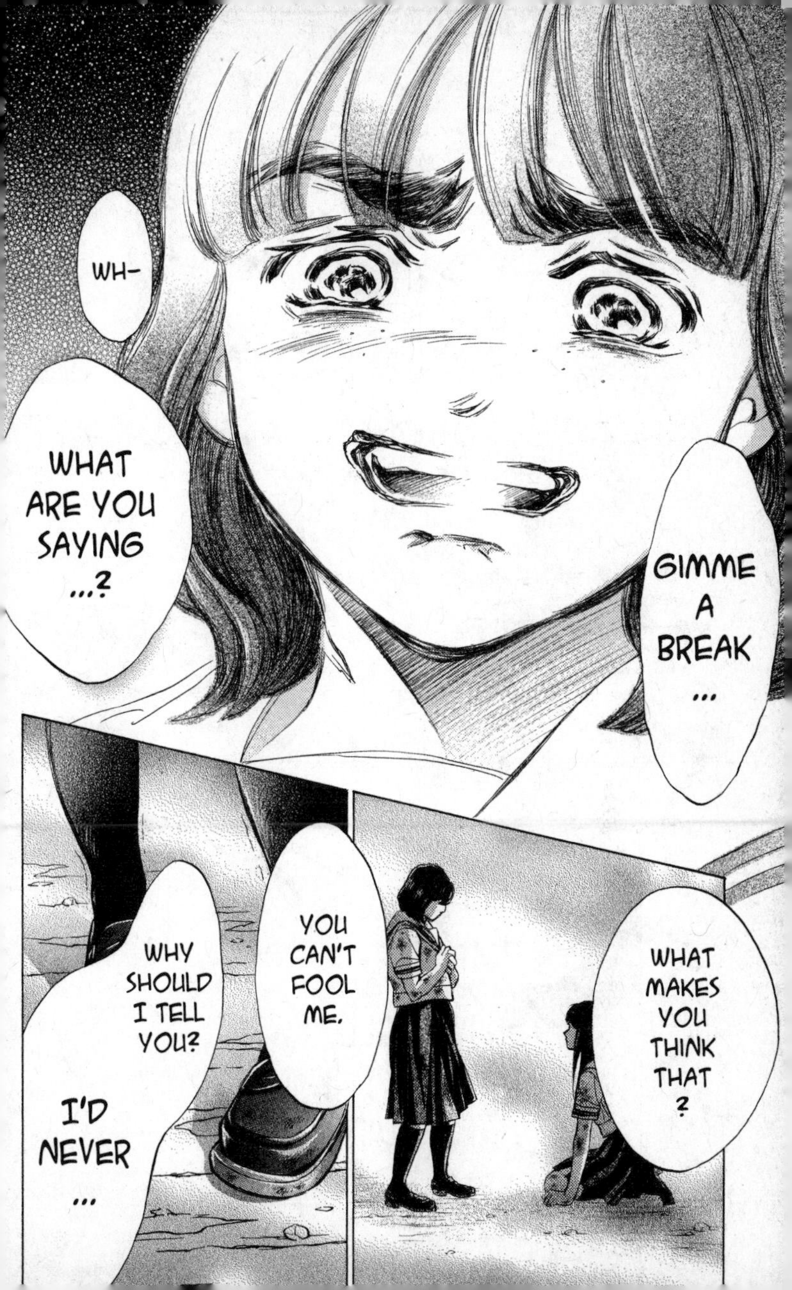
GIMME A BREAK ...
WH-
WHAT ARE YOU SAYING ...?
WHAT MAKES YOU THINK THAT?
YOU CAN'T FOOL ME.
WHY SHOULD I TELL YOU?
I'D NEVER ...

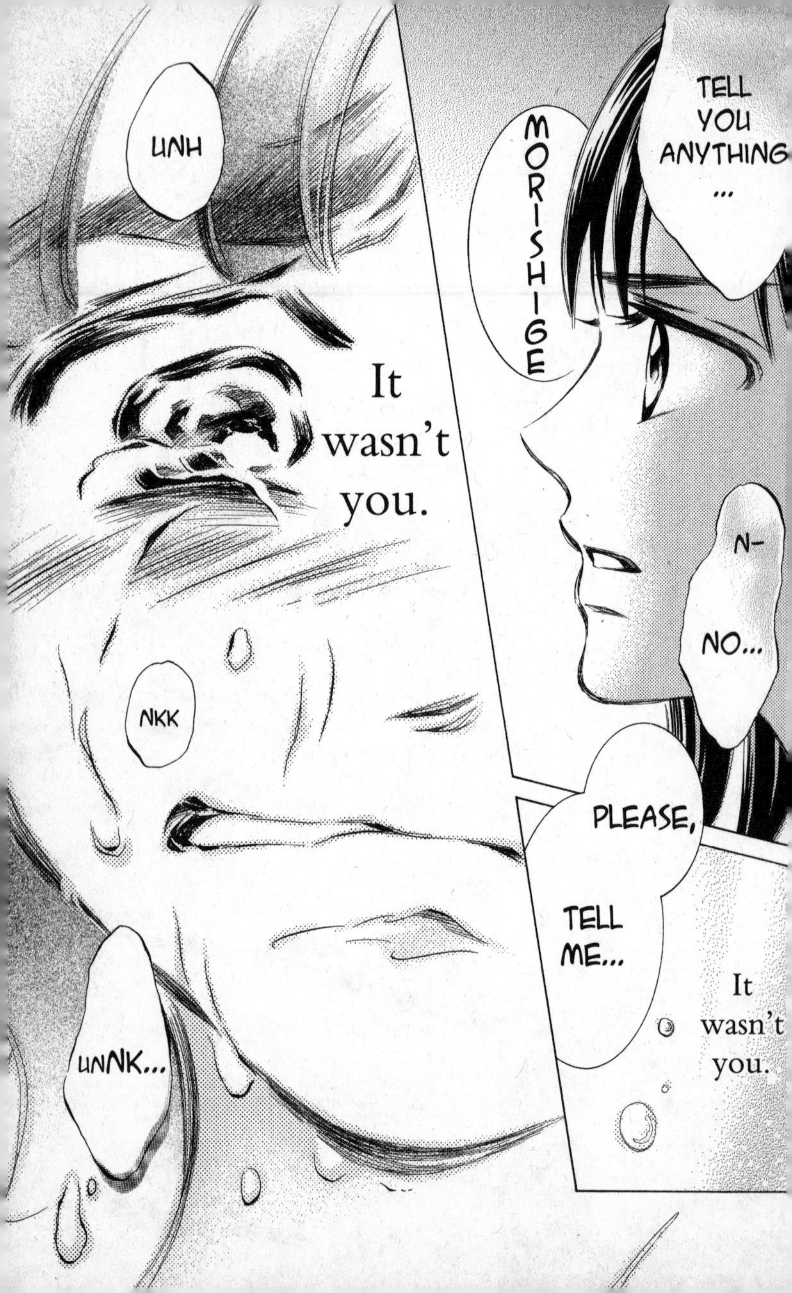
TELL YOU ANYTHING...
MORISHIGE
N- NO...
PLEASE, TELL ME...
It wasn't you.
UNH
It wasn't you.
NKK
UNNK...

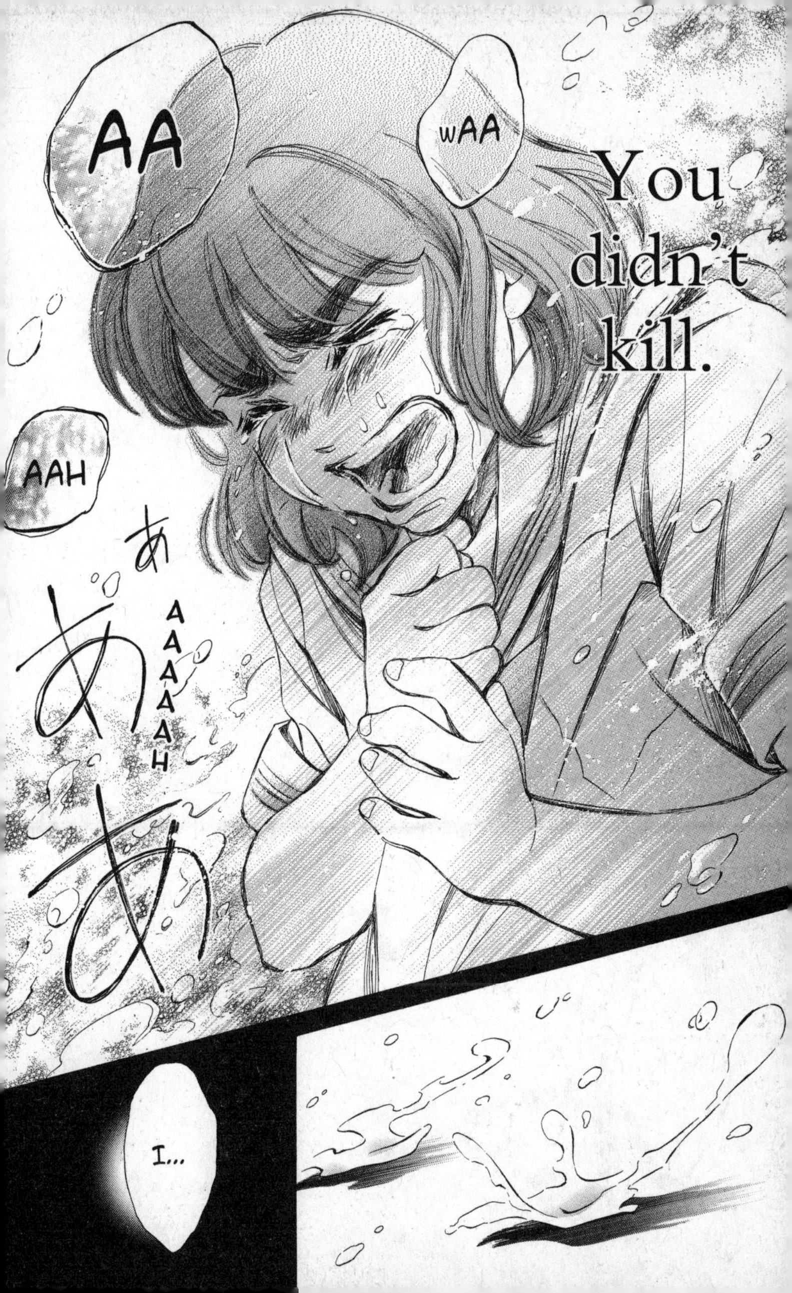
You didn't kill.
WAA
AA
AAH
あああ
AAAAAH
I...

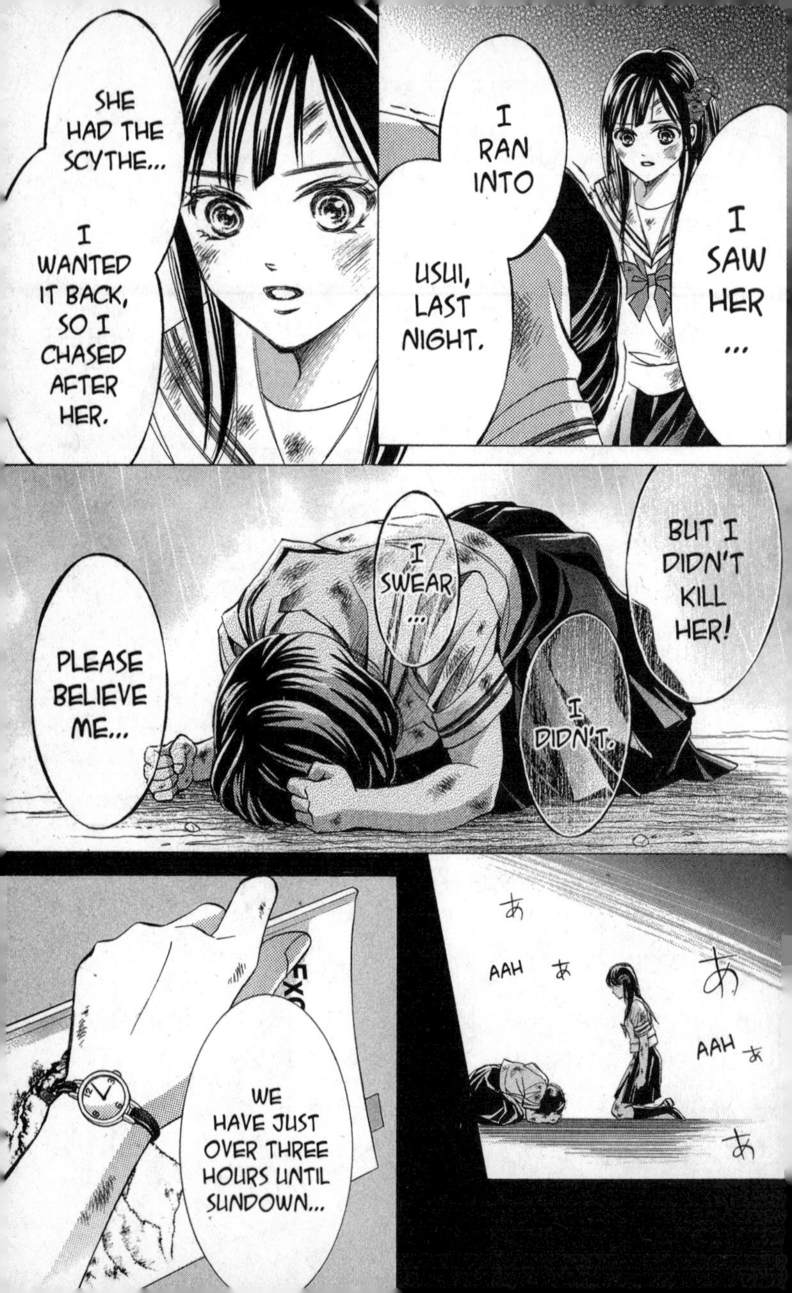

I SAW HER...
I RAN INTO USUI, LAST NIGHT.
SHE HAD THE SCYTHE...
I WANTED IT BACK, SO I CHASED AFTER HER.
BUT I DIDN'T KILL HER!
I DIDN'T.
I SWEAR...
PLEASE BELIEVE ME...
あ
あ
AAH あ
AAH あ
あ
WE HAVE JUST OVER THREE HOURS UNTIL SUNDOWN...

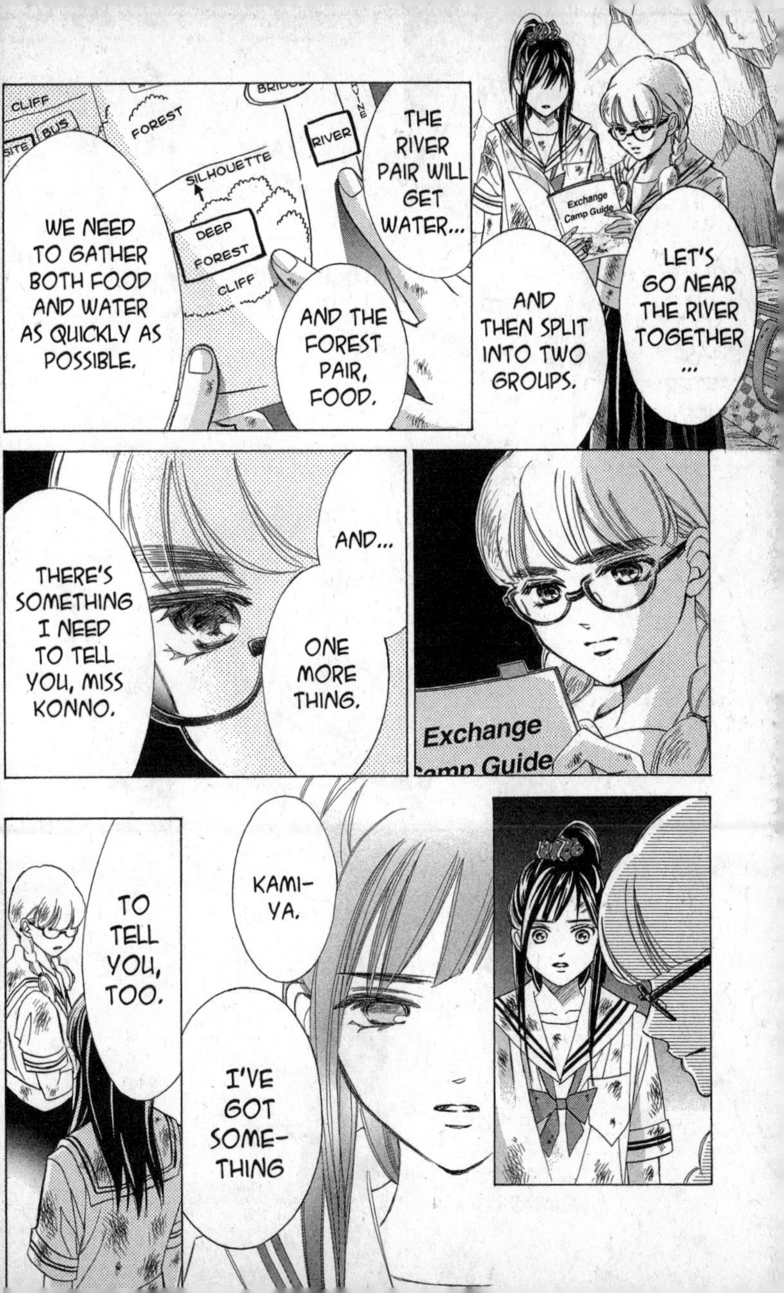
Exchange
Camp Guide
LET'S GO NEAR THE RIVER TOGETHER ...
AND THEN SPLIT INTO TWO GROUPS.
THE RIVER PAIR WILL GET WATER...
AND THE FOREST PAIR, FOOD.
RIVER
FOREST
SILHOUETTE
DEEP FOREST
CLIFF
CLIFF
BUS
SITE
WE NEED TO GATHER BOTH FOOD AND WATER AS QUICKLY AS POSSIBLE.
Exchange
Camp Guide
AND...
ONE MORE THING.
THERE'S SOMETHING I NEED TO TELL YOU, MISS KONNO.
KAMI-YA.
I'VE GOT SOME-THING
TO TELL YOU, TOO.

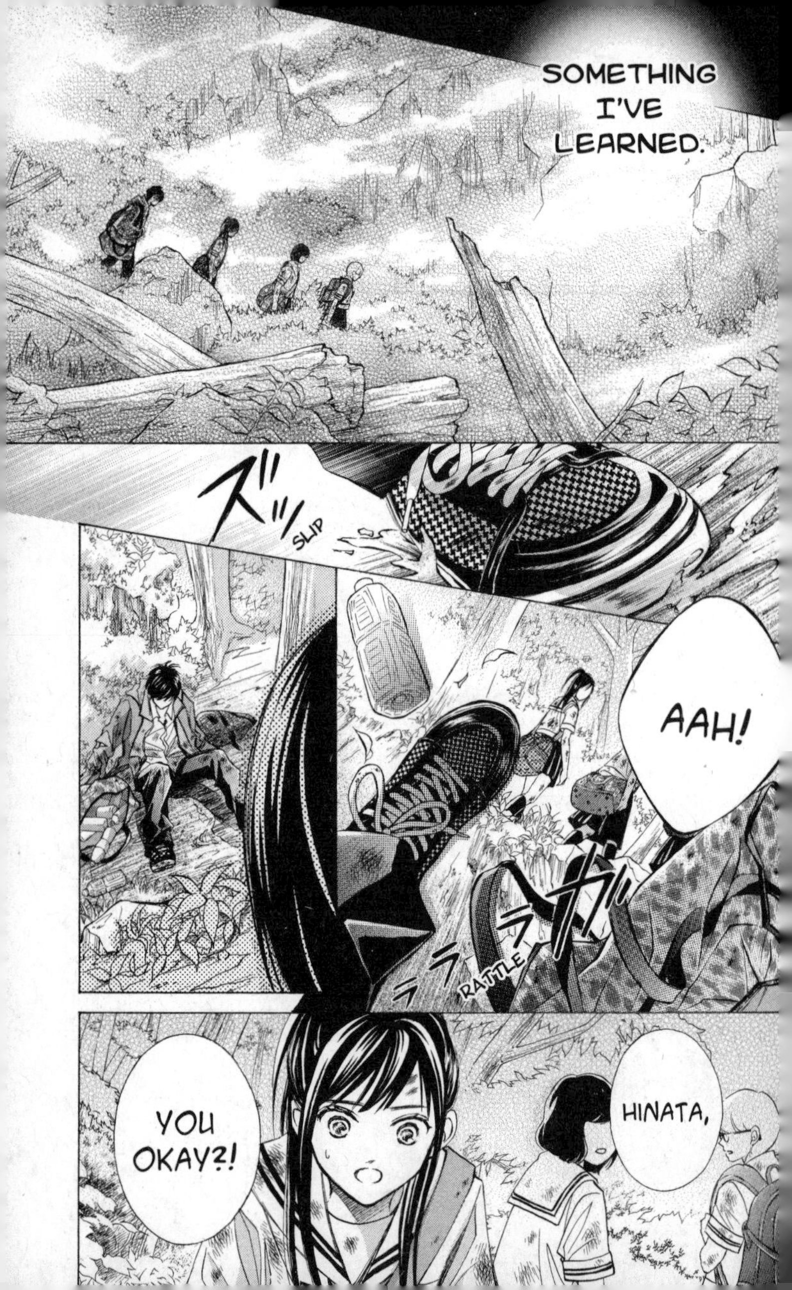
SOMETHING I'VE LEARNED.
ズッ
SLIP
AAH!
RATTLE
HINATA,
YOU OKAY?!

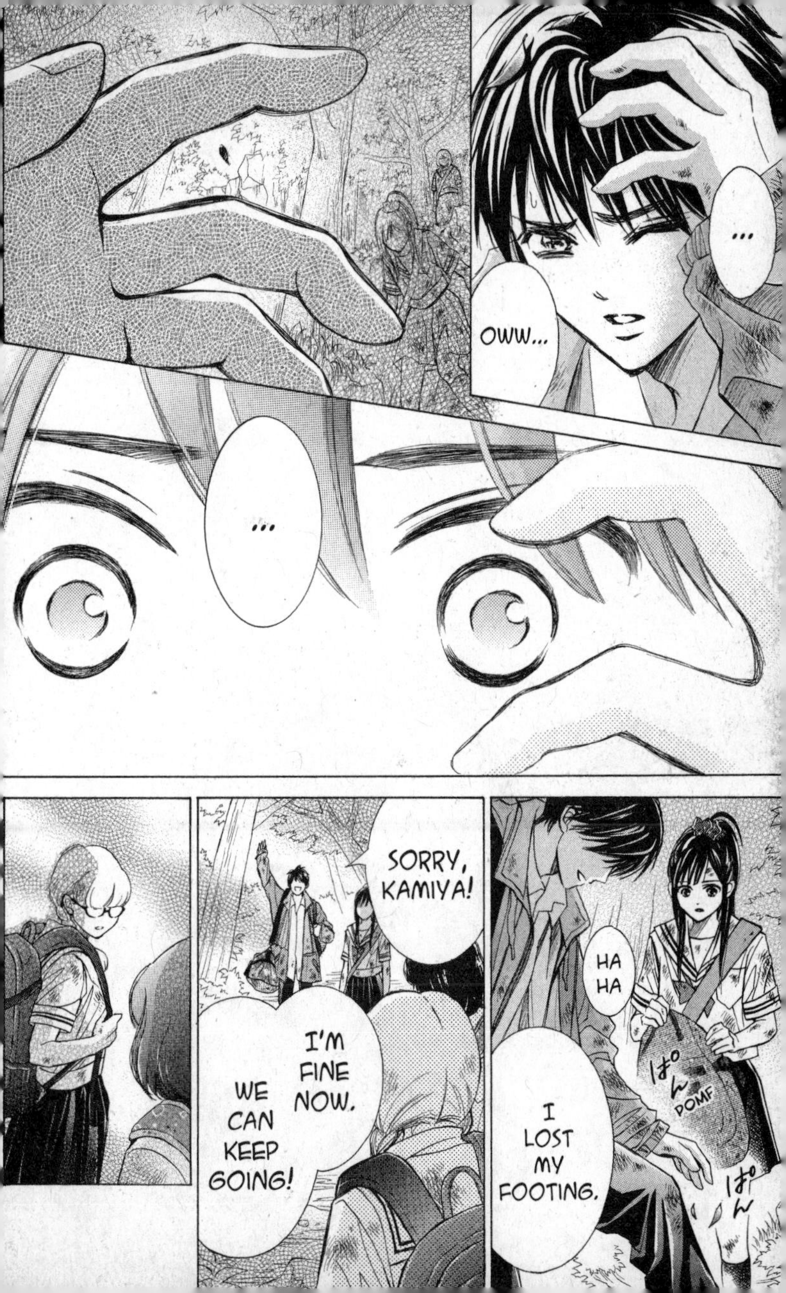
...
OWW...
...
HA
HA
I LOST MY FOOTING.
ぱん
POMF
ぱん
SORRY, KAMIYA!
I'M FINE NOW.
WE CAN KEEP GOING!

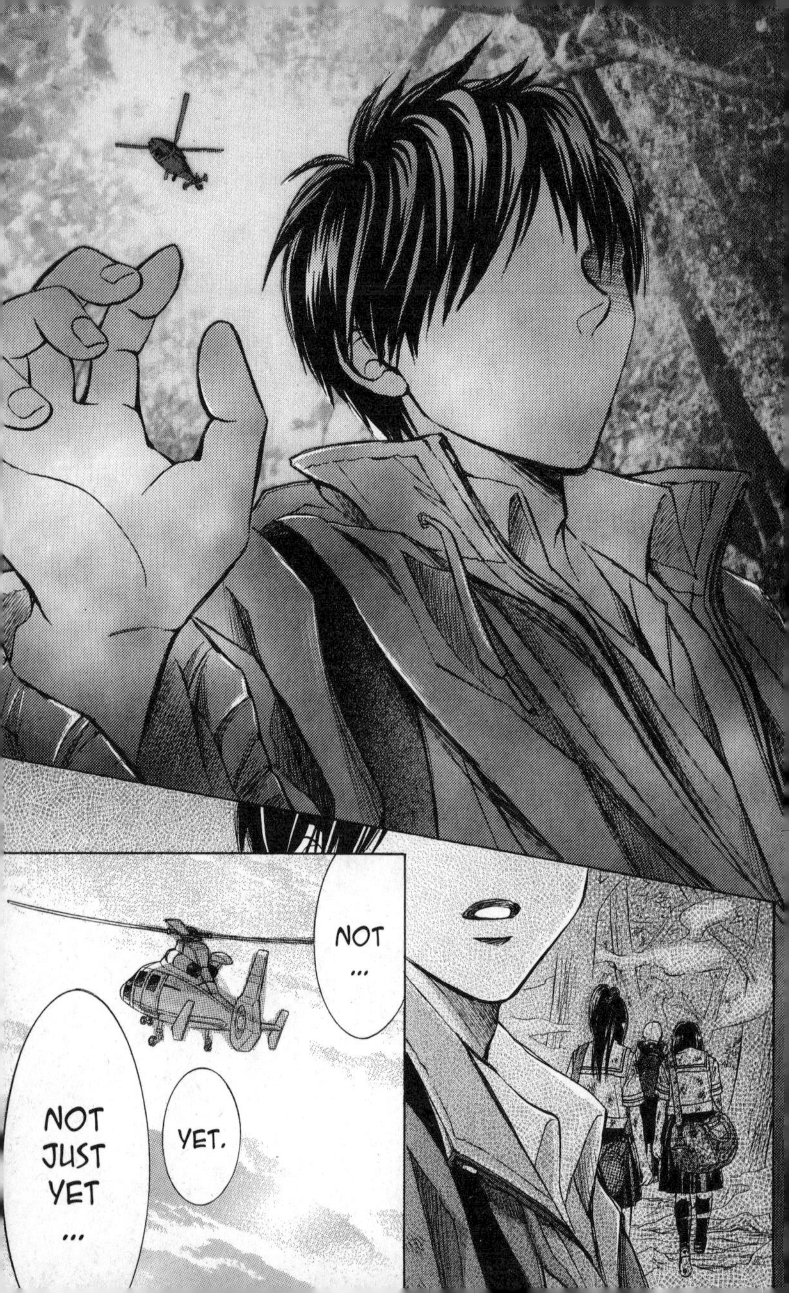
NOT ...
YET.
NOT JUST YET ...

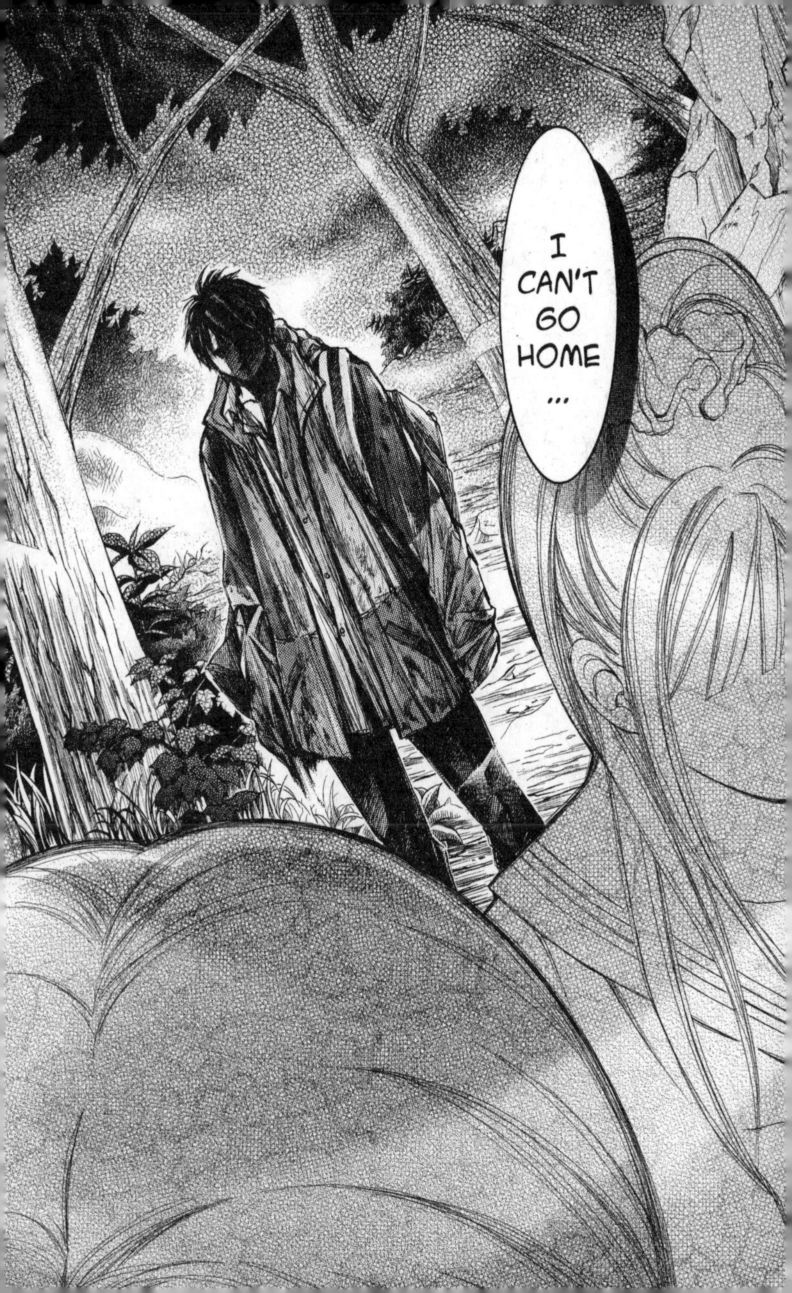
I CAN'T GO HOME ...

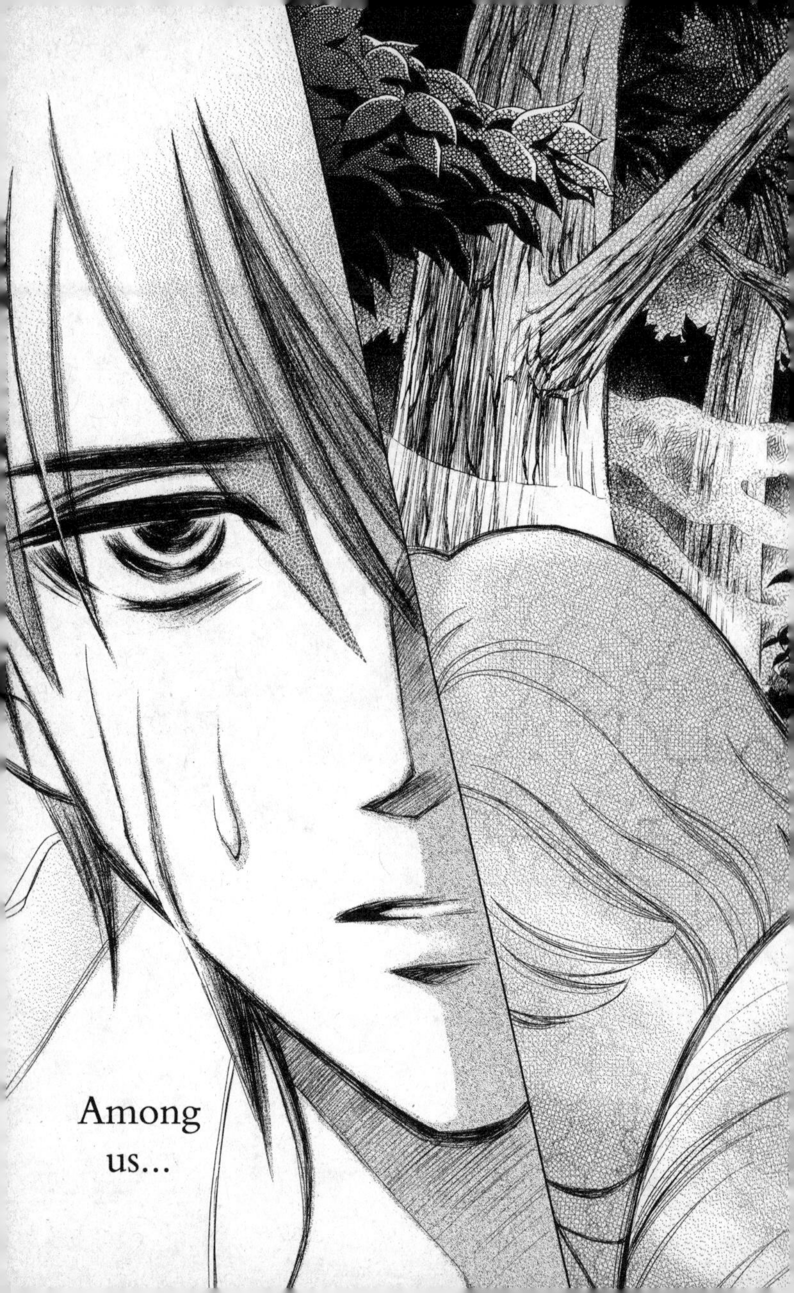
Among us...

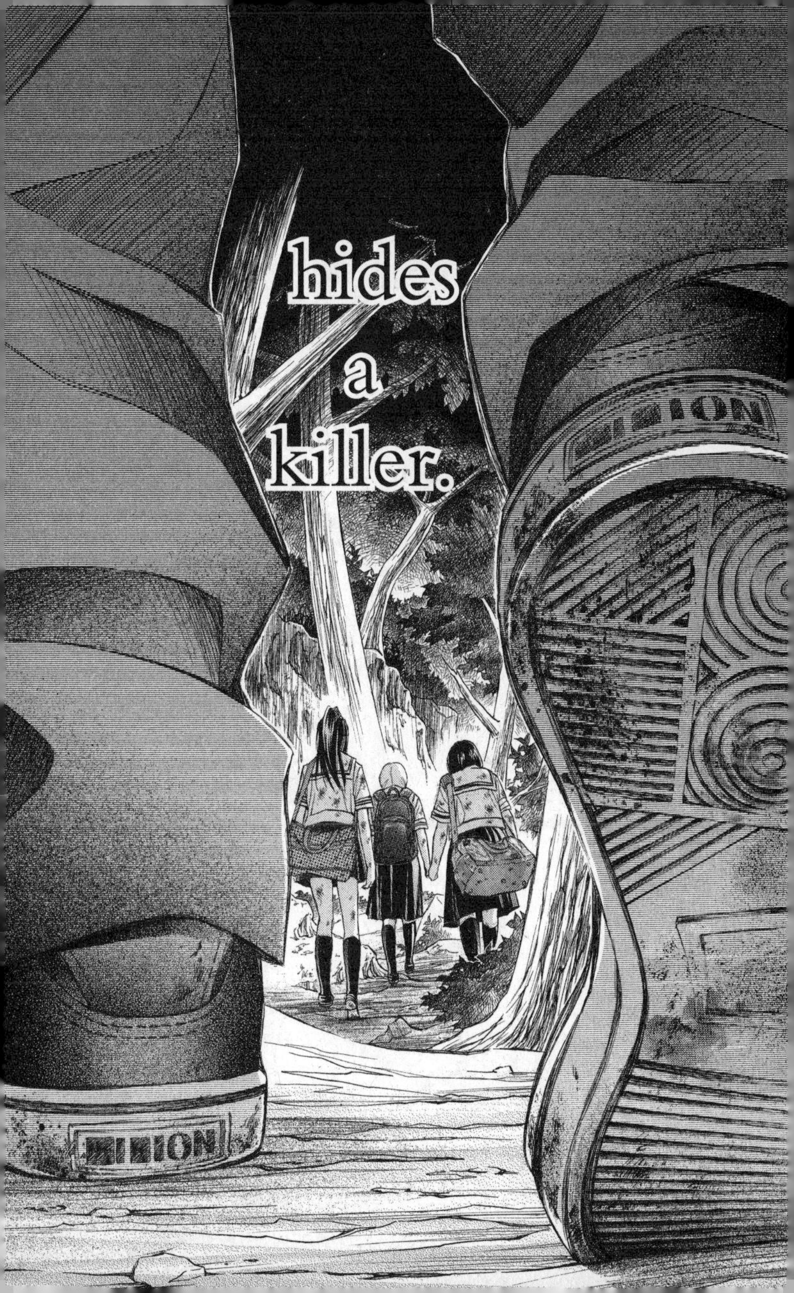
hides
a
killer.

**To be
continued...**

MY WORKROOM

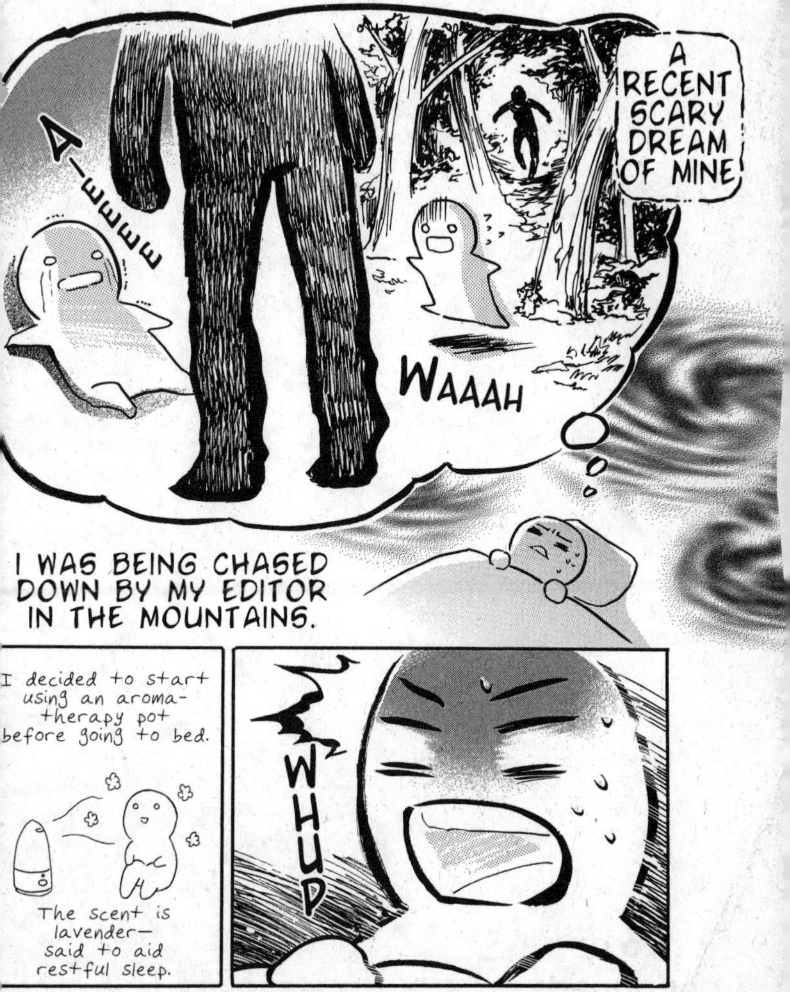

A RECENT SCARY DREAM OF MINE
A—EEEEE
WAAAH
I WAS BEING CHASED DOWN BY MY EDITOR IN THE MOUNTAINS.
WHUP
I decided to start using an aroma-therapy pot before going to bed.
The scent is lavender—said to aid restful sleep.

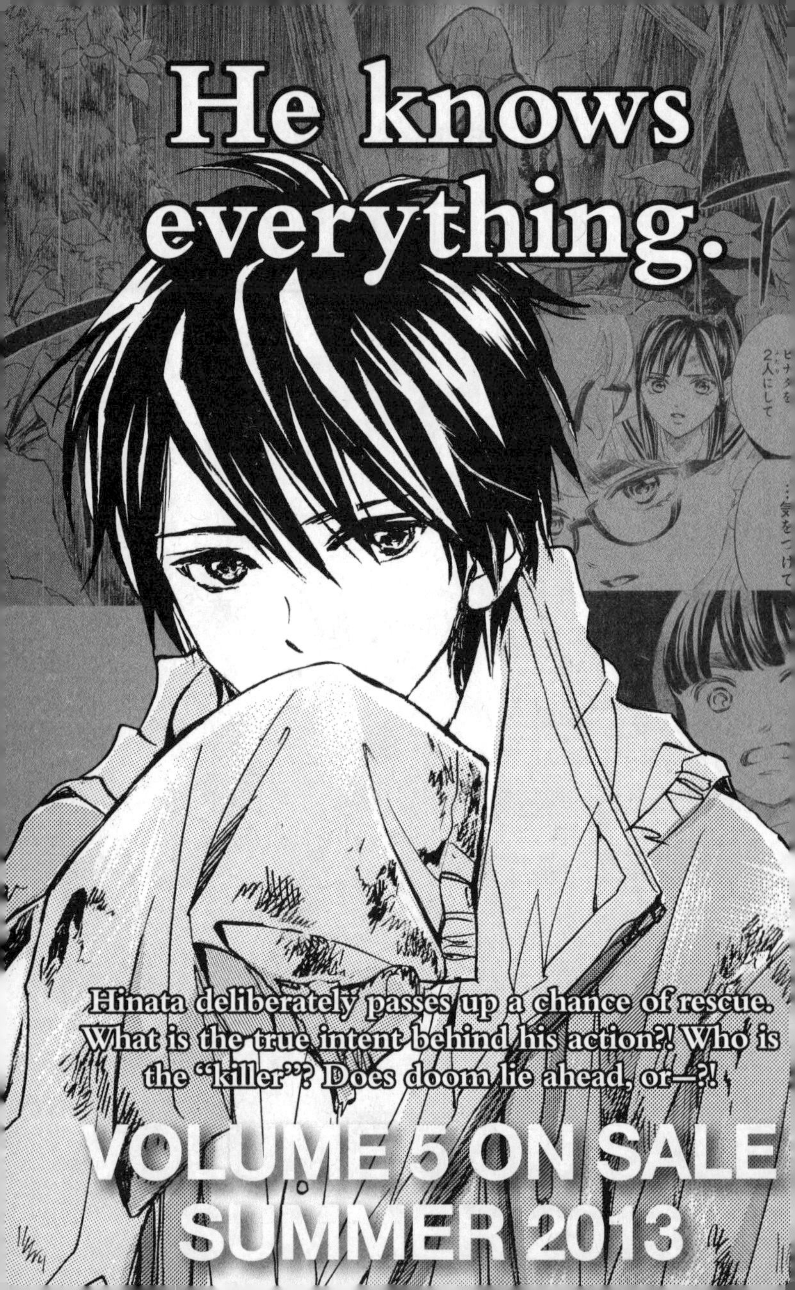
He knows everything.
ヒナタを2人にして
…気をつけて
Hinata deliberately passes up a chance of rescue. What is the true intent behind his action?! Who is the "killer"? Does doom lie ahead, or—?!
VOLUME 5 ON SALE SUMMER 2013

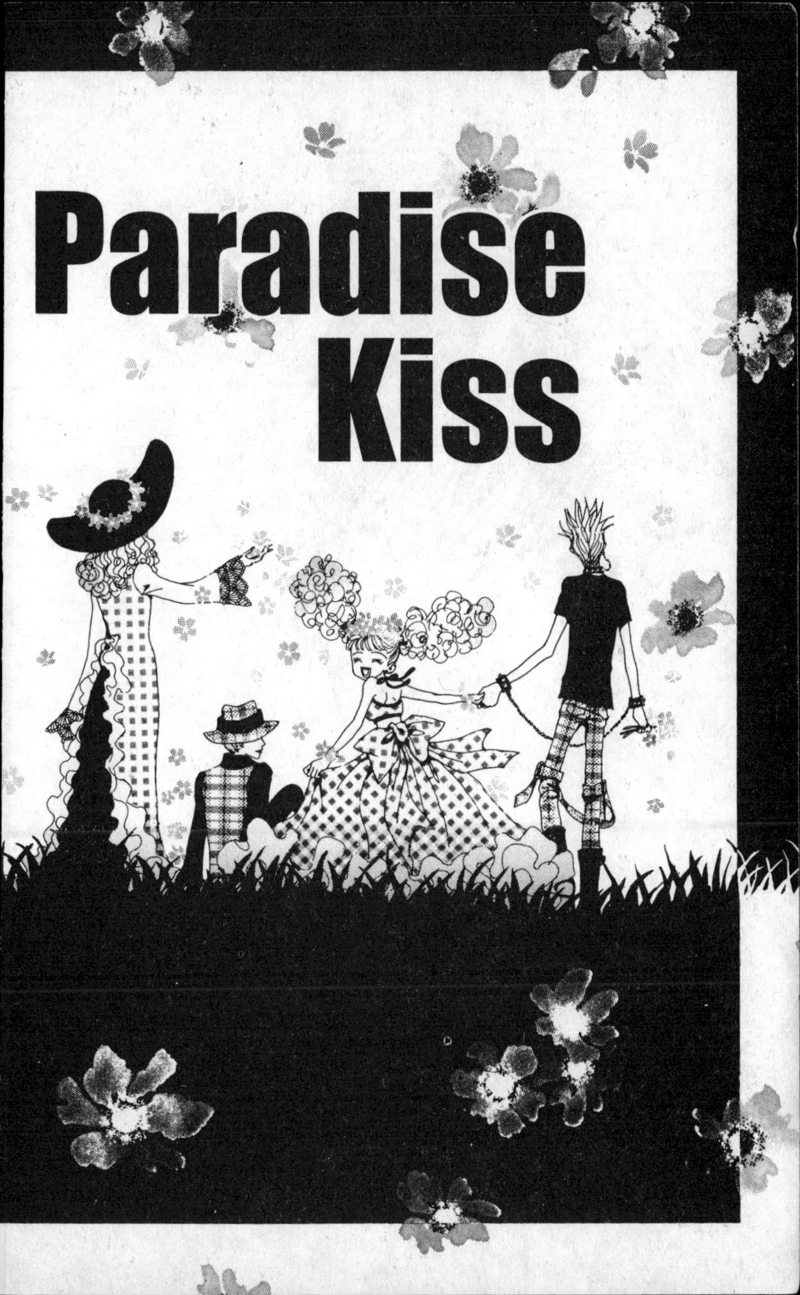
Paradise
Kiss

Fashion Forward

Ai Yazawa's breakthrough series of fashion
and romance returns in a new 3-volume
omnibus edition, with a new translation and a new
gorgeous trim size. Relive this hit all over again,
'cause good manga never goes out of style!

All volumes available now
280-320 pages each, Color plates, $19.95

LIMIT

D0829715

Limit: Volume 4

Translation: Mari Morimoto
Production: Risa Cho
Nicole Dochych
Daniela Yamada
Jeremy Kahn

Copyright © 2013 Keiko Suenobu. All rights reserved.
First published in Japan in 2011 by Kodansha, Ltd., Tokyo
Publication for this English edition arranged through Kodansha, Ltd., Tokyo
English language version produced by Vertical, Inc.

Translation provided by Vertical, Inc., 2013
Published by Vertical, Inc., New York

Originally published in Japanese as *Limit 4* by Kodansha, Ltd.
Limit first serialized in *Bessatsu Friend*, Kodansha, Ltd., 2009-2011

This is a work of fiction.

ISBN: 978-1-935654-64-3

Manufactured in the United States of America

First Edition

Vertical, Inc.
451 Park Avenue South
7th Floor
New York, NY 10016
www.vertical-inc.com

CENTRAL ARKANSAS LIBRARY SYSTEM
OLEY ROOKER BRANCH
LITTLE ROCK, ARKANSAS